W9-ADF-809

Euxinus (Sea)

PAPHLAGONIA

BITHYNIA

GALATIA

CAPPADOCIA

SYRIA

Antioch

PISIDIA

Iconium
LYCAONIA
Lystra

Derbe

Perga

CILICIA
Tarsus
Seleucia

Antioch

Seleucia

CYPRUS
Paphos

Great Sea

(Mediterranean Sea)

Tyre
Magdala
Damascus

Caesarea

Tiberias

Joppa

Jerusalem
Bethlehem

palacios

EGYPT

SALEM COLLEGE
LIBRARY

The Road to Bithynia

THE ROAD TO BITHYNIA

FORT EVERGLADES · THE STUBBORN HEART

DIVINE MISTRESS · SANGAREE

THE GOLDEN ISLE · IN A DARK GARDEN

A TOUCH OF GLORY · BATTLE SURGEON

AIR SURGEON · SPENCER BRADE, M.D.

THAT NONE SHOULD DIE

by FRANK G. SLAUGHTER

The Road to
BITHYNIA

A Novel of LUKE, *the Beloved Physician*

by FRANK G. SLAUGHTER

Garden City, N.Y., 1954 DOUBLEDAY & COMPANY, INC.

With the exception of actual historical personages identified as such, the characters are entirely the product of the author's imagination and have no relation to any person or event in real life.

COPYRIGHT, 1951, BY FRANK G. SLAUGHTER
ALL RIGHTS RESERVED
PRINTED IN THE UNITED STATES AT
THE COUNTRY LIFE PRESS, GARDEN CITY, N.Y.

To JANE, FRANK, *and* RANDY

46549

Almighty God, who callest Luke, the Physician, whose praise is in the Gospel, to be an Evangelist, and Physician of the soul; May it please Thee that, by the wholesome medicines of the doctrine delivered by him, all the diseases of our souls may be healed; through the merits of Thy son Jesus Christ our Lord. Amen.

Collect for St. Luke the Evangelist's Day, Book of Common Prayer

Author's Preface

STUDENTS of the New Testament will recognize that portions of this novel are dramatizations from the The Acts of the Apostles. This is to be expected, since the chief characters of this book also played prominent parts in The Acts, and St. Luke is generally credited with authorship of both it and the Gospel which bears his name. Where appropriate, dialogue attributed to the characters is taken from actual records of the speeches made by them in The Acts, as well as from the Epistles of St. Paul. Except for a few passages from the Authorized or King James version of the Bible, easily recognizable as such, all this quoted material is taken from the Charles B. Williams translation of the New Testament, published by the Moody Press, Chicago 10, Illinois. I am indebted to the Moody Press for their kind permission to quote from this translation without crediting individual passages, which would, of course, be impossible in a work of fiction. I am also indebted to Dr. Williams for the hours of genuine pleasure which his beautiful "Translation in the Language of the People" has given me.

It would be impossible to list the many hundreds of references consulted in writing this novel. I should like, however, to acknowledge my indebtedness to Mr. Graham Chambers Hunter, whose book, *Luke, First Century Christian* (Harper and Brothers), helped immeasurably to crystallize my concept of Luke, as well as giving me invaluable facts about his life, and to Dr. Edgar Goodspeed, through whose fine biography of St. Paul (John C. Winston Company), I first learned of the historical existence of the leading feminine character.

My purpose in writing *The Road to Bithynia* is twofold: First, to study the events of the life and ministry of Jesus, and the growth and spread of the early Christian church, through the eyes of an educated Greek physician of the period who possessed an unusual warmth and breadth of character. And second, to seek in these events and in the philosophy of the early Christian faith lessons which this most beautiful of all written stories has for us in the troubled world of today. Where I have succeeded in these aims, credit is due the man through whose eyes I have been privileged to look at this fascinating and inspiring period of history, Luke, the physician. Where I have failed, the fault is my own. To those who will quarrel with me over the character of Paul—and there will be many—I offer no apology. Although there is ample authority in theological writing for all controversy portrayed in this novel, I have tried to see and understand Paul as first of all a human being, with all the frailties and virtues which such a state implies, remembering that it was a humble carpenter of Nazareth who showed men the Way, before ever they knew he was the Son of God.

It is my sincere wish that many will see in these pages, as I have been privileged to see through the eyes of Luke the physician, Luke the man, and Luke the Christian—THE ROAD TO BITHYNIA.

Contents

The Road to Bithynia

Book One: THE SCROLL

*Whosoever cometh to me, and heareth my
sayings, and doeth them, I will shew you to
whom he is like.*

Luke 6:47

THE SUN was a thin blood-red crescent above the low-lying
range of hills to the west as two men climbed a winding stone stairway
in the fortress of Antonia that towered above the city and served as
headquarters for the Roman garrison. The older man was grizzled, his
face craggy, and his skin seamed by the sun and wind of military cam-
paigns in the far-flung climates of the Empire. His toga was of fine
wool, dyed a rich purple according to the custom of high-ranking
Roman officers, and over it he wore the harness and jeweled short
sword of a centurion. The other man was young, a youth just eighteen,
but as tall as a full-grown man, although hardly out of the *toga prae-
texta* of childhood. There was a gravity about his regular even features
and warm brown eyes that belied his youth. His well-muscled body
and eager spirits made nothing of the climb, but the old centurion was
puffing long before the two of them reached the top of the stairway
and came out on a broad balcony. The soldier leaned against the stone
parapet to get his breath. "There is what you have been so anxious to
see, Luke," he said. "Jerusalem, the Holy City of the Jews."

The young man looked eagerly out over the city, for he had heard
much of it from Jews in Antioch. But what he saw did not impress
him. "Is that all there is to it, Silvanus? Surely there must be more."

"It is a mean city," Silvanus agreed. "Nothing like our Antioch or
Rome. But look up, not down. The glory of Jerusalem is on the hill-
tops. Look at the towers there by the west gate, where the road to
Joppa enters the city."

I

The young man's gaze followed the soldier's pointing finger. From the broad stone wall on the west, three great battlemented towers reared toward the sky. Windows, breaking the solid stone of the walls, marked the rooms inside them, and from the battlements and turrets above a small army could have loosed a hail of missiles upon any attackers.

"Herod the Great named those towers after his relatives and friends," Silvanus explained. "The tallest is called Phasael, after his brother. The next Hippicus, for his friend. The smallest is Mariamne, after his Queen."

"I remember reading of her. He had her murdered, didn't he?"

"That is the story. Some say because he was afraid she might be unfaithful to him, although others insist that he was afraid she would poison him. All the Herods have a penchant for evil. But look to the east; there is the crowning glory of Jerusalem."

The youth caught his breath, as had many another, at his first glimpse of the Holy Temple of the Jews. His eyes widened and he leaned his elbows on the stone parapet, resting his chin in cupped hands to stare at it. Here was something of what he had expected from Jerusalem. Walls of polished granite enclosed the square structure on the summit of a little hill. It rose in three broad terraces, each supported by colonnaded archways. Through the open arches Luke could see protected arcades surrounding each terraced level. The dying rays of the sun, reflected from the polished metal columns, blinded him for a second. "Look, Silvanus," he cried. "The columns are of gold."

"Not quite." The centurion smiled. "But they are of Corinthian bronze, perhaps the next thing to it."

The momentary flash from the columns had been the last of the day's sunlight, but although darkness was now falling rapidly, the polished granite walls and the pure-white marble of the terraces and gates continued to glow with the warmth stored in them during the day. For a long moment the youth did not speak, enraptured still by what he saw.

"Others have been stricken dumb by the beauty of Herod's temple," Silvanus said. "I brought you up here because I knew you would appreciate it, Luke."

"Why do you call it Herod's temple?"

"Several temples have stood here before this one, but Herod built the most magnificent of all, I suspect because he hoped that a monument to their God would make the Jews forget his heavy taxes."

"It would have been simpler and cheaper to erect statues to him, as we have in Antioch."

"The Jews abhor idols, Luke. Their law forbids them."

"Do they have laws? I thought Rome governed here."

2

"Rome does, in civil matters," Silvanus explained. "But the religious laws of the Jews go back for centuries to a man called Moses, who led them out of bondage in Egypt."

"But they are still a Roman state," Luke protested. "And the laws of Rome are just and good."

"The Jewish God, Jehovah, is a jealous god. He will let the Jews put no other laws above those he gave to Moses centuries ago."

"Where does this Jewish God dwell, Silvanus?" Luke asked, smiling. "Is he so jealous that he must have an Olympus of his own?"

Silvanus caught the irony in the young man's voice. "They set him so far above all others as to place his dwelling in the sky, Luke," he said somewhat severely.

"Such as on the planet Venus?" Luke pointed to the evening star. "Some of the old Greeks believed the planet might be inhabited."

"I am a soldier, not a philosopher," Silvanus reminded him.

"But you have visited many lands, Silvanus, and you found each with its own gods. I find it easier to believe that all gods exist only in our minds, than that each country has a different one and even the Roman emperors are divine."

"It is not good to believe in no gods whatsoever," Silvanus told him. "Besides, it is not wise for a Roman to openly question the divinity of the Emperor."

Luke grinned. "I will take the Jewish God then, since he seems to be the most powerful one of all."

For a moment Silvanus said nothing, but stared into the dusk where the great white temple still glowed faintly. Then he shook his head slowly and said, "You would not like Jehovah, Luke."

Luke sensed the seriousness of the old centurion's manner, and his own voice lost its sarcastic note. "Why, Silvanus?"

"Some years ago a young Jewish teacher named Jesus of Nazareth was crucified here in Jerusalem. He was a kind, harmless man whom the people loved." Silvanus turned somber eyes upon his young friend. "There are many who believe that Jesus was the son of Jehovah."

"His son!" Luke repeated. "But you said their God dwelt in the stars, Silvanus. How could his son—if you grant that Jehovah does exist and could have a son—live and be crucified as a mortal man?"

"I am only telling you what they say."

Suddenly a thought struck Luke. "Did you ever see this teacher?" he asked.

Silvanus seemed to be looking at something far away. "Yes," he said slowly. "I saw him once and heard him teach."

"Do you believe that he is the son of the Jewish God?"

The centurion fiddled nervously with the sword at his belt, a habit of

3

his when worried or uncertain. "I don't know what to believe, Luke," he admitted. "There are things about Jesus you can't explain. But it is getting late. We had better prepare for the evening meal."

"Wait, Silvanus," Luke said. "This criminal, this man Stephen that Theophilus has come here to judge. Does he have anything to do with the teacher you spoke of, Jesus of Nazareth?" Theophilus, deputy governor and chief magistrate of Syria, was the youth's foster father. Luke's real father, a Roman freedman, had been a trusted member of the Roman judge's retinue for many years before his death.

"This man Stephen has already been tried and found guilty," Silvanus said. "Theophilus is only here in case he stands upon his rights as a Roman citizen and appeals to Rome."

"But why do we have to go to all the trouble of traveling from Antioch to Jerusalem to interfere in a religious controversy?"

"This has become more than just a religious controversy, Luke," the centurion explained. "Ever since Pontius Pilate allowed Jesus to be crucified there has been unrest throughout Judea. Stephen is a follower of Jesus, and Sixtus, the proconsul, is afraid of more trouble if he is executed."

"Why doesn't Sixtus forbid them, then?"

Silvanus smiled. "You may understand books, Luke," he said tolerantly, "but you know nothing of political affairs. The Romans cannot interfere in a strictly religious matter such as this without stirring up a lot of trouble. But because Jesus has followers who are important in the Empire, Theophilus must report to Rome that Stephen has been granted all of his rights under Roman law."

"When is the trial of Stephen to take place?" Luke asked.

"Tomorrow morning. And you can be present," Silvanus added with a smile, "since you would pester me to death about it anyway."

Luke linked his arm affectionately through that of the grizzled soldier. "Come along then, old friend," he said with a warm smile. "Let us see if the food in Jerusalem is any better than the looks of the city."

ii

Although the hour was early, the narrow streets of Jerusalem were thronged with people as Luke followed the soldiers escorting the prisoner Stephen from the dungeons of the Antonia to the council chamber of the Jewish high court, the Sanhedrin. For the most part, the populace stayed well out of the way of the soldiers; those who did get too close were elbowed summarily aside by the brawny men of the legions. Everywhere there was the clatter of voices speaking in many tongues,

4

for it was a season of holiday and feasting and many people had come to the city, some to worship, others to trade.

The streets were narrow and lined with shops. Once, in a section of wider streets, Luke hurried forward to get a good look at this prisoner who had caused the most respected judge in the Roman provinces along the eastern end of the Mediterranean to be sent here by Rome. The man marching along in the center of the square of guards was of middle stature, his robe torn and dingy, of poor stuff indeed. But his head was erect, and he held his manacled hands before him as he walked, more as if they were a badge of honor than a sign of his lowly status as a prisoner. He glanced to neither side, although crowds lined the street and shouted curses at him.

Stephen was obviously part Greek, his ancestry visible in his olive skin and dark hair. His face was pale from confinement in the dungeons, his beard short and ragged, and his long hair unkempt. In his eyes, however, burned an intense, fanatic light, a look of fierce pride, not at all what one would expect in a man who, according to rumor, was already doomed.

As he walked along looking at Stephen, Luke noticed just ahead of him a tall, striking figure in just such a sorry robe as the prisoner wore. The man was heavily bearded and obviously a Jew, but there was something about him that particularly attracted Luke's attention. For even though his robe was cheap, the big man radiated a kindly majesty, and infinite wisdom and tolerance shone from his deep-set eyes as they swept over the crowd and the prisoner.

Suddenly the tall man stopped and seized a fish from a stall before which he was passing. Luke thought for a moment that he was trying to steal the fish, but he only lifted it high above his head, shouting in Greek, "Stephanos! Stephanos! Take courage in the name of Jesus!"

The effect upon the prisoner was startling. He turned his head, and at the sight of the fish held above the heads of the crowd, his face suddenly shone with an unearthly radiance. Exultantly he raised his manacled hands above his head and shook them in a gesture of triumph.

"Fear not, Stephanos," the tall man shouted. "*His words* will be saved."

Stephen nodded then and marched on, his head even more proudly erect than before.

Luke was so intent upon this odd happening that he stumbled into the tall man and would have fallen into the street to be trampled underfoot by the crowd swirling around them had he not clutched at the dingy robe for support. The proprietor of the fish market was waving his arms and shouting indignantly, but the big man calmly transferred the fish to one hand and put the other arm around Luke to

5

support him. Then, placing the fish upon the counter from which he had taken it, he set Luke on his feet, patted him on the head as if he were a child, and strode off through the crowd. Surprised by this odd occurrence, Luke stood there dumbly until the tall figure disappeared around a corner into another street. Then he turned to the proprietor of the fish market. "Who is that man?" he asked in Greek, which was spoken in Jerusalem as often as the Aramaic tongue, which he did not understand.

"He is a member of the accursed Company of the Fish." He spat out a string of curses, then, noticing the rich material of Luke's toga and cloak, held up the fish. "A valuable fish has been ruined," he whined. "I am but a poor merchant, sir, and cannot afford the loss."

Luke could not see that so much as a scale of the fish had been disturbed. He tossed the man a coin from his purse, anyway, and hurried to catch up with the Roman party. But his mind was seething with questions. Who was the big man with the strangely majestic mien, so out of keeping with his garb? What was the Company of the Fish, so obviously hated by the Jews? And what had the tall man meant by "His words will be saved"?

Luke found no answer to his questions, for the party escorting the prisoner was already climbing the steps leading to the lower terrace of the temple, where the council chamber of the Sanhedrin was located. Great signs in Aramaic, Greek, and Latin adorned the walls, warning all those not of the Hebrew faith to remain at this lower level. Only Jews could ascend the nineteen steps of polished marble leading to the second terrace, and most of these were priests who would take part in the sacrifices of the feast day which was now in progress.

Luke saw no sign yet of Sixtus, the proconsul, and his party. Knowing that the hearing of the Sanhedrin could not start until the Romans arrived, he decided to make a brief tour of this most popular portion of the temple while waiting for them. As he walked along the cool terrace in the shade of the broad arcades, he was jostled by Jews, Greeks, Romans, dark-skinned Asiatics, Egyptians, Nubians, men of every race. From the booths ranged along the walls rose many strange scents. The delicate aroma of myrrh and frankincense from Egypt mingled with all manner of diverse perfumes, while from the next stall came the strong odor of goats or sheep as tender kids and lambs were sold to the chatter of bargaining voices. The sellers assured the Jewish pilgrims that all were equally pleasing to the nostrils of their God when sacrificed on the altars of the temple, but added shrewdly that of course the Most High expected every man to sacrifice according to his means. Wrinkling his nose against the smell, Luke wondered how they could have much respect for the perceptions of their divinity, if the odors of rare perfume and burning goat flesh pleased him equally well.

A special area aloof from the stalls of the merchants was reserved for the money-changers. Silvanus had told Luke that the Jews did not accept foreign coins as offerings in the temple, since their religion forbade any graven image, and Roman coins were adorned with the heads of the Caesars. Seated behind little tables covered with stacks of coins, the money-changers were doing a thriving business changing coins for the Jewish pilgrims from all parts of the Empire who had thronged here for the feast and religious holiday.

Antioch, where Luke lived, was a city to which came many caravans from the wild lands to the east, as well as the merchants from Rome, Greece, and Egypt who landed at the neighboring port of Seleucia. And familiar as he was with the currency of the Empire, he saw at once that the money-changers were shamefully cheating the pilgrims, who had no other choice but to change their money to Jewish coin if they were to make the gifts which they had traveled so far to lay before their God. Disgusted by such obvious chicanery, he moved on to the booths where the sellers of written scrolls displayed their wares.

The scrolls, wax tablets, and papyrus sheets found in such places held a fascination for Luke, who had the true scholar's weakness for anything containing written information. He stopped now at the booth where an intelligent-looking Jew was busy copying a scroll from Aramaic into Greek, setting down the letters in a fine, scholarly script. "Can I serve you, sir?" the Jew asked pleasantly in Greek.

"I am interested in the history of your people," Luke told him.

The man opened one of the parchment rolls. "Here is a copy of the very words of Moses translated into the Greek tongue."

"I will take it," Luke said promptly, remembering that this same Moses was supposed to have received from Jehovah the very laws which the prisoner Stephen was accused of breaking and for which he would be tried today.

"These others here contain the sayings of our prophets," the seller continued. "You will find them as interesting as the writings of your Greek philosophers."

Luke purchased these scrolls too. Then, obeying a sudden impulse, he asked, "Do you have a scroll containing the teachings of Jesus of Nazareth?"

The Jew's face paled and he backed away, almost upsetting his small worktable. "Why do you ask?" he said almost in a whisper. "Who sent you?"

"A friend of mine, a Roman centurion, told me of him," Luke explained.

"Are you one of the Company of the Fish?" There was a curious urgency in the Jew's voice.

Luke shook his head, puzzled by the man's obvious agitation over such a simple question. "I am a Greek of Antioch, a student of medicine."

The man looked at Luke closely. "There is said to be such a scroll of the sayings of Jesus," he admitted. "But I know of no one who has seen it, unless it is one who is to be stoned to death this day."

"Stephen?" Luke asked in surprise. "My foster father, Theophilus, is here because of the trial of Stephen."

The man's manner became friendlier. "Theophilus is known to be a good man and a just one, and you appear to be like him. What is it that you wish to know?"

"Can you tell me something about the Company of the Fish?"

"It is the name which the——" Whatever he was going to say was never finished, for suddenly he gave Luke a shove and shouted, "You have made your purchase, Roman. Be off with you now. No one has cheated you."

Luke stumbled backward, clutching the packet of scrolls he had purchased. Then he saw the reason for the sudden change in his informant. A priest was almost upon them, and undoubtedly the scroll seller had been afraid their conversation would be overheard.

This was the second time within the hour Luke had heard that strange phrase, the "Company of the Fish." But there was no prospect of learning more just now. The seller of scrolls stepped quickly out on the terrace and began to harangue the passers-by, extolling the virtues of his merchandise. And just then a Roman trumpet sounded on the steps of the temple, warning Luke that the party of the proconsul was arriving. Clutching the scrolls under his arm, he hurried to join the group, fearful lest he miss the trial he had come to see.

A tall, handsome youth in military dress was in the van of the procession. This was Apollonius, the natural son of Theophilus, and Luke's foster brother, who would sail in a few days from Joppa for Rome and an eventual commission as a tribune in the Roman Army. Luke and Apollonius had grown up together, brothers in everything but reality. "Hah! Little brother." Apollonius jeered as Luke arrived, panting. "Wasting your coin on scrolls again, I see."

"It is better than snoring your life away in bed," Luke retorted.

"Let Tanos carry your burdens to the Antonia and return to wait upon us." Tanos, the personal slave of Apollonius, carried the short spear and small round shield affected by the servants of Roman officers. Shifting the shield, he took the bundle of scrolls and placed it under his arm while Luke and his handsome foster brother followed the party of the proconsul into the chamber of the Sanhedrin and found seats beside Silvanus, where the Roman officials were seated to one side of the chamber.

iii

Barely a dozen members of the Sanhedrin, highest religious and judicious council of the Jewish people, were ranged behind a long table at the end of the chamber. Before them the prisoner sat quietly on a stool, his manacled hands in his lap. His eyes, fixed on some point above the heads of the judges, burned with a strange look of exaltation, as if he were seeing something invisible to the others.

"Will they crucify him, Silvanus?" Apollonius asked in a whisper.

The centurion shook his head. "The crucifixion of Jesus of Nazareth has already caused no end of trouble," he said. "Sixtus tells me that he and Theophilus have decided to allow only death by stoning."

"But Stephen has not been convicted yet," Luke protested.

"This trial is only an official formality," Silvanus explained. "The Sanhedrin has already sentenced him. That is why only a few of them are here. This is only to allow Sixtus to approve the verdict for Rome."

Caiaphas, the high priest, rapped for order, and the hum of conversation died. The other two sides of the room were packed, and the crowd filled the door and extended back along the terrace outside. A short man had been talking to the high priest in low tones. Now he stepped into the open space between the court and the prisoner. Barrel-chested, bandy-legged, and not impressive of stature, he somehow seemed to radiate an inner quality of power that gripped the interest of the onlookers. Without effort he dominated both the crowd and the council even before he spoke.

"Who is he?" asked Silvanus in a whisper.

"Saul of Tarsus, prosecutor of the Sanhedrin. He has been commissioned to destroy the followers of Jesus."

Saul seemed to be about thirty, Luke judged. The most striking thing about him was his majestic, almost godlike head. The wide, mobile mouth, the broad planes of the face, the deep caverns in which his eyes burned with a fanatic zeal, and the broad high forehead gave individuality to a face that was not easily forgotten. Slowly he looked around the room, waiting for the crowd to grow completely quiet. Then, unrolling a thin scroll from the table before the high priest, he began to read the charges against Stephen in a deep, vibrant voice. It was an astonishingly puerile list of crimes, Luke thought, having to do with what was called "blasphemy" against their God and their

9

prophets. A Roman judge would have disregarded them entirely, but they seemed to be serious accusations according to Jewish law, judging from the manner of the judges and the crowd.

Following the reading, Saul brought a succession of witnesses before the court. They had obviously been well coached, for they recited their accusations as if by rote. At the end of each account Saul turned to the prisoner with studied courtesy and inquired if he wished to question the witnesses. But Stephen only shook his head and continued to look afar off, seemingly unaware that he was convicting himself when he could easily have proved the absurdity of the evidence.

As he listened to the arraignment, Luke's anger rose steadily, fanned by pity for the prisoner and indignation at the trumped-up charges. His every sense of fairness was appalled by the way Saul was building a tissue of obvious untruths to justify the death penalty requested by the Sanhedrin of its Roman masters.

One witness said, "I have heard him speak a blasphemy against God and Moses." But he was not even asked to specify the nature of the blasphemous utterance.

Another recited, "He has blasphemed against the temple, saying that Jesus of Nazareth shall destroy it and set at naught the laws of Moses." All of which Luke recognized as absurd, for Silvanus had told him that Jesus had been dead for several years.

Finally, when a third witness stated, "Stephen has been heard preaching that Jesus is King of the Jews," Luke could contain his indignation no longer. Leaping to his feet, he cried, "What crime is this? Obviously a dead man cannot be King of the Jews."

There was an instant of stunned silence at this sacrilege. The prisoner turned to Luke and smiled, as if to thank him for the protest. Then Luke felt Silvanus tugging at his sleeve and sat down again, appalled now at his own temerity. Sixtus turned, a look of displeasure on his face, but seeing the cause of the disturbance, he hesitated to order the son of his distinguished colleague ejected from the room. Fortunately Silvanus saved the situation. "He is young, noble Sixtus," the centurion volunteered. "I will see that he remains quiet."

The Romans laughed, and Luke shrank down in the seat, his cheeks burning with humiliation. Turning to the high priest, Sixtus said courteously, "Forgive the interruption, please, respected Caiaphas. The young man does not understand your law."

"It is forgiven," the high priest said. "Proceed, please, O Saul."

Seeing that he was not to be summarily executed, Luke dared to lift his head again, and his eyes met Saul's. The prosecutor was staring directly at him with a strange expression upon his face. It was, Luke thought, a look of doubt, perhaps of momentary uncertainty in regard to what he was doing. Then Saul turned back to Stephen. "What say you, Stephen?" he asked, his voice oddly gentle.

The prisoner got to his feet, and his eyes moved around the room slowly. But his gaze was neither angry, beseeching, nor condemning, as might have been expected. Rather, the tender smile on his face was one of compassion, as if those who sat in judgment upon him were children who should not be held accountable for their actions.

"Men, brethren, and fathers, listen," he began, his voice soft, yet vibrant with conviction and power. "I hold it not against you that you persecute me and seek to take my life when I have committed no crime. For one greater than I also laid down his life that men might know the truth and through it live forever with him."

There was a rumbling of anger from the crowd, and Caiaphas spoke sharply in their tongue.

"You make much of the holiness of this place which Herod builded to blind you to his many sins, O Priests of Israel," Stephen continued. "And I am accused of blasphemy against the temple when I say that Jesus of Nazareth will one day destroy it. Yet you, yourselves, blaspheme against it when you turn it into a den of money-changers and thieves who cheat pilgrims coming here from far-off lands to worship the Most High."

A fanatic-looking individual at the front of the crowd cursed Stephen, then spit upon him. The spittle struck the prisoner's face and ran down his cheek, but he made no move to wipe it off. Before Caiaphas could reprimand the offender, Stephen turned and spoke directly to him.

"Why do you spit upon me, you Pharisees? You claim to keep the law, but you are stiffnecked and uncircumcised in heart and ears, for you continue to resist the Holy Ghost, even as your fathers did. Which of the prophets did not your fathers persecute?" he thundered at them suddenly. "And did they not slay those who spoke of the coming of the Just One?"

The accused had now become the accuser, and the council squirmed under the lash of his voice. "And why do you set so much store on the temple and the forms of your worship, O Priests," Stephen continued, "when the prophet says that the Most High dwelleth in temples not made with hands? You know his words: *'Heaven is my throne, and earth is my footstool: what house will ye build me: or what is the place of my rest? Hath not my hands made all these things?'*"

Stephen's eyes lifted to the ceiling and his voice rose in a shout of exaltation: "Behold, I see the heavens opened, and the son of man standing at the right hand of God! Repent, you who crucified him, acknowledge your sins while there is still time that they may be forgiven!"

When Stephen thus accused the high priest and the Sanhedrin of killing the man he served, the rumblings of the crowd became voice now in a full-throated roar, an animal-like clamoring for blood. The soldiers at the door were forced to lower their spears to keep the excited crowd from surging into the chamber.

The high priest looked questioningly at Saul in the midst of this hubbub, but the prosecutor was staring at the prisoner with a strange look on his face, and only when Caiaphas spoke sharply to him did he recover his attention. "Have you finished, Stephen?" Saul asked.

The prisoner did not answer but remained standing, his eyes uplifted, his face glowing with exaltation. When it was apparent that he would not speak further, Saul nodded to Caiaphas and the members of the Sanhedrin filed from the chamber.

"What do you think of this man Stephen, Luke?" Apollonius asked as the murmur of conversation filled the room.

"I would choose him before I would the priests," Luke said promptly.

"He seems to possess a strange power," Apollonius agreed. "I wonder if all followers of Jesus have it."

"If you had seen Jesus you would understand from whence comes this power to move the hearts of men," Silvanus volunteered.

Luke would have questioned Silvanus further, but just then the Sanhedrin members returned, their farce of deliberation over. The council filed solemnly into the room and took their seats.

"We have reached a decision, O Sixtus," the high priest announced.

Sixtus rose to his feet. "What is your verdict?"

"The prisoner Stephen is guilty of breaking the laws of Israel and of having blasphemed against the Most High and the temple of the Lord."

A hum of approval came from the crowd outside.

"What is the punishment for these crimes specified by your laws?" Sixtus asked.

"The punishment is death, by crucifixion or by stoning."

The Roman official turned to the prisoner. "You have heard the punishment prescribed by the Sanhedrin, Stephen. Since you are a Roman citizen, you may invoke the authority of Rome and be tried by a Roman court. What is your desire?"

Stephen's voice came clearly, without faltering. "I invoke no authority save that of the Most High God and his son, Jesus Christ, to whom I commend my soul."

Sixtus said slowly then, "I declare it the will of the Emperor Tiberius that the prisoner Stephen shall be executed, as prescribed in the laws of the Jewish people, by stoning."

Luke suddenly felt a little sick, as he had the first time he saw a woman torn to pieces by lions in the arena at Antioch. Sixtus and his party filed from the room, but when they reached the terrace outside Luke plucked at Silvanus's sleeve. "When will the execution take place?" he asked.

"As soon as the crowd can drag him outside the gates. Come along, stripling," the centurion added kindly. "We could all use a glass of wine."

Luke shook his head. "I am going to the execution."

"Don't be a fool," Silvanus cried. "This is only another religious quarrel between two sects among the Jews. Let them settle their own affairs."

But an impulse he did not himself understand told Luke he must see this tragedy through to the end. "I've got to go, Silvanus," he said. "Don't ask me why."

"Be careful, then," the centurion admonished. "And for Diana's sake, keep your mouth shut."

As the Roman party left the temple, the crowd rushed unimpeded upon Stephen and dragged him from the chamber. Luke followed in the crowd as they surged toward the city gates, struggling to keep his footing in the mass of shoving and cursing men.

iv

A small rocky clearing just outside the gates of the city was the customary site for ritual executions by stoning. As Luke worked his way through the crowd to get a clear view, he saw several of the men who had been witnesses drag Stephen's battered body over to the wall. Slowly the bloody pile of flesh stirred and the prisoner pushed himself painfully to his knees. His eyes were half shut and his face swollen from the blows of the crowd as he had been dragged through the streets to the place of execution, but he still managed to lift his head and turn his eyes to the sky. Then, oblivious of the crowd, he began to pray.

Saul was directing the execution, as he had the trial, and now the witnesses began to remove their outer garments and lay them on the rocky ground before him. As was the custom in religious executions, they would cast the first stones. At a nod from Saul one of them took up a jagged rock from the ground and threw it expertly at the kneeling man.

The first stone struck Stephen on the shoulder and twisted him about, but he ignored the pain and continued to pray. The second laid open a cut on his forehead, and blood began to drip down across his face and into his eyes. Then a hail of missiles poured upon the kneel-

13

ing figure as more and more of the crowd joined in the stoning. Cursing and shouting, those at the back tried to push their way to the front to join in the persecution of the helpless prisoner. Although sick with horror at such a display of brutality and blood lust, Luke could not have looked away if he had tried. Soon Stephen's body lay on the rocky ground, while the hail of stones continued to rain upon it, gradually beating it to a pulp.

Finally, when Saul shouted a command in Aramaic and held up his hand, the crowd stopped stoning. The prosecutor walked over to the victim and stood looking down at him, then turned back to the crowd. "It is not right to continue stoning this man if he is already dead," he said. "Is there a physician among you who can tell us whether he still lives?"

Some impulse made Luke step out from the crowd. "I am a student of medicine," he volunteered. "I can tell you whether or not he is dead." He had seen many dead men while studying with the physicians in Antioch, and the signs of death were clearly set down in the writings of Hippocrates.

"Examine him, then," Saul said gruffly. "But expect no pay."

Luke knelt beside the bleeding form and felt for the pulse. He did not expect to find it, for he could not see how Stephen could have lived through the horror of the stoning. But to his surprise he felt a faint throbbing under his fingers. Stephen's lids fluttered open at his touch, and though the doomed man's eyes were already filmed over by death, they seemed to plead with Luke to understand something, some message he wished to impart before death claimed him.

"His words . . ." Stephen's whisper barely reached Luke's ears. "The scroll . . . in . . . my robe." Then, as if by magic, all pain was suddenly erased from his face and he smiled. "Lord, lay not this sin to their charge," he whispered clearly, before his lips grew slack with death.

"Is he dead?" Saul demanded impatiently.

"I must listen for the heartbeat to be certain." Luke needed no further assurance of death, but he knew that somehow he must remove from Stephen's robe whatever it was that the dying man had wished him to take. It was almost as if Stephen had somehow managed to keep himself alive during those last moments in order to impart his dying message to one who would be sent to hear it, but logic assured Luke that such an assumption was absurd.

Carefully Luke put his ear to Stephen's chest, as prescribed by Hippocrates in listening for the heart and the lung sounds. The heart was still, but as his hand fumbled surreptitiously inside Stephen's robe his fingers touched something hard and cylindrical in shape. He recognized the object immediately as a small scroll and, with a deft movement, slipped it from the dead man's robe and into his own toga. Then, rising to his feet, he announced loudly, "This man is dead."

"Get your garments, then," Saul told the witnesses curtly, as if he were anxious to get away.

"Is no one to remove the body?" Luke asked.

"If he has friends, they can take it," Saul said coldly. Just then Stephen's legs gave a convulsive jerk, as the limbs of an animal sometimes do even after the head has been removed. One of the crowd shouted, "The body moved! The Greek lied when he said Stephen is dead." And as others took up the cry some of the foremost among them seized a handful of small stones and cast them at Luke, eager for another target upon which to turn their still unsatiated blood lust. One small stone laid open a cut over Luke's eye, and at the sight of blood the crowd began to bay again in earnest. A shower of stones rained about the youth as he turned desperately and ran toward the gate, seeking to escape their pelting. With the crowd in their present temper, a hail of missiles would have followed and Luke would have been battered to death in a matter of minutes, but Saul's voice whipped them to a standstill. "Stop, fools!" he shouted. "This man is a Roman; do you want to feel the swords on your necks?"

The threat of vengeance by the legions checked the crowd for a moment, but some of the more rabid shouted again, "Kill the Roman!" As others took up the cry Luke realized that Saul would not be able to control them alone.

Over this tense situation a welcome sound reached Luke's ears, the beat of marching feet. Looking around desperately for a glimpse of the soldiers, he spied the tall form of Apollonius beyond the crowd. "Apollonius!" he shouted desperately. "Help me! Help me!"

Recognizing the fear in Luke's voice, Apollonius plowed into the crowd with half a dozen Roman soldiers, knocking struggling bodies unceremoniously aside with the flat of his sword. He took in the dangerous situation at one quick glance, the threatening looks of the crowd, the dirt on Luke's tunic and toga where the stones had struck him, and the bleeding cut over his eye. "What is this?" he snapped angrily. "Do you dare attack the son of Theophilus?"

Cowed by his voice and manner, the crowd shrank back. But it was not so with Saul. "They are angered because he lied and would have let the condemned man live," the short man said defiantly.

Apollonius wasted no time in argument. "It is a good thing for you that he is not badly hurt," he told Saul curtly, and turned to Luke. "Come along, brother. We leave for Joppa at once to meet my ship."

Now that the tension was over, Luke's fear was replaced by a burning anger. Unreasonably—for Saul had saved him from serious injury, whatever his motive—he snapped at the prosecutor, "May your God punish you, Saul, for murdering a good man like Stephen."

Saul recoiled, almost as if Luke had struck him, and a strange look came into his eyes. It flashed through Luke's mind that Saul already felt guilty for the death of Stephen, but just then Apollonius seized him by the arm and drew him away, with the soldiers holding back the crowd at spear point.

"As usual," Apollonius said, grinning, "I arrived in time to get you out of a bad mess."

"How did you happen to come?" Luke asked.

"Wherever you are, there is always trouble," Apollonius said. "You can thank Silvanus for the rescue, though. He's been fretting ever since we left the temple. As soon as he heard that my ship is in Joppa, he jumped at the chance to send me for you. What stirred up the Jews, anyway?"

"An argument over whether the man was dead or not. They abhor a corpse, so no one else would touch him." But he did not tell Apollonius about the scroll safely hidden in his tunic. That had been Stephen's secret. Until Luke could decide what to do with the scroll, it would be his own as well.

Now that he was safe, Luke had time to wonder at the strange succession of events which had characterized this day, beginning when he had encountered the tall, majestic man before the fish market on the way to the temple that morning and first heard of the Company of the Fish. Equally strange was the behavior of the scroll seller in the temple and the unfortunate interruption by the priest just when Luke had thought to satisfy his curiosity. Most puzzling of all was the fact that Stephen, although dying, had immediately trusted Luke and given him the scroll, almost as if he thought he had been sent to get it. And yet Luke knew that Stephen had never seen him before that same morning at the trial.

v

It was midafternoon when the party in which Luke traveled left Jerusalem by the western gate that gave access to the Joppa road, leading to the seaport city through which passed traffic to and from the Jewish capital. Night fell when they were only halfway to Joppa, and they made camp near a spring in a grove of olive trees beside the road. Luke and Apollonius shared a tent, as they had a bedchamber most of their lives in Antioch. But tonight both were saddened by the thought that Apollonius would leave soon for Rome, breaking their companionship for the first time. It would be several years before the taller youth's training would be completed, and meanwhile Luke himself would soon be leaving for Pergamum, where he was to enter the final phase of his medical training in the famous Temple of Asklepios. Neither spoke much, for both were saddened by the thought of tomorrow's parting.

Apollonius removed his outer garments and hung his sword and harness upon a peg projecting from the center pole of the tent. Then with a husky "Good night," he wrapped himself in his robe, lay down on his sleeping rug, and began to snore almost immediately. Luke was filled with a strange restlessness and felt no desire to sleep. At home he would have read from the writings of the Greek philosophers, as he often did, until late at night, but his books were in Antioch.

Then he remembered the scroll he had taken from Stephen's body. Carefully he took it from the bag containing his clothing and other belongings and unrolled it in the light of the small lamp hanging from the center pole of the tent. The scroll was thin and stained with several dark spots which he recognized as blood. The penmanship was exquisite, and it was written in Greek. The first words told him that this was a collection of the sayings and doings of Jesus of Nazareth, perhaps the very scroll of which the seller had been speaking that morning when the appearance of the rabbi had broken off their talk. Glancing over the parchment, Luke began to read at random:

And he came down with them, and stood in the plain, and the company of his disciples, and a great multitude of people out of all Judea and Jerusalem, and from the sea coast of Tyre and Sidon, which came to hear him, and to be healed of their diseases . . .

Luke's interest was immediately attracted. Was this Jesus, then, a physician? he wondered, and read on eagerly.

And they that were vexed with unclean spirits: and they were healed. And the whole multitude sought to touch him: for there went virtue out of him, and healed them all.

No physician cured all who consulted him, Luke knew. Was this, then, a new method of healing, one unknown to ordinary physicians? Had this gentle teacher made some remarkable discovery before they nailed him to the cross, one which enabled him to cure all disease?

And he lifted up his eyes on his disciples, and said, Blessed be ye poor: for yours is the kingdom of God.

Blessed are ye that hunger now: for ye shall be filled. Blessed are ye that weep now: for ye shall laugh.

Blessed are ye, when men shall hate you . . . and cast out your name as evil, for the Son of man's sake.

Rejoice ye in that day, and leap for joy: for, behold, your reward is great in heaven: for in the like manner did their fathers unto the prophets.

The picture of Stephen before the Sanhedrin came into Luke's mind, for the doomed man had said something very much like this to the judges. Now Luke could begin to understand how Stephen's belief in this doctrine could carry him through the ordeal of stoning and death, trusting in the promises made by Jesus of greater rewards.

What proof was there, Luke's logical mind asked, that this teacher had the power to give the things he promised, unless he were, as his followers believed, the son of Jehovah? And that was impossible, Luke assured himself, for if no gods existed, how could there be a son of a god? Turning to the scroll, Luke read on, for he wanted to learn whatever he could about this new method of healing.

But woe unto you that are rich! for ye have received your consolation.

Woe unto you that are full! for ye shall hunger. Woe unto you that laugh now! for ye shall mourn and weep.

Woe unto you, when all men shall speak well of you! for so did their fathers to the false prophets.

Such teachings would appeal to the great multitudes, who were constantly in hunger and want, since they promised that the rich would suffer in the future while the poor would be comforted. But the merchants and moneylenders such as Luke had seen cheating pilgrims in the temple, and the well-fed priests who were obviously paid to let them sell and exchange there, would naturally hate Jesus and his followers and wish to destroy them.

All at once Luke realized that he was not alone in the tent and started up, chilled by a sudden fear. Stumbling over his rolled-up sleeping rug, he reached instinctively for Apollonius's sword hanging in its scabbard from the center pole. Then his hand dropped, for he recognized the visitor as the same man who had figured in the episode of the fish that morning. Something told him that this giant of a man standing just inside the tent came in peace.

"H-how did you get in?" Luke stammered, his heart pounding from the shock of finding another in the tent.

"You were reading and did not see when I opened the flap." The big man glanced down at Apollonius. Luke realized with a start that his foster brother's rasping snore had stopped, and his breathing was as deep and even now as that of a baby. "He will not awaken until after I have gone," the guest said with calm certainty. "May I sit down? I am very weary."

"Forgive me my discourtesy." Luke unfolded his sleeping rug. "This is all I have."

"No one can give his brother more," the visitor said with a smile. He lowered his body to the rug and stretched his legs with a sigh of deep weariness. The soles of his sandals were worn through and his feet were raw and bleeding.

"Your feet," Luke cried with immediate concern. "What happened to them?"

"It is a long walk from Jerusalem."

"But that is impossible. Unless you left before we did."

"It was three hours before sunset when I left the city."

Luke stared at the big man dumfounded, for their party had left Jerusalem fully three hours before him and had traveled rapidly. "I have long legs," the visitor explained with a smile. "Besides, nothing is impossible to those who trust him."

"Him . . . ?"

"Jesus of Nazareth. I see that you were reading the scroll of his words."

Luke put his hand to the scroll, as if to protect it, although some instinct told him that this man had no designs against it. That morning when he had held up the fish for Stephen to see, it had been evident to Luke that the two were friends. And the shopkeeper had identified the tall stranger as a member of the Company of the Fish, to which Stephen also must have belonged, for it was apparently a designation used to distinguish the followers of Jesus.

"You need have no fear, Luke," his visitor said reassuringly. "I am Simon, who is called Peter."

The name meant nothing to Luke, but somehow he felt as if he had known this majestic, kindly man a long time and that he was a friend. "You knew I had it, then?" Luke asked.

"Why else would I have walked from Jerusalem to find you?"

"But no one saw Stephen give it to me," Luke protested. "How could you know?"

"It was not on Stephen's body when we took it away," Peter pointed out. "You were the only person to whom he might have given it." He smiled. "But I would have known it anyway."

"This morning," Luke cried, "when you told Stephen, 'His words will be saved,' you meant the scroll."

Peter nodded. "I knew it would be saved, but not how."

"Did you come to take it from me?" Luke asked.

19

Peter shook his head. "The time has come for the teachings of Jesus to be spread abroad so that they may be read by those who did not hear them from his own lips. Stephen was commissioned to set the sayings down in a scroll." He sighed as if in deep sorrow, and Luke remembered that the dead man had been his friend. "Those who crucified Jesus heard of it and took Stephen to kill him. But for your kindness, Luke, they would have found the scroll on his body and destroyed it."

Luke did not ask how Peter knew these things. Here in his presence it was easy to believe that he could look into the future if need be, and that whatever he said would be true. "Then you must be one of the disciples of Jesus of Nazareth," he said.

Peter lifted his head proudly. "I am he who was chosen by Jesus to lead those who believe."

"The Company of the Fish?"

"That is what we call ourselves," Peter said, then added briskly, "But our time is short. The centurion Silvanus will be coming soon to see why a light burns so late in your tent, and I must be gone before he comes. Listen carefully, Luke. You go from Joppa to Damascus as soon as Apollonius sails."

"How could you know that?" Luke asked in surprise. Silvanus had only told him of the change in their plans as they were leaving Jerusalem. The new route would take them back to Antioch by way of Damascus, northward through the populous cities along the Lake of Tiberias, which the Jews called Galilee, and the city of Tiberias, where Herod had his seat.

"There is one who knows all things," Peter said. "Now listen closely, Luke. Keep the scroll with you and let no one but those you trust know that you have it."

"Not even Silvanus?"

"The centurion knew Jesus. He is one of us already in his heart. And Theophilus will one day believe. But let no others know. When you reach Damascus, go to the street called Straight and inquire there for the shop of one Judas, a cobbler. In his house you will find Nicanor, who is one of the Seven, as was Stephen. You may give him the scroll."

Luke did not question Peter's right thus to instruct him, for the big man had said he was the leader of those who followed Jesus, and the scroll rightly belonged to them. "But how shall I be certain of this Nicanor when I find him?" he asked. "Those who killed Stephen to get the scroll may figure out that I have it and try to get it from me."

"Do you remember the words of Stephen just before he died?" Peter asked.

"Yes. I was the only one who heard them."

Peter smiled. "Someday, Luke, you will know that there is really one

20

who heareth all things. What Stephen said to you was, 'Lord, lay not this sin to their charge.' Nicanor will repeat those words to you in Damascus."

Luke's mouth went slack with astonishment, for he would have sworn by all the gods that no one other than himself could know those words. Before he could question Peter further, the big man rose. "Silvanus is near and I must go," he said, laying his hand upon the youth's dark head. "Blessings be upon thee, Luke, for in thee our Lord has found a faithful servant and a tongue like unto his own with which to speak to the hearts of men."

Then he was gone through the flap of the tent, so quickly that the fabric hardly moved and Luke was left alone, staring at the scroll and wondering if he had been dreaming. When Apollonius's snore began again, however, his eyes fell to a dark spot in the sand that formed the floor of the tent, and he knew his senses had not deceived him. For that stain could be nothing else but blood which had dripped from Peter's wounded feet.

vi

Placing the scroll in his clothes bag again, Luke stepped outside the tent. The moon was shining brightly, and in its light he could see Simon Peter limping along the road that led back to Jerusalem. The sentry was not ten paces away, and Luke walked over to him. "Did you see the man who just left my tent?" he asked.

"No man left it, sir," the sentry stated. "I have been in this spot for fully one turn of the glass."

For a moment Luke wondered again if he had been seeing a vision, in spite of the blood spot in the sand. But when he looked down the road he could still see Peter trudging along in the moonlight. "Never mind," he told the soldier. "I was only testing you."

Silvanus appeared from the shadows in time to hear the last words. "What is this, Luke?" he asked severely. "Are you an officer that you test my soldiers?"

Obeying a sudden impulse, Luke said, "Look down the road, Silvanus, and tell me what you see." For he could still see Peter in the distance.

Silvanus jerked his head impatiently in the direction of Jerusalem, then back at Luke. "The road is empty," he said. "What is the name of this ghost you have been seeing?"

Luke spoke in a low voice so that only the centurion could hear. "He called himself Simon Peter."

Silvanus stiffened as if the point of a sword had been pressed against his back. To the sentry he said, "Move along now," and then to Luke, "Come inside the tent."

When he had secured the tent flap, Silvanus demanded, "Now what is this all about, young man?"

"Just as I told you," Luke insisted. "A man who said he was named Simon Peter came here tonight and talked to me in this very tent. When I asked you to look down the road I could still see him. Perhaps your eyesight is failing, Silvanus," he added, smiling.

But the centurion was in no joking mood. "Do you have any real evidence that this man Peter was here, Luke?" he asked.

"Look there in the sand. It is blood from his feet."

Silvanus knelt and rubbed some of the sand between his fingers. "It is blood," he agreed. "But why were his feet bleeding?"

"He had walked from Jerusalem and his sandals were worn through. Now do you believe me?" Luke asked triumphantly.

"I believed you the moment you said it was Peter who had visited you," Silvanus told him.

"Then you know him?"

"I saw Peter some years ago. Is he large, broad-shouldered, and heavily bearded?"

"It is the same man," Luke told him. "But why couldn't you and the sentry see him?"

Silvanus settled himself comfortably on Luke's sleeping rug. "Strange things are always happening where this man Peter is concerned, Luke. He is the leader of those who follow Jesus of Nazareth and is said to have been given many of Jesus's powers."

"Are you trying to tell me that he has supernatural powers, Silvanus? How could you believe in such things?"

The centurion stared at the blood spot on the sand. "I don't know what to believe," he admitted candidly. "Can you explain how neither the sentry nor I could see Peter just now?"

"Hippocrates speaks of people whose vision is poor at night," Luke insisted.

"My vision was always good before tonight," Silvanus pointed out. "What did Peter want with you?"

"He came about the scroll."

"What scroll?"

There was nothing to do now but tell Silvanus what had happened that morning at the stoning of Stephen and show him the scroll. Besides, Peter had said that Silvanus and Theophilus could be trusted.

The centurion took the slender spool and turned it in his hands. "So Stephen gave up his life because of this," he said softly.

22

"I see nothing in the teachings of this Jesus to make such a disturbance about," Luke said. "They differ but little from the philosophy of Plato, for example."

"Read me some of it," Silvanus said.

Luke unrolled the parchment from the spool and read again the portion that he had been reading when Peter came. When he finished, Silvanus nodded. "Those are the things Jesus taught. They have set them down correctly."

"Did you hear Jesus teach?" Luke cried eagerly. "With your own ears?"

"Yes. I heard him once."

"And did you see him heal the sick?"

"Yes. In fact, Jesus once healed Gaius, my body servant."

"Tell me about it," Luke urged. Here was an opportunity to learn at first hand something of the strange powers of healing which this Nazarene seemed to have possessed.

"It was several years ago," Silvanus began. "I was living in Capernaum, a city on the Lake of Tiberias. Jesus and his disciples came through one day. He was young, about thirty years, I would say, with a soft brown beard. I remember particularly his eyes." Silvanus stopped for a moment. "They were the kindest eyes I ever saw. From the moment you saw them you knew that he could be trusted, even with your life."

"But the healing," Luke said impatiently. "How did he do it?"

"I don't know what he did," Silvanus admitted. "Gaius was sick with a fever of the brain, and we had given him up to die. When I heard that Jesus was healing the sick, I sent some Jewish friends to ask him if he would heal my servant. I still don't know what made me think Jesus could help Gaius, but when I met him I knew that he could. And when I returned home Gaius was well."

"It must have been some strange new treatment," Luke suggested, but Silvanus shook his head.

"I think not, Luke. This was something beyond drugs and physicians."

"I have seen a man get well when he seemed to be dead," Luke objected. "It was an affliction of the mind, and he was cured suddenly so that he seemed to rise from the dead."

Silvanus smiled tolerantly. "Suppose I tell you that Jesus fed almost five thousand people with a few loaves and fish."

"Did you see this yourself?"

"No. But it was told to me by people who were there."

"You know how such things are magnified in the telling," Luke scoffed. And then he had a thought. "Is that why the followers of Jesus call themselves the Company of the Fish?"

"It might be," Silvanus admitted. "Jesus taught them that he would provide for them. They may be using his feeding fish to the crowd as a symbol."

"But all this doesn't mean that Jesus had to be divine, Silvanus. Does it make sense that the God of an obscure tribe like the Jews should have power over all the gods that men believe in? And if he were so powerful, would he have let his son become a mere man, an obscure teacher? And then let the Jews kill him?"

"I know little of gods and religions, Luke." Silvanus got to his feet and tightened his harness. "Jesus was no mere man, I am sure of that."

"But you can't really believe that he was divine, Silvanus."

Then the centurion said a strange thing. "Perhaps I am afraid to believe what I know in my heart is true, Luke. What did Peter tell you to do with the scroll?"

Luke repeated Peter's instructions. "Do you think I should obey them?" he asked.

The older man smiled and rumpled the youth's hair with a gnarled hand. "Have no fear, Luke. I don't think you could keep from carrying out his instructions even if you tried," he said enigmatically.

vii

Luke bade Apollonius farewell on the quay at Joppa before his ship sailed. As he watched his foster brother standing on the deck, straight and tall in military trappings, he felt a moment of envy, for Apollonius would be a tribune, an important official in the Roman Army, while he would be only a physician. Romans of that day looked down upon physicians, particularly Greek ones, and made mock of them. But Luke had noticed that even the proudest Roman hurried to seek the advice of a Greek medical practitioner when he was ill, for they were known to be more learned and skillful than Roman physicians. Then he reminded himself sharply that he had no right to envy Apollonius but should be thankful that he had been reared through the generosity of Theophilus as a foster son, although his father had once been a slave. And it was entirely through the influence of Theophilus, he knew, that he would shortly enter the Temple of Asklepios at Pergamum, the most famous training ground for physicians of that day.

Theophilus's party left Joppa the following morning. Their way led northward along the great Via Maris, called the Way of the Sea because it touched the large lake which the Jews called the Sea of Galilee

24

and the Romans the Lake of Tiberias. The Romans had built this great road upon the oldest highway in the world, the route from Mesopotamia on the north and east to Egypt far to the south. Through the Plain of Sharon to Pirathon they traveled leisurely, and thence through a mountain pass to the fortress city of Megiddo. It was wild and mountainous terrain, like much of the country they had traveled through in this troubled land. Luke found himself wondering, as he rode his mule at the end of the column, why the Jewish leader Moses had led his people here from the fertile lands along the Nile in Egypt.

He had been reading the scroll while in Joppa, and as they neared Nazareth, the city where Jesus had lived, he wished to stop and make some inquiries about further miracles of healing. But a messenger brought word to Theophilus on the road, inviting him and his party to stop for a few days at the palace of Herod Antipas, tetrarch of Galilee, in the city of Tiberias. And since the hospitality of Herod was known to be lavish, the rest of the party was anxious to push on, so Luke did not get to see Nazareth.

It was hardly an hour before sunset when they reached the city of Magdala through what the Jews called the Valley of the Doves. As tired as he was, Luke could not repress an exclamation of pure delight as they emerged from the narrow defile through the mountains ringing the lake. Suddenly it lay before them, a jewel of unbelievable beauty, sparkling in the afternoon sunlight far below. Now he knew why the Jews had come from Egypt and why they would return from the very ends of the earth to what a poet had called "the entrance to Paradise."

To the north a plain curved beside the lake for several miles. It seemed, from this distance, to be about a mile in width and was so thickly planted with vines and fruit trees that the fertile strip of earth itself could not be seen, the whole looking like a green carpet.

Silvanus stopped beside Luke. "What do you think of it?" he asked.

Luke took a deep breath. "Is there a more beautiful spot on earth?"

The centurion smiled, and there was a faraway look in his eyes. "Yes, there is one more beautiful." Then he seemed to recover his wandering thoughts. "That plain is one of the most fertile spots in the world, Luke. The Jews keep its fruits away from the markets of Jerusalem on feast days lest they prove a greater attraction than the rites in the temple."

"I wonder why all the Jews don't live here," Luke said.

Silvanus laughed. "Walk around the lake and you will think they do. The whole shore on the west is almost one continuous city. Capernaum, where I lived, lies to the northward there," he said, pointing to it in the distance.

Capernaum was a familiar name to Luke, for it was mentioned several times in the scroll. Jesus, he was sure, had loved this fertile shore, and looking down upon it now, he could easily understand why.

"That is Tiberias to the south," Silvanus said. "We had better be going if we are to dine tonight at Herod's table." Luke could see the lovely city built along the hills beside the water, with the white marble villas of the Roman officials shining in the sunlight, and amid them the dazzling splendor of Herod's palace. Marble stairways led down to the water's edge, where sumptuous pleasure barges lay. Nowhere in the world, not even in Rome, did the officials of the Empire live more sumptuously than in this lovely city which Herod had built in honor of the Emperor Tiberius.

But it was not Tiberias or the life of the palace that interested Luke most. He had seen Roman splendor in other cities and found it not very attractive to one of his serious purpose. The occupants of those beautiful houses, he knew, spent most of their time in gambling, drinking, feasting, and making wagers on their favorite sword fighter in the next games. Always discontented, they bickered constantly among themselves, and often blood was shed over nothing more important than the question of which was the deadlier weapon in the arena, the short sword or the net and trident.

The scroll had said Jesus healed many people on the shores of Galilee, and Luke was anxious to talk to some of them. In a few days they would be leaving this region and he would have no other chance to learn the truth about how Jesus healed from the very people who had been cured by him. Gaius, unfortunately, had been able to tell him nothing, for the servant knew only that he had been deathly sick but suddenly became well.

Luke roamed the teeming cities along the fertile coast of the lake during the next few days, walking in the very streets where Jesus had walked and upon the very shores where, according to the scroll, he had fed a multitude of many thousands upon a few loaves and fish. But he found no man who did not look away when he spoke of the Nazarene, and none would tell him of the healing miracles Jesus had performed, for Herod was seeking to stamp out this new faith and, in addition, the Romans were determined to let no opposition rise again among the Jews.

Every day Luke saw prisoners being marched through the streets in chains, some to be executed, others to pour out their lifeblood under the claws of wild beasts in the arenas of Rome, and still others to sweat out their lives on Roman galleys. Roman justice was swift and impartial, but its weight was heavy on those who failed or were unable to pay the heavy taxes imposed by the conquerors. Daily, as Luke set out from the palace through the sparkling capital city of Tiberias, he heard the screams of slaves being whipped in the courtyards of the Roman villas. What he saw and heard sickened him at first, but it also made him think. Although by birth a Greek, he was also a Roman citizen, as his father had been before him, and he had always prized that citizenship highly. It had been his belief that the rule of Rome was always a just one, bringing peace and order to lands whose history had previously been that of strife and bloodshed. Now he was beginning to see how that rule was maintained, and for the first time he doubted the rightness of Roman justice.

Herod, Silvanus told Luke, was fearful that the followers of Jesus sought to dethrone him and set up another kingdom in one of the rapid changes of government which had been almost the rule in this land until the firm hand of Rome had settled upon it. And so few were willing to admit any connection with Jesus of Nazareth, fearing the wrath of Herod and the Romans.

"But I find nothing in the scroll to indicate that Jesus sought to overthrow the government," Luke protested. "It seems to me that his concern is only with things of the spirit."

Silvanus smiled. "You are not a ruler, Luke. Those who rule obtain their office by climbing over others, so they always suspect someone else of the same ambitions."

"But that is selfish and deceitful."

"You are young, Luke. When you know more of the world you will realize that many men are selfish and deceitful. It is part of their nature."

"Socrates did say that an evil spirit, the daimonion, lives in every man and constantly battles for control," Luke agreed. "Perhaps what the teachings of Jesus do is to strengthen and bring out the good in man."

"To the Jews who believe in him, Jesus is also a great deliverer they call the Messiah," Silvanus pointed out.

"There are messiahs in every religion," Luke objected. "Why should men look for someone to deliver them from the results of their own misdeeds, when they know in their hearts that peace and happiness come only through kindness and love and repaying good for evil?"

Silvanus smiled. "Do you realize that you were repeating the principles of Jesus then, Luke?"

"Yes," Luke admitted. "But all good men know these things in their hearts, Silvanus."

"Men do know them," the centurion admitted. "But they need something else. In battle, a good commander always sees that the standard bearing the eagles of Rome goes ahead of the troops. It gives them courage and strength to fight on."

"Then Jesus must be a symbol to his followers of all that the good in men stands and fights for."

Silvanus looked at him keenly. "Could you set those things down in writing, Luke?"

"Why, yes," Luke said in surprise. "But there is nothing new about the idea. Plato and Socrates said the same thing."

"I don't mean that. I mean about Jesus being a symbol."

"Yes. But why?"

"It may be just what most people are looking for," Silvanus explained. "You could show them Jesus as a symbol of what his teachings seek to bring out, the fundamental goodness in everyone. Any man could understand a principle as simple as that, whether he believed Jesus to be the son of a god or not."

"But who would read it? After all, I am only the son of a Roman freedman; my father was once a slave——"

"Jesus was a carpenter," Silvanus reminded him. "But you may be right at that. You have the scroll and can study it. Later, when you are a famous physician, you can set these things down and publish them abroad. Then many will read them because you are famous."

Luke smiled. "Are you that certain of me, Silvanus?"

The grizzled centurion put his arm about the youth's shoulders. "If you can always speak and write the truth as simply as you have told it to me today, Luke, I am sure that men will read your writings as long as the world shall last."

viii

The road to Damascus led upward along the slopes of the mountains that ringed the Lake of Tiberias. From time to time, as his mule plodded along in the bright morning sunlight, Luke would lose sight of the blue oval lying hundreds of feet below in its natural cup, only to see it appear again unexpectedly as the path rounded a craggy bluff. So entranced was he by the ever-changing panorama of lake and mountain that his mule often wandered from the road and stopped to munch grass without his realizing it.

Even after a full hour of climbing the road was still below the elevation of the seacoast, for the lake lay about the eighth part of a mile below the level of the sea. The air, which had been humid and oppressing by the lake, grew cooler as they ascended, and the marching foot soldiers began to joke and sing bawdy songs in the invigorating mountain heights. Ahead towered the snow-capped peak of Mount Hermon.

The party halted for rest and food where the Way of the Sea crossed the river Jordan at a point called Jisr Benat Ya'kub, or the Bridge of Jacob's Daughters. Since it was spring, melting snows pouring down into the river Jordan had swelled it to a rushing torrent fully thirty paces in width. The water was icy cold and bluish-green in color, and along the banks of the river grew flowering oleanders, the tall fanlike papyrus, and a balsamlike tree from which came the nuts whose oil was made into the famous "balm of Gilead," much prized for its flavor and its healing properties.

They paused by the river only long enough to eat and fill the waterskins, for much of the Via Maris that lay ahead traversed very dry country, and water must be carried on mules for the party, sometimes for several days at a time. When the column stopped again at the top of the long hill above the river so that the mounts and the walking soldiers could catch their breath, Luke dismounted for a last look at the Sea of Galilee.

Against the blue of the lake was set the green of the vineyards and groves, the brown wharves, and the dazzling white palaces of the Romans and richer Jews. And upon its surface bobbed the bright sailed boats of the fishermen. Both Tiberias and Capernaum were plainly visible, their buildings reduced to the proportions of dollhouses. And across the lake the mountains dropped precipitously to the water level.

Then Silvanus shouted the order for march, the column moved out along the straight ribbon of road leading northward and eastward to Damascus, and the compelling beauty of Galilee was left behind. Luke's place was at the rear of the column so that his medical knowledge would be available in case any of the party fell out of line and needed attention. He settled back on his mount, conserving his strength for the long, hot journey ahead.

Ten days later the city of Damascus was a welcome sight from a hilltop several hours' journey away. A low walled square of white buildings, it lay on the south bank of the river Barada, with the green of trees sometimes hiding the buildings. Thoughts of the cool shade and refreshment that waited ahead cheered the whole column and it seemed to take on new life, so that Luke had to kick his mule to keep up. Hardly had they started down the hill, however, when there was a shouted order, and the long train halted. Luke rode ahead to see what had happened.

A knot of gesticulating men were gathered in the road, and as Luke came closer he saw that they were Jews. Silvanus and a pair of brawny soldiers had just pushed their way into the crowd, and Luke dismounted quickly and entered the breach they formed. Everyone seemed to be talking excitedly at the top of his lungs.

Then Luke saw that a man was kneeling in the center of the excited crowd. His face was pale, sweat beaded his forehead, and he held out his hands in a gesture of supplication, as if begging for help or praying. The man seemed to be in the grip of utter terror, for his whole body was trembling. Luke recognized him with a start of surprise.

The kneeling man was Saul of Tarsus!

Silvanus saw Luke in the crowd and beckoned to him. Having lived in Capernaum, the centurion understood the barbarous tongue they called Aramaic. He was listening to a tall, bearded man who was pouring an impassioned oration into his ear. And as he listened a strange look came into his face.

"What has happened, Silvanus?" Luke asked, but the centurion only shook his head in a warning to be silent and continued to listen to the tall Jew.

Luke turned his attention to Saul, who still knelt in the dirt, his staring eyes moving ceaselessly about, as a blind man's do. Obviously some great change had come over Saul; he was no longer the arrogant, assured prosecutor who had questioned witnesses at the trial of Stephen. Luke wondered what could have happened to bring about such a change. Saul might have fallen, striking his head, and leaving him partially bereft of his senses, but there were no marks upon him. Actually, he looked more like a person who had just experienced a frightening dream.

Silvanus came over to Luke. "That fellow I was talking to is Hyrcanus, a member of the Sanhedrin," he explained. "He and Saul were on the way to Damascus to continue their persecution of the followers of Jesus, when a strange thing happened." He hesitated, as if reluctant to speak further and Luke asked patiently, "What was it?"

"You will not believe this, Luke, but Hyrcanus insists there was a blinding flash of light that stopped them in their tracks. Then Saul claimed to have heard a voice say, 'Saul! Saul! Why do you persecute me?'"

"Who was speaking?"

"Hyrcanus says they could see no one, but Saul seemed to hear it, for he asked, 'Who art thou, Lord?' Then he claims that the same voice answered, 'I am Jesus, whom you have persecuted. It is hard for you to kick against the pricks.'"

It was a strange story, and for a moment Luke was tempted to believe that it really was one of the miracles such as the followers of Jesus often described. But just then he happened to glance at the city of Damascus, and the sun was reflected from the gilded roof of a palace in a sudden glare that hurt his eyes. "There is your bright light," he cried in a flash of inspiration. "A perfectly natural explanation. See the way the sun is reflected from the dome of that palace."

Silvanus and the Jews all looked at it, and some of them put their hands before their eyes to shield them against the glare. Hyrcanus spoke to the others, and they all began to talk excitedly.

"That could account for the light," Silvanus admitted. "But what about the voice?"

"It mentioned the pricks," Luke suggested. "Why not the pricks of Saul's conscience? And remember, the others did not hear it."

"But they say Saul acted exactly as if he were hearing someone speaking to him from heaven."

"It could have been a hallucination," Luke said confidently. "They are sometimes very real to people who are laboring under great excitement." He pointed to the kneeling man. "Look at him. You can see that he is still tremendously disturbed."

Silvanus was impressed by the explanation, for he fiddled unconsciously with the sword at his belt, a habit of his when trying to make up his mind. Hyrcanus had been listening to Luke's explanation intently, and he turned now to translate for the other Jews, who were pointing to the gilded roof from which the sun still shone in a bright glare, then back at the kneeling figure of Saul, who seemed completely ignorant of the commotion he had stirred up on the road to Damascus. Luke could understand only one word in the flood of Aramaic that Hyrcanus was pouring upon the rest of the party. It was "Jeshua," their word for Jesus. But as the Jewish official continued to talk, the faces of the crowd became threatening and several moved toward the kneeling figure, lifting their heavy walking staves to strike him.

Silvanus noticed them and barked an order to the two soldiers, who moved up beside Saul to protect him. "Why are they turning against Saul?" Luke asked.

"Hyrcanus told them that Saul has been converted to belief in Jesus."

"He has no reason to say that," Luke protested.

"I am not sure but that he is right," Silvanus said. "Saul told them that after the voice spoke to him he asked, 'What would you have me do, Lord?' And the voice told him to go into the city."

One of the men with Hyrcanus spat upon Saul with the peculiarly vicious gesture which they used to express contempt. Silvanus casually knocked him sprawling with the back of his hand and turned back to Luke. "This is a serious business, Luke. If Saul goes into Damascus and tells that Jesus spoke to him on the road to the city, many people will think it a miracle and might follow Jesus because of it. We have enough trouble with these people already, without Saul stirring up more."

Luke saw that Hyrcanus, too, was worried. It would be no tribute to the Sanhedrin if its most trusted emissary were suddenly converted on the road to Damascus to the very beliefs he had been so active in trying to stamp out. Hyrcanus might even be held accountable by the high court. Now he bowed before Silvanus and said, "Release this man to us, O Centurion, and we will return with him to Jerusalem at once."

Return to Jerusalem would mean death for Saul, probably by stoning, if he had indeed espoused the belief in Jesus. And Luke could not find enough anger in his heart even against Saul to wish this fate for him. "Why not go on to Damascus?" he suggested to Hyrcanus. "You must have Jewish authorities in your synagogue there."

But that suggestion only made Hyrcanus more excited. From a babble of Greek and Aramaic, Silvanus managed to translate, "Saul tore up the letters of authority they were bringing from the Sanhedrin so that they could persecute the followers of Jesus. That leaves Hyrcanus without authority, and Saul can do as he pleases in Damascus." The centurion pulled his sword half out, then shot it home in the scabbard decisively. "Stay here, Luke," he said. "I will go back along the column and discuss this with Theophilus."

But first he stopped beside Saul. "You are of Tarsus, Saul," he said. "Are you not then a Roman citizen?" The prosperous city of Tarsus had been a part of the Roman Empire for many years, and many among its population were Roman citizens by birth.

"Yes." Saul spoke the words tonelessly, as a man does whose mind has wandered from reality. "I am a Roman."

The colloquy between Theophilus and Silvanus was short, and the centurion returned with a relieved look on his face. "This man is a Roman," he told Hyrcanus. "As such he is entitled to our protection. We will take him with us into Damascus."

The Jews would far rather have taken Saul back to Jerusalem, where the Sanhedrin reigned supreme in religious matters, but Silvanus ignored them. "Get up, Saul," he ordered. "We are taking you into Damascus."

Saul got stiffly to his feet, swaying, as if uncertain of his footing, although he stood on level ground. "The light has blinded me," he said tonelessly.

"Blind?" Silvanus echoed. "How could it?"

"I can see nothing," Saul insisted.

"Can you tell if he is really blind, Luke?" Silvanus asked.

"Not for certain. He could feign blindness easily." Luke said to Saul, "Try to walk, please."

Saul took a few halting steps, groping before him as a blind man does. Then he stumbled over a rock and would have fallen if Luke had not caught him by the shoulders. "He must really be blind," Luke said, "or he would have seen that rock."

"Help him on his mule, then," Silvanus said with disgust. "He can ride along with you."

As the column moved on, Hyrcanus and the others were left wrangling among themselves on the road, but when the Roman party was about a mile away, they finally mounted and followed. As they rode along, Luke tried to question Saul, but the short man answered in the same toneless voice, and he learned nothing that Hyrcanus had not already told them about what had taken place on the road to Damascus.

While they waited at the city gate for a message to be sent to the governor announcing the arrival of so important a party, Silvanus came back to where Luke and Saul were sitting on their mules. "Did you learn anything else from him, Luke?" he asked.

"No. He tells the same story that Hyrcanus did."

The centurion nodded thoughtfully. "Where was it that Peter told you to take what you are carrying, Luke?"

"To the house of Judas, a cobbler. In the street called Straight."

"I remember now; many Jews live on that street. Some of them will undoubtedly know Saul and take him in. You will take an escort of four soldiers, Luke," Silvanus said in a relieved voice. "Deliver the scroll and then ask in the neighborhood if anyone knows Saul of Tarsus and will take care of him. Deliver him to them and come on to the governor's palace."

ix

The street called Straight ran in a direct line entirely through Damascus. It was lined with beautiful colonnades and partially roofed over in the center of the city. Many shops opened upon the street, and Luke was directed at once to the establishment of Judas, the cobbler. Leaving the soldiers with Saul in the street a little way from the house, he entered the shop, which was open to the street. As was the custom here, the family living quarters were at the back, grouped around a small open garden visible through an open door. The whole place resounded with the tapping of many hammers as apprentices and artisans worked at benches around the wall. A man who was cutting patterns for sandals out of beautifully soft leather rose and came forward, bowing courteously. "What is it you wish, noble sir?" he asked.

"I am seeking one Judas," Luke said.

"I am called Judas."

"My name is Luke."

33

Instantly Judas seized his hand. "You have the scroll?" he asked in low, excited tones.

"How did you know?" Luke said, caught off guard. Then he began to back toward the door and the street, thinking that this might be a trick.

But Judas turned and called into the back of the shop, "Nicanor! Nicanor! Luke has arrived from Jerusalem."

Luke stopped, for Nicanor had been the name of the person to whom Peter had told him to give the scroll. When a man hurried forward from the back of the shop, Luke's first thought was that he looked like Peter. And yet there was no physical resemblance, for he was of medium height only, with a distinctly Greek face, and was beardless. What he and Peter did have in common, however, was a look of calm majesty, of peace and tolerance.

"I am Nicanor," he said, bowing. "Welcome to Damascus, Luke. We had word of your coming from Cephas."

"Cephas?" The name was not familiar.

"He is also called Simon Peter. Do you have the scroll?"

"Peter instructed me to give it only to one who would repeat the last words of Stephen."

A spasm of pain crossed Nicanor's face and Luke saw tears start in his eyes. "Stephen and I were as brothers, Luke," he said in a choked voice. "Forgive me if I weep for my friend." Then he put his lips close to Luke's ear and whispered, "His last words were these, 'Lord, lay not this sin to their charge.'"

Luke took the scroll from his tunic then and gave it to Nicanor. As it left his hand he experienced a strange feeling, almost of reluctance to give it up, as if he were losing something precious. Nicanor took the scroll tenderly in his hands and ran his fingers over the stains where Stephen's blood had seeped into the parchment. "You have earned the undying gratitude of all the members of the Company of the Fish everywhere, Luke," he said sincerely. "Be sure that the Most High will reward you as you deserve. Will you not stay and break bread with us?"

"Perhaps another day," Luke said courteously. "Now I must find quarters for a man who was blinded on the road a few hours ago."

"You may leave him with us too," Nicanor said. "We have been expecting him."

"You must be mistaken," Luke protested. "The accident only happened a few hours ago, and no one passed us on the road to bring you word."

"Would you believe we knew of his coming if I told you his name?" Nicanor asked, smiling.

Luke turned to look through the doorway out into the street. Saul and the guards were not visible from inside the shop, and Nicanor had come from the back of the room, so he could not possibly have seen and recognized Saul. How, then, could he know?

"No, Luke." Nicanor's quiet voice interrupted his thoughts. "I cannot see him in the street, but I can tell you that the blind man is Saul of Tarsus."

"H-how did you know?" Luke stammered.

"There is one to whom nothing is hidden," Nicanor said gently. "Someday you, too, will know him." It was almost exactly what Peter had said on the road to Joppa.

All the way to the palace of the governor Luke puzzled over the strange fact that Nicanor had known of Saul's coming before they had arrived. By the time he reached the palace he was sure he had a simple answer. Seeking out Silvanus, he told the whole story to the centurion in his quarters while he dressed for the evening meal.

Luke's answer to the whole thing was simple. Saul, being active in the Jewish religion, would be known to many Jews in Damascus. One of them must have recognized him when Luke had stopped to ask for the shop of Judas and had run ahead to warn those in the shop. And since Nicanor was known as a leader of the Company of the Fish, word would naturally be brought to him of Saul's coming.

"Does it occur to you that you may have turned Saul over to his enemies in Jerusalem?" Silvanus asked when Luke finished. "Nicanor and the rest of the Company of the Fish are the very people Saul was sent to destroy."

"I hadn't thought of that," Luke admitted. "What will they do with him?"

Silvanus smiled. "Suppose you go back there in a day or two and see." But it was obvious to Luke that the centurion did not believe Saul would be harmed.

"What is your explanation, then?" Luke demanded, a little aggrieved that his explanation had not been accepted.

"Suppose Jesus is what his followers believe him to be, the son of Jehovah," Silvanus suggested. "Nicanor could have been warned by Jesus of Saul's coming."

"But you don't really believe a man who has been dead for several years spoke to Saul from the sky, Silvanus. That is absurd."

It was a long moment before Silvanus spoke. "You are young, Luke, and far more learned than I am. But someday you will admit that there are things for which we can find no answer, except that there is some sort of divine being watching over us."

"How can you believe in something you cannot even understand?" Luke insisted doggedly.

The centurion smiled. "I heard Jesus speak of that once, Luke. He used a word, *faith*. Some things we must accept without trying to explain them. In youth, death seems far away. But I am almost sixty years old now. You must not blame me if, toward the end of my days on earth, I cling to something which assures me a life beyond this one."

The grizzled old soldier had never confided in Luke to this extent, and the youth was deeply moved. He tried to laugh and did not succeed very well. "Would you have me bawling like a child?" he demanded. "Let us talk no more of age and death. As for me, I would rather believe there is a place somewhere on earth where man remains forever young, as some of the philosophers have claimed."

"There is such a land, Luke," Silvanus said to his surprise. "I have seen it."

"Where?" Luke demanded eagerly. "Where is it?"

"A long way to the north, on the shores of the Pontus Euxinus, which some call the Black Sea. It is a province called Bithynia."

"Bithynia." The word had a pleasant rhythm, a pleasant taste, and Luke repeated it again. "Do people really stay young there, Silvanus?"

The centurion shook his head, smiling. "No, Luke. Nor anywhere else in this world, I suspect. But it is a beautiful land surrounded entirely by mountains, except on the shores of the sea. The sands are white and the water is warm and clear. And in the valleys that come down to the sea all manner of fruits and vegetables grow, merely with stirring the soil. The people of Bithynia are forever happy, or so it seems, and those who are contented are always young."

"Are you going back?" Luke asked.

"Yes. If only to die in Bithynia."

Impulsively Luke said, "Take me with you when you go, Silvanus."

The centurion smiled fondly. "I will send for you when I am ready to go to Bithynia, Luke," he agreed. "That is a promise. Now don't forget." He added briskly, "I want you to go back to the shop of Judas and find out what happens to Saul of Tarsus."

That night Luke unrolled his sleeping rug on the balcony outside his chamber, for it was still hot inside. As he lay there under the stars, his thoughts turned to Bithynia. It must indeed be an earthly paradise, he thought, if everyone was truly happy there, for he had seen few signs of real peace and happiness anywhere in his travels. Idly he tried to think who, among all those he knew, were really happy, and suddenly he realized that the only really happy people he had seen all had one thing in common. They were followers of Jesus of Nazareth.

Peter, who had known imprisonment and whose feet on the night he had visited Luke beside the road to Joppa were raw and bleeding, had still radiated a calm happiness. Stephen had gone to his death with the same look of peace in his eyes, and today it had been in the faces of Nicanor and Judas. These men had found something not possessed by most men, Luke realized, some private kingdom of peace, a place of the mind which must be amazingly like the province of Bithynia that Silvanus had described.

Luke found himself wishing that he had the scroll again. Perhaps through reading it once more he might find there the secret of their happiness. Presently he drifted off to sleep, only to dream of a fair land beyond the mountains to which he tried to go but was held back by a small man with a large head who seemed to be Saul of Tarsus. And when finally he awakened he was drenched with sweat and shaking in the grip of a terror he could not name.

x

There was much to interest a youth of eighteen in Damascus, the oldest city of the world: the long caravans from the mythical lands to the east with their great ungainly beasts of burden; the shops of the metalsmiths where furnaces glowed to a white heat and boys trod madly upon great bellows skins to keep the coals glowing so that shining blades of steel could be forged by the skilled hammers of the workmen; the magic of strange dark-skinned men who charmed poisonous serpents with little flutes; the loose-robed conjurers making balls appear and disappear with startling ease; the thin-faced Egyptian who worked spells with a glass ball and forced men into a deep sleep in which they did his bidding, so that sometimes the lame walked and the blind saw again. Everything was new and strange, and it was three days before Luke thought again about Saul of Tarsus and returned to the shop of Judas, the cobbler.

When Luke entered the cool gloom of the shop, neither Nicanor nor Judas was working, but one of the apprentices directed him to the garden in the back that gave access to the living quarters. He went on into the garden, and Nicanor came to meet him, hands outstretched, smiling in welcome. "One of the men in the shop told me to come back here," Luke explained.

"You are always doubly welcome in this house," Nicanor said. "For it was you who brought Saul to us."

Luke started involuntarily. Could Silvanus have been right, after all, about his turning Saul over to his worst enemies? "Are you happy about his coming?" he asked incredulously.

37

"Oh yes. Very happy indeed."

"But Saul came here to persecute you."

"Jesus has revealed himself to Saul," Nicanor explained. "It happened just before you found him on the road. He is one of us now."

"And you trust him?" Luke asked, still unable to believe that a man who had persecuted the Company of the Fish so diligently in Jerusalem could change sides so quickly.

"It is not what a man does before Jesus calls him that counts, Luke," Nicanor said gently, "but what he does afterward. Come and see for yourself. Saul is praying in the garden here."

"Is he still blind?"

"Yes. But it has been revealed to Saul in a vision that a disciple here in Damascus named Ananias will soon visit him. Ananias has the gift of healing and will restore his sight."

"I should like to be here when he heals Saul," Luke said immediately, hoping for the opportunity to see at first hand one of the acts of healing which rumor had it that some disciples of Jesus possessed the power to accomplish.

"You may see it. We are waiting for Ananias to come now."

"How long since you sent for him?" Luke asked.

Nicanor smiled. "The Lord sent for him, Luke. He has revealed to Saul that Ananias is coming."

Luke followed Nicanor across the shady garden to where Saul was kneeling, his hands held out in supplication, his eyes moving constantly as they had on the road to Damascus. From his lips poured a steady stream of words in Aramaic. Judas knelt beside him, his eyes uplifted, ecstasy shining in his face, as he prayed in the same tongue. Looking at Saul, haggard and supplicant, Luke could hardly believe that this was the strong, confident man who had prosecuted Stephen a few weeks ago before the Sanhedrin in Jerusalem. A great change had indeed come over him.

There was a stone bench under the spreading fronds of a great palm, and Luke and Nicanor sat there, sipping wine and munching some dates that were on a small table before the bench. The dates were delicious, and Luke had already become quite fond of the sweet wine that was favored by the Jews. "You still do not trust Saul, do you, Luke?" Nicanor asked.

"He killed Stephen," Luke said bluntly. Then he added, "But it doesn't matter now. I don't think Saul will ever persecute anyone else but himself. He seems quite mad to me."

"Others have mistaken the ecstasy that comes from God for madness, Luke. Men older and wiser than either of us."

Luke started to reply, but suddenly Nicanor stood up, saying, "Here is Ananias!"

A short, plump man stood in the doorway leading to the shop, looking about him with an air of uncertainty. When Nicanor hurried over and greeted him, Luke heard the newcomer ask, "Is there one here who is called Saul of Tarsus?"

"Yes. Saul is here," Nicanor assured the visitor.

"I was told in a vision to come here and heal him of his blindness."

"We have been expecting you, Ananias." Nicanor led the healer to where Saul knelt, still praying. Luke was forgotten in the excitement, so he moved closer in order to see what new medicine Ananias might use in curing blindness.

Nicanor tapped Saul gently upon the shoulder. "Ananias has come to heal you, Saul," he announced.

Saul lifted his face and smiled. It was the first time Luke remembered seeing him smile, and even haggard as he was, the blind man's face lit up so that he seemed a different person. Ananias went over and stood behind him, laying his fingers on Saul's eyelids. "Brother Saul," he said, "the Lord, even Jesus, has sent me, that you might receive your sight and be filled with the Holy Ghost."

Luke found that he was holding his breath, carried away by the tension of the moment, and looked around to see if anyone had noticed his absorption. But every eye was fixed on the scene before him, and he turned his gaze upon Saul once more. Indeed it was a gripping picture, the godlike head of the kneeling man thrown back, his sightless eyes lifted to the sky, and the pudgy figure of Ananias, somehow impressive in spite of his small stature, standing behind Saul, fingertips resting upon his eyes.

Suddenly Saul shouted, "I see! I see! Thanks be to God, I see!" He staggered to his feet and, throwing his arms about Ananias, wept upon the healer's shoulder. The others were embracing each other and weeping. Luke knew that if he remained he would soon be blubbering himself, so he slipped through the deserted shop into the street outside.

He did not leave the vicinity, however, for he wanted to talk to Ananias when he came out. Apparently the healer had used no medicine, but Luke was sure that there must be some explanation for such an immediate cure. When the chubby form of the healer emerged from the shop and started along the street, Luke fell into step beside him. "My name is Luke," he said in explanation. "I am a student of medicine. May I talk to you as you walk along?"

"Certainly, Luke," Ananias said graciously. "You were in the garden of Judas. Why did you leave?"

"I—I am not a Jew," Luke explained. "I felt out of place."

39

"Are you of the Company of the Fish?"

"No. I am a Greek and worship no gods."

Ananias smiled. "Yet Nicanor tells me that you ministered to Stephen as he lay dying and guarded the scroll containing the sayings of Jesus. And that you cared for Saul when he was stricken blind on the road."

"I am going to be a physician," Luke explained. "Naturally my first duty is to care for the sick and wounded."

"Would that all physicians were like you, Luke. What is it you wish of me?"

"I would learn the secret of how you were able to give Saul his sight. Or purchase it, if you will sell it."

Ananias looked at him quizzically. "I have nothing to sell, Luke. There is no secret."

"But you seemed to know exactly what to do."

"I only did as the Lord instructed me in a vision," Ananias explained patiently. Then, seeing the disappointment in the younger man's face, he added, "I know nothing about the power by which I am sometimes able to heal disease, Luke. But you are already more learned in medicine than I, and perhaps you may discover it for yourself. Come and we will break bread together, then I will take you with me on my visits to the sick."

xi

Ananias was a weaver by trade, and his shop, located on a side street under the very walls of the city, was filled with the pungent smell of cloth and dyes, the clash of scissors blades, and the clicking of looms. In a corner was a stack of large wicker baskets, almost as long as a man was tall, in which weavers placed their goods to protect them on the long trips by mule or camel caravan to markets in other cities. They tarried only a moment in the shop while Ananias inspected a strip of fine cloth which had just come from the looms, then entered the garden around which the living quarters of the house were arranged on two sides, the third being the shop, and the fourth the wall of the city itself.

It was the most pleasant house Luke had seen in his journey, more attractive by far, he thought, than the ornate palaces of Tiberias. Ananias had told him as they walked through the city that the house and shop had once belonged to a smuggler who had become rich by hauling goods over the adjacent city wall with ropes, thus evading the usual customs charges collected at the gates, and he could see now that it was admirably suited for the purpose. A fountain bubbled in a small pool beside the wall, and around it vines and ferns grew thickly, with flowering vines climbing trellises halfway up the walls of the building. A great cedar stood in the center of the garden, its outflung branches shading the entire area from the heat of the sun, but letting enough of its rays through to dapple the green carpet of grass with a stippling of gold. The song of birds here was as pleasing to the ear as the flowers were to the eye, and everywhere was the fresh, enticing smell of growing things.

A girl was sitting on a bench beside the fountain. When they approached, she put down the scroll she had been reading and stood up, smiling. She was slight in stature and young, about fifteen, and her features were almost as pure Greek as a classic statue. Her hair was jet black and confined only by a bandeau of white silk falling unhindered to caress her shoulders in rich, soft waves. She wore a robe of white silk, its lines of classic Greek simplicity bound about the waist with a tasseled cord, and sandals were upon her tiny feet. She was, Luke thought as he stared at her with openmouthed admiration, like a perfect figurine carved from marble by loving hands. But this was living marble, glowing and breathing with a healthy, unstudied beauty.

Ananias went over and kissed the girl on the forehead; then, turning with his arm about her waist, he said, "This is Luke, my dear. A fine young man and a student of medicine. My daughter, Mariamne, Luke."

The girl smiled graciously and held out her hand. "You are welcome to our house, Luke."

Tongue-tied for the moment by her beauty, Luke fumbled with her fingers. Somehow he managed to touch them with his lips while he mumbled an incoherent greeting. The girl sensed his confusion, perhaps because her beauty often struck young men dumb when they saw her for the first time. "Do you like my garden?" she asked to put him at ease.

Luke found his tongue then. "It is exceeded in beauty only by its mistress," he said gallantly.

Mariamne clapped her hands and laughed with pleasure at the compliment, while Ananias beamed proudly upon them both. "You are nimble of tongue and wit, Luke," he said approvingly. "But watch her, for she is no chucklehead. You must keep your wits about you."

"The Queen Mariamne is reported to have been both wise and beautiful, Ananias," Luke said. "Your daughter is a worthy namesake."

Mariamne's lips parted, and soft color rose to her cheeks. Luke could see that she was pleased by his remembering the name of Queen Mariamne, wife of Herod the Great, who had built the magnificent temple at Jerusalem. "I was looking at the tower named for you only a few weeks ago, Mariamne," he told her.

"You have come from Jerusalem?" she asked excitedly.

"And Tiberias." Luke was human enough to want to impress her with the fact that he had also visited Herod's capital.

Impulsively Mariamne took him by the hand and pulled him over to the bench. "Tell me about it," she urged. "I have never traveled beyond Damascus." There was nothing of coquetry in the gesture, for she seemed completely unspoiled, in spite of her beauty.

"I must go to the shop for a little while," Ananias said, laughing. "Be careful, Luke. She will worm all of your secrets from you."

Luke had known some young girls in Antioch, but his studies had left him little time for frivolous pursuits. Besides, most of the girls he knew were shallow, it seemed to him, knowing nothing of philosophy or science, interested only in preening to attract the attention of young men, or chattering endlessly about clothes, jewelry, and entertainment. Mariamne was different, however, and he found himself describing for her the Sea of Galilee, painting in words the blue of the water, the green of the olive trees, and the marble-white of the Roman villas. But he said nothing of prisoners driven through the streets with chains dragging from their ankles, or the heavy burdens imposed upon the people by rascally tax gatherers to pay the tribute that Rome demanded in return for its protection. Nor did he speak of Stephen and the horror of his death outside the walls of Jerusalem.

"Where do you go next, Luke?" she asked when he finished the account of his travels.

"Back to Antioch, and then to Pergamum, to continue my studies in medicine at the Temple of Asklepios there."

"Will you pass through Tarsus?" the girl asked. "My mother was from there. She was a Greek, like yourself, but she died when I was a little baby and we moved to Damascus. Father says she was very beautiful."

"She must have been," Luke agreed fervently.

Mariamne put her hand upon his and said softly, "I like you, Luke." And then she repeated in a whisper, for her father had come into the garden, "I like you very much."

The noonday meal was served in the garden, but Luke hardly knew what he ate, for Mariamne continued to chatter gaily throughout the meal. She possessed a talent for mimicry and imitated the traders who came to her father's shop to buy cloth, now puffing out her cheeks to represent a fat Persian from the East, now stroking her chin as an oily Arab pirate from the desert, or again assuming the pompous mien of a Greek who bought for the markets of Rome. She kept them helpless with laughter, and Luke was completely smitten with love long before it was time to go with Ananias upon his daily round of visits to the

42

sick. He willingly promised to return on the morrow and tell her about the theater in Antioch.

Luke learned little from Ananias about healing, however. In some cases the pudgy weaver apparently healed instantly. But these people, it seemed to Luke, were ill only temporarily in their minds and were helped by the kind manner of Ananias and his assurance of the power of Jesus to help if they trusted him. Ananias himself obviously believed completely in such a power, and Luke wondered if his healing ability might not come as much from this confidence as from any other source.

As he made his way back to the governor's palace Luke's thoughts were of Mariamne rather than of healing. He found himself remembering with a warm glow of pleasure how pretty she was, how soft her fingers had been as they lay on his, the music of her laugh, and the way the rich color rose in her cheeks when she was pleased or excited.

Several times, as Luke sat with Silvanus and the others at the feast that evening, the centurion was forced to speak twice to him before he heard. Finally Silvanus said in exasperation, "Who is she, Luke?"

And without thinking, Luke answered promptly, "Mariamne," then blushed in confusion at having betrayed the cause of his reverie.

xii

Matters of state lengthened the stay of Theophilus's party in Damascus to more than ten days, but Luke was not at all displeased by the delay, for he was spending part of every day with Mariamne. With her beauty, she needed no particular learning or intelligence, the ways of pleasing men and attracting their attention being things that a woman knows by instinct, but her mind was keen also. And she was very well read, particularly in the works of the great Greek dramatists, of whom Luke knew but little, his own studies having been largely confined to the writings of philosophers and physicians.

With intentional mischief she led him into the *Plutus* of Aristophanes, that satirical comedy which takes physicians and the pretensions of their art so severely to task. They laughed at it together, for Luke could see how truly it depicted many members of his chosen profession. He was happy during these carefree days in the garden by the city wall, for Mariamne was showing him a side of life, a gay and delightful one, far removed from the revels which he had vaguely thought accompanied music and the theater. The enjoyment of such pleasant things, he assured himself as a physician, must inevitably be reflected in heightened well-being for both body and spirit.

Mariamne was an accomplished player on the lyre and possessed a

43

very pleasing voice. Luke loved to lie on the grass at her feet beside the fountain while she sang. Sometimes her songs were in Aramaic, which he hardly understood at all. They were very pleasing to the ear, but when he pressed her for the meaning of the words, she only blushed a little and put him off. Some had been written by David, she told him, a great king of the Jewish people. And others by Solomon, said to be the wisest man who ever lived. But when she also told him that Solomon had many hundreds of wives, Luke stoutly maintained that he could not have been so wise, for who would want more than one if she were as lovely and desirable as Mariamne? At this Mariamne suddenly put down her lyre and, leaning over, kissed Luke full on the mouth, creating such a confusion in his senses that everything for the moment reeled before his eyes.

It must have had a similar effect upon the girl, for Luke heard her gasp. Then she dropped the lyre and, cheeks crimson, ran into the house. While he waited for her to return, Luke considered this strange effect from contact with her lips but was totally unable to account for it. Nevertheless, he decided to repeat the pleasant experience at the earliest opportunity.

When Mariamne came out again, however, she gave him no such opportunity, promptly saddling him with a large market basket and taking him off on a shopping expedition. By the time they returned, with Luke staggering under the weight of the loaded basket, Luke had to go back to the palace, so he was alone with her no more that day.

He was back the next morning, however, and Mariamne was her own sweet self again. So the time passed and only two days remained until Luke must leave for Pergamum and his studies. He was sad as he joined Ananias and Mariamne for the evening meal that day, but he tried to hide his feelings. As they sat in the twilight, enjoying the cool fragrance of the garden, it seemed to Luke that Ananias was not himself either. Mariamne sensed it, too, for she stopped her gay chatter and asked, "Is anything wrong, Father?"

Ananias rumpled the dark waves of her hair with loving fingers. "Nothing to trouble your pretty head, child." Then he turned to Luke. "I hear that you and your party will be leaving soon, Luke."

Luke had delayed telling Mariamne of his coming departure, planning to do it later in the evening when something might take Ananias to the shop, leaving them alone in the garden. Their relationship had somehow changed since the day she had interrupted her singing to kiss him. Some of the quiet sense of companionship they had shared before had been replaced by an indefinable reserve, a tingling sense of expectancy when they were alone together, which was far more exciting than their comradeship had been before. Now he was forced to break the news that his departure was set for the day after the morrow. The animation faded from Mariamne's face at his words. She caught her breath and said in a whisper, "Do you have to go, Luke?"

Had she waited for him to answer, Luke almost might have decided not to go back to Antioch, for he was strongly tempted to stay always close to her. Then she laughed, although her eyes were wet with tears. "Of course you do. You must become a great physician." She puffed out her cheeks and threw back her head in such a devastating caricature of a pompous medical man that he could not help laughing. Then she jumped up and went running into the house, although she had hardly finished her meal.

When Luke started to follow Mariamne, Ananias put his hand on the younger man's arm. "She will weep and then feel better," he said. "It is the way with women. You have been very good for Mariamne, Luke," the weaver continued. "She has not known much of the world, and you have let her see it through your own eyes. I hope you will remember us when you leave Damascus."

"Oh, but I will," Luke protested. "I will never forget Mariamne—or you, sir," he added, blushing at thus having revealed his feelings.

The weaver smiled. "Perhaps we may hope that you will return when your studies are finished. It would please me to think that you and my daughter might someday mean much to each other."

"She means a great deal to me now, sir," Luke assured him. "And I shall certainly return." Then he changed the subject to hide his own feelings. "You are troubled about something, Ananias. Can I help you?"

The weaver looked at him quizzically. "You will make a good physician, young man; your perceptions are very keen. Yes, I am worried about Saul."

"But you cured him of his blindness."

"It is his life I fear for, not his eyes. Do you remember a man named Hyrcanus in Saul's party when you found him on the road?"

"Yes. He is from the Sanhedrin in Jerusalem."

"Then you know that Hyrcanus followed Saul to Damascus. And you have probably heard that Saul has been telling people everywhere how the Lord spoke to him on the road."

Luke could not have escaped hearing of Saul's activities, for all of Damascus was seething with stories of his eloquence and his dramatic description of how Jesus had called him to join those who called themselves the Company of the Fish. More startling, however, was Saul's insistence that Jesus still lived, although unseen by ordinary men, and that he himself had seen Jesus when he had been blinded. Great crowds were listening to Saul nightly, and each day hundreds of new believers were immersed in the river Barada in the rite of baptism which Jesus had prescribed for those who believed in him.

"Last night," Ananias went on, "there was a riot at one of the synagogues where Saul was speaking. We are sure it was stirred up by Hyrcanus. Several of our people were hurt, and Nicanor and Judas were barely able to keep Saul from being seriously injured."

"Why not send Saul from the city until things have quieted down?"

"Saul is willing to leave Damascus," Ananias explained. "He wants to go into the desert for a while. But Hyrcanus has gotten the ear of Paphos, the governor, and has persuaded him that Saul is a troublemaker and should be sent back to Jerusalem for trial before the Sanhedrin."

"That would mean his death."

"Yes, and we must keep it from happening at all costs. Paphos has already issued the order for Saul's arrest, but Nicanor has hidden him away for the time being. Even worse, Hyrcanus has learned that the scroll containing the sayings of Jesus is here in Damascus and has made a public vow to find and destroy it."

"Where is the scroll now?" Luke asked.

Ananias reached into his robe and brought out the small parchment roll, holding it reverently in his two hands, as if it were a precious jewel. "Nicanor gave it to me because he feared his house would be searched, since he is known to be the leader of the Company of the Fish in Damascus."

The bloodstains and the jagged tears from the stones which had lacerated Stephen's body were still plainly visible on the scroll. It seemed a small and unimportant thing to be the object of a search in which one man had already lost his life and still others might follow him.

"This parchment contains the hope of the world, Luke," Ananias said. "Whatever happens, these teachings must not be lost."

Luke understood why Ananias had shown him the scroll, but logic argued that it was none of his worry. The Company of the Fish believed that the sayings of Jesus were especially sacred because they had been spoken by one whom they vowed to be the son of Jehovah. But Luke himself believed no such thing, for he could not admit either that there was such a god or that his son, if he really existed, could have taken human form on earth and been crucified by ordinary men. And yet, some deep inner voice kept reminding Luke, the principles set down in that torn and bloody roll of parchment did contain a way of life which could bring peace and happiness to the world if men could be brought to follow it. With that thought, a decision crystallized in his mind. "If you will trust me with the scroll," he told Ananias, "I will try to see that it leaves Damascus safely."

The weaver's face cleared. "I was hoping you would make that offer, Luke. Traveling in the party of Theophilus, you would not be searched. The sayings will be safe with you."

"What shall I do with the scroll once I am clear of Damascus?" Luke asked.

Ananias put the slender parchment roll into Luke's hands. "Jesus will tell you when to pass it on to another," he assured him. "Have no fear of that, Luke."

"What of Saul?" he asked. "Are you going to arrange for him to leave the city?"

"We have no plan," Ananias admitted. "But be sure that the Lord will give us one when the time comes." He stood up. "You had better go now and put the scroll in a safe place, Luke. The guards may search my house at any time, since I am known to be among the Company of the Fish. You must come again before you leave the city and say good-by to Mariamne."

"Yes, I will come," Luke told him. He could not leave Damascus without seeing her again and begging her to wait until he could return.

"God guard you, then," Ananias said, embracing him, "for with you goes the hope of the world."

xiii

Silvanus listened gravely to Luke's account of what Hyrcanus was doing, his vow to destroy the scroll, and his plan to take Saul back to Jerusalem in chains. "Paphos was speaking to me of this today," he said. "The ethnarch Aretas has ordered him to keep the good will of Herod, which means that Paphos will do everything he can to help Hyrcanus."

"Was I wrong in accepting the scroll?" Luke asked. It was one thing to foil the Sanhedrin and its agents, but quite another to evade the lawful rulings of a governor in the Roman Empire.

Silvanus shook his head. "You did no wrong, Luke. It is part of a plan."

"What plan?" Luke asked, mystified.

Silvanus did not answer but went over to the window and stood there, staring out upon the city and fiddling with his sword. Finally he turned back to Luke. "You hate Saul, don't you, Luke?" he asked.

Luke shrugged. "Why should I do anything else? He was responsible for the murder of Stephen and persecuted the followers of Jesus, while I have found nothing but good men in the Company of the Fish."

"A man who executes another on the orders of a state is not a murderer, Luke," Silvanus said severely. "You heard Sixtus pronounce the death sentence in the name of the Emperor."

"Would you have executed Stephen if ordered to do so?"

"Of course," Silvanus said crisply. "Any soldier would have obeyed the order."

"But that doesn't make it right to kill innocent men."

Silvanus put his hand upon Luke's shoulder. "You will find much in the world that is not right, Luke. And who knows, perhaps you might become an instrument through which many men may know right from wrong, for you are kind, courageous, and wise. Let us suppose you believed that this man Saul was more than you think he is right now, perhaps as important to the world as the teachings of Jesus set down there in the scroll. Would you help him escape death at the hands of the Sanhedrin?"

"If I believed those things, I would," Luke said promptly.

Silvanus smiled then, for Luke had given him the answer he was seeking. "I do believe them, Luke. Just why, I don't know, but something tells me they are true. And I want you to help arrange Saul's escape from Damascus."

"Why me?"

"Because I can trust you, and I know your courage is beyond question."

"But how could we get him out? They will certainly be watching for him at the gates."

"He could be disguised."

Remembering Saul's stature and his godlike head, Luke was doubtful about any disguise hiding him from detection. "He would be out of place in a Roman column," he objected, "and would be easily spotted."

Silvanus admitted the validity of his objections. "Can you suggest anything?"

"There might be a way," Luke said thoughtfully, and told Silvanus the story Ananias had told him about the smuggler who had lived in the house he now owned, and how a fortune had been made by hauling goods up and down the walls with ropes to avoid paying customs duties.

The centurion's eyes lit up. "It could be the answer," he admitted. "But Saul still might be challenged close to the city. Many travelers reach the gates after they have closed when the sun sets and are forced to camp outside the walls until morning. I know that Paphos maintains a small detachment of the guard outside the walls every night to keep order among these people."

"Saul must be hidden, then."

"Yes, but how?"

"I know," Luke cried in sudden excitement. "In one of the weavers' baskets. There is a stack of them in Ananias's shop. One basket could easily hold a short man like Saul. I could disguise myself and take him out through the gates inside it."

"But suppose the guards make you open the basket?"

"Why not take an empty one out of the city? Saul can be let down over the wall later when it is dark."

"It might succeed," Silvanus admitted. "But I hate for you to risk it. If you are caught it would go hard with you, and Theophilus might not be able to keep you from being punished severely."

But Luke's youthful enthusiasm was kindled by the daring nature of the stratagem they proposed. This was like the games he and Apollonius had played as children, when the Roman spy escaped from the barbarians just before he was to be executed and led the legions through a secret pass to a surprise attack and victory. Only this time it would be far more exciting, for the danger would be very real indeed.

xiv

Less than an hour remained before the gates of Damascus would close when Luke stood in the garden with Mariamne, beneath the very wall over which, if all went well, Saul would escape about midnight. They had decided to make the attempt then, for the city would be asleep. Saul was hidden somewhere else; he would be brought to the house of Ananias when it was dark enough to escape detection.

Mariamne's eyes were red, and Luke knew that she had been weeping because he was leaving. They stood now in awkward silence close together beside the fountain, their hearts brimming over with things each wished to say in this hour of parting, but too shy still to speak them. Then she put her hand on the rough fabric of the cheap homespun robe Ananias had purchased to hide Luke's regular clothing, and her fingers moved up to touch his cheeks, stained a light brown by walnut juice, for he was to play the part of a lad from the streets of Damascus.

"You will be careful, won't you, Luke?" she whispered.

49

He took her soft hand and put it to his lips, thinking that it was like touching them to the soft inner petals of a flower. "Yes, dearest Mariamne," he said. "Will you wait until I come again?"

"I will wait always, Luke, my darling," she whispered. Then suddenly she put her arms about his neck and, rising on tiptoe, pressed her soft mouth to his, clinging to him as if she could never let him go. But when he would have caught her in his arms and held her, she broke from him and ran sobbing into the house. As he stood irresolute, wanting to follow her but knowing it would only prolong the parting, Ananias called from the shop, "Hurry, Luke. Sometimes the gates are closed early."

A mule waited patiently in the street before the shop, one of the large baskets securely held by a harness on its back. Ananias put his hands upon Luke's shoulders and embraced him fondly. "Farewell, Luke," he said in a choked voice. "Be sure and come back to us."

Luke stumbled through the dusty street leading to the gate, for his eyes were still blurred by tears. He had planned to reach the gate in the rush of people leaving just before it closed, but tonight the rush was smaller than usual. One of the guards stopped him with the lowered blade of his sword. "What is in the basket, boy?" he demanded gruffly.

Luke pitched his voice to the nasal whine of a street beggar. "Nothing of any value, master."

"We shall see about that." When the other guards began to laugh, Luke knew that he was to be made sport of, a cruel custom of the soldiers with those too poor to strike back. The guard slapped the side of the basket with the flat of his sword. "Open it," he commanded.

"Please, sir——" Luke's voice trembled with honest fright now as he fumbled with the ropes, searching desperately for some means of diverting their attention from the basket. If they found it empty, he knew they would become suspicious that he was engaged in smuggling and hold him inside the city. "My father just died, master," he whined, hoping to play upon the sympathy of the guard. "And I am carrying his few belongings to the house of my uncle in Antioch."

"Your dead father needs no money, boy." The guard laughed. "I can sell his belongings and buy wine." He slipped the blade of his sword under one of the ropes, severing it easily, and, when Luke tried to stop him, knocked the youth sprawling in the dirt.

"Please, master," Luke whined, fighting back the tears brought by the pain and humiliation at having to grovel in the dirt before a common soldier. "My father was a leper. Do you want to——"

"A leper!" The guard recoiled from the basket.

"He died only yesterday, but already it had eaten away his——"

50

"Go!" the soldier shouted, booting Luke roughly to his feet. He looked with horror at the hand which had touched the basket, as if momentarily expecting to see the dread white spot of leprosy appear there. "Begone!" he screamed again, and kicked the mule so that the surprised beast leaped through the gate and trotted down the road with the lead rope dragging. Luke plunged through the gate and seized the rope, hot still with resentment, but already feeling a surge of relief at having gotten out of the city with no damage to anything but his pride and a few bruises.

xv

During the early hours of the night Luke rested close to the walls of the city so that he could hear the crier shout the passing of the hours. Damascus should have been asleep long before midnight, the time they had chosen for the escape, but as time passed he could hear the sound of marching troops inside the walls and occasionally a scream of agony as some poor devil was beaten or prodded with the sharp point of a sword. Something was happening inside the city, he realized with a sense of foreboding, and it could mean no good for the project he was embarked upon. If the guards discovered Saul hiding in the house of Ananias, they would certainly arrest the entire household, and the thought of Mariamne in the rough hands of the jailers was almost more than Luke could stand.

Shortly before midnight Luke led his mule with its empty burden along the wall toward the spot where he judged the house of Ananias to be. He had made a reconnaissance the morning before with Silvanus, under the guise of a walk outside the gates. He could not tell exactly where the house lay, and since those above would not dare to show a signal light lest there be guards outside tonight looking for smugglers, they had agreed upon a signal by which he would know when he had reached the portion of the wall against which the house of Ananias was built.

Now his heart leaped, for clearly through the cool night air came the notes of a lyre and the lovely voice of a young girl singing in Aramaic one of the songs which the Jews attributed to the wise king Solomon. It was a signal which none would suspect to be a signal, a young girl singing to her lover in the garden.

Luke whistled a low note, and at once Mariamne sang the words, her voice faltering a little: "Luke. Is it you?"

"Yes, dearest one," he called.

Dropping all pretense of song, she said quickly, "You must hurry,

Luke. The soldiers are searching the city; they may be here at any moment."

"I am ready," he called. "Let down the basket."

Scraping sounds came from the darkness overhead, and then he saw the dark shape of the basket sliding down the wall a few yards ahead of him. As he moved the mule toward it, he loosened the rope holding the empty container upon the animal's back and, dropping it to the ground for the moment, settled the much heavier basket into the harness.

The animal grunted at the sudden change in burden, but Luke soothed it with one hand and untied the rope from around the basket with the other. Then he quickly attached the free end to the empty basket he had taken from the mule and jerked three times. It was whisked up the walls at once, showing the urgency felt by those in the garden of Ananias. A few seconds sufficed to lash the container in which Saul lay to the mule's harness and, picking up the lead rope, Luke urged the mule away from the wall in the direction where he knew the road leading from Damascus to the north lay. As he stumbled along in the darkness Mariamne's lovely voice sang to him in farewell, this time in Greek. It was a tender love song, and the words, plus the realization that it might be years before he saw her again, brought a lump to his throat.

He was almost to the road he sought and beginning to breathe easier when he saw torches bobbing through the night toward him. There was no way of telling who it could be or what was their purpose, so he seized the mule's bridle and stood dead still in the darkness, hoping not to be seen. But the mule snorted, and immediately the lights turned and converged upon him. A cold fear gripped Luke now, for he was sure that the guards had somehow learned of Saul's escape from the city and had come out to capture them. Silvanus had warned him, too, that his fate might not be an easy one if he were captured while helping an important figure like Saul to escape.

Then a torch was lifted high, outlining him and the mule against the night, and a voice hailed sharply: "You, with the mule. Stop!"

Luke had no choice but to wait numbly. The soldiers gathered around him, and the leader peered at his face by torchlight. His terror was evident, for the leader said kindly, "Where are you going at this time of night, boy?"

"I am lost, master," Luke whined, remembering to play his role. "I seek the road to Antioch."

"Antioch! Why do you go there, and by night?"

"My father died yesterday, and I am going there to live with my uncle. They tell me robbers are on the road by day."

The man laughed. "Do you carry such valuable things, then?"

"Nothing of any real worth, master. Nothing you would want."

"We want not your paltry belongings, boy," the leader said. "A criminal has escaped from the city, a Jew named Saul." He nodded to one of the soldiers. "Open the basket so that we can be on our way. It would hardly harbor a Jewish criminal, but we must make sure."

"The basket is unclean," Luke cried, remembering the success of that stratagem before. "My father died of leprosy."

The soldier drew back and the group around him widened noticeably, but Luke feared that in a moment the leader would order him to open the basket, and he would have no course but to obey. In the moment of awkward silence that followed his warning cry he heard the tramp of more feet, and new torches appeared from the direction of the gate. "Sasa!" a voice shouted. "What have you found?"

"Only a boy with a mule," the leader called Sasa replied. "We are going to look into his basket and then go on."

Luke recognized the voice of the man who had called. It was the soldier with whom he had had the trouble earlier at the gate. "Ask that one who spoke if I do not tell the truth about the basket," he suggested quickly. "He was at the gate when I came through."

The other group had approached now and, seeing Luke, the one who had been at the gate shouted, "Touch not the basket, Sasa! It is unclean from leprosy."

Sasa stepped back then, apparently satisfied. "The road to Antioch lies two hundred paces ahead, boy," he said kindly. "See that you lose no time in reaching it."

Luke's knees were trembling as he led the mule along the road, but not enough to keep him from setting as fast a pace as the plodding animal would allow. He wanted no more searching parties stopping him, even if it did mean shaking up Saul a little as he crouched in the basket.

It was several hours later and weary miles lay between them and Damascus before Luke felt that it was safe to stop. By then the moon had risen and he led the mule off the road into a small grove of apricot trees growing beside a brook. His feet, unaccustomed to walking on the hard dusty road, were blistered and sore, and he was glad to get off the road and onto the smooth carpet of grass growing beside the brook. Tying the mule's lead rope to a sapling that grew over the water so the animal could drink its fill, Luke loosened the ropes holding the cover on the basket and removed it. Saul lay with his knees drawn up nearly to his chin, for there had barely been room for him.

"I will help you out," Luke said. "You must be stiff."

He had to lift Saul bodily from the basket and set him on his feet, and even then cramped muscles refused to function and his legs buckled. With Luke's help Saul hobbled over to a large flat rock and sat down. Beads of sweat stood out on his forehead from the intense agony as feeling returned to his numb limbs. Luke limped over to the mule and detached the waterskin from the harness, along with a package of bread, cheese, and dates which Ananias had thoughtfully provided. He held the skin for Saul to drink and afterward drank long and deeply himself. While the mule sucked up water noisily, he spread the food on a rock beside them. They ate awhile in silence, until Luke said, "We barely escaped capture back there. Did you hear it all?"

Saul nodded. "You are a quick thinker, Luke. I am sure I owe my life to you." Then he added thoughtfully, "But I wonder if I should not have remained in Damascus."

"Hyrcanus would have taken you back to Jerusalem, and you know what that would have meant."

"Yes. I have sent men to their deaths for just such an offense as I myself have committed against our religious laws."

"Do you feel any remorse?" Luke asked curiously.

"I was wrong," Saul admitted soberly. "But I was obeying the law as I knew it then. Only later did I learn another and better way."

Perhaps it really was unjust to blame Saul for Stephen's death, Luke thought. It could be that the man who had persecuted the Company of the Fish had really changed, moved by some powerful inner force which could make a new man of him in the instant of time when he had been blinded on the road to Damascus by sunlight reflected from the gilded dome of a palace. "What are you going to do now, Saul?" he asked.

"Do?" Saul lifted his head. "Whatever the Lord wills me to do, of course." Then, almost as if he were talking to himself, he continued. "As a boy I studied the Greek philosophers as religiously as I did the scrolls which tell the history of the Jews and the words of the prophets. Later I went to Jerusalem to study under the greatest teacher of our race, the rabbi Gamaliel. And in time I was given a high place before the Sanhedrin and one day would have been a member of the ruling council of the Jews."

"But you were not satisfied with what you were doing," Luke pointed out. "I could see that on the day you prosecuted Stephen before the Sanhedrin."

"A man does not change his beliefs and his whole life in an instant," Saul admitted. "Much must go before and after such a change. And yet I have endured much since that day when you and your friend, the centurion, found me on the road to Damascus. For three days I was blind. I was forced to hide from the guards and escaped over the walls like a common criminal, although guilty of no crime. Do you think this is better than what I had in Tarsus or Jerusalem?"

"Why did you do it, then?"

Saul turned somber eyes upon his young companion. "Because I heard a call which tells me there is a higher purpose for me than anything which has gone before." His voice sounded as if he were seeking encouragement in that conviction, but Luke could not help him, for here was something he had never experienced before, a troubled man pouring out his innermost thoughts. Later—when he had many years of experience in the calling of medicine—Luke would know that the highest duty of a physician is thus to receive the troubled thoughts of those sick in mind and body and give them the confidence and assurance they so badly need. But tonight Luke was only a youth, learned in science and philosophy, but knowing little indeed about life.

"Nicanor tells me you saved the scroll of the teachings of Jesus," Saul said. "And tonight you risked your life to help me. Why did you do those things, Luke?"

Luke did not answer, for he really did not know why he had acted as he had, except that Silvanus had asked him to help Saul, and he had taken the scroll in answer to the request of a dying man. Yet he could not help feeling in his heart that something beyond either of those reasons had actually moved him, something he could not express in words.

"I think I know why both of us have changed the pattern of our lives, Luke," Saul continued. "We must be part of a larger plan, something we can only obey but not yet understand."

"Silvanus said the same thing," Luke cried in astonishment.

"There was a centurion at Capernaum whose servant was healed by Jesus."

"That was Silvanus," Luke interrupted excitedly. "I—I think he believes in Jesus."

"Do you believe in Jesus yet, Luke?" Saul asked. Then he shook his head. "No, you are a Greek and intelligent. You must search out the truth for yourself."

"Have you found it?" Luke asked impulsively.

"Not yet. That is why I must do what Jesus did when first he realized what destiny had in store for him. I shall go into the wilderness." Then he changed the subject abruptly. "Where were you to meet your own party, Luke?"

Luke fumbled in his robe, striking his hand against the scroll, and drew out the rough map Silvanus had drawn for him of the road leading northward from Damascus. "The Via Maris leaves the road to Antioch about two hours' journey or so from here," he explained to Saul as they studied the map in the bright moonlight. "Our way lies north and west, toward the coast, while the Way of the Sea continues eastward toward the great desert and Mesopotamia."

"*Your* way lies to the west, Luke," Saul corrected gently. "Mine goes eastward, into the desert."

"But you will starve—or die of thirst."

"Jesus taught his disciples to carry neither purse, nor scrip, nor shoes. Should I carry more?" Saul got to his feet. "We should be on the road again; I want to reach the fork by sunrise."

Together they removed the basket from the mule and hid it in the bushes that grew along the bank of the creek. Luke took off the rough cloak he had been wearing over his toga and washed as much of the walnut stain from his face as he could in the water of the brook. While Saul filled the waterskin Luke bathed his feet, but when he tried to replace his sandals, the blisters had swollen so that he could not tie the thongs, and the thought of walking on that hard road again made him shudder.

Saul saw the blisters and came over from where he was fixing the waterskin to the mule's harness. "You cannot walk with those blisters, Luke," he said concernedly. "I will lead the animal and you can ride."

Luke got on the mule without protest, for he could not have hobbled much farther on his wounded feet. Thus they left in quite the reverse order from that in which they had arrived, with Saul, formerly the hunted one, now unquestionably the leader of the small caravan.

The sun was already several hours high when the road divided before them at the top of a hill. Looking back, Luke could just make out the white pattern of the city of Damascus like a strange geometric cloud on the horizon. A pillar of dust much nearer to them marked the progress of Silvanus and the rest of the party.

Over Luke's protests that he was not hungry and that Saul should keep the food for himself, the older man divided it into two parts, and they ate and drank. Luke insisted that Saul take the mule, however, for there would be plenty of them with the approaching party, and Saul could use the animal during his journey into the desert to carry water for the two of them. Besides, it was in Luke's mind that Saul could always sell the mule and thus be assured of food and drink. Finally the food was finished and Saul took up the lead rope of the mule.

"Come with us to Antioch, and Theophilus will see that you are protected," Luke urged once more. "Then you can go with me to Tarsus when I travel to Pergamum."

"In times of crisis a man must be alone to think, Luke. It is better this way."

"But this is not a crisis. You have already joined the Company of the Fish."

Saul shook his head. "I am not yet worthy to join that noble company, Luke. Most of them walked and talked with Jesus, but I have heard his voice only once, from the heavens."

Luke was beginning to understand now what was troubling Saul. Intelligent and well educated, he would know that others, too, had heard what they thought were voices speaking to them alone. Even Socrates admitted such in his experience. A man of Saul's intelligence would not be content with what had happened to him on the road to Damascus; he must ponder upon it and the things which had preceded that dramatic moment. Perhaps he also had some warning through his experience in Damascus—his being set upon in the synagogues and the plot to take him back to Jerusalem in chains—of what the future might hold for him if he kept on in the way he had chosen so recently. A man would be a fool to undertake such a course of action with the obvious hardships and risks it promised, without considering in advance where such a path would take him. And as Saul had said, alone in the desert with his thoughts, there would be a time of crisis indeed, a time when he must decide once and for all to continue traveling what was obviously going to be a rocky road indeed.

Moved by an impulse he could not explain, Luke took the scroll from his toga. "Here are the words of Jesus himself," he said. "Perhaps they can help you."

Saul took the scroll in his hands. "Was it for this that Stephen lay down his life?" he asked wonderingly.

"Yes. He gave it to me as he lay dying."

Tenderly Saul touched the dark bloodstains upon the parchment and the jagged tears made by the stones. Then with trembling fingers he put the scroll carefully inside his robe and turned to Luke, his eyes shining, his face transfigured.

"Now I know I am obeying God's will," he said confidently. "And I think I understand why you and I and the words of Jesus have come together here on this hill." He put his hands upon Luke's shoulders. "It must be part of God's plan, Luke. There is no other answer." Then, dropping his hands, he picked up the lead rope and, followed by the patient animal, moved down the road to the east. Some fifty paces away Saul turned, still smiling, and called joyously, "Farewell, Luke, my brother. Be sure it is God's will that our paths shall cross again."

Luke watched Saul and the mule descend the hill and move out across the dusty plain to the east toward the desert. And as he stood there, something deep inside him urged that he forsake the comfort and luxury of Theophilus's home in Antioch, his chosen profession, even his promise to Mariamne to return, and give up everything that lay before him to follow the man whose figure was steadily growing smaller as the distance between them widened. So strong was the impulse that Luke actually struggled to his feet and took a few steps along the road Saul had taken. But the pain from blisters made him cry out in agony and stumble, so that he tripped and fell. Finally, weeping with frustration and impotence, he pushed himself up on hands and knees and crawled back to the rock beside the road to Antioch upon which he had been sitting.

It was thus that Silvanus found him several hours later, staring at two black dots that were barely visible now among the sands to the east, all that could be seen of Saul of Tarsus.

Book Two: THE MIRACLE

*And he sent them to preach the kingdom of
God, and to heal the sick.*

Luke 9:2

Night had fallen over the Temple of Asklepios in Pergamum. Before the door of the abaton, the doubly sacred inner temple, torches lighted the statue of the divine Asklepios with the sacred serpents twined about the staff in his hand. In the outer court the bubbling of water from the sacred springs sounded a muted obbligato to the voices of the night, and the soft tones of lute, lyre, and cymbal floated from the quarters of the priestly physicians, where a banquet was in progress.

The multitude of the sick who thronged the outer court had already received their evening meal of gruel, fruit from the temple orchards, and goblets of the bitter mineral waters from the sacred springs whose purgative action, scoffers maintained, was more beneficial than the ministrations of the God of Medicine. Some had finished the prescribed three days of preparatory dieting and purging and tomorrow would be admitted to the abaton at sunset for the sacred sleep called *incubatio*. Others, newly arrived at the temple, discussed their sicknesses with the more experienced as they bathed in the pools into which the mineral springs emptied, before placing their offerings upon the altar of the god. Strategically placed in the outer court, flaming torches illumined votive tablets erected in honor of the divine Asklepios by grateful worshipers who had been cured at the shrine:

Julian [one of them stated], being in a hopeless state on account of a spilling of blood, was directed by the god to take pine seeds from the altar, mix them with honey, and eat them during three days. He recovered and returned thanks openly before the people.

59

Still another tablet gave pointed notice that the god, however divine, worked for profit to himself, as well as for the good of those who did him homage:

A certain Hermo of Pasos was cured by the god from blindness. He, however, made the mistake of refusing to pay the honorarium to the sanctuary. The god promptly smote him again with blindness as a punitive measure for the oversight. When he returned again and paid, he slept once more in the temple, and the financially satisfied god once again healed him.

The great hostel just outside the gates of the temple grounds was filled with patients who could not yet be admitted to the healing shrine. Not many of the poor were to be found in the luxurious hostel; they were forced to fare as best they could while waiting for admission, sleeping under the temple walls, at one of the meaner inns which catered to the poor, or even in stables. In the hostel gouty silversmiths from Ephesus, rich from trade in the statues of Artemis for which their guild was famous, argued with fat merchants from Tarsus and beyond the Cilician Gates, through which came the rich caravans from the Far East, bringing spices for the sophisticated palates of the rich in Antioch, Ephesus, Rome, and Alexandria, exotic cloth for the gowns of their wives and mistresses, and shining steel swords and cutlery from the blacksmiths of Damascus. A priest of Diana, fat and jaded from too much venery, belched reflectively after a meal of rich viands which tomorrow would be denied him, once he entered the temple and placed himself in the hands of the priestly physicians. And to one side a Roman judge, hoping the water and the god could cure his gouty toe, dined in splendid isolation and haughty silence, his striped toga of nobility drawn tightly against his body lest the merchants passing his bench soil the fabric with greasy fingers.

There was much going and coming, for tonight a performance was being given in the theater which formed a part of the temple grounds. Also under the direction of the priests of Asklepios, and contributing no little to the coffers of the god, were a stadium for the games, a gymnasium, vast kitchens from which special foods were sold, and shallow stone lakes where the waters from the springs were allowed to evaporate, after which the bitter salts which gave them their mineral action were scraped up and sold in packages to those who would continue to take the waters in their homes.

Tonight Mnesilochus, the favorite actor of the Ephesian theater, had brought his troupe of players to present the *Thesmophoriazusae* of Aristophanes, drollest and most facile of all the plays by that inimitable writer of comic drama. No tragedies were presented in the theaters of Asklepios, for the thoughts of those who sought healing of the god must never be disturbed by the contemplation of death. The priests boasted that none ever died in the temples of Asklepios, but they said nothing of those who, admitted by some mischance to the shrine while nearing death, were summarily ejected by order of the chief priest, to die unattended by any medical aid outside the walls.

Not even Mnesilochus would have dared to present here the *Plutus* of Aristophanes, that whimsical allegory satirizing the activities of the Asklepian deity and his priests, in which Plutus, god of riches, regained his sight under the healing tongues of the divine serpents. After four hundred years Greeks and sophisticates the world over still laughed as the barbed shafts pricked the bloated priests of Asklepios and ridiculed their pretensions to divine power. Nor did the followers of Asklepios swear the Oath of Hippocrates, for that prince of physicians had eschewed priestly rites to allege that nature, aided by the physician, healed disease, rather than through any mystic intervention by the God of Healing, who some irreverent Greeks vowed did not even exist.

ii

In the darkened abaton the sick chosen for communion tonight with the god were lying on low couches. Most of them dozed quietly in the healing stupor of the *incubatio,* or "temple sleep," a state of semiconsciousness induced by the mystic laying on of hands by the temple priests, plus the warning that only in such a state would the god reveal to them the measures necessary for their cure. Aiding in the production of the divine stupor was a drink administered to each of the sick as he entered the abaton, a shrewdly prepared decoction of poppy leaves, mandragora, and the East Indian drug, hashish, much prized by libertines in those lands and by the more decadent Roman nobility for its power to produce fantastic dreams. Wax tapers burned before the small altars along the walls, where the patients had placed their offerings in the hope of luring the god to visit them personally in their dreams.

At the back of the room a door opened gently and an odd wailing note filled the inner temple, a monotonous trilling repeated in endless melody until the very droning became a palpable force, oppressing the breathing. In the gloom that filled the abaton the forms of the two men moving through it were barely distinguishable. Tall, with shaven heads, they wore flowing white robes, and their faces were whitened with clay. Small snakes extended their heads from the full sleeves of the white-robed acolytes, giving them the strange appearance of having serpents for arms.

Through the room the acolytes moved on their nightly mission, stopping to lift an eyelid or prod an irregular snorer, until they were satisfied that all who lay there were already in the divine stupor. Then they returned to the door through which they had come and knelt beside it, their heads bent, their arms and the writhing snakes extended in a gesture of supplication.

Now a startling figure emerged from the door, surely the divine Asklepios himself! He was unnaturally tall, the effect produced by a high mask that covered his head and hid the face which, according to tradition, no man might see upon pain of death. The features of the mask were noble, a handsome man with curling hair and a short beard arranged in ringlets after the manner of the Olympian gods, but the eyes of the god behind the mask were brown and quite human.

A strange procession began to move among the beds, with the god in the lead. Beside him was a tall man with a sheaf of wax-covered tablets under his arm and a slave bearing many boxes and jars of medicines in a basket. The slave carried also a burning taper, and on top of the basket containing the medicines lay a large emerald. The tall man was the apothecary-scribe, an important member of the god's retinue, for not only did he keep the records of the hundreds of patients who passed through the abaton every month, but he also compounded the medicines prescribed by the god and dispensed them to the sick.

Behind the apothecary-scribe walked the acolytes, and after them another slave bearing a large empty sack suspended from his belt. The procession stopped beside the first sleeper, and the apothecary selected one of his tablets and held it up to the light of the taper on the wall. The flame showed a lean, intelligent face with an ironic quirk to the lips, as if the man found humor even in this stately procession of healing, and his eyes twinkled in a very unpriestly manner as he read from the tablet:

"'Janos, a merchant of Philadelphia, suffers from a bloating after his meals which is made worse by wine and rich food. He has already been considerably benefited by the fasting and the waters, but seeks to keep this improvement, if it be the will of the divine Asklepios.'"

The scribe put down the tablet and, bending over the sleeper, lifted his left eyelid with a skillful movement of the right thumb and forefinger. The slave now handed him the emerald, which the tall man manipulated until a beam of light from the taper was directed into the wide-open pupils of the sick man. "Janos," he said sharply. "The divine Asklepios favors thee in person."

The sleeper's pupils contracted from the light, and he stirred as if in a dream. "I hear, O Divine Healer," he said in a voice slurred from the stupor.

"Abstain from spices and wine," the god recited in a bored voice. "Be not a glutton, and avoid foods cooked in lard and butter. Drink daily of the waters from the springs or the salt mixed in your drinking water." He lifted his staff, and the small snakes twined about it reared their heads and hissed. "Asklepios has spoken to thee in thy dream, Janos. Thy prayers have been heard and answered."

The apothecary took a package of the evaporated salt from the basket carried by his assistant and left it beside the couch. Then the procession moved on to the next patient, while the slave at the rear of the group scooped the offering from the altar into his bag, sniffing audibly at the stinginess of the merchant from Philadelphia. The ritual was repeated with every sleeper, and where one was found who did not respond to shaking and the concentrated light of the emerald, the divine instructions were written on a wax tablet by the apothecary-scribe and left by the couch.

A sufferer from the stone was told that he would be cured by the temple lithotomist, one of those whom Hippocrates had spoken of in his oath as "cutting for the stone." And a man with bleeding from the stomach was warned that a diet of ass's milk would soothe the angry passions that griped his belly. In each case the procedure was the same, and as they went from row to row the scribe noted in exquisite Greek script upon the tablets the treatment prescribed by the god.

It was almost midnight before the visit of the divine Asklepios was finished. Each of the small altars had been swept clean of its offering, and when the procession filed out of the abaton, the sack of the slave at the rear was so heavy that he carried it slung over his shoulder and staggered with its weight, while the basket of the apothecary's assistant was empty save for the emerald used to focus the light.

Now the abaton was silent while those who had experienced the divine visit during the rite of *incubatio* slept. Tomorrow new cures would be recited to the glory of the godly Asklepios and new tablets would be chiseled attesting his power. Meanwhile in the outer courts a new throng would soon greet the dawn eagerly, looking to the night when they, too, would enter the abaton to receive the favors of the god.

iii

In the luxurious anteroom outside the abaton where the priests put on and off their ceremonial robes two men were busily occupied. One was the apothecary, who was helping the tall figure wearing the mask of Asklepios to remove it. Bereft of the mask, the god revealed himself to be mortal, a slender man in his early twenties, fairly tall, with warm brown eyes, a mobile face, and the facile fingers of a surgeon. Dumped unceremoniously in the corner, the divine Asklepios was a far from arresting visage.

"Thank you, Probus." The young man accepted a towel from the tall scribe and went to wash his hands at a basin in the corner of the room. Probus, the apothecary and scribe, uncovered a small table upon which was placed a platter of cold meat and bread, with a bottle of wine beside it. It was the custom of the priestly physicians, after taking their turn at impersonating the god in the rite of *incubatio,* to take refreshment here before going to their quarters. Probus poured wine into two goblets and handed one to the younger man. "You were magnificent tonight, Luke," he said. "I almost thought Asklepios himself had favored us with his presence. Mnesilochus, the actor, could have done no better."

Luke smiled and took a fragment of meat from the platter. "My last performance should be my best," he said. After five years of study Luke was now a full-fledged priest-physician, respected in the temple because of his knowledge of medicine and his skill with the scalpel. Of the apothecary-scribe, Probus, he still knew next to nothing, except that he was a kindred spirit, for all his outward sarcasm, a man of great learning and deep philosophy, whose speech revealed familiarity with cities throughout the far-flung reaches of the Empire. In the year that the lean and sardonic man had been chief scribe and medicine compounder for the temple he and Luke had become fast friends.

"Did the chief priest beg you to stay?" Probus asked.

"Not exactly." Luke smiled. "I think he was relieved when I told him I would leave at the end of my term of study."

"Well he might be," Probus grunted. "With your skill, you could have had his office within a few years. Naturally he would be glad to get rid of you." He drank deeply of his wine goblet. "Anyway, you would be a fool to stay here. Physicians of less than your caliber are getting rich in Antioch, Ephesus, and Rome." Then for a moment his blue eyes were serious. "But I pity the sick who come here after you leave. You should hear the pronouncements of the divine Asklepios when some of your brother physicians are wearing the mask."

Luke sipped the wine and ate a piece of beef from the platter. "I wonder," he said thoughtfully, "how much longer this mockery of medical science will keep up."

"Careful," Probus warned. "That is heresy, and you are still in the temple."

64

"But Hippocrates dared to treat the sick without wearing the mask of a god that does not exist. And Celsus did the same recently in Rome."

"Rationalem quidem puto medicinam esse debere," Probus intoned in Latin, then translated expertly into flawless Greek: "I am of the opinion that the art of medicine ought to be rational."

"Where did you learn the words of Celsus?"

"Among other things, I once studied medicine. And remember that Chiron, the father of apothecaries, is also the father of medicine."

"Why did you not keep on?" Luke asked.

Probus shrugged. "An apothecary charges as much for his medicines as you physicians receive for prescribing them. And rich men will pay a philosopher well merely to insult them in words they cannot understand." He put down his goblet and went to the bag containing tonight's offerings which the slave had deposited in the corner. "Hah! Asklepios is well paid tonight. He will not miss these." From the bag Probus took a handful of gold coins and put them in the pouch that hung at his girdle. "You should have adopted this habit long ago, Luke. Your brother physicians rob the god regularly."

Luke smiled. "I have no need for money. Theophilus, my foster father, is rich. I can always live with him in Antioch and practice my profession."

"Are you going to Antioch, then? When last we talked you were not sure."

"No. I think I will join the army as a surgeon."

"The army!" Probus looked at his young friend as if he had suddenly gone mad. "Why the army?"

Luke took a small scroll from his robe and handed it to the apothecary. "Here is a letter from Silvanus that came only yesterday."

"Silvanus? Oh yes. He is the centurion you spoke about." Probus began to read the letter:

I write you, knowing that your term of study is almost at an end and that you will soon be returning home. Petronius, the governor of Syria, has been ordered by the Emperor to send an army to join those now being prepared by Sergius Paulus for an expedition to Paphlagonia, where some have dared to defy the Empire and refused to pay taxes. Apollonius, your brother, has come from Rome to march with the Syrian Legion and I go, too, so that I may be near him, for he is inexperienced yet in warfare. I have spoken to Theophilus of this, and it is his hope that you will accompany us, since your time in the temple is so nearly finished. We have received excellent reports of your skill as a physician, and I know that Theophilus would rest easier on account of Apollonius if he knew you were with us. If

65

you can find it in your heart to come with us, both Apollonius and myself will welcome you with open arms. You will not even have to journey back to Syria, for we join the forces of Sergius Paulus at Pisidian Antioch, which is only a few hundred miles from Pergamum.

As for me, I shall not return there when the campaign is finished, since my soul yearns for the peace which awaits me in Bithynia. It joins Paphlagonia, where we are going, so I shall remain when our work is finished.

If you can join us for at least the duration of this expedition, I know that Apollonius and I will welcome you, and Theophilus will rest easier at home.

All here send love to you,

SILVANUS

Probus frowned. "Why does he want to go to Bithynia?"

"Silvanus is getting old. When I was a boy he used to describe the land to me. I am sure he thinks of it as something of a heaven on earth."

"It is a beautiful country."

"I did not know you had traveled there," Luke said.

"There are few places I have not seen," Probus said with a shrug.

"Is there truly peace in Bithynia?"

Probus smiled. "I suspect that the only peace man ever attains lies within himself, Luke. When do we leave for Antioch?"

"We!" Luke exclaimed. "But you aren't going, Probus."

The apothecary looked pained. "So you no longer wish the company of your friends now that you will be associated with important people?"

"B-but," Luke stammered, then realized that Probus was making sport of him. "You are jesting."

Probus walked over to the mask of Asklepios and gave it a sharp kick. "Not at all. I have been planning to leave for some time; only my devotion to you, Luke, kept me here. Now that you are going, there is no need for me to remain longer. Especially when I take this with me," he added, picking up the emerald which lay in the basket with the wax tablets and putting it into his purse.

"But your position. You are the chief apothecary."

"For which I am paid no more than I would make as a *circumforaneus*.* If I did not rob the god regularly, I could not afford to stay."

"There will be even less pay for an apothecary in the army," Luke reminded him.

Probus lifted his eyebrows. "Remember that I am also the best scribe in the world, in addition to being a roller of pills. When we join the legions I will seek out the military commander and become his per-

---

*A traveling dispenser of medicine, literally a quack.

66

sonal scribe. In war men say and do things they would never think of doing in peace, and thus I shall learn all of his secrets, who his supporters are, and to whom he owes money. When he has won the battle and comes back a hero, he will remember what I know about him and make me rich, as a reward for keeping my mouth shut."

"And if he loses?"

"Then his enemies will pay me well to write a memorial telling the things that he did wrong. Good night, Luke. Do we leave tomorrow?"

"No. The day after. I had planned to purchase a mule and ride to Pisidia over the Via Augusta."

Probus made a wry face. "My backside cries out already in protest, but I am a philosopher, so perhaps the pain in my bottom will stimulate the thoughts in my mind. Good night, Luke."

"Good night, Probus," Luke said, smiling. "And I am very glad that you will be with me."

Luke did not feel sleepy, although the hour was late, and he let himself out into the temple gardens. The night was cool, for it was late summer, and as he walked among the pools and beds of growing flowers and shrubs, his thoughts went back over the past five years since he had first come here to study. This great establishment had been his home, school, and working place in one. As an acolyte he had assisted the priest-physicians in the small audience chambers to which the sick were admitted during the preliminary days of fasting and purging. Here he had studied disease and its effects upon the human body, for the pretense of godly intervention was only a front behind which the priest-physicians went about the practice of medicine, just as did more skillful physicians outside the temples who dealt directly with their patients, rather than through a theoretically divine agent.

In these small examining chambers he had learned to recognize symptoms and the body changes which caused them. And he had learned, too, the treatments prescribed by physicians through the years and handed down by word of mouth from master to apprentice, or set down in scrolls. These same prescriptions were later uttered by the priest wearing the mask of Asklepios during the rite of *incubatio*. Luke's hands, facile and sensitive, had been trained by the skilled temple lithotomists and surgeons until no one in the entire establishment was more skilled with scalpel and forceps. In the hidden inner chambers of the temple he had cut up the bodies of animals to study their organs, and sometimes the temple lithotomists could be bribed to arrange a dissection of human bodies outside the walls. The priest-teachers of the temple were conveniently blind to such activities, for they, too, realized the truth of the admonition of Rome's famous physician, Celsus: *"Mortuorum corpora incidere discentibus necessarium* [To open the bodies of the dead is necessary for learners]."

In the library Luke had found his greatest pleasure. Studious by nature, he had spent many hours among the racks of ancient manuscripts summing up the total of medical knowledge. Here were the mythical pronouncements of the real Asklepios, a physician of ancient Greece, later deified, and accounts of the daring feats of those skilled surgeons and sons of Asklepios, Machaon and Podalirius, who had ministered to the heroes of the Trojan War. In other scrolls were descriptions of medical treatments by many races, including clay models of the livers of sheep used by the *haruspex,* or soothsayer, in diagnosing disease and predicting the future by studying the livers of animals killed for the purpose.

Set down, too, were ethical rules governing the conduct of physicians, going back as far as the earliest of medical codes, that of the Babylonian physician, Hammurabi. Reading them, Luke had felt thankful that he lived in more enlightened times, for one rule went: "If a physician shall produce on anyone a severe wound with a bronze operating knife and kill him, or shall open an abscess with an operating knife and destroy the eye, his hands shall be cut off."

Looking back on these five years, Luke knew that they had been a busy and profitable period when he had grown from a youth to a man and during which he had learned much. He had been an overserious youth when he had journeyed from Antioch to Jerusalem, Joppa, Tiberias, around the jewel-like Sea of Galilee, and thence to Damascus, and back to Antioch to take ship at nearby Seleucia for Ephesus and Pergamum to begin his studies, and the memory of that journey had soon grown dim. Letters from Mariamne had arrived regularly for a while, brought by caravans passing through Damascus on the way westward along the Via Augusta, the great highway through Lesser Asia. But Luke had been too busy with studies to be a good correspondent, and there had been no word from her for a year now, since a hurried note told of persecution against the Company of the Fish in Damascus and the flight of Mariamne and her father to their old home in Tarsus, which, being primarily inhabited by Greeks and Romans, was a much more tolerant city.

Of Saul of Tarsus, whom he had last seen going into the wilderness beyond Damascus, and of the scroll containing the sayings of Jesus, Luke had heard not a word. Remembering Saul, he wondered now what could have happened to the dynamic Jew whom he had almost followed into the wilderness that day on the road to Antioch.

Yes, he told himself as he turned back to his quarters in the temple, they had been good years. Lately, however, he had been filled with a strange unrest, a feeling he could not name, but certainly a sense of inadequacy, of lack of purpose. Perhaps a change was just what he needed, he thought, and there could be no sharper change from the quiet and peace of the temple than the rigorous life of a surgeon in a military campaign.

iv

Antioch-in-Pisidia lay some two hundred and fifty miles to the east of Ephesus on the frontier of the district of Phrygia. A highly civilized Greek and Roman city, it was one of the sixteen Antiochs established by Seleucus I Nicator and had been a Roman colony for nearly fifty years. Located on the lower slopes of the mountain range rising on the right bank of the Anthius River, it was admirably situated as a base for military operations. A network of excellent Roman roads converged upon the strongly fortified city, and a large aqueduct, built also by the Romans, brought an ample supply of water from the foothills of the mountain range above the city.

The Camp of Mars, as the Roman military camps were always called, was located outside the city on a low plain beside the river. Luke had never visited this lesser Antioch before, and he looked about him with interest as they rode through it on the way to the Camp of Mars. Nowhere in his travels had he seen sculpture and architecture so effectively combined.

"The Roman part of the city was built by Augustus," Probus lectured him. "That upper square was constructed in his honor and is called the Augusta Platea. The lower one is the Square of Tiberius and dates from a later period."

A broad flight of steps connected the two squares, and at the top were three archways of the triumphal Propylaea erected to the glory of the Emperor Augustus, while the reliefs in the spandrels that studded the arches commemorated the great victories of that emperor on land and sea.

"Look at the temple there on the Augusta Platea," Probus directed. "I have never seen anything to compare with that frieze of bulls' heads."

"Who is their god?" Luke asked.

"A local deity called Men, the God of Agriculture. I believe his worship is related to that of Mithras. This city is an important stop on the travel route from east to west. The Via Augusta from Babylon to Ephesus runs through here, and another road leads northwestward to Troas and the northern cities of the coast."

They emerged from the city and rode out on the plain where the Camp of Mars stood. Seeing it at close range, Luke was startled by its size, but Probus, who was more experienced in such things, sniffed, "This must be a small-scale war. There are not more than three legions here."

"That is almost twenty thousand men," Luke protested. He knew that a legion numbered about six thousand, besides auxiliary troops.

"The barbarians can easily mount fifty thousand soldiers. These are not the days of Julius Caesar, Luke, when a handful of Romans could conquer the world."

As they rode nearer, Luke scanned the banners waving in different parts of the camp, indicating the legions already there, but saw no sign of the men from Antioch and northern Syria. The camp itself was arranged roughly in the form of a rectangle, the long side running parallel to the river and extending back for about a quarter of a mile. The tents of the legions were pitched in orderly rows, like streets in a city, the rich purples and blues of the officers' quarters contrasting with the drab goat's hair fabric of the men's. Small groups were drilling in open spaces here and there, but the thud of their sandaled feet and the rattle of their harness were drowned out by the clang of blacksmiths' hammers and the roar of armorers' forges. Close to the river hundreds of horses were tethered in parallel rows; behind them were the chariots and carts upon which the mobile part of the army moved. Down the roads from the mountains and the country back of the city moved a steady procession of farmers' carts, loaded donkeys, and camels bringing fodder for the animals and supplies for the troops.

They were stopped at the entrance to the camp by a sentry, who demanded the nature of their business. Luke answered, "I am a physician, and this is Probus Maximus, an apothecary and scribe. We seek the legion from Antioch-in-Syria."

"They have not yet arrived," the sentry said, "but are expected daily."

A centurion came out of a small building that served as a sentry post. "Did you say you were a physician?" he asked.

"Yes," Luke said.

"Then Sergius Paulus will want to see you. He is in the devil of a temper with gout and refuses to let the camp physicians into his tent."

They were conducted by a slave to the tent of the Roman commander in a grove of trees beside the river. When Luke and Probus were ushered in, Sergius stared at them with eyes red from pain and lack of sleep. He was a tall, commanding figure, a typical Roman aristocrat, but now he sat in a chair with his right foot swathed in bandages and resting on a cushion, his expression truculent. "Well," he barked irritably, "what do you want?"

Luke spoke courteously. "I am a physician, come to join the legion of Antioch. My name is Luke."

The commander's face brightened. "Can you relieve the gout? I know there is no cure."

Luke knew better than to make rash promises. Gout was a knotty problem indeed. A strict regimen of diet, avoiding all rich foods and taking only a little thin wine, sometimes helped, but relief was uncertain and recurrence frequent.

Sergius Paulus divined his thoughts, for he said resignedly, "Well, you might as well look at it and tell me to starve myself and drink no wine, as the others have done. But I am doing that already and the toe is worse."

Luke unbandaged the officer's foot gently. It was a classic case of gout in the very acute stage, the toe swollen, red, and exquisitely tender. He rewrapped the foot carefully and got to his feet, but he felt no optimism. "I must see what drugs your medical supplies contain," he temporized. "Perhaps I can compound a remedy which will help you."

Sergius Paulus shrugged. "You will fail as the others have done, but join us, anyway. We are badly in need of physicians. Half my troops are raw levies, and already there is fever among them. Who are you?" he demanded of Probus.

The tall man bowed low. "My name is Probus Maximus. By occupation I am an apothecary, but by inclination a philosopher and student of religion. I am also the most skilled scribe in the world."

"A plague on all scribes," Sergius burst out irritably. "My personal secretary was killed only yesterday in a brawl over a country wench."

"Then you cannot afford not to enlist my services," Probus said promptly. "I can more than take his place."

"He was a graduate of the university at Athens," Sergius warned dourly.

"And I of Alexandria, which is better."

"He had visited half the great cities of the world and knew them intimately."

"I know them all like the back of my hand," Probus boasted. "Including those of Gaul and Britain."

Sergius Paulus laughed then. "At least you are an engaging and original liar. You shall be my secretary and historian, and if you cannot do the things you say, I shall have you whipped out of the camp." He called to a centurion who acted as his adjutant. "Find a tent nearby for these two; I would have both the physician and the scribe near me."

When they were alone in the large tent assigned to them Probus said, "When I was in Gaul, where gout is frequent, I heard of a remedy that is said to be very effective."

"Tell me what it is," Luke begged. "Perhaps they will have the drug among their medical supplies."

"No army medicine chest will contain this drug. It is a powder made from the dried plant of a flower, the autumn crocus."

"But where could I find it?" Luke asked, his hopes dashed again.

"You can thank the gods that, being an apothecary, I am always on the lookout for medicinal herbs," Probus told him. "I noticed the plant growing along the roadside a few miles out of the city."

Luke wasted no time. By nightfall he had gathered a sack of the pale flowers and had them drying in an oven he had commandeered for the purpose. Later he ground the plants into a powder and mixed a liberal dose with an equally large measure of powdered poppy leaves for the narcotic effect. Then he went to the tent of the commander, where a light still burned.

Sergius Paulus was sweating with pain and ready to try any remedy. He drank the mixture in a little wine, and in a few minutes the pain began to diminish from the effect of the poppy. "By Diana!" he said gratefully. "You have brought me more relief already, Luke, than a dozen other physicians. But I tasted poppy in that dose; will there be any permanent effect?"

"I have compounded a new drug," Luke told him truthfully. "One never before used by medical science. The benefit will be permanent if you take it as I direct."

"I would put my head in a noose at your orders," Sergius told him wryly, "so long as you can ease the pain."

The crocus flower worked almost magically. By the third day of Luke's new treatment Sergius Paulus was able to hobble about with only a little pain and the inflammation had begun to subside. In gratitude he showered his new physician with gifts and honors, but Luke insisted that the credit belonged to Probus, who had put him on the track of the new treatment, and divided everything with the tall scribe.

Had he chosen to do so, Luke could have lolled at his ease, with no work save measuring out the four daily doses of powdered crocus leaves for the commander. But military medicine was a new and fascinating study for him. He noted that, while the older and more hardened soldiers seemed immune to many diseases, fevers developed and spread with alarming rapidity through the raw levies. Yet when he talked to the older troops he found that they, too, had suffered just such epidemics when they had been green recruits. From which he judged that men tended to develop a resistance to some diseases when they came in contact with them, sometimes apparently without actually having the diseases themselves.

One cohort developed an alarming epidemic of dysentery, laying nearly all of them low and killing a number of men. Looking for a cause, Luke discovered that these troops, not wanting to carry water from the aqueduct, had been taking their drinking water from the river nearby, where the men bathed and the horses watered and into which, at another level, the cloacas of the city emptied. When he asked Sergius Paulus to issue an order forbidding the taking of any drinking or cooking water from the river, the commander demanded his reason.

"A physician named Marcus Terentius Varro," Luke explained, "wrote a hundred years ago as follows: *'Advertendum etiam qua erunt loca palustria, et propter easdem causas, et quod arescunt, crescunt animalia quaedam minuta, quae non possunt oculi consequi et per aer intus in corpus per os, ad nares perveniunt, atque efficiunt difficiles morbus.'*"

Probus, who was also in the commander's tent, translated promptly: "Perhaps in swampy places small animals live that cannot be discerned with the eye, and they enter the body through the mouth and nostrils and cause grave disorders."

"You might be right," Sergius Paulus admitted. "I contracted a quartan fever in the swamps near Rome. But these waters are not swampy."

"The same could hold true for rivers as well as swamps, particularly when men bathe in the waters."

"Issue the order, then, Probus," Sergius directed. "We will see what happens."

When shortly the dysentery epidemic subsided, Luke's reputation was enhanced. There was also a profusion of wounds to be treated, for the raw troops were always cutting themselves with swords or accidentally jabbing others with lances. Fights, too, broke out between men from rival cities and sometimes resulted in grave wounds. When one of the blacksmiths was kicked in the head by a horse and subsequently fell into convulsions, Luke trepanned the man's skull as described in the teachings of Hippocrates, boring into the bone until the brain was exposed. A quantity of blood escaped through the trepanned opening, and shortly the injured man recovered.

By the time the legion from Antioch marched into the Camp of Mars, Luke was already established as the most skillful physician and surgeon in the entire army. He embraced Silvanus and Apollonius and took them to Sergius Paulus, who also greeted them warmly. Apollonius, Luke saw, had changed a great deal. He wore the trappings of a tribune with gravity and was more thoughtful than he had been as a youth, although even handsomer than before he had gone to Rome. Silvanus, except that he was a little more grizzled with age, was the same.

Sergius Paulus promptly invited them all to dine with him that evening, and since there was work for Silvanus and Apollonius to do, getting their troops quartered and established in the routine of the camp, Luke saw no more of them until they met together in the luxurious tent of Sergius Paulus. Probus had lost no time in making good his boasts to the commander; already he was more of a confidant than a secretary, and it was natural that he should join them at the table.

Sergius came in from his evening inspection and threw his velvet cloak down on the cushions before the table. "Wine!" he called to the slaves, and when it came they drank first to the Emperor and then to the legion of Antioch. The toasts over, they settled down on cushions around a low table for the meal. It was a luxurious one, for the Romans never stinted themselves even when in the field. Sergius, because of his gout, ate sparingly, as Luke had prescribed, and drank only a little wine. While they ate, Probus entertained them with tales of his travels that kept them laughing throughout the meal.

"You can see why I am so fond of this fellow," Sergius said after a particularly outrageous tale. "He is the greatest liar in the Empire."

"Not so, noble Roman," Probus objected. "I am a disciple of Democritus, who was called the 'Laughing Philosopher' because he taught that we should live for each day only."

"Is this the same Democritus who said everything is composed of tiny particles called atoms?" Luke asked.

"The same," Probus agreed. "Or, as Lucretius wrote:

> *"That you may know*
> *That forms dissimilar coalesce in one,*
> *And things are formed of differing elements;*
> *As in our verse you many letters see*
> *Common to many words, yet words and verse*
> *As wholes dissimilar . . .*
> *Thus common atoms may exist in things,*
> *The compound whole be yet dissimilar."*

"You are more recently from the halls of learning than any of us, Luke," Sergius Paulus said. "What does all that mean?"

Luke smiled. "It may be true that everything is composed of atoms, just as it may be true that animalcules cause disease, as Marcus Terentius Varro claimed. But I am so busy treating disease that I have little time now for philosophical matters."

"Plato warned against trying to separate the soul from the body, Luke," Probus reminded him. "Perhaps it would be better for you to study the souls of men as well as their diseases."

74

"Do you believe in the immortality of the soul, Probus?" Sergius asked.

The philosopher took a long draught of wine. "If a man has known a good measure of happiness on earth, why wish for immortality? The best he can hope for is a repetition of what he has already experienced. And one grows weary from the same pleasures oft repeated."

"But who is really happy?" Apollonius asked.

"Myself," Probus replied promptly, "for I ask of a day only that which it gives. A sensible man's prayer to the gods should be only, *'Give me that which I deserve.'* Then if he gets much, he deserved much. If he gets little, he deserved little and therefore has no right to be unhappy because of what he did not get."

"I am not sure I agree with that philosophy, Probus," Luke protested. "It justifies the rich and excuses the poor. I lean to the teachings of another who said—let me see if I can remember it. Yes, it was, *'As ye would that men should do to you, do ye also to them likewise.'*"

"An admirable way of life," Sergius Paulus admitted, "but not a very practical one, I am afraid. Who is this philosopher?"

"A Jew called Jesus of Nazareth."

"He was the Galilean executed by Pontius Pilate!" Sergius exclaimed. "There has been trouble in Judea ever since."

"Think twice before you endorse such teachings, Sergius," Probus warned. "If you believed them, you would not make wars."

"By the Ephesian Diana! You are right. Then it can never be popular with the Romans; we live by war."

"Or with the Jews, who profit by business," Apollonius added. "I cannot see a religion surviving long which antagonizes the most influential people in the Empire. It seems to me that this sect works toward its own destruction."

"It would except for one thing," Silvanus interposed quietly. "Jesus, according to those who believe in him, is more than a man."

"Is?" Sergius Paulus exclaimed. "But he was crucified."

"His followers believe that Jesus rose from the dead," Silvanus explained. "As the son of God, they look for him to return at any moment and rule over the world."

"Hah! Would he overcome Rome?"

"They believe he will," Silvanus admitted.

"Then I know they will not survive long," Sergius said positively. "The Emperor will not let any sect live which advocates his downfall." Then he changed the subject. "You have been in Paphlagonia, Silvanus. What do you think of our chances against the barbarians?"

"It is a mountainous region," the centurion said, "and poorly adapted to military campaigning."

"Exactly what I told the Emperor and Petronius," Sergius exploded. "And yet to punish a few people who do not pay taxes, they send me into dangerous country with half the men I need and most of them untrained and untested in battle. I only hope that we get safely home."

"I for one am not returning," Silvanus said.

Sergius gave him a startled look. "If you are so sure of death, you need not go, Silvanus. I will need someone to guard supplies here at the camp."

"I only meant that I am going on to Bithynia," Silvanus explained. "I am going to live there when the war is over."

"Bithynia is a barbarous country," Sergius protested. "Why would you choose such a place?"

"Away from the cities it is a pleasant land, and the climate is mild."

"There are hundreds of cities in the Empire where you can have all that, without burying yourself in such a faraway place."

"I think I understand what Silvanus seeks in Bithynia," Probus interposed. "All men long for a place where none of the troubles of the world exist. Most religions offer such a heaven after death, but Silvanus thinks he can find it on earth."

For a long moment no one spoke, then Sergius Paulus said softly, as if he were speaking to himself, "There is a bay on the island of Cyprus . . ."

"And I would choose a hunting lodge in the mountains above Antioch," Apollonius added.

"You are all wrong," Probus said. "It is along the banks of the river that the Britons call Thames, near their city of Londinium."

"And I insist upon Bithynia," Silvanus said doggedly.

"You are strangely silent, physician," Sergius said to Luke. "Or are you too young yet to think of a place to die?"

"No," Luke said, smiling. "I am attracted to Silvanus's Bithynia, to Apollonius's lodge, even your Cyprian bay and the far-off river that Probus loves. But I wonder if you are not all talking about the same thing, a state of mind. None of you could hope to be happy in the places you mention unless your mind was at peace. It seems to me that if a man has achieved peace in his own mind, it makes no difference where he is."

"By Diana! You are right," Sergius exclaimed. "But how does one attain peace?"

"I am not sure yet," Luke admitted. "Perhaps by first doing the things which it is your lot to do on earth."

"What sort of an answer is that?" Probus snorted. "My way is better. Live for the day and pray only for what you deserve."

Sergius yawned. "Well, I have lived enough for this day. Since I cannot eat or drink, I can at least sleep." At this pointed invitation to leave, they all bade the commander good night.

Outside the moon was shining and the camp was quiet as Luke and Silvanus walked along the riverbank, Apollonius having gone to make a final check upon his troops. "I was interested to hear you speak of Jesus of Nazareth tonight, Luke," the centurion said. "During these past few years I have become a believer in the Galilean."

"I remember you were very near to being one when we were in Jerusalem five years ago."

"Yes, I suppose I was. But only lately have I found in him the real peace of mind of which you spoke. That is why I am ready now to go into Bithynia."

"Can I go with you, Silvanus?" Luke asked impulsively. "You promised, remember?"

The old centurion put his hand on the younger man's shoulder. "You gave the answer tonight, Luke. No man can reach his private Bithynia until he has done his own particular work on earth."

"But how will I know what my task is?"

"God will tell you, Luke. Why else would he have selected you as the agent by whom the sayings of his son were preserved five years ago if he did not have some purpose for you?"

"It could have been chance," Luke pointed out.

"Yes, it could have been chance. But then chance may be only another name for the workings of God's will on earth."

For which thought Luke had no answer at the moment.

v

North of Ancyra, in the province of Galatia, the southern borders of Bithynia and Paphlagonia lay along the top of a range of mountains towering above the icy currents of the river Halys. Here the three provinces joined near a pass giving access to the fertile plains of Bithynia and Paphlagonia, where the river Synape wound through them both. Beyond the mountain range the rebellious Paphlagonians had gathered in force, and on a flat plateau south of the pass leading into their territory Sergius Paulus halted his troops and prepared for battle.

The cool air of the mountains, already crisp with the promise of frost, brought a sharp drop of temperature at night, and a fresh epidemic of coughs and fevers broke out among the troops. Luke was kept busy prescribing medicines for the cough and pain, leeching, cupping, and administering cataplasms. He had seen little of Silvanus or Apollonius during the march northward, for the Syrian legion traveled as a rear guard for the army, and Luke's place was in the train of the Roman commander near the front of the long column. When Silvanus appeared at his dispensary after the evening meal a few days following their arrival, Luke's face lit up with a smile. "Don't tell me an old campaigner like you is already suffering from the cold, Silvanus," he greeted his friend.

The centurion shook his head. He carried a blanket rolled up under his arm and wore a heavy cloak. "I came because I want to show you something, Luke. Can you leave?"

"I am just finishing up for the night," Luke said, glad of an excuse to close the dispensary.

"Get a blanket and wear a heavy cloak," Silvanus directed. "We will sleep out and return in the morning."

"Are we going to spy on the enemy?" Luke's eyes kindled with excitement.

"Not unless we meet him by accident," Silvanus said with a smile. "No, I have other plans."

Luke rolled up a blanket and threw a heavy cloak about his shoulders. Silvanus took him along the mountain road that led to the narrow pass. In the defile itself they were halted by the Roman advance guard but were allowed to go on when the centurion gave the password. Perhaps a quarter of a mile beyond, where the road began to descend, he led the way off the road into a small wooded glen, one side of which was a vast empty darkness where the mountains dropped precipitously to the plain below.

"What have you brought me to see, Silvanus?" Luke asked, mystified.

"Sleep first," the centurion advised. "I will wake you at dawn."

Luke lay down on a level spot and wrapped himself in the cloak, drawing the blanket around him, for it was already growing cool. No sound disturbed the peace of the night, nothing to remind them that the Roman Army was encamped behind them and an enemy in front. Luke was asleep at once, for he was tired from the long trip north and the days of hard work.

When Silvanus awakened him by shaking his shoulder, Luke sat up and rubbed his eyes. Then he remembered where they were and looked around, but there was as yet only a little light, and he could see nothing beyond the confines of the small glen. While waiting for the sun to come up they munched the bread and goat cheese which Silvanus had carried and drank from his canteen.

As the dawn brought light Luke could see that one side of their glen ended in a precipitous craggy drop, although the fog curtain still shielded the lowlands from view. Slowly, as the gray tendrils of the fog dissolved before the rising sun, the valley below them began to take form. Luke saw a small river winding its way to the north and west through a broad green carpet of fields and pastures. Distantly to their ears came the lowing of cattle, the neighing of horses being led to water, and the sound of human voices as people began to stir in the farmhouses below. To the west another mountain range towered, its craggy tops dark blue against the morning sky, but the plain below extended as far to the north as Luke could see, ending in a bluish haze upon the horizon. It was a calm and peaceful land of small farms and farmhouses, fields, orchards, and pastures, with the bright colors of flowers painted against the green background of the fields and the brown thatch of the housetops as if by the brush of a divine artist.

Luke turned to Silvanus, his eyes shining. "It is the most beautiful land I have ever seen," he cried. "Surely this must be Bithynia."

The centurion smiled. "Yes, Luke. This is Bithynia. The plain stretches northward to the Pontus Euxinus, which the inhabitants call the Black Sea. Paphlagonia lies to the east, and there is more of Bithynia behind the mountains there to the west, more mountains and more valleys like this one. The climate is mild in those valleys," he continued, "and on the shores of the Black Sea the sand is sometimes as white as the snow on the mountaintops to the east there. I wanted you to see it as I always picture it in my mind."

"Take me with you when you go, Silvanus," Luke begged again. But the old centurion only shook his head. "You will take the road to Bithynia soon enough, Luke," he promised. "But only when you have fulfilled your personal destiny, as we all must do to find peace and happiness." He gathered his cloak about him. "Come now. We must get back to the troops; our place is with them on the eve of a battle."

vi

The Paphlagonians had managed to choose their own battleground, thereby accomplishing the unusual feat of forcing Roman soldiers to fight on ground not of their own choosing. And worse still, since the battle was joined in many narrow defiles and small pockets among the mountain peaks, the Romans could fight only in small groups and were unable to use the famous "square of shields" by which Julius Caesar and the generals who had followed him were able to batter great holes in the ranks of other armies. The Paphlagonians were cunning fighters. As soon as one band of them isolated a small group of Romans, others, climbing like goats about the mountain crags, loosed a shower of arrows and spears from above upon the luckless soldiers of the Empire.

Casualties from the very first were heavy. Luke, because of his skill in surgery, had been ordered by Sergius Paulus to set up a hospital at the advance camp upon the small plateau. Here he worked tirelessly, suturing wounds, removing arrow- and spearheads, splinting broken bones, and measuring out liberal doses of the powdered poppy which was his main weapon against pain. Many of the wounds were hopeless, spear thrusts into abdomen or groin, and compound fractures where splintered bones tore through muscle and skin as the wounded man dragged himself away from the fighting, grinding gravel and dirt into the exposed tissues. Wounds of the chest rarely reached Luke's hospital; for the most part they died upon the field, as did severe wounds of the skull.

All day long the battle raged back and forth. Dispatches from the front indicated that the Romans were holding desperately although being cut to pieces in a multitude of tiny conflicts in the craggy pockets among the mountain peaks. Just before nightfall a litter was borne through the trees to where Luke was working. When it came closer Luke recognized Silvanus, his face chalk-white and drawn with pain. He ran to steady the litter while the soldiers set it down under a tree near the improvised surgery.

Silvanus opened his eyes. "There is nothing you can do, Luke," he said quietly in a voice taut with pain. "I got word that Apollonius and his troops were surrounded and led a party to open a path for them to retreat. One of the barbarians thrust a spear into my side, but the boy is safe."

Luke examined the wound, an ugly, gaping spear thrust in the right flank, penetrating deeply into that vital area. There was little external bleeding, almost surely meaning an internal hemorrhage. Silvanus had spoken the truth, Luke agreed silently. There was no hope in cases such as this, nothing to do but wait for the inevitable. As the hemorrhage continued, death would come with increasing swiftness.

"Attend those who can be helped by your skill, Luke," Silvanus whispered. "If I could only have something for the pain."

Luke poured a liberal dose of the powdered poppy and mixed it in a little wine. He lifted Silvanus's head while he drank the medicine, then covered the wounded man with his cloak. "I sent word to Apollonius that my wounds are only minor," Silvanus gasped. "He is troubled enough already without worrying about me."

Luke nodded, and the centurion closed his eyes. Presently his deep, even breathing told Luke that he was sleeping under the influence of the powerful narcotic.

There was no rest for Luke that night, and shortly before dawn one of the less severely wounded came for him where he was dressing wounds. "The centurion Silvanus is awake and calling for you," he reported.

One look told Luke that the end was not far away, for already the grayish pallor of death was creeping into the bearded cheeks of the centurion. Luke knelt beside the litter and took one of the gnarled hands in his own. "What do you wish, Silvanus?" he asked.

The old man opened his eyes. "My time is almost up, Luke," he whispered. "Grant me a last favor."

"Anything." Luke's voice broke. "Anything I can do."

"I would die in Bithynia, in the glen where we were this morning."

"I will get men to carry the litter," Luke said promptly.

"Hurry, my son," Silvanus urged. "There is but little time."

The bearers deposited the litter upon the grass carpet of the little glen overlooking the plain of Bithynia, close to the edge of the crag so that Silvanus could see over it. Luke sent the litter bearers back and knelt beside his dying friend, weeping unashamedly. Silvanus opened his eyes. "Do not grieve for me, Luke," he said softly. "I have found the way to eternal life and I have seen Bithynia. I want nothing else." His voice trailed off for a moment, and Luke reached for his pulse, thinking that the end might have come, but the heavy-lidded eyes opened and the low whisper came once more. "I have been honored, Luke; Jesus, too, died from a spear thrust in the side." He tried to raise himself up on his elbows. "Can you see the plain below?"

"Not yet," Luke said. "But the fog is thinning, and I will lift you up when the valley can be seen." A few moments later the sun shot through the fog, dispelling it, so that the fertile plain below was revealed, as if a curtain had been drawn back. When Luke lifted Silvanus by the shoulders, the dying man's eyes searched eagerly the scene of peace below them and a smile broke over his face, erasing the pain. "Bithynia!" he gasped. "Bithynia at last!" Then the tortured body went suddenly limp and the lines of pain about Silvanus's mouth were eased by the peace of death.

Luke lowered the body of his friend back on the litter and got slowly to his feet. His eyes were still fixed upon the land below the mountain, the green fields and the pastures, and the golden ribbon of the river winding through it in the morning sunlight. "Bithynia," he repeated softly. "Peaceful land."

Suddenly Luke's heart was sick of fighting and death and he longed for the peace of that scene below him. But the words of Silvanus came again to his mind: "You will take the road to Bithynia soon enough, Luke." Bithynia lay before him, almost within his grasp, as it had been almost within the grasp of Silvanus. A narrow road wound along the face of the mountain; he had only to take it now to be free. But Silvanus had died before he reached Bithynia, and with scores of wounded needing his skilled care, Luke knew that his place was with the army. The path leading down the mountains, the road to Bithynia, seemed farther away than ever now.

Stumbling through the pass toward the battle lines where he knew he would find Apollonius, Luke came upon Probus riding toward the front in a chariot with messages for the commanders from Sergius Paulus. The scribe stopped the chariot. "You have no business up here, Luke," he said severely. "Are you mad?"

Luke looked up at him dully. "I am looking for Apollonius. Silvanus is dead and we must bury him."

Probus knew how much Luke and Apollonius had loved the centurion. "Step into the chariot," he said. "I am going to see your brother now and will bring both of you back with me."

There had been an early-morning sortie in force, and the dead and dying littered the small pocket where the battle had been fought. Bodies from the day before still lay on the ground, swollen with the bloat of death, and the stench of war was appalling. Apollonius had led the Romans in their last sortie and was resting now with his battle-weary troops. Since the way was too rough for the chariot, Probus sent the driver ahead for Apollonius while he and Luke waited.

An old and battle-scarred centurion, the short sword in his hand dripping with blood, was walking over the battlefield. Twice they saw him kneel beside a body on the ground, then rise and quickly plunge the sword into the soldier's neck. Luke felt a wave of anger and revulsion at what looked like an act of wanton murder and took a step toward the centurion, but Probus gripped his shoulder. "Steady, Luke," he advised. "Those men are beyond help. He is only performing an act of mercy; the soldiers want it that way."

"What do these men gain, Probus?" Luke asked, a little unsteadily. "The ones who are fighting and dying, both ours and the enemy?"

"What do the little people of the world ever gain from wars, except the privilege of dying? If their armies win, they know a short period of pride in naming themselves victors. And if their armies lose, they change masters and death comes a little sooner."

"Is life, then, without either purpose or hope of happiness?"

"I did not say that." Probus sniffed as a breeze enveloped them with the scent of the battlefield. "The driving force in every man is the need to convince himself that he is better than his fellows. Eating fine food, drinking spiced wine, satisfying the animal passions, overcoming other men in combat, war, or politics, acquiring great wealth and power—all give a man the illusion of being nearer to a god than other humans, so those are the things that men risk their lives for."

"But there can never be peace so long as every man strives to be better than the other."

Probus grunted. "When has there ever been peace? You remember the Jewish concept of the creation of man, don't you?"

"The story of Adam and Eve? Yes."

"Then you remember that in the Garden of Eden everything was perfect and Adam and Eve were created in the image of Jehovah, which should have satisfied them at least. But when they learned of a tree whose fruit would let them know things they did not know, they needs must eat of it so that they might think themselves better than they had been before. And even when they had sons, the two fought and one was killed."

"Do you believe those stories?" Luke asked.

Probus shrugged. "They are nothing but allegorical tales, of course. The writer was showing that the base impulses which make each man seek to triumph over the others were present in the very beginning, just as they will be present in the last man on earth, the one who finally triumphs over all others and stands alone."

"What then? After he has triumphed?"

"He will realize, too late, of course, that he is a fool. For if there is a god, then man is under him and can never be supreme. And if there is no god, there is always death, which he cannot vanquish." Probus smiled wryly. "My philosophy is better, Luke. Live for today—tomorrow comes soon enough. Pray for what you deserve, and think yourself better than no man, for then you must try to be better than the man above him."

A chariot whirled across the littered battlefield with Apollonius at the reins and the driver they had sent to find the tribune standing beside him. Apollonius was tall and handsome driving the chariot, but when he stepped down from it Luke saw that his shoulders drooped with the despondency of near defeat. Remembering the carefree and happy youth with whom he had played in Antioch, fishing under the great stone arch that carried the road to Seleucia across the yellow flood of the Orontes, throwing stones at wine jugs floating in the stream, and swimming in the strong current, Luke felt a new sense of depression grip his spirits.

"Luke!" Apollonius cried, embracing him. Then his face grew serious again. "You should not be so near to the battle, little brother," he said, using the nickname of their childhood together. "Tell me of Silvanus; I heard he was wounded yesterday."

"Silvanus is dead," Luke told him.

"Dead!" The tall tribune's voice broke. "B-but he saved my life only yesterday when he led a party to rescue me."

83

"He was wounded then, but he didn't want you to worry and would not let me send word to you. He died about an hour ago; I came for you because I thought we two should bury him."

Apollonius nodded, but tears were in his eyes. "He did enough for us; we can at least do that for him. Fontinus!" he called to the centurion who had been dispatching wounded on the battlefield. "You will command until I return. Come, Luke, you and Probus can ride with me; my chariot is larger and faster."

Apollonius wiped sweat from his forehead. He and Luke had just finished erecting a small cairn of stones over Silvanus's grave. "So that is Bithynia," he said, looking out over the valley. "Now I can understand why Silvanus loved it. Did he see it again before he died?"

"He brought me up here the morning before he died to watch the sunrise," Luke said. "And he died happy, Apollonius, for he told me he would live again with Jesus of Nazareth."

"I know. He often talked to me of these things in Antioch. But I am too weary to think right now; we had better be getting back." Apollonius started toward the mouth of the little glen, where Probus was waiting with the chariot, but Luke lagged behind for a last look at Bithynia. He turned quickly when Probus's shout of warning reached his ears, and what he saw sent a chill of apprehension through his body.

From the rocky wall of the glen three men were in the act of leaping to the grassy floor, swords in hand. Their clothing and weapons stamped them as Paphlagonians, and Luke saw at once what had happened. The three must have been climbing along the craggy face of the mountain, seeking to get behind the Roman lines, where they could lie in wait beside the pass and leap upon the chariot of any high-ranking officer who happened to be passing, killing him and escaping for another foray. But the three in the glen were even easier prey, for only Apollonius was armed.

Caught off his guard, Apollonius barely had time to draw his sword before the men were upon him, forcing him backward, so that he stumbled and dropped to one knee to keep from falling. The tribune fought desperately, but the Paphlagonians were huge men, obviously intent upon dispatching their victim quickly. One of them beat down Apollonius's weapon even as a second lifted his heavy sword for the fatal thrust into the young officer's heart. Acting by instinct, Luke seized a rock from the cairn at Silvanus's grave and threw it with all his strength at the attackers.

There was no time to aim the stone well, but some remnant of the skill he had developed as a youth breaking wine jugs floating on the Orontes still remained. The rock went true, striking the shoulder of the man whose sword was intended for Apollonius's heart, deflecting his aim so that the blade was buried instead in the tribune's upper breast and shoulder. His shoulder shattered by the blow, the Paphlagonian let out a scream of agony and reeled backward while the other two whirled to meet this unexpected attack, converging upon Luke where he stood almost at the edge of the cliff.

From the mouth of the glen where Probus was holding the horses Luke heard a sudden rumble of wheels and the spatter of gravel as the horses leaped from the cut of a whip. But he had no time to watch anything except the two men whose swords were almost at his throat. Unarmed as he was, he could only retreat, expecting at every step to go plummeting backward into space, but knowing that only death awaited him at the hands of the attackers. Then he heard Probus shout, "Jump, Luke! Jump!" and obeyed without looking to see what the scribe was doing.

As Luke dived sideways, landing on his breast in the dirt and sliding along the gravel, he had a glimpse of Probus, his face contorted, driving the chariot and whipping the horses like something possessed. One wheel of the heavy vehicle struck the Paphlagonian with the shattered arm, bowling him over beside Apollonius, who lay on the ground with the blade of the sword in his upper chest snapped off almost at the skin. The chariot wheels spattered Luke with gravel, so close did they come to him as he lay on the ground. The other two attackers had no chance to escape as Probus drove over them, sweeping men, chariot, and horses over the edge of the cliff. At the last moment the scribe leaped from the vehicle, a flying jump that carried him clear. He struck the ground almost at the edge of the cliff and rolled along the precipice until he came up short against a boulder.

Luke struggled to his feet, still dazed by the plunge into the dirt and the rapid sequence of events which had changed certain death into victory. He saw Probus getting up and, judging that the scribe was not seriously injured, hurried over to where Apollonius lay unconscious on the ground. The wound was high, through the muscles of the breast, almost up to the shoulder, where the arteries and veins to the arms coursed. Seeing it, a cold sweat of apprehension broke out on Luke's forehead. If the point had penetrated a vein, there could be internal hemorrhage, as had been the case with Silvanus. Only when he removed the broken sword, as he must do soon if Apollonius were to live, would he be able to tell whether or not the wound was fatal. In any event, it was a very serious injury.

Since there was nothing to be done immediately for Apollonius, Luke turned his attention to Probus. The apothecary-scribe was bending over the stone cairn, selecting one of the rocks with his left hand;

his right arm hung limp at his side and there were beads of sweat on his face from pain. He took up a sizable stone and, moving to where the wounded Paphlagonian was just beginning to stir, pounded on the man's head with savage intensity until the rock cracked his skull and there was no question of his stirring any more. Then Probus straightened up and managed a wry grin. "Two minutes ago we were all closer to death than we're ever likely to be again and escape, Luke. We must have deserved to live."

"It was you who saved us," Luke said gratefully. "Is your arm hurt badly?"

"From the way it grates, I suspect that Sergius Paulus has lost the writing arm of his chief scribe for several months. What about the tribune?"

"I can't tell until I remove the blade."

"Then we must get him back at once. Splint this broken wing of mine so the bones stop moving, and I will go for help."

Probus's arm was broken just below the shoulder, Luke saw when he examined it. The broken sword of the enemy, save the point which was in Apollonius's breast, made a satisfactory splint which Luke bound in place with strips torn from the clothing of the dead Paphlagonian. When he had finished and suspended the arm in a sling, Probus was white, but he stood up and moved around, testing the efficacy of splint and bandage. "There is little pain now," he reported. "I will go for a litter to move Apollonius." When he left the glen, Luke was alone with the unconscious tribune and the grave of the man who had guided them both through the years of their youth.

vii

In his improvised surgery at the main encampment of the Roman Army, Luke surveyed his preparations for the operation which might mean life or death for his foster brother. They were pitifully small in the face of such a job as this, he thought, but comforted himself with the knowledge that the determining factor in any difficult feat of surgery was always the skill and courage of the surgeon. And he knew that no one else in the camp was sufficiently skilled for such delicate work. His instruments lay on a small table: *scalpri,* sharp knives of the best Damascus steel; strong-jawed forceps for removing arrow fragments and spear points; *specilli,* the long metal sounds for probing into wounds; *unci,* curved hooks for holding muscles apart; and thin metal *spatulae,* flat separators for tissue searching. There was also a special instrument in the shape of a V to hold open wounds while extracting arrowheads. To one side, since he did not expect to use them in this task, were the *rhissagra,* a specially hooked forceps for removing the roots of teeth; *trepannes* with the *meningophylax* for holding back the membranes of the brain as the skull was drilled; lead catheters for bladder wounds; and, of course, amputation saws. Everything was spotlessly clean, for Luke had always followed both Hippocrates and Celsus in this respect.

Apollonius was sleeping quietly under the narcotic effect of an extra-strong dose of poppy powder. Beside the table burned a brazier of charcoal in which rested the cauterizing irons in case it became necessary to control bleeding by searing the flesh with the hot irons. And four brawny soldiers stood ready to hold the wounded tribune if he struggled from the knife.

Sergius Paulus stood to one side, for he had become attached to Apollonius, and the son of the deputy governor of Syria was naturally important to the Roman commander. Watching the broken end of the sword pulsate faintly in the hurried rhythm of the pulse, Luke knew that the point lay very close to an artery, if not actually inside the vessel. Hippocrates, he remembered, had considered that the arteries carried air, but more recently Celsus had written, *"Interdum etiam, ut sanguis vehementer erumpat, efficit."* Which could only mean that the great Roman physician had observed the arteries to spurt blood when cut and concluded that they carried blood, not air. A wound of the pulsating vessels, then, could be a source of dangerous hemorrhage. And even worse, a fragment of Apollonius's cloak had been carried into the flesh by the blade and could now be seen at the edge of the metal point. Wounds containing clothing were notoriously poor risks in wartime, frequently resulting in fatal gangrene.

Holding in his left hand a pad of the washed wool which Hippocrates recommended as a dressing for wounds, Luke placed the point of his scalpel in the edge of the wound beside the sword point and cut outward for about two finger breadths, then turned quickly and cut the same distance on the other side. Apollonius groaned and tried to twist away from the pain of the knife, but the soldiers held him firmly.

"Why do you not simply extract the point, Luke?" Sergius Paulus asked.

"It is so deeply embedded near the blood vessels and the lungs," Luke explained, "that I may need room in case there is serious bleeding. Besides, the torn portion of cloak must be removed, or there will be a severe inflammation afterward." Holding the wound open with his left hand, he next separated the muscles on each side of the sword point. Working slowly and carefully, he went deeper into the tissues, deeper than he had ever before gone in such an operation, but the instincts of a surgeon told him that here daring meant saving life.

Now Luke put down the scalpel and took up a forceps. The sword point had originally been broken off flush with the skin, but now that the muscles were pushed away on either side, a full half inch of metal projected. He set the jaws of the forceps upon the metal and exerted a gentle, slow pull. For a moment it resisted, and he thought with a sudden cold fear that the point must be embedded in bone, making the job far more difficult. Then it loosened and Luke breathed a deep sigh of relief.

Another danger had come into being now. A large blood vessel could be injured and the bleeding blocked by the sword point. With the point removed, blood would begin to gush, perhaps uncontrollably. Slowly he drew out the sword point and put it on the table, then turned his attention to the open wound. Blood, old and dark, gushed from the opening for a moment as he had expected, but there was little of the bright red flow which would have been a harbinger of serious trouble. Luke drew a deep sigh of relief and covered the wound with a pad of the washed wool. "The sword does not seem to have injured any vital structure," he told Sergius Paulus. "He should have a good chance for recovery."

"Asklepios should be proud of you today, Luke," Sergius said. "You have saved one of the Empire's most valuable young officers."

Carefully Luke extracted the fragment of cloak from the wound and washed the wound thoroughly with a mixture of oil and wine. Then he applied a clean dressing and bandaged it firmly into place. Wounds like this usually suppurated, exhibiting the classical signs of inflammation described by Celsus, *"dolor, calor, tumor, et rubor,"* or "pain, heat, swelling, and redness." But with the sword fragment removed and the wound thoroughly cleaned out, Luke had done all that he could. Apollonius's fine young body must do the rest.

Fighting desperately during the next few weeks, the Romans managed to stave off defeat, leaving something like an armed truce in effect, with scouting operations and sudden vicious battles to the death between small parties occurring every day. Luke was busy, largely with caring for Apollonius, for in spite of the tribune's strength, his convalescence was very stormy. Suppuration set in almost immediately, with a raging fever, weakening rigors, and delirium. More than once Luke was ready to give up, but as the weeks passed, the fever began to subside and it seemed that the worst was over, if there were no further complications.

The nights were cold and raw and, protected only by tents and temporary shelters, the troops suffered constantly from exposure. Hardly a day passed without one or more soldiers complaining of pain in the chest, followed by fever and chills, rapid breathing, cough, and a sputum rusty with blood. Case after case died of such a fulminating form of pneumonia that Luke grew more apprehensive daily, for if this should happen to Apollonius in his weakened state, he stood little chance of recovery.

Luke told his fears to Sergius Paulus in his tent one evening as the Roman commander sat, gaunt and unshaven, before his desk, dictating letters to be sent back to Rome and the colonies, begging for more troops. Sergius frowned and asked, "What would you recommend to prevent such a danger, Luke?"

"Perhaps he could be sent to some less mountainous region where the climate is milder?"

"Where would you suggest?"

"There is the plain of Bithynia nearby."

Sergius shook his head. "I like not the idea of sending him farther away from home." Then his face brightened. "I have it. How many men do we have recovering who will not be fit for action within the next few months but could travel by wagon?"

Luke made a quick estimate. "Roughly two hundred or more."

Sergius thumped the table with his fist. "Then we will send them back to Pisidian Antioch in a train which you and Apollonius can accompany, along with these letters asking for more troops. The wagons can return with supplies we need, and you and Apollonius can go on to Antioch."

Probus was standing by and now he said, "Since I cannot work, should I not go with Luke? I can report directly to the governor of Syria on the numbers and disposition of the enemy and make out a stronger case for support."

Sergius smiled. "Tired of military life so soon, Probus? But then you are a philosopher, and a military camp is a poor place for thinking. Yes, you may go."

And so Luke and Probus, with Apollonius lying on the floor of a light cart, traveled to Pisidian Antioch with the train of wounded and sick. Leaving the train at the base camp, they pushed on southeastward along the Old Way, probably the most famous highway of the Roman Empire, toward Tarsus, where they planned to take ship for the short trip by sea across the Gulf of Issus to Syrian Antioch.

The road was lined with caravans moving in both directions, but Luke did not even notice the plodding dromedaries or the many-hued robes of the turbaned drivers. He was in the wagon with Apollonius, watching apprehensively the heightened color of his foster brother's cheeks, the increased rate of his breathing, and the short hacking cough which had developed on the way. Apollonius's eyes grew brighter as his fever rose, and he talked incessantly, but not always coherently, warning Luke of an impending delirium. When his foster brother complained of a pain in his chest distant from the wound and coughed up rusty sputum, Luke knew with chill finality what had happened. Pneumonia! It could be nothing else.

Probus frowned when Luke told him his diagnosis. "We are two days from Tarsus. Is it safe to carry him that far?"

"We have little choice. There is no place nearer than Tarsus where a sick man can be cared for."

By the time they reached the Cilician Gates, Apollonius was already in a desperate state. Luke blistered, cupped, applied leeches to the sick man's chest, and covered painful areas with potent cataplasms. He exhausted the resources of his medicine chest, following the directions of Hippocrates in such cases, first administering a purge, then following it with oxymel, and after that a clyster, but with no effect. Ptisan mixed with honey was equally valueless, as were galbanum and pine fruit in Attic honey, southern wood in oxymel, and a decoction of pepper and black hellebore, all classic remedies in this disease. As the miles passed beneath the wheels, Luke's certainty that Apollonius would die grew stronger and stronger.

Under other circumstances he would have been very much interested in the region through which they were passing, for history had been made in the narrow defile through the Taurus Mountains called the Cilician Gates, which gave access to the teeming population centers of the Lycaonian plains from the storied lands to the east and south. Through it ran the important trade routes formed by the junction of the roads from the Euphrates to the east and Syrian Antioch to the south.

Through the chasm where a stream tumbled beside the narrow road Hattic races from Cappadocia had poured to inhabit the fertile basin between the Euphrates and the Orontes rivers, and to act as a buffer state separating the Babylonians and Assyrians to the east from the Egyptians to the south. Northward from the city of Tarsus and the Cilician plain came the Persians to conquer the whole of Lesser Asia, and southward again streamed the legions of Alexander to fight the armies of Darius on the plains of Issus.

The Romans, moving eastward in their successive waves of conquest under the Caesars, poured through the pass to conquer and hold permanently the fertile plains and seaports. As was their custom, they built roads and brought stable governments with them, and now long caravans from the land of man's beginning plodded in safety to Ephesus and the home cities of the Romans. Tarsus, with its ready access to the sea by way of the river Cydnus which split the city, had been an important center for a thousand years. It had prospered especially under the Romans and was now a busy and important shipping point as well as a station on the overland trade routes. In all of Asia no city was more famous for the manufacture of tents. On the slopes of the Taurus Mountains goats thrived and their hair grew long and silky. From it was woven the tough fabric known as *cilicium,* a favorite material for tentmaking.

Luke was busy as the wagon moved through the Cilician Gates and out on the plain toward the city of Tarsus, some forty miles away. Now Apollonius's hoarse breathing filled the wagon, and it took all of Luke's strength to control him in his delirium, plus the crippled efforts of Probus. During one of the few periods when Apollonius was dozing Probus said, "I have been wondering where we can go in Tarsus. Innkeepers are superstitious about people dying in their establishments, and I doubt if any will take us in."

Luke had been worrying about just that, but now a thought struck him. Ananias and Mariamne! Why hadn't he thought of them before? Mariamne's last letter had told of their flight to Tarsus. And Ananias was a healer as well as a friend.

"But how can we find them?" Probus objected when Luke told him his thoughts. "Tarsus is a city of weavers."

"Ananias is a follower of Jesus. Someone in the community of weavers will certainly know of him in that connection."

As it happened, they found Ananias sooner than they expected. Hardly had the wagon entered the city when Probus spied a man haranguing a crowd on the street and heard him utter the word "Christos." "I believe there is a member of the Nazarene sect preaching out here," he called to Luke inside the wagon. "Perhaps he will know your friends."

The preacher was a tall man with a white beard. When Luke tugged at his robe he stopped and said in a kindly voice, "What is so important that you would interrupt me in teaching the words of Jesus, my brother?"

"I seek the house of Ananias, who is a weaver and a follower of Jesus. My brother is dying in the wagon and I have hopes that Ananias can heal him."

"I will take you to his house at once," the preacher said promptly. "In all of Tarsus there is not one more devoted to our Lord Jesus than the weaver Ananias. We will all pray together for your brother's life, and if it be the will of God, he will live."

viii

The house of Ananias was situated near the river Cydnus, on a cool street shaded by giant oaks. As usual, the shop was at the front with the living quarters at the rear. Ananias got up from his loom at the back of the shop as they entered, and Luke saw that the years had dealt rather heavily with him, for he was stooped and his hair was almost white. But there was the same look of quiet joy in his eyes. "Luke, my son," he cried, embracing the young physician. "You have come back to us."

Luke explained his errand, and Ananias and the preacher helped to carry Apollonius into the house. They placed him in the best chamber, one whose draperies showed a definite feminine touch. "This is Mariamne's room," the weaver explained. "She is out buying food but will soon return. You will hardly know her, Luke, for she is no longer a child."

Luke's memory of Mariamne had faded considerably in the past five years, and he was too worried about Apollonius now to think of anything else. "Apollonius is dying with a congestion of the lungs," he explained to Ananias. "My art has proved worthless. If you would but touch him and pray over him, as you did over Saul in Damascus . . ."

The pudgy weaver looked at him keenly. "Have you come to us because you have no other hope, Luke?" he asked gently. "Or because you believe that Jesus can help your brother?"

Luke bowed his head. "I have no other hope. And he is dear to me."

Ananias smiled. "You are honest, Luke, and Jesus turns away no one who comes without evil in his heart."

"Then you will heal him?" Luke asked eagerly.

"I will do what I can. Better still, I will go for one whose faith is greater than my own and through whose hands many have been healed."

Just then Apollonius began thrashing about in delirium and Luke missed the name of the other healer, if Ananias spoke it before he went out. Probus came into the room while Luke was quieting the sick man. "His breathing is more labored," he observed. "Are you sure that you have done everything possible for him, Luke?"

"Everything but draw blood."

"Why not that?"

"Hippocrates says, 'Bleed in the acute affections, if the disease appear strong, and the patients be in the vigor of life, and if they have strength.' I am afraid Apollonius is not strong enough, and Ananias has already gone for a healer whose power he says is great. . . ."

"Be sensible, Luke," Probus urged. "You know that such cures are in the mind and not for serious cases like this. Would you let Apollonius die without bleeding him, while you wait for a healer, when drawing blood may be the thing that would turn the tide in his favor?"

Luke looked down at the sick man. Already the bluish pallor of death was upon his lips, the rattle was in his throat, and a bloody froth bubbled faintly from his lips. When Luke felt the pulse it was full and bounding and the veins on the back of the sick man's hands seemed ready to burst, so filled were they with blood. Noting all these signs, Luke's mind began to work alertly once more. It appeared from the dilated veins that there was a plethora, an excess of blood in the veins, perhaps brought on by the congestion of the inflamed lungs. But if that were true, then bleeding was indicated, as Hippocrates had said and Probus urged. And there was no time to lose. "Hand me the basin on the table there in the corner, Probus," he directed as he opened the small case of instruments which he always carried with him. "Then hold the arm while I incise a vein."

The sharp point of the scalpel penetrated the skin and the bluish swelling of the vein beneath. Blood, dark and unhealthy in color, spurted from the cut into the basin, while Luke held the wound open by turning the blade. He let the bleeding continue until he estimated that a full goblet had escaped before removing the scalpel and binding a pad of wool against the tiny puncture wound. The whole operation had taken only a few minutes.

"See!" Probus cried. "He is better already."

There did seem to be a shade less rattling in Apollonius's lungs when he breathed and perhaps a slight lessening of the unhealthy bluish tinge of his lips, but the delirium continued and the pulse still raced. Neither Luke nor Probus realized that anyone else had come into the room until Luke heard a faint cry and saw a slender feminine figure slump to the floor.

It was Mariamne. He recognized the delicate beauty and the dark hair. Her body had filled out with the promise of maturity, and her beauty had blossomed in the five years since he had seen her last. She wore a tunic of lightest yellow that fell softly about her slender ankles, around which were bound the lacings of light golden sandals. And over the tunic was a peplum of pure white, in narrow light folds, as if pleated by one of the specially trained slaves the Romans called *vestispicae*. She wore no ornaments except a slender gold chain about her neck from which hung a tiny cross of gold.

"By Diana!" Probus said. "A goddess has come to visit us."

Luke's fingers sought Mariamne's pulse and found it slow and strong,

93

so he judged that she had merely fainted from the sight of blood. Just then she opened her eyes and stared at him dazedly.

"It is Luke," he said with a smile. "In the flesh."

"Luke!" she cried, sitting up. "How did you get here? And all that blood . . ." She stopped and shuddered.

Luke explained his presence and that of Probus and Apollonius. Mariamne spoke pleasantly to Probus, then looked down at the sick man. "He is very handsome," she said softly, as if to herself, and then blushed. "Is he very sick, Luke?"

"Desperately. Nothing I have done seems to help."

"I—I am counted as having some skill in nursing. Can I help?"

"I am afraid he is already beyond all help," Luke warned her.

Mariamne touched the pale hand of Apollonius on the bed, and her slender fingers curled about his, as if she would transmit to him some of her own blooming health and strength. "No one is beyond help, Luke," she said in gentle reproof, "if God wills that he shall live. Jesus Christ raised the very dead from their graves."

Luke saw Probus lift his eyebrows, but when the apothecary spoke it was only to say, "The operation Luke has just performed is sure to help Apollonius, Mariamne. Luke has not slept for three nights, and naturally he is much concerned about his brother."

There was the sound of voices in the other part of the house, and Ananias came in, his face concerned. "I was delayed," he said anxiously. "Is he——"

"Apollonius still lives," Luke told him. "I have drawn some blood."

"Then there is still time; we must pray for him."

From the background Probus said, "Theophilus, the boy's father, is rich. Perhaps if we made a suitable sacrifice to your God——"

"The Lord Jesus Christ was a living sacrifice for us all," Ananias said a little sharply. "Nothing is needed save his blood." Then he turned back to the door and held the curtain aside.

A short man came into the room. His body was not remarkable in stature, but his head was of noble proportions, and his deep-set eyes glowed with a compelling fire. Luke stared at him unbelievingly, and a feeling akin to terror began to surge up within him, a sense of fear and respect for something, a will or a purpose, which transcended his own. A flash of memory took him back to a hilltop beyond Damascus when a man named Saul of Tarsus had said, "We are a part of a larger plan, Luke, something we can only obey but not yet understand."

This same Saul of Tarsus stood before him now, smiling warmly, his hand held out in the strange but friendly greeting of those who followed Jesus of Nazareth. "We meet once more, Luke," Saul said. "I told you on the road from Damascus, it was God's will that our paths shall cross again."

Luke had been so startled by the unexpected appearance of Saul that for the moment he could not speak. Sensing his emotion, Saul said kindly, "Ananias tells me that your foster brother is very sick."

"He is near to death," Luke admitted. "I can do no more to help him."

"Then it is time for prayer." Saul dropped to his knees beside the bed, and the others followed suit. Luke found himself on his knees, too, but Probus stepped back into the shadows near the curtained doorway and stood watching. Saul's voice was low and vibrant, an oddly compelling tone, not of supplication, but almost of comradeship and trust. "God of our fathers," he prayed, "who has sent Jesus Christ, thy son, to save men from their sins, and who brings to us all good things and punishes us for our sins, look down, I pray, upon the young man who lies upon this couch. Search his heart, O God, and make him know the grace and strength of thy son to forgive sins and give new life. If it be thy will, grant to him thy healing power that he may be well and, rising from this couch, praise thee and speak the power and grace of thy son, Jesus Christ."

The prayer went on, with now Ananias and now the bearded preacher taking up the flow of words. Luke had seen the followers of Jesus engage in their custom of continuous prayer in the house of Judas, the cobbler, in Damascus when this same Saul had been blind. Now, kneeling while the others prayed, he experienced a strange feeling, as if some other presence had entered the room and pushed him aside while this new agency took control of Apollonius and his fate. When Probus touched him on the shoulder, Luke got up from his knees and followed the scribe into the other room. Food and wine had been set out for them and, realizing for the first time that he was hungry, he joined Probus in eating.

"Do you realize that these so-called healers have pushed you entirely out of the picture in there, Luke?" Probus asked severely.

Luke did not tell his friend of the strange feeling he had experienced of being pushed gently aside by some unseen but reassuring hand. Probus, he sensed, would not understand. Instead, he said, "I had already done everything I could, and it was all worthless."

"Your perceptions are dulled by worry and fatigue," Probus insisted doggedly. "There was distinct improvement after you drew the blood. If anything saves Apollonius, it will be your medical skill and not this business of mumbling prayers to a provincial deity."

"So long as he is healed, I care not who gets the credit."

"This fellow Saul will claim it, then. I can see that he is not one to

95

step aside and let others take rewards which are rightfully his. By the way," Probus continued, "is he the same fellow you mentioned to me once, the one who was stricken blind on the road to Damascus?"

"Yes. He is the same."

"Do you believe what he says about it being God's will that your paths should cross again?"

"I don't know," Luke admitted thoughtfully. "How else could you explain it?"

"How else but that Saul, being a native of Tarsus, would naturally return to his own city to live?"

"Can you explain why Apollonius became ill on the road just before we got to Tarsus, where Saul is now living?"

"The road now called the Via Augusta has run from Pisidian Antioch to Tarsus for a thousand years, Luke. Naturally we traveled it on our way to Antioch. And since strong men get pneumonia, as you saw the soldiers doing at the front, why shouldn't it happen to one who was weakened by illness as Apollonius was?"

"You may be right." Luke rested his head in his hands. "I am too tired to know. But I will rebuff no power which might help Apollonius, merely to build my own self-pride."

Before Probus could answer, Saul came into the room. He was smiling, and Luke started up eagerly. "Is Apollonius better?" he asked.

Saul put his hand upon Luke's arm in a comforting gesture. "We have prayed to Jesus Christ that he will save your brother from death, Luke. No one can do more. Go to him now and give him the benefit of your skill as a physician."

"B-but——" It was on the tip of Luke's tongue to say that the case was out of his hands, but he stopped, for Saul had been kind enough to try to help, and he did not wish to appear ungrateful.

"Christ himself told his disciples, '*They that are whole need not a physician; but they that are sick,*' Luke. He came to the earth as a living proof that God will work side by side with us in all our labors if we but let him." With a final squeeze of Luke's arm, he was gone.

Ananias and the bearded preacher came out of the room where Apollonius lay. "We go to gather the followers of Jesus to the house of God to pray for your brother, Luke," the weaver said. "Be not dismayed. Victory will be ours."

When Luke entered the sickroom Mariamne was sitting beside the couch, still holding Apollonius's hand in her own. The pulse still raced under his finger when Luke examined his foster brother, the bluish pallor of his lips had not lessened, and his breathing was still labored. There was no real change, he knew, nothing from which to take hope. Mariamne saw the despair in his face and touched his hand reassuringly. "Do not give up hope, Luke," she said. "In my heart I feel that he is going to live. Remember, the servant of your friend, the centurion, had been given up for dead, yet he was healed by Jesus."

The thought brought Luke little comfort, for he had seen too many men die of pneumonia in the Roman camp in just this manner. But there was nothing to do now but wait for the end, and he pulled up a cushion and sat beside the couch, leaning his head in his hands. Apollonius had quieted as soon as Mariamne took his hand, as if somehow her presence had penetrated even into his delirium. Now there was no sound except the sick man's stertorous breathing, and soon Luke dropped off to sleep sitting upright, so near to complete exhaustion was he from the long vigil in the wagon.

He had been dozing about an hour when a cry from Mariamne brought him wide awake. His first thought was that the end had come, but then he saw that Mariamne was standing beside the bed with tears of joy pouring down her face. "Luke!" she cried. "It is a miracle! Look! The disease is leaving his body."

There was indeed a startling change in Apollonius. Perspiration covered his skin, which had been dry and hot with fever a short time before. His breathing was deeper and less labored, and the bluish color of the lips and ear lobes was already fading into a more nearly normal pink tint. When Luke fumbled for the pulse he found that it, too, had slowed and become stronger.

Probus had been dozing in the adjoining room. Roused by Mariamne's cry, he came through the doorway and stopped, gripped by the picture that met his eyes. Mariamne, her face radiant, still held the sick man's hand; Luke stood looking down at his foster brother as if he could not believe the evidence of his own eyes, and Apollonius was perceptibly stronger now that the raging fever had broken so dramatically. A frown wrinkled the forehead of the apothecary, and he moved closer to the couch in order to see more clearly what was happening.

Then Mariamne dropped to her knees and began to pray, pulling at Luke's hand until he knelt beside her. To the confused jumble of sobbing and hysterical laughing in which she poured out her prayer of thanksgiving, Luke could only add a mute paean of thanks of his own, "God, or gods, if such there be, I thank thee for the life of my brother Apollonius."

ix

By morning Apollonius was definitely out of danger. Mariamne had remained beside him throughout the night while Luke, exhausted com-

pletely, slept in the adjoining room. It was Mariamne's face that Apollonius saw when he opened his eyes with a clear vision shortly after
daybreak. "I am Mariamne," she said, smiling. "We are all so happy
that you are better."

"Then you are not an angel?" he whispered.

"I am real." She laughed. "Here, pinch me."

Obediently he pinched her firm round arm, then managed to smile.
"I don't seem to remember much since we left Pisidian Antioch."

"You have been very sick, but Jesus has made you better in answer
to our prayers."

"Your prayers?"

She blushed then, but when he reached for her fingers again she did
not draw them away. "The prayers of all of us," she explained, "including your brother Luke." Then she drew her fingers away. "I will get
you some broth. Luke will want to know that you are conscious."

When Luke came in, rubbing his eyes from sleep, the tribune's first
words were, "Who is that girl?"

"She is Mariamne, the daughter of a weaver named Ananias. I met
them in Damascus five years ago."

"Are you—are you sweethearts?"

Luke shook his head. "We are friends." Then he smiled. "I think she
has fallen in love with you, though. She hasn't left you since we reached
this house."

Apollonius flushed with pleasure, and when Mariamne came in with
a bowl of broth, he followed her around the room with his eyes. Nor
could Luke blame him for being smitten with the girl. She had been
lovely enough as a mere girl five years ago. Now she had bloomed into
an extraordinarily beautiful young woman, slight of figure but innately
graceful, her skin smooth and unblemished, her dark hair richly alive,
and the small head on the slender neck as symmetrically perfect as the
work of any classic sculptor. Seeing that the two of them were quite engrossed with each other, Luke tiptoed from the room.

Probus was gone all day but returned in time for the evening meal,
a look of quiet satisfaction on his face. "How is Apollonius?" he asked.

"Improving steadily," Luke told him. "There is no fever today and
he is taking food."

"Would you say that he is out of danger?"

"The crisis is past, I am sure of that."

"Hah! Then you admit there was a crisis?"

"Yes. Why do you ask?"

"If the disease improved by a true crisis," Probus said triumphantly,
"then the cure was a natural phenomenon."

Luke had been asking himself the same question, but he was still not

98

sure of the answer. "I don't know, Probus," he admitted candidly. "I never saw such a dramatic recovery before."

"Zut!" The scribe spat out a date pit explosively. "Just because this sect make a ceremony of what they call healing and a beautiful girl looks at you, must you forget all your medical science?"

Luke started to protest, but Probus paid no attention to him. "I have just come from the library of the university here," he continued, "where I took the trouble of copying on a wax tablet—as best I could with this broken arm—something I want you to hear. Listen:

"In Abdera, Anaxion, who was lodged near the Thracian Gates, was seized with an acute fever; continued pain of the right side; dry cough, without expectoration during the first day, thirst, insomnolency. On the sixth, delirious; no relief from the warm applications. On the seventh in a painful state, for the fever increased, while the pains did not abate, and the cough was troublesome and attended with dyspnoea. On the eighth I opened a vein at the elbow and much blood, of a proper character, flowed; the pains were abated, but the dry coughs continued. On the eleventh the fever diminished; slight sweats about the head; coughs with more liquid sputa; he was relieved. On the twentieth, sweat, apyrexia, and a crisis, with recovery."

Probus looked up from the wax tablet. "What do you think of that?"

"It could be a history of Apollonius's illness," Luke admitted.

"It could. But it *is* the history of a case of pneumonia treated by Hippocrates several hundred years ago. You will note that there was a crisis and that it followed bleeding. I tell you, Luke," the scribe insisted, "Apollonius was saved by your hands when you drew blood to relieve the plethora, and not by prayers and incantations."

"You may be right, Probus. And yet if credit is due something or someone else, I would not withhold it."

Probus put away the tablet. "So long as you yourself know that your own skill and knowledge of medicine saved him, I am satisfied," he said. "How long do you propose to remain in Tarsus?"

"Apollonius will not be able to travel for several weeks, at least."

"Why not leave him here until he is entirely well, then? Theophilus will gladly pay Ananias for his care, and Apollonius would just as soon stay close to that girl. Besides, we really should go on to Antioch and notify the governor of Sergius's needs."

Luke recognized the logic of Probus's arguments, and when he broached to Apollonius and Mariamne the question of the tribune's staying on there, he found no objection. "In fact," Apollonius said with a smile as he put his arm about the slender waist of the girl beside the couch, "I was just telling Mariamne that she and I will always be indebted to you, Luke. If you had not remembered that Ananias was now living in Tarsus, I might not have found her. I have asked Mariamne to marry me, Luke. And she has agreed, if my father consents. We want you to plead our case with him in Antioch."

"Perhaps you and Luke could discuss this better without me," Mariamne suggested. "I will go and make preparations for the evening meal." Before they could protest, she was gone.

"Have you considered how Theophilus will feel about this?" Luke asked. "After all, Mariamne is part Jewish and her father is an artisan, a mere weaver, and a follower of Jesus besides."

"Would that make any difference to you, Luke?"

"No. But my father was a freedman and before that a slave of your grandfather. Theophilus is one of the noblest judges in the Roman Empire, and you are his heir."

"I would still wager on your judgment," Apollonius insisted. "You picked Mariamne first, remember. She has told me of your friendship in Damascus."

Luke smiled. "Then all will be well, I am sure. I might even persuade Theophilus to come here and see for himself what kind of people Mariamne and her father are."

"What do you think cured me, Luke?" Apollonius asked.

"It could have been a miracle," Luke admitted. "Mariamne and her father and Saul believe that it was. But Probus has discovered a case recorded in the writings of Hippocrates which closely parallels your own. This patient improved after bleeding, as you did."

"But you do not deny that it could have been a direct intervention by Jesus or God, as they believe?"

Luke smiled. "The important thing is that you are well, that is enough for me."

"Would it surprise you that I am near to believing as Mariamne and Ananias do?" Apollonius asked.

"You could do much worse," Luke said sincerely. "The teachings of the Galilean are the finest set of principles a man could wish to live by."

"Then why do you not believe in Jesus, Luke?"

"This sect believes Jesus lived after death and that he is the son of Jehovah," Luke explained. "They even say that he will someday return to rule over the world. But all of my studies in science tell me that such a thing is impossible and that there are no gods."

Apollonius shook his head in bewilderment. "You were always too deep for me, Luke. I prefer to leave such questions to philosophers, but I love Mariamne and I find it easy to believe as she does."

"Then you cannot go wrong," Luke told him, smiling. "If there *is* a god over everything, the love of a man for the woman who will bear his children must spring from him. And if there is none, then love is the only force that can bind everyone together in happiness."

Luke had one more duty to perform before he sailed for Antioch. He must see Saul and express his appreciation for the tentmaker's efforts in behalf of Apollonius, whether or not he believed that they had been effective. He had no trouble finding the shop where Saul plied his trade, but Saul was not in the shop. While he waited Luke watched the men spin the tough fabric of goat's hair called *cilicium,* after the name of the province, and making it into the tents for which Tarsus was famous.

In the back of the shop the spinners worked, making threads from the tough goat hair. A treadle kept the crude machines spinning while the operator moved his arms backward and forward, advancing and retreating from the hardened point upon which the wisps of hair were twisted into a continuous thread so strong that a man could hardly break it with his hands.

In the center of the shop the weavers worked, sitting at ground level under their looms, with their legs in a pit over which the heavy machines rested. The yarn beams were of the weighted type which had been weaving *cilicium* here for a thousand years, and the shuttle flew back and forth in the skilled hands of the weavers almost faster than Luke could see. At the top of the loom the fabric was rolled up on a wooden spool as it was woven, ready to be transferred to the tables of the tentmakers, who cut and sewed the cloth into the finished product.

While Luke was watching the men as they stitched, Saul came in. "Welcome to the Street of the Tentmakers, Luke," he said in greeting. "How is the health of the noble Apollonius?"

"He rests well and gains daily although smitten with love."

"For the gentle Mariamne? I noticed that when I was last at the house. How will the noble Theophilus take the idea of his son marrying a Jewess?"

"I don't know," Luke admitted. "Apollonius and Mariamne have commissioned me to plead for them."

"Then they can be sure of an eloquent advocate," Saul said, smiling. "But the kingdom of the Master may come at any moment, and then there will be no marriage or giving in marriage."

Startled by Saul's statement, Luke asked, "Do you really believe Jesus will reign on earth, as some have claimed?"

"The earth is the Lord's, why should his son not rule over it?"

"I haven't thought much about it," Luke admitted. "But I judged from the scroll of his sayings I read that Jesus was referring to a spiritual kingdom."

"Why not both?" Saul demanded. "Would the son of God bow down to earthly rulers?" Then he smiled. "Mere man cannot understand the inscrutable working of God's will, Luke. I am sure that the Lord has something more in store for me than to weave tents in Tarsus, just as sure as I am that it was the will and plan of God that we should meet again here in Damascus."

"But logic tells me there is no god and that a human being could not be his son."

"No man knows God or his son in his mind alone, Luke, but in his heart as well. You need not seek to prove his existence through logic. When you are ready to know Jesus as the Saviour of mankind, be assured that he will be revealed to you in the only place where you can know him, in your heart. Tell me," he continued, "have you seen or heard anything else of the scroll that contained the sayings of Jesus?"

"Not since I gave it to you on the road to Damascus. Did you lose it?"

"No. When I returned from the wilderness I journeyed to Jerusalem and gave the scroll to Simon Peter. Later I heard that it had been lost."

"Do you think it may have been destroyed?"

"The words of Jesus can never be destroyed so long as they are written in the hearts of men, Luke." Saul smiled and held out his hand. "Good-by, Luke. Go your way, but rest assured that our paths will cross again. You and I have been chosen as agents of God's will; perhaps the pattern of that will may be revealed to us soon."

Two days later Luke and Probus sailed from Tarsus on a coastal sailing vessel bound across the Gulf of Issus for Syrian Antioch. With him Luke carried a letter from Apollonius telling his father of his decision to become a follower of Jesus and to marry Mariamne.

x

Theophilus looked at Luke with incredulous eyes. "Apollonius marrying a Jewess? Has he lost his mind?"

"Not his mind, but his heart," Luke said. "And you will lose yours when you know Mariamne."

The gray-haired jurist sat down and put his hand to his forehead. "How soon is this wedding to take place?"

"They have set no date. Mariamne refuses to be wed without your consent."

Theophilus shook his head. "I have always tried to be a good and tolerant father to both of you. But for my son to marry a Jewess. I must think."

"Apollonius also plans to become a follower of Jesus of Nazareth," Luke added, but to his surprise Theophilus did not seem to be disturbed by this information. "Silvanus was a believer in the Galilean," the jurist said. "I myself lean toward the worship of Mithras, as do most Romans outside of Rome today, but there are many fine people here in Antioch who have espoused the Nazarene faith." He stood up. "We will talk more about Apollonius and this girl—what is her name again?"

"Mariamne. She was named for a very beautiful Jewish queen."

"I remember now. One of the Herods had her murdered. But we had better get to the bath if we are not to be late for the dinner at Junius Gallio's apartment."

"What brings Gallio to Antioch?" Luke asked while they soaked themselves in the tepidarium before being rubbed by the *balneator,* a slave trained particularly in massage. As deputy governor of Syria, Theophilus occupied a lesser palace on the *insula,* the island formed by the division of the river Orontes on the northern side of Antioch which housed the palaces of the governor and other officials and the administrative center of the province. The baths in the palace of Theophilus were not so elaborate as those of the governor, Petronius, or those which a triumphant Caesar had built on the side of Mount Silpius to the south, but they sufficed for the simple needs of Theophilus and the members of his establishment.

Now that he was back in Antioch, Luke found it pleasant to take up once more the familiar routine which he had left five years before to begin his studies of medicine at Pergamum. There were deft servants to attend every need and cool breezes from the river to refresh them as they sat at dinner in the evening. And as the foster son of the deputy governor, Luke was invited to the frequent entertainments and feasts at the governor's palace and the luxurious homes of the richer Antiochians who lived along the bank of the river within sight of the island.

Theophilus emerged from the water and entrusted himself to the hands of the *balneator,* who began to rub his body with fragrant oils. "Junius Gallio is something rare in the Roman Empire these days," he said as Luke seated himself on a bench to await his own turn at the hands of the deft slave. "He is a statesman, but more attached to the Empire than to bettering his own fortunes. The Emperor trusts him explicitly and keeps him busy with special missions."

When his own massage was finished, the older man waited while Luke's strong young body was pummeled and kneaded. "I haven't asked about your plans, Luke," he said almost hesitantly. "Do you expect to return to the army?"

"No. Military medicine requires little skill, except in dressing wounds and an occasional surgical operation. I had thought of setting up as a physician in some city."

"Why not Antioch?" Theophilus asked, his eyes lighting up. "You could continue to live here with me then."

Luke smiled. "I did have Antioch in mind."

"Then it is settled," Theophilus said happily. "There is a small building at the edge of the grounds which is unused; it would make a fine surgery for you. And its proximity to the palace will certainly not hurt your practice." He looked at the water clock and exclaimed, "We must hurry! Gallio is expecting us in less than an hour."

Junius Annaeus Gallio was a small, roly-poly man with twinkling, deep-set gray eyes. Although a brother of the Stoic philosopher Seneca and of Mela, father of Lucan, the poet, Gallio had no need to bask in the reputations of his kinsmen. He was seated in the atrium of the luxurious palace apartment which had been placed at his disposal by the governor, his bandaged foot extended upon a cushion. "A thousand apologies for not being able to accept your hospitality, Theophilus," he said in greeting. "But I cannot get about with a toe which seems inhabited by a legion of devils."

Theophilus introduced Luke. "So you are a physician." Gallio's face brightened. "Can you cure the gout?"

"I treated Sergius Paulus with a new drug," Luke admitted, "and was able to give him some relief."

"By Mithras!" Gallio exclaimed. "Where can I get this preparation?"

"A friend of mine, one Probus Maximus, is opening an apothecary shop near the palace. I will visit him in the morning and order a supply for you."

"Good! Good!" Gallio rubbed his hands. "Then maybe I can get on with my travels. By the way," he continued, "you spoke of Sergius Paulus. When did you treat him?"

Luke told of his experience with the army, and Gallio questioned him shrewdly. "You have saved me a trip to the front, Luke," he said finally. "The Emperor asked me to report on this affair with the Paphlagonians. From what you say, Sergius has saved us from a serious defeat."

"I am sure of it," Luke agreed.

"I will report as much to the Emperor before I leave for Cilicia," Gallio stated. "Sergius Paulus and I are friends, but his enemies are circulating rumors that he has failed miserably in Paphlagonia, and Rome is always ready to believe the worst of its generals in the field."

"If you are going on to Cilicia, Junius," Theophilus said, "perhaps I shall join you. Luke brings me the disquieting news that my son Apollonius is planning to marry a Jewess in Tarsus."

"A Jewess!" Gallio exclaimed. "She must be rich." The office of tribune in the Roman Army carried a relatively modest stipend but a high social position in military circles, so the young officers nearly always made advantageous marriages.

"No," Luke volunteered. "She is the daughter of a weaver."

"The weavers are influential in Tarsus, almost as much as the silversmiths in Ephesus."

"Ananias is a follower of Jesus of Nazareth," Luke explained. "And that sect does not believe in the accumulation of great wealth."

"Hah!" The ambassador's eyes lit up. "Do you know much of these Nazarenes, Luke?"

"A little, sir. I have met a number of them in my travels."

"Isn't this faith spreading rather rapidly for a mystery cult?"

"I know very little about the mystery religions," Luke admitted. "But it seems to me that the beliefs of the followers of Jesus are different from the others, such as those of Mithras, for example."

"I had already decided as much," Gallio agreed. "The Emperor is very much interested in the Nazarenes, since there has already been trouble in the Empire because of them."

"Petronius has condemned a number of members of this sect to death," Theophilus added. "They refused to be conscripted for military service and affirm allegiance to the Emperor. I advised against such a penalty, but he felt that he must make an example of them."

"My interest in the Nazarenes is more than a casual one," Gallio admitted. "The Emperor has been informed that they teach the coming of a leader who will overthrow the Empire and set up a new kingdom in which the Jews will rule the world."

"Jesus taught nothing of the kind, sir," Luke said earnestly. "I have studied a scroll of his sayings, and they contained no such statements."

The ambassador's eyes brightened. "Do you still have the scroll? I would like to read it."

Luke shook his head, but Theophilus said, "Tell Gallio of your experiences with the scroll, Luke. I have heard Silvanus speak of them."

Luke told the story again and gave Gallio a brief description of the teachings of Jesus. "There is nothing in them that many Greek philosophers, even my brother Seneca, has not said before," Gallio said when he finished.

"Both Plato and Socrates taught similar truths," Theophilus agreed.

"Whence comes this talk of destroying the Roman Empire and setting up another?" Gallio asked. "It seems to me that Jesus was merely another philosopher."

"The Jews believe they are a chosen race," Luke explained, "and that their God, Jehovah, will one day rule over the world. Some of their prophets told of the coming of a son of Jehovah that they call the Messiah, and the followers of Jesus think he is that son."

"Is?" Gallio echoed. "Was he not crucified? I can hardly see an all-powerful god letting that happen to his son."

"I think the Jews who follow Jesus have confused the teachings of a great and good man with their prophecies about a messiah who would rule the world," Luke explained.

The ambassador sighed. "It is the same everywhere. Why are these small countries not content to be simply parts of the Roman Empire? Even Herod Agrippa would betray us if he could, so he plays the different factions among the Jews against each other in order to gain power for himself. It was he who reported that the Nazarene sect is stirring up the Jews to revolt."

"Then they are not following the teachings of Jesus," Luke assured Gallio. "He taught only that people should help and love one another and respect the dignity of the individual."

"I shall write the Emperor tomorrow, then," Gallio said happily. "You have told me what I need to know. Now I can have a holiday in peace."

But as he walked home with Theophilus after the dinner, Luke's thoughts were troubled. For he had failed to tell the ambassador of his last conversation with Saul of Tarsus and he remembered now the short, dynamic preacher's words: "Since the earth is the Lord's, why should his son not rule over it?" And again, "Would the son of God bow down to earthly rulers?"

Had he been wrong to withhold these facts, Luke wondered. But after all, he told himself, they were the words of only one man. And how could one man's words affect a people and an empire?

xi

Probus had opened an apothecary shop just off the island containing the palace of the governor, and when Luke told him of the need of Ambassador Gallio for the powdered crocus leaves which had so effectively relieved the gout for Sergius Paulus, he immediately procured a supply and took it to Gallio himself. Relief was immediate, and Gallio was so grateful that he sang the praises of both Luke and the apothecary to all he met. In addition he had them both as his guests at a state dinner, where they were introduced in extravagant terms as experts in the diagnosis and treatment of all diseases. As a result the shop of Probus had more business than it could handle, and Luke quickly became the favorite physician of the Roman officials and the rich Syrians through whom they ruled the city and the province.

Probus thrived on popularity, and gold poured into his shop in return for the medicines he compounded. But as the months passed, Luke felt a strange unrest stirring within him again. He recognized it as the same dissatisfaction which had moved him to leave Pergamum at the end of his five years of instruction rather than remain there in the post of priest-physician. The busy life of the Roman military expedition into Cilicia and Paphlagonia had for the time being dissipated the unrest, but now it returned in full force.

The sun was shining brightly and the air was warm with the promise of spring one morning when Luke came out of the palace, where he had been treating a mild indisposition of the governor's wife. It was only a short walk to the palace of Theophilus and his small surgery at the edge of the grounds, but he turned instead toward the bridge that led from the *insula* into the city itself. To the east, in the famous grove of bay trees that marked the suburb of Daphne, the Temple of Diana shone like the snowy top of Mount Silpius in winter, the pristine purity of the marble walls quite at variance with the rites practiced there.

Almost directly ahead, bearing only slightly west, was the broad colonnaded street that bisected the city, the Via Caesarea, ending where the foothills of Mount Silpius led upward to the craggy peaks of the mountain itself. On one of these summits towered the castle which the Romans had built long ago to dominate the city and guard it from invasion. On another crag stood the beautiful Temple of Jupiter Capitolinus, and to the eastward were the luxurious baths and the aqueduct constructed by Julius Caesar in honor of his defeat of Pompey.

The apothecary shop which Probus had opened was on the north bank of the river. Luke strolled past the magnificent homes of the Romans and the luxurious shops catering to their whims and stopped before a small building over which a sign announced:

SEPLASIA
PROBUS MAXIMUS—MEDICAMENTARIUS

Medicamentarius was the Latin term for a dispenser of medicines prescribed by a physician, in contrast to the Greek *pharmacopeus,* who was often a quack and a poisoner as well. Probus saw Luke standing outside and came to the door. "Luke," he cried, embracing the young physician. "You must come in and inspect my establishment. I have enlarged it since last you were here."

Luke entered the shop and looked around admiringly. "You certainly have a complete stock of medicines," he observed.

"The most complete in the whole Empire," Probus admitted modestly. "Here are the *malagmata.*" He pointed proudly to jar after jar of ointment arranged on shelves. "And here are the *eucharista,* to be applied as embrocations. On this shelf," he continued, "are the *katapotia.* See, there are all sizes of pills among them and all the usually prescribed drugs."

He moved off to another section. "Here I have a special room for treating the eyes and all manner of *collyria* for the purpose."

They were at the door of a room in which a half dozen men sat, all bald or partially so, and all richly dressed and obviously well to do. "What are you treating here, Probus?" Luke asked.

"It is a new cure for baldness," Probus admitted. "I was preparing to give some treatments, so you may watch if you like."

A slave waited in the room, standing near a small table filled with jars of ointment. Upon the table lay a strange object, a rectangular piece of hard yellowish substance with a fragment of woolen cloth beside it. Probus indicated an empty chair beside the table and said, "Paganos, the merchant, can be the first today."

Paganos waddled over to the chair and sat down. His hair was gone except for a fringe over the temples and extending around the back of his head. Probus began to rub the rectangular piece of yellowish material with the woolen cloth. "This is called *elektron,*" he told Luke in a low voice. "Actually it is a form of amber which exhibits special properties when rubbed with a woolen cloth." He held the piece of amber about an inch above the merchant's head and began to move it back and forth. Before Luke's startled eyes the individual hairs fringing the man's scalp began to rise, as if attracted to the substance called *elektron,* although they touched at no point. As the amber block was moved back and forth over Paganos's head the hairs rose and fell in a wavelike motion. Like Luke, the onlookers were agape, eyes popping.

Probus finished the treatment and handed Paganos a jar of ointment. "Rub this into the scalp daily," he directed. "And return in a week for another treatment with the *elektron.*" The merchant got up and, digging into a fat purse, handed Probus a gold piece which Luke noted was as much as he usually received for treating an entire illness.

Probus treated each of the remaining patients in the same way, stopping to rub the *elektron* before each treatment, and receiving a substantial fee in each case. When he finished and the patients were gone, Luke asked, "How does this stone obtain its peculiar properties, Probus?"

"It comes from the rubbing, I am sure. Almost any piece of amber will perform in the same way."

"But how does it help to grow hair?"

The apothecary smiled. "Bald men usually have bald fathers, but a vain and wealthy man will pay well for anything which he thinks will give him his hair and make him look younger."

"And the ointment?"

"It is a prescription I had from an Egyptian magician, who found it in the tomb of an Egyptian queen, and contains equal portions of date blossoms, the flesh of an Abyssinian greyhound, and asses' hoofs, boiled in oil and evaporated to a solid."

"It sounds formidable enough."

"I have another, in case you ever want to treat baldness, made from a mixture of the fat from a horse, a crocodile, a hippopotamus, a cat, a snake, and an ibex."

Luke laughed. "I shall leave the top of the head to you, Probus. I have enough to do, treating gouty toes and the imaginary complaints of rich women."

Probus looked at him keenly. "They pay you well, do they not?"

"Of course."

"Then why are you unhappy about it?"

"Money is not the prime concern of a physician," Luke protested.

"Not yours, perhaps," Probus corrected him. "But you know very well that most of your brothers in Asklepios are money grabbers of the worst sort. You need a change. Why not take up a religion?"

"A religion? Why should I?"

"Everybody should have a religion. I have been studying Mithraism. It is an interesting faith and one practiced by our richest people, so it is not bad business to be a believer in Mithras."

Luke shook his head. "I have business enough. No, it is not religion that troubles me."

"Well, it will not hurt you to see a Mithraic ceremony," Probus insisted. "I am going to a taurobolium this morning. Why not come along?"

"Taurobolium? What is that?"

"The most colorful and interesting ceremony in the Mithraic faith. I can guarantee that you will be diverted, to say the least."

"But I should visit some patients."

"Let them wait," Probus said airily. "Remember the words of Hippocrates: 'The physician visits a patient suffering from fever or wound and prescribes for him. On the next day, if the patient feels worse, the blame is laid upon the physician; if, on the other hand, he feels better, nature is extolled and the physician reaps no praise.' "

"All right," Luke agreed, laughing. "Perhaps a change will do me good."

Neither Mithras nor any other of the new cults which were gradually supplanting the old gods in the religious life of the Greeks and

Romans boasted such fine temples as those of Diana, Apollo, and the others. But the Mithraeum to which Probus took Luke was large for that cult, capable of holding perhaps two hundred people, Luke estimated as they stood just within the grottoed building before a gate which held them back from the temple itself.

The room, seen through the bars of the gate, was really a grotto, carved from the rock of the hillside against which the building stood and roofed over with timbers that rose in graceful arches. Stone benches stood empty, waiting for the *sodalicium,* as the congregation was called, to enter when the gate was opened. Tapers burned in brackets against the wall, lighting up the interior.

The altar was made of stones, smoothed flat and lying across stone supports. Beneath the altar a pit had been dug to perhaps the depth of a man's waist, with the dirt piled up on either end, as if it were to be filled up again at the end of the ceremony or as though someone were to be buried in the sanctuary itself. Around the walls of the altar recess candles burned in banks, illumining the carved bulls' heads forming a frieze just under the vaulted timbers that supported the roof. Bordering the altar itself was a smaller frieze of exquisitely carved heads of bulls.

A young bull was lashed securely upon the altar, eyes wide open and bulging with fear as it strained against the ropes. In front of the large altar was another, smaller one, on which lay a gleaming sword, as long as a man's arm, with a richly chased hilt of ivory into which precious stones had been set. To one side of the two altars stood a low throne over which a covering of rich velvet had been placed, draping and almost hiding the stone chair itself.

"Today's candidate must not be rich," Probus said in Luke's ear. "I never saw a smaller bull for the taurobolium." Mithraism, Luke already knew, was the favorite religion of the Roman soldiers, and since they were poorly paid, it boasted no such elaborate ritual as did the ceremonies honoring the older gods, whose temples and priests were rich from centuries of votive offerings.

"What is the significance of it all?" Luke asked.

"The ultimate step in all these rituals," Probus explained in low tones, "is the ritual of death and rebirth to immortality. The ceremony of the taurobolium is the highest grade of Mithraic worship, that of 'Father.' Most worshipers never get beyond the 'Soldier' grade. Look, there comes a priest to begin the ceremony."

On a small table to one side of the large altar a fire was burning in a brazier. The white-robed priest now took a brand from the old brazier and turned to a small altar which Luke had hardly noticed for it was in a corner of the open space where the bull lay. The small altar had been prepared with some readily inflammable substance, for it took fire at once and flared up brightly. And as the flames danced, a choir of some ten persons filed into a choir stall beside the altar and began to chant in a low tone.

"Watch this," Probus said softly. Slowly, moved by no force that Luke could see, the gates of the Mithraeum began to open, sliding back into the wall. There was a murmured "Aah!" of amazement from some of the spectators, but Probus said contemptuously, "An old trick. A Greek named Hero invented it two hundred years ago."

"How does it work?"

"The heat of the fire causes air to expand in a pig's bladder and activates levers which open the gates."

The congregation poured into the sanctuary. On either side of the wall stood a curious-looking machine. Luke saw several people stop before the machine and drop a coin into a narrow slot in the wooden cabinet. Each time a spray of water spurted from the machine upon them, again without any visible human agent. "The worshipers think it is a magic machine activated by Mithras," Probus whispered. "When the coin strikes a lever, it opens a tank and douses them with sacred water. Then the coin rolls off and shuts it off again. Hero invented that too."

As the temple filled with the waiting crowd, the chant of the choir rose steadily in volume. Luke could distinguish the word "Mithras" repeated again and again, as if they were invoking the deity to appear. Then a massive gong sounded inside the Mithraeum, its reverberations jarring even the walls, and a bizarre figure appeared behind the altar. The lower part was that of a man, a priest clad in flowing robes, but the entire upper half of his body was hidden by a great mask simulating the head of a bull. For a second Luke was reminded of some mythical beast, like the centaur Chiron so revered in the ritual worship of Asklepios, but he could see this was only a man wearing the mask of a bull's head, from the nostrils of which smoke curled thinly.

"Mithras! Mithras!" the worshipers chanted with the choir. "The god himself," Probus explained. "Or as near as he has ever come to actual existence. Look! The *virgines.*"

Four white-robed young women emerged into the open space around the altar, leading a tall man who wore a robe of rich silk, corded at the waist in gold, with golden tassels and a crown of garlands upon his head. They took him to the low throne and seated him reverently, then knelt, touching their foreheads to the floor. As the music of the choir and the distant orchestra of flutes, lyres, and cymbals rose in a hymn of adoration, the priestesses rose and began a slow dance about the throne.

"Why do they revere him instead of the god?" Luke asked.

"The initiate, the *tauroboliatus,* pays for the ceremony. This is his religious birthday or *natalicia,* the day he becomes immortal through the taurobolium and a lesser god in the Mithraic dynasty."

"It all sounds like gibberish to me."

Probus shrugged. "There is much gibberish, as you call it, in all successful religions. People seek the mysterious and the unnatural, so that by claiming kinship with something superhuman they can rise above ordinary men. Thus the *tauroboliatus,* because he has money to buy a bull, rent the temple, and pay the priests and the choir, becomes immortal and a god.

"Watch this," Probus warned in a sibilant whisper. "It is the symbolic burial of death before he is resurrected."

"Tauroboliatus!" The voice of the priest issued from the bull's-head mask in stentorian tones, magnified, Luke realized, by a cone inside it. The initiate stood and the white-robed *virgines* sank to the floor again while the chant of the choir rose in volume:

"Let all nature listen while we hymn our praises to Mithras, Lord of Creation. Let the heavens open and let the sun and the stars give praise to his great name. Hymn, O Truth, the Truth, O Goodness, the Good. Life and Light come from thee, O Divine and Eternal Mithras, we receive blessing and the life eternal which we seek through the sacrifice of the Blood."

The chant died away and the *tauroboliatus* spoke:

"By thy spirit, O Mithras, I declare that I perceive. To the author of my new birth, I, mortuus, offer this reasonable sacrifice. O Mithras, Father of the Universe, and of the Sun, and the Stars, Lord of Creation, accept this sacrifice. Enter, thou, into my spirit and my thoughts, for thou art I and I, thou."

The *tauroboliatus* stepped down from the throne now and entered the pit beneath the altar upon which the young bull lay. Sitting on the floor of the pit, he was barely visible as the *virgines* circled it in solemn funereal procession, tossing handfuls of earth upon him while the choir chanted a dirge. The symbolism was easy to understand. The initiate, having given up his life, was now being buried as a symbol of the finality of death for those not granted immortality by Mithras. As the music died away, his voice, somewhat muffled, came from the pit once more:

"In this grave I die and am covered with earth, that through the divine blood of this taurus, which becomes thy blood, O Mithras, I may rejoice that even in my mortal body thou didst deify me, and grant to me eternal life through the vision of thyself."

Suddenly the great cymbal clashed and the chant of the choir changed to a paean of joy. The women prostrated themselves before the bull on the altar, and the priest wearing the bull's-head mask seized the sword and held it aloft as the music rose to a crashing climax. Looking around him, Luke saw that most of the worshipers really believed this gibberish, for they were quite carried away by the ritual. All eyes were intent upon the drama being played out before them, and at the end of one of the benches a woman, anticipating the climax, began to twitch, then rolled to the floor in a spasm.

A deep sigh from the crowd brought Luke's attention back to the altar. As if realizing its fate, the bull had begun to struggle and one of the cords snapped. The sword in the hand of the priest plunged downward, entering the animal's throat and searching deep inside the body for the heart. But the bull still struggled, and another rope snapped with the death agony. In another moment it might have crashed from the altar into the pit beneath, upon the *tauroboliatus,* but the priest, withdrawing the sword quickly, slashed across the animal's neck, cutting the great blood vessels there.

"Mithras should get another butcher," Probus whispered.

Blood gushed from the animal's neck with the second stroke, spattering the robe of the priest, and poured down through the crevices between the stones of the altar to drench the *tauroboliatus* in the pit. The initiate, far from cringing, lifted his face so that the red tide poured down upon it and, opening his mouth, let the warm, sacrificial blood run into it with evident pleasure. He lifted his arms and allowed the blood to pour over his flowing sleeves and down over his shoulder. "Mithras!" he cried in ecstasy. "Mithras!"

"*Resurrectionis! Resurrectionis!*" the voice of the priest boomed.

"*Resurrectionis! Resurrectionis!*" The choir and the *virgines* took up the cry as the *tauroboliatus* rose from the pit while the bull quivered in the final throes of the death agony. Dripping blood, the initiate ascended to the throne, where he stood with arms upraised. When the chanting died to a low murmur, he intoned:

"*I, a man of mortal womb, having been this day begotten again by thee, out of so many myriads rendered immortal in this hour by thy grave, O all-powerful Mithras, am become divine, saved by thee. I rejoice that even in our mortal bodies thou didst deify me by the vision of thyself.*"

Above the chant of the choir now rose the shrieks and groans of the worshipers, who rolled and jerked on the floor in religious ecstasy.

"Let's go," Luke said in disgust. "This place has become a shambles."

"The priests will dine tonight on tender beef," Probus agreed as they made their way from the temple. "What did you think of it?"

"How can they call that a religion?"

Probus shrugged. "It pleases the worshipers, else they would not pay for it. Which reminds me, I have some more bald heads coming in for treatment. Will you go back to the shop with me?"

Luke shook his head. "No. I think I will walk through the city for a while. I need some fresh air after that butchering exhibition we just visited."

xii

Luke ate the midday meal in a little shop on the banks of the river. The strange restlessness still assailed him; in fact, it was only intensified by witnessing the barbaric rite of the taurobolium. He could not help comparing that repulsive ceremony with what he had witnessed of the way Ananias, Saul, Mariamne, and even Simon Peter seemed to feel about Jesus. Their religion was almost a comradeship, and they prayed to Jesus as if he were in the room, waiting to help them.

Luke had been walking aimlessly, but now he found himself in the midst of a stream of people all moving in the same direction. Turning to a plump Greek who waddled along beside him in the press of the crowd, mopping his forehead, Luke asked, "Where is everybody going?"

"To the theater for the games, of course. Today is the greatest event of the season. Dacius, the champion with the short sword, will fight a net and trident wielder from Cyprus. And there will be a *venatio* with the black-maned lions from Africa."

Luke knew the word. The *venatio,* or wild-beast hunt, was not yet so popular in other cities of the Empire as it was in Rome, but he had seen it once in Ephesus, and also in Athens when he had gone there on a holiday from his studies in the temple at Pergamum. In Rome, he had been told, the condemned were often thrown to the beasts instead of formally executed.

"It should be a fine spectacle," the Greek said. "You are going, are you not?"

"I think I will," Luke decided suddenly. He had found some forgetfulness for the strange unrest in military life; perhaps he might find it again in the games, the nearest approach to a military combat outside the battlefield.

The crowd was in a festive mood, laughing and joking with each other as they pushed past the small booths where the tickets were sold. Huge posters on the walls announced today's events:

"A Great Battle of the Mightiest Gladiators of the Empire," one declaimed in the extravagant language which characterized such postings. *"Twenty Fighters Furnished by Anaxios of Ephesus Will Battle*

Twenty of the Champions of Antioch. The Reputation of Our City Is at Stake."

Another stated: *"The Greatest Venatio Ever Seen in Antioch. Ten Lions and Eight Lionesses."*

The bright afternoon sun shone upon the great façade of the stadium and the graceful travertine arches of the lower stories, framed in the prevailing architectural styles, Doric, Corinthian, and Ionic. The topmost story was of wood, and set upon it were metallic sockets bearing tall masts which held broad canvas awnings to protect the audience from the sun. Bearing a ticket purchased at the booth, Luke entered the building through the arch marked upon it. A stream of people wound through the corridors and up the stairs leading to the *vomitoria*, passages that gave access to the seats themselves. Luke had purchased one of the better seats and so was only about halfway up the broad shell of the theater, but the circular arena, covered with fresh white sand, still seemed far below. The fat Greek had remained just behind Luke in the crowd and had purchased the seat next to him. While Luke bought a cushion from a passing vendor, the Greek hailed still another seller and bought a sweetmeat, which he began to suck noisily.

The stadium at Antioch was not so magnificent as the great theater for the games at Rome, but it ran the capital a close second. Around the arena a strong metal fence separated the participants from the spectators, protecting each from the other and from the wild beasts of the *venatio*. Above this fence a high platform of stone encircled the arena, studded with thronelike seats before which a gleaming balustrade partly overhung the arena itself. The next fifteen rows of seats constituted the *cavea* and were enclosed by walls with a special corridor and *vomitoria* giving access directly to them. Restricted to the nobility, the equestrian order, and the officials and military leaders, as well as the richer Syrians and Greeks, this section was already half full. Only a few were as yet in the thronelike seats directly above the arena, and the luxurious center throne was empty. Reserved for the use of the Emperor when in Antioch, and for the Roman governor when he attended the games, it was used on ordinary occasions by the promoter, known as the *editor,* who financed the performances.

Above the *cavea* began the seats for the crowd, thousands of them reaching upward, tier on tier, to the very rim of the outer wall of the stadium. The people were cheerful, and there was much good-natured shouting back and forth. Occasionally, when a richly dressed figure moved into one of the box seats or into the *cavea,* there was a burst of applause as the crowd voiced its approval of one of the more famous names in the city. Over it all sounded the shrill cries of the vendors, who kept up a constant din hawking cushions, syrupy drinks, and trays of pastries and sweetmeats.

Suddenly there was a blare of trumpets and the crowd rose, cheering. Upon the lower steps of the dais occupied by the throne two trumpeters appeared, followed by two slaves bearing banners. Beside Luke, the Greek said, "Petronius, the governor, sponsors the games today, and Dacius fights under his banner." He grinned. "If Dacius wins, as he is sure to do, Petronius will win a small fortune in bets with Cyprians who favor the net and trident fighter."

"Suppose the Cyprian wins?"

The Greek shrugged. "There will be another champion for a while. That is the way it goes."

Another wave of applause swept the crowd as Petronius emerged. A tall, hawk-nosed man with a haughty, arrogant face, he bowed once, then took his seat upon the luxurious throne. When he raised his hand as a signal, a burst of martial music sounded from beneath the amphitheater, and a colorful procession marched out upon the sand of the arena. Two giant Nubians in the lead beat a compelling rhythm upon huge drums; after them came a quartet of trumpeters, then fife players and wielders of the cymbals. In the wake of the musicians marched a group of acrobats and tumblers, cavorting in perfect rhythm, whirling and leaping, quickly forming human pyramids from which one of their number was tossed expertly through the air to land on his feet.

Behind the acrobats were the fighters themselves, heavily armed Samnites, lighter-clad Thracians, Gauls and Britons from the westernmost provinces of the Empire, driving the chariots from which they fought a moving battle. At the rear of the procession marched a giant of a man in armor, his sword uplifted in salute to the governor.

"Dacius! Dacius Victor!" the crowd shouted, breaking into a frenzy of applause. The slender figure of the net and trident fighter, the *retiarius* who marched beside Dacius, was almost ignored. His weapons seemed pitifully inadequate beside the massive armor and shield of Dacius, for they consisted only of a three-pronged spear upon a long handle and a net of heavy cords carried over his shoulder, large enough to cover a man's head and torso and deep enough to enmesh his arms, once it was thrown over them.

Once around the arena the procession marched, to stop before the throne of Petronius. As the music rose to a climax and ended with the crash of drums and cymbals, the governor stood and lifted his clenched fist in the Roman salute, while the gladiators unsheathed their weapons and held them high before their faces, thundering the traditional salute of the arena: *"Morituri te salutamus!"* Then as the crowd

116

roared its approval once more, the procession wheeled smartly and marched from the arena.

Six men now ran out and started to belabor each other with blunt weapons, each trying to strike down the other by brute force rather than by skill, for their arms could inflict no cutting wounds. The crowd soon tired of this preliminary bludgeoning, however, and began to shout, *"Sine missione!"* the cry of the bloodthirsty for a fight to the death.

At a signal from the trumpets the blunt-weaponed fighters ran off and six Samnites took their places. The traditional beefy, heavily armed gladiators of the Roman arena, they wore steel helmets bearing the crest of the impresario to whose stable of gladiators they belonged. One leg was protected by a metal greave, a leg armor extending from above the knee to the ankle. On their left arms they carried great oblong shields with which to protect their bodies against the blades of the heavy Roman short swords. They were skilled fighters, and the crowd kept up a continual hubbub as now one and now another brought blood from an opponent. Luke found himself gripped by the rising excitement and the sheer thrill of man-to-man combat, although the principals meant nothing to him.

One of the fighters went down, his sword arm slashed by a long cut. Lying in the sand with blood pouring from his wound, the fallen gladiator managed to raise himself up and cried, *"Missus! Missus! Mercy! Mercy!"*

From his throne Petronius waved negligently to the crowd, indicating that the decision was theirs. The man had fought well and the people were in a good mood. A burst of applause and a sea of waving handkerchiefs gave their approval to his plea, so the leeches ran out to apply cloths to his wounds and bear him from the arena.

Next a bevy of light-armed Thracians fought each other. Protected only by helmets and small round shields, they used a short curved sword and fought in close formation. The lightness of their armor gave them more mobility than the ponderous Samnites, and their long, graceful leaps and parries, the skilled strokes and counterstrokes stirred up the enthusiasm of the crowd. They took the fighters to their hearts, applauding a skillful cut and shouting with blood lust when the sharp point of one of the curved swords entered a fighter's neck and slashed through it, bringing a fatal gush of blood.

After them, Britons and Gauls fought from chariots, creating a magnificent spectacle as they careened and wheeled across the arena in the fleet vehicles, each seeking to overturn the other and leave the driver at the mercy of a long spear. But these battles were mere preliminaries to the main event, the epic conflict between Dacius, the champion *secutor,* or sword-bearer, and the *retiarius* with the net and trident.

When the fight began, Dacius stood like a rock, slashing and jabbing at the *retiarius.* The slender fighter, unhampered by weight of armor, leaped with remarkable agility about his opponent, now striking with the trident, now tossing the net expertly so that Dacius was forced to lumber backward lest he be entangled in the cords. Once the net wielder managed to throw his tough web over Dacius's head and shoulders, quickly leaping in to strike with the trident at a vital spot in the unprotected groin of his heavier adversary. But somehow Dacius managed to loosen his shield and drop it enough to ward off the spear. A blow of his huge arm sent the *retiarius* sprawling, giving the *secutor* time to free himself from the net.

Like everyone else in the great theater, Luke was on his feet shouting encouragement to the agile Cyprian, for the sympathies of the crowd were now all with the graceful fighter against whom the odds had seemed hopelessly weighted at first. Again the cat-and-mouse play began, but now the *retiarius,* emboldened by his near victory, became more daring in his attack, moving in swiftly to jab at the burly figure, whirling the net above his head as a constant threat of entanglement to Dacius. The crowd was screaming, and Luke found himself shouting hoarsely with the rest, hoping the slender man could win by sheer agility and courage.

Suddenly the net swooped through the air and enveloped Dacius, tying up both his shield and sword arms. The *retiarius* leaped in for the kill now, striking with his spear for the great veins that coursed through the *secutor's* groin. But Dacius, although his shield and sword were still unusable because of the net, managed to twist his body with desperate strength and avoid the fatal thrust. As it was, the points of the trident buried themselves in his massive buttock muscles, and the long handle snapped in two. Blood stained his thin tunic and the pain must have been agonizing, but Dacius somehow managed to slash through the cords with his sword and, dropping his shield, let the net fall around his feet with the shield still entangled in it.

The *retiarius* had been thrown off balance by the breaking spear and was for the moment at the mercy of the huge gladiator. Sensing that unless he killed his opponent at once the crowd would give him his life, Dacius jabbed savagely at the helpless figure on the ground, finding the throat with the point of the sword and bringing a gush of blood. A second stroke severed the man's head from his body. As the slender form collapsed in a red pool on the sand, an angry roar broke from the crowd at the unfairness of Dacius, who, by the laws of the arena, should have given his fallen adversary an opportunity to cry for mercy and receive the verdict of the crowd. Only the heavy metal fence kept the people from surging down into the arena itself to destroy Dacius with their bare hands as the wounded gladiator hurriedly limped from the arena, the trident still buried in the thick muscles of his buttock.

Sick with excitement and revulsion, Luke got to his feet and started for the exit. Around him the crowd still screamed insults at Dacius, but when some took up the cry of *"Venatio! Venatio!"* others joined in the demand for the wild-beast hunt to begin. Just then the Greek beside him shouted, "Look! They are bringing in the traitors!"

Luke turned, curious to see who dared to defy the might of Rome and its Emperor. Six people were being driven into the arena by guards bearing whips; all were naked. A tall man and a beautiful girl marched proudly in the lead, as if defying the crowd, each helping an older person who was hardly able to walk. Another man, middle-aged but strong, carried the frail body of a white-haired woman, perhaps his mother, in his arms. Luke could feel nothing but pity for these people, whatever their crime, for they seemed wholly defenseless there on the sand.

Before the throne of the governor the guards left the small group, driving into the ground three short-handled spears which the men could use if they chose to fight against the lions. But one of these men was crippled, another could hardly rise from the sand, and the middle-aged one simply stood with the older woman in his arms. The young man put his arm around the shoulders of the girl, and she leaned against him as if to gather courage from his strength.

Then a full-throated roar broke from the crowd as a black-maned African lion bounded from one of the arena gates. He paused, a magnificent specimen of animal beauty and ferocity, while behind him a lioness and another male padded out on the sand. For a moment the lions did not see the little group of humans huddled helplessly on the sand, then their scent reached the leader. He growled menacingly, and his ruff stiffened. Slowly the great tail began to lash the sand and, crouching, he moved forward, the others following, converging upon the doomed men and women.

"What is their crime?" Luke asked the Greek beside him.

"Treason against the Empire. They refused to acknowledge the divinity of the Emperor or to serve with the army."

"For what reason?"

The Greek shrugged. "It is said that they belong to some sect that worships a strange god, one they call Christos."

"But Christ was a Jew," Luke protested. "And these people are not Jews."

The Greek's eyes narrowed. "How do you know so much about Christos——" he began, but a sudden roar from the crowd drew his attention back to the arena.

As the lions came nearer, no one in the group made any move to fight them except the tall young man, who stood in front of the group with the girl. Luke could sense his agony at the thought of the claws of the lion tearing into the beautiful young body of his beloved, and everyone in the theater heard his sudden cry of anguish. Then, stooping to kiss the girl quickly in farewell, he seized one of the spears and jerked it from the ground, moving out before the others to face the lions alone.

Not ten feet away from the doomed group the black-maned lion crouched and launched his body through the air, ignoring the puny threat of the spear. But the lone defender stood firm, and as the lion's claws raked his body he stabbed at the soft underbelly of the beast, driving the spear completely through it and pinning the thrashing animal to the sand. Then, leaping to jerk another spear from the sand, he turned to face the other two lions, jabbing at the lioness, who turned and retreated, snarling, well beyond reach of the spear. The third beast, as if amazed that a naked human dared stand against them, stood irresolute.

The crowd had surged to its feet, screaming with excitement, and Luke was seized by the hope that the young man would somehow win his battle with the beasts and be pardoned. He saw Petronius make a hurried signal to the trumpeters and thought he might be giving the prisoners their lives, but when the blast sounded, a full dozen lions surged into the arena and bore down upon the doomed humans. It was all over in a matter of seconds then; wild beasts surged over the group, snarling and tearing at unprotected bodies, clawing the young man and the girl and going on to slash open the flesh of the others.

Dizzy with revulsion and nausea, Luke stumbled through the nearest exit, leaving the pandemonium of the kill behind him. He staggered blindly through the empty corridors and down the stairways, with no idea where he was going save that the way to the street lay downward. Finally, when there were no more stairways, Luke realized that he was lost in the lowermost passages of the amphitheater where the cages of the animals were located and the rooms in which the gladiators awaited their turn in the arena. The cooler air in the stone-lined passages relieved some of the nausea and dizziness engendered by the horror he had witnessed, but not knowing in which direction the outside lay, he could only walk along, hoping to reach an exit. Then the door of a cell appeared and he hurried to reach it, thinking that someone there might give him help.

Luke was already inside the room before he realized its use. Sickened by what he saw, he stopped short at the door, for somehow he had managed to stumble into the room below the walls where the dead were dragged from the arena to await the carts which hauled them away. The slashed body of the *retiarius* was there, and the gladiator upon whom the crowd had turned thumbs down, the traditional signal by which one not favored by them was condemned to death. The mangled bodies of the people who had been thrown to the lions were piled to one side, torn almost beyond recognition. He was turning away when he heard a low whispered word, "Christos."

Startled, Luke bent over the mangled bodies. Somewhere in the pile there must be life, and as a physician he could not leave until he was sure that person was beyond help. Then he saw the lips of the young man who had fought the lions move slightly and knelt beside him to feel the pulse. It beat faintly under his fingers, and as he knelt there he saw the dying man's lips move again. "Lord . . . lay not"—he could barely hear the whispered words—"this sin to . . ." Then the pulse under Luke's fingers faded away, and he saw the dying man's lips go slack.

Luke got to his feet slowly and thoughtfully. He had heard those words before, from the lips of Stephen as he lay dying outside the walls of Jerusalem. Was it purely coincidence that he should hear them again deep beneath the theater of Antioch, from the lips of a man who had been torn to death by lions because he refused to disavow the Galilean in whom he had trusted? Or was it another of those strange coincidences which seemed to occur in his life?

"What do you do here, my son?" a deep voice asked behind him. Startled, Luke turned quickly to face the newcomer. A big man stood in the door. His robe was coarse and cheap, and his massive head was crowned with red hair and a red beard, while a calm majesty shone from his eyes.

"I—I was seeking the way out and stumbled into this room," Luke explained. "I am a physician and stopped to see if all were beyond help."

The big man came into the room and stood looking down at the group of bodies, his eyes warm with compassion. "I came to comfort the dying," he said, "but I see that I am too late." And then, as if it were an afterthought, he said, "My name is Barnabas."

The name meant nothing to Luke, but there was something familiar about the other, something strangely reminiscent of another man whose size had been distinctive, a man named Simon Peter. Then he realized what it was. Barnabas had the same look, the same calm majesty which Peter possessed.

"Cletus was my friend," Barnabas said, kneeling to close the dead man's eyelids with gentle fingers. "I thought I heard his voice as I came into the room."

"He was praying," Luke explained, " 'Lord . . . lay not this sin to . . .' He died with the sentence uncompleted, but I think the rest of it would have been 'their charge.' "

Barnabas looked up at him, his eyes bright with interest. "How do you know that? Did you ever hear those words before?"

"Yes. From the lips of a man named Stephen outside Jerusalem."

Barnabas got slowly to his feet, but his eyes never left Luke's face. "What is your name, my son?" he asked.

"I am called Luke, a physician."

The red-haired man smiled. "I know of you from Simon Peter, Luke," he said. "Wait a moment. I must pray for our friends." He raised his eyes, as if he were looking to someone above him, and when he spoke his voice had the same note of assurance that Luke had heard in Saul's voice when he had prayed for Apollonius. "Lord, we commend to thy tender mercy the souls of these our brothers and sisters who have died in thy service, trusting in the promise of eternal life which thou hast made to all who believe and trust in thee. Amen."

Barnabas turned to Luke. "You had better go," he said. "That passage there will take you to the street; it is the one used by the death carts. I will return through the dressing rooms of the gladiators, who are my friends."

"But why——" Luke would have liked to stop and talk to Barnabas about Simon Peter.

"Petronius is persecuting those who follow Jesus," Barnabas interrupted. "It is better if you are not seen with me." Then he smiled. "Be patient, Luke, the plans of God mature slowly. We will speak another time of Simon Peter and the purpose of God which has brought us together here this day." Then he was gone.

By following the directions of Barnabas, Luke found his way safely out of the stadium. But as he walked home through the streets he was troubled by a strange feeling that he should have followed the red-haired man. He had felt that same desire once before, he remembered, when he had watched Saul of Tarsus disappear into the desert from a hilltop beyond Damascus. And with it now went a strange conviction that some force beyond his knowledge had taken control of him, the same force, perhaps, which had gently pushed him aside as he had knelt beside Apollonius with Saul and the others in the home of Ananias at Tarsus.

Book Three: THE CHRISTIANS

*And the disciples were called Christians first
in Antioch.*

Acts. 11:26

THEOPHILUS returned from Tarsus after a month. Not only had
he given his blessing to the marriage of Apollonius and Mariamne, but
he had stayed for the ceremony as well. He brought other news, too,
particularly about the spread of the Nazarene faith in Tarsus and
Cilicia and the decision of Junius Gallio to recommend that all provincial governors cease, for the time being at least, persecuting the
followers of Jesus.

Luke continued to be busy with his medical practice. Largely confined to the richer people of the city, it earned a great deal of money
for him but did nothing to stimulate his zeal, since his work consisted
largely of treating the effects of overeating, drinking, and debauchery,
or administering potions to relieve the headaches of women whose
major activity for a day was dressing for the evening banquet. More
and more Luke had been troubled by the same sense of dissatisfaction
and depression which had driven him with Probus to the taurobolium
and afterward to the games, in a vain search for something which
would ease his mind and give him some purpose. But he had found
none, and now, as he stood in his room on the second floor of the
palace of Theophilus and watched the lights go on in the city this
spring evening, he wondered if he would ever again feel the thrill of
searching for knowledge and using his skill to save lives instead of
pleasing those who sought his advice.

A knock on the door broke into his thoughts. When he opened it,
the *nomenclator,* a slave who announced guests, informed him that
the apothecary, Probus Maximus, waited to see him downstairs. Luke

123

hurried across the atrium to embrace his old friend. "I thought you had forgotten me, Probus," he said happily. "We see so little of each other these days."

"So long as you prescribe well and I compound the proper medicines, our paths do not cross very often," Probus admitted, smiling.

"I am glad they crossed tonight," Luke said. "What brings you here?"

"A friend of yours needs medical help."

"A friend? Who?"

"He was once called Saul of Tarsus, but lately he has adopted the Latin name, Paul."

"Saul of Tarsus!" Luke exclaimed. "What is he doing in Antioch?"

"He has been teaching here for several months," Probus explained, "with Barnabas and some others. I think you know Barnabas."

"Yes. I met him after the games. But how do you come to know these people, Probus? And why were you sent for me?"

"I thought I told you I had been operating a small apothecary shop on the Street of the River for several months," Probus said, "dispensing medicines and treating disease as best I can. There are few physicians in the slums, you know."

"Have you been giving your services to the poor?"

Probus grinned. "Let us say rather that I have been robbing the rich, treating bald heads, to buy medicines for those who cannot afford them."

"You are a fraud, Probus," Luke said, laughing. "Where is your philosophy of live only for today?"

The apothecary looked pained. "My prayer has always been, 'Give me that which I deserve.' Naturally, since I give to the poor, I deserve more from the rich. If you were more familiar with mathematics, my boy," he added with an impish grin, "you would understand that such things work out according to the law of inverse proportions as propounded by the Pythagoreans."

"This is no time for one of your lectures," Luke said, smiling. "I will get my medicine case and we will visit my friend Saul—or Paul, as you say he prefers to be called now."

Across the bridge from the *insula* they turned westward along the winding street that followed the south bank of the Orontes, just beneath the older wall of the city. The houses, many of them mere hovels, were packed closely together, and the street teemed with poorly dressed and often emaciated people. The elegant and cynical Probus Maximus seemed more than ever out of place here, and finally Luke's curiosity led him to ask, "How did you get interested in the people below the river, Probus?"

"As a philosopher I am interested in men, Luke, wherever they be, and were I to limit my observations to the rich who come to my shop across the river, I must shortly conclude that man is no better than the animals, who also gorge themselves on meat and crawl away to sleep it off, although they are considerably more sensible in matters of drink and animal pleasures. Down here I see men facing the elemental forces of hunger and sickness, and even of nature when earthquakes shake the city, as they so often do."

Luke nodded. "I have thought the same things," he admitted.

"Here on the Street of the River," Probus continued, "a philosopher can find some hope for the human race. Look yonder!" He pointed to where a blacksmith could be seen through the open front of his shop, plying the treadle that pumped his bellows and kept the coals glowing in his forge. "There is the best blacksmith in Antioch, perhaps in all the world, although he welds only iron bands for carriage wheels and sharpens cutlery for housewives. Yet he is as proud of being a good blacksmith as you are of your diploma from the temple at Pergamum, Luke."

Across the street Luke noticed a shop with a painting of a beautiful iris displayed in the window, its blue-tinted throat as graceful as any Grecian column, its colors so naturally lovely that at first he thought it was really a living flower posed against an empty frame. The colors and the artistry would have demanded a high price in shops across the river. "That flower you are looking at," Probus said, "was painted by an old man whose limbs are so gnarled by age and the ague that he can hardly move his hands an inch at a time. He could paint for kings and emperors and yet he chooses to half starve down here so that poor people may see in his paintings things they would otherwise never know."

They stopped before a house which was somewhat larger and in better repair than the others. It stood next door to a large, circular-domed building which Luke remembered from his childhood as a synagogue. "This is the house of Barnabas," Probus said. "Paul is here."

A group of boys were playing in the dirt, and as Luke and Probus stopped before the door one of them jumped up and spat a single sneering word, "Christian!" It was obviously a term of insult, for the rest now leaped to their feet and began to dance about in the jeering manner of children the world over, chanting, "Christian! Christian!" very much as a Persian might have said, "Dog!"

Probus flushed with anger and, seizing a stone from the street, threw it at the boys, shouting, "Scum! Rabble! Be off with you!"

Amid this hubbub the door opened and Luke saw Barnabas standing inside. He shook his head gently at the apothecary in reproof at his anger. "Those who listen to the sneers of children, Brother Probus, will have no time for the music of the heavens," the big red-haired man said, and gave Luke his hand. "I have been looking forward to seeing you again, Luke. But first you had better see to Paul. I believe his fever is rising."

The house was old but clean. Neither its furnishings nor the surroundings gave any impression of luxury, yet Luke sensed here a certain assurance, a feeling of peace which he remembered feeling in no other house in Antioch, not even in the palaces of Theophilus and the legate Petronius. Paul lay on a couch in a back room, his cheeks burning with fever and his eyes very bright. He breathed quickly, but with no cough or effort, and Luke judged the increased respirations to be from fever alone. "I remember telling you in Tarsus that our paths would cross again, Luke," the sick man said in greeting. "But I did not know it would be so soon."

It seemed to be a clean-cut case of intermittent fever, probably tertiary, with rigors accompanied by debilitating sweats every other day. The fever would burn itself out in time if there were no complications, Luke knew, but would return again and again. He gave the patient a powder to help bring on the sweats and lower the fever, and promised to return the following day.

In the front room Barnabas and several others besides Probus were gathered around a small table, talking and munching spiced cakes with the sweet wine that the Jews seemed to love. Barnabas introduced two of them as Lucius of Cyrene, and Manaen, who, he said, had grown up with Herod Agrippa, now King of all Judea and the surrounding provinces. The third man was a tall Negro called Simeon Niger whose ears were slit in the traditional mark of slavery. Seeing Luke's eyes upon his mutilated ears, Simeon said proudly, "Yes, Luke. I have been a slave, but Christ set me free. My master was present when Jesus was crucified in Jerusalem; afterward he became a believer and gave all his slaves their freedom. As a physician you know it is a simple matter to burn the slits with a hot iron so that they heal almost without a scar and then no one would know I had been a slave." He lifted his head. "But so long as my ears are slit every man can know the power and mercy of Jesus to free men."

Barnabas said easily, "You see we are an odd company, Luke. I, a Jew, was a merchant of Cyprus; Simeon, a slave; and Lucius, a scribe. Manaen could have been chief steward to Herod Agrippa, who now oppresses our brothers in Jerusalem. Probus has a fine apothecary shop above the river. Yet we all work together here in Antioch in the cause of Jesus Christ."

"What are you going to do about those children, Barnabas?" Probus asked. "They shouted 'Christian' at Luke and myself when we came in."

"We were discussing that today, Probus. I know of nothing that we can do."

"But they are insulting you."

"Christ was insulted more than once," Barnabas said mildly. "Do you have any suggestions, Luke?"

"I had never heard the word before," Luke admitted. "What does it mean?"

"Literally, I suppose, it would be 'follower of Christ.' The children have heard their parents shouting it as an insult directed toward us, so they are not to be blamed. Perhaps I should explain something to you," Barnabas continued. "Some time ago Simon Peter, upon whom the mantle of our Lord has descended, received a vision in which he was instructed to tell the Gentiles of Jesus and to baptize any who believed, admitting them to full fellowship in the Church of Christ. Unfortunately, many orthodox Jews, particularly the Pharisees, believe that admitting Gentiles to the synagogues and the fellowship is breaking the ancient laws set down by Moses. They do not yet understand that Jesus came to make the grace of God free to everyone. We here in Antioch have been foremost in preaching to the Gentiles, and so there are those who seek to revile us and stop our work. 'Christian' is the term they have chosen as an insult to us."

"But it is not an insult," Luke protested. "You are really followers of Jesus and therefore 'Christians.' If you openly call yourselves by that name, then their insults will mean nothing."

Barnabas was obviously impressed by his reasoning. "I never thought of that before," he admitted. "What say you to this?" he asked the others.

Simeon spoke first. "Luke is right. We should be called 'Christians' for the same reason that I keep my ears slit, because we are proud of our faith, not ashamed of it."

The others agreed. "It shall be so, then," Barnabas decided. "The disciples shall be called 'Christians' first in Antioch." He turned back to Luke. "We were planning to leave in a few weeks for Jerusalem, taking help to our starving brethren there. Do you think Paul will be well soon?"

"He has had such attacks before," Luke said. "This one should subside in a few weeks." He went on to ask a question which had been in his mind since Probus had come to the palace. "Why does he call himself Paul now, instead of Saul?"

"Paulus is his Roman name," Barnabas explained, "since he is also a citizen of Rome. As Saul of Tarsus he was active in persecuting those who followed Jesus, and there are still many who remember him in that role, so it seemed better to use his other name."

"I remember how much trouble he stirred up in Damascus," Luke agreed.

Barnabas smiled. "There will always be trouble where Paul goes, Luke. The Spirit burns in him with too hot a fire not to scorch others, but many of us believe that just such a fire is needed now. Perhaps Paul may be the very 'pillar of fire' described by our ancient prophets to lead the world to God again through Jesus Christ.

"We have brought Paul from Tarsus to join us," he continued, "because we are sure the time has come to carry the teachings of Jesus to men everywhere. If Peter and the elders in Jerusalem approve, Paul and I will set out on a journey, first to my home island of Cyprus and thence to Tarsus, where we plan to take the Via Augusta to the cities of the Lycaonian plains and the highlands. If that venture is successful, we might even go as far as Ephesus."

Walking back to the *insula,* Probus said, "I have been talking to Paul lately, Luke. What do you think of his story of how the Lord spoke to him on the road to Damascus?"

"It could have been true. If you admit that Jesus is the resurrected son of God, as the Christians do."

"But if Jesus was just an extraordinarily wise and good teacher instead of a divine being, then what Paul heard must have been a hallucination. You know the sort of things people imagine they see while in a trance."

"I had thought of that," Luke admitted. "Why are you so concerned with Paul's visions?"

"I have been studying what Barnabas likes to call the Christian religion. The teachings of Jesus are easy to believe, but not the resurrection. And because I do believe so strongly in the principles that Jesus preached, I hate to see them imperiled by discord."

"Do you mean with Herod Agrippa?"

"With Herod, yes. He is the first King of all the Jews for several generations and certainly is ambitious for all the power he can get. But there is something else. You heard Barnabas say tonight that the mantle of the Lord had descended upon Peter and they look on him as something of another messiah."

"When you meet him you will understand their feeling," Luke interposed.

"But Paul believes God singled him out on the road to Damascus to be the personal representative of Jesus Christ on earth."

"Then one of them must give way to the other," Luke observed.

"It will not be Paul, you can be sure of that. One reason why Barnabas is so anxious to take Paul to Jerusalem is to arrange an agreement whereby Peter will preach to the Jews and be their leader, while Barnabas and Paul do the same for the Gentiles."

"Do you think such an arrangement would work?"

Probus shrugged. "There is an old Greek parable—you should know it."

"United we stand, divided we fall." Yes, he did know it. And he wondered just how much it was going to apply to this fledgling faith which had so much to offer to the world if the humans within it did not forget the teachings of the meek and lonely man who founded it and gave his life on the cross that it might be known to every man.

ii

Luke visited Paul daily at the home of Barnabas and soon formed the habit of dropping in at the small surgery-apothecary shop which Probus had opened. There he gave his knowledge and skill to those who could not have afforded his services otherwise. Gradually he found himself spending more and more time on the south side of the river Orontes and less on the north, where his rich clients lived. He was finding in the new work a happiness and satisfaction he had not known since his early days as a student at Pergamum, for now he was fulfilling the real duty of a physician, ministering to the truly sick for whom his knowledge and the skill of his gentle hands might mean the difference between life and death.

Even more satisfying to Luke was the contact with the men who formed the nucleus of the thriving Christian Church in Antioch. They came from all walks of life, from several races and creeds, but all ministered to the sick and poor, working at their several occupations to earn bread for themselves and their families, and giving the rest of their time to the needs of the Church. It took deep convictions and an abiding faith, Luke recognized, for men of so varied backgrounds and interests to submerge their own personalities and ambitions to the greater one of making known the teachings and principles of Jesus.

As Luke had predicted, Paul was much better in ten days, and by the end of the second week the dynamic tentmaker was able to be up part of the day. Luke could not help noticing what Probus had mentioned, Paul's firm conviction that God had chosen him personally for a divine purpose, speaking to him from the heavens and striking him blind as a token of the truth of the visitation. But Paul burned with an even greater conviction of the imminent return of Jesus to set up his kingdom. All else, the normal activities of life other than those necessary for survival, he thought should be subordinated to the single fact of Jesus's coming from heaven to reign on earth.

Toward the end of the second week of Paul's illness Luke was leaving the house late one night when Barnabas, who was reading in the front room, called to him. The red-haired man put down a worn scroll. "You are staying late tonight, Luke," he observed.

"Paul and I have been arguing again."

"About the scroll, and Simon Peter, and the things which happened on the road to Damascus?"

Luke smiled. "Our voices must have been louder than we thought."

"Paul will give in to no one who questions the truths he believes in. But I am sure that the teachings of Jesus can stand up under any examination. I had troubling word from a ship that touched at Joppa recently, Luke," Barnabas continued more seriously. "Herod Agrippa may arrest Peter and the elders before we can get their sanction for Paul and myself to begin our missionary journey."

"Paul should be able to travel in another week."

"We should go sooner," Barnabas said with a worried frown. "Paul is very important to the Lord's work, Luke; we are all sure of that here. But Jerusalem is a long way from Antioch, and we need to convince Peter and the elders that we should carry the Word to the Gentiles. Besides, Manaen knew Herod as a boy; we hope he may have some influence on the King." Barnabas leaned forward. "If it is necessary for us to leave before Paul is completely well, Luke, would you come with us?"

Luke was startled by the request. Before he could answer, Barnabas went on, "This is not just an impulse, Luke. Since you have been helping us here below the river I have realized what a powerful influence for Christ a really dedicated physician can be. Tell me, is it not true that you are really happier down here with us than up there on the *insula?*"

"Yes, I am," Luke admitted. And in truth these past few months were the happiest and most rewarding ones in his memory.

"I wonder if it isn't because your conscience tells you that you were prostituting a great life-giving talent by wasting it on the rich, when the poor need men like you so badly." Barnabas took up the worn scroll he had been reading. "Listen to this, Luke. It is called the 'Prayer of a Physician' and is from the ancient writings of the Jewish people:

> *"O stand by me, my God, in this truly important task;*
> *Grant me success! For—*
> *Without Thy loving counsel and support,*
> *Man can avail but naught.*

130

Inspire me with true love for this my art
And for Thy creatures,
O grant—
That neither greed nor gain, nor thirst for fame, nor vain ambition,
May interfere with my activity.
For these I know are enemies of Truth and Love of men,
And might beguile one in profession
From furthering the welfare of Thy creatures.
O strengthen me.
Grant energy unto both body and soul
That I might e'er unhindered ready be,
To mitigate the woes,
Sustain and help
The rich and poor, the good and bad, enemy and friend.
O let me e'er behold in the afflicted and suffering,
Only the human being."

Barnabas laid down the scroll. "I think you already live closer to these precepts than many of us, Luke, and to what Jesus taught as well. That is why I did not mind asking you to come to Jerusalem with us."

"I will go," Luke agreed. Then he added, "And after tonight I have a strange feeling that if you had not invited me I would have asked you myself."

Theophilus was still reading in the atrium when Luke reached the palace. He listened gravely while Luke told him of his plans to go to Jerusalem. "My only advice to you is to be careful in Jerusalem," he said. "Herod has strong nationalistic designs, and it is no secret that he controls the Jewish people through their high priest! He has already refused to comply with Gallio's recommendations that these people you call Christians be let go in peace, so there will be trouble between the Jews and Christians in Jerusalem as long as Herod Agrippa sits on the throne."

"I shall have nothing to do with political controversy," Luke protested. "I am going merely as a physician."

Theophilus smiled. "You were only a youth when you traveled with me nearly six years ago, but you managed to become very much involved with those people then. Neither Petronius, the governor, nor myself has been blind to your association with the Christians," the jurist continued. "I do not object to what you are doing, but remember that the lines between classes in a city are almost as definite as the boundaries between countries. Soon you may be forced to decide where your real loyalty will lie, either above the Orontes or below."

"What would you advise, sir?"

Theophilus went to the window and stood looking out upon the great city below. "A year, perhaps as little as six months, ago I would have been sure of the answer," he admitted. "But since then my son has married a Jewess, a race which as a Roman I was taught to despise. The proudest blood of the Empire runs in my veins and that of Apollonius, but the future mother of my grandchildren is the daughter of a weaver. Yet I found in the home of Ananias a joy and a pride and a strength of purpose that I had never known before."

He came back from the window and put an arm about the younger man's shoulders. "I am beginning to have some inkling now of the source from which springs the joy these Christians seem to have found in what is otherwise pretty much of a joyless world, Luke. I shall not tell you the way you should go. Perhaps a higher force really does guide our individual destinies, a force which we must all obey, although often without understanding. Every man must travel the road that leads to his own particular destiny; may your steps be firm and strong. Good night, my son."

A few days later Luke stood in the bow of the small coasting smack which was carrying them southward to Joppa and Jerusalem. The wharves of Seleucia and the white houses upon the hillsides at the mouth of the Orontes made a lovely picture as they faded into the late afternoon haze; Luke's eyes were turned to the west, where the sun was poised in a bower of scarlet-lined clouds before its plunge into the sea. There had been another day, another time, like this when he and Silvanus had climbed the steps leading to the tower of the fortress of Antonia guarding the same city of Jerusalem to which he was going. Then, too, the sun had been low in the west. And then, too, a star had begun to twinkle already. "Where does this Jewish God dwell, Silvanus?" he had asked mockingly. And the centurion had answered, "They set him so far above all others as to place his dwelling in the sky." The glory of the setting sun, Luke thought now, did indeed befit the dwelling place of a god who should be above both earth and sky.

"You are pensive, Luke," a familiar voice said beside him. "Is it that you are so reluctant to leave Antioch?"

He made a place for Barnabas. "No. I was just thinking that if you believe your God, Jehovah, dwells in the sky, yonder sunset must be in his honor."

Barnabas smiled. "Listen to this. It is part of a song written by David in praise of God:

> *"When I consider thy heavens, the work of thy fingers,*
> *The moon and the stars, which thou hast ordained;*
> *What is man, that thou art mindful of him?*

132

And the son of man, that thou visitest him?
For thou hast made him a little lower than the angels,
And hast crowned him with glory and honour.
Thou madest him to have dominion over the works of thy hands;
Thou hast put all things under his feet."

"I can understand how your King David was moved to write such a tribute," Luke admitted. "It *is* hard to see how the heavens and the earth, the moon and the stars, could have been created without the hand of some all-powerful being."

"Then you must believe in a god who is above everything."

"Yes," Luke said with a new feeling of conviction that was like coming from darkness into light. "I do know it now."

"It makes me very happy to hear you say that, Luke," Barnabas said warmly. "Now you are truly a Christian."

"But I do not yet accept that Christ is the son of God," Luke protested. "Or that he rose from the dead. Those are things you Christians believe."

"Yes, we do believe them," Barnabas said gently. "But we do not demand them of every man who would live rightly and love and respect his fellow man, which is also the way of Christ. There are also the words of God to guide men, as revealed to Micah, one of our ancient prophets: *'What doth the Lord require of thee, but to do justly, and to love mercy, and to walk humbly with thy God?'* Those who follow God's precepts are also truly Christians."

iii

Approaching Jerusalem from Joppa, the seaport which gave access to the Holy City of the Jews, Luke could see little change in the five years since he had last visited it. The three towers of Hippicus, Phasael, and Mariamne still ornamented the walls, and the great white Temple of Jehovah shone with dazzling glory upon its hill across a narrow valley from the grim fortress of Antonia, symbol of the might of the Empire. As usual the city teemed with people of all races, and all the tongues of the Empire could be heard in its streets.

Over the temple hung the eternal smoke of the sacrifices, and dimly from across the Vale of Kedron came the sound of clashing cymbals and the chanting of the Levites as they marched in the ritual processions. To the north of the temple the sun glinted from the metal corselets of the eternally watchful Roman guards atop the Antonia. Behind the temple lay the Upper City of the wealthy, its beautiful terraces and magnificent villas in sharp contrast with the mud-daubed houses of the poor which dotted the hillsides and spread out far beyond the gates of the city.

Vying with the glory of the temple were the marble walls of the palace of the high priest and of the Maccabees, but dwarfing everything save the Sanctuary itself was the magnificent palace of Herod Agrippa, King of the Jews. In the center of the business district of the Tyropoean, with its bazaars and shops, stood the Hippodrome built by another Herod, an abomination in this city of Jehovah which the older Jews still resented as a symbol of the subservience of their King to the heathen Emperor at Rome.

The Christian sect in Jerusalem—although not yet called by that name as they were in Antioch—was centered around the house of James, the brother of Jesus, who had become patriarch of the new faith. As in Antioch, a nearby synagogue was used by them as a church. Located in the poorer section of the city—for the teachings of Jesus inevitably appealed more to the poor than to the rich—it was an unimpressive building in keeping with the simple living habits of those who followed Jesus. The travelers were welcomed by James himself, a slender bearded man with kind eyes and a look of humility. When Luke was introduced as a physician, he said, "There is much sickness in Jerusalem because of the famine. Your skill can be put to a good use in the service of Christ." Then he turned to Paul. "And a friend of yours is here, Paul. His name is Glaucus."

"Glaucus of Iconium?"

"Yes. He became ill while on a pilgrimage to Jerusalem."

"Is his daughter with him?" Paul asked eagerly.

"Thecla? Yes, she is here. They are both in the other room."

Paul left the room at once, which surprised Luke, for James was giving them an account of the recent troubles in Jerusalem. It was disquieting news, for Herod Agrippa had finally dared to kill one of the twelve disciples. James, the brother of John, a gentle man whom Jesus loved, had been arrested, but was killed, Herod claimed, while resisting arrest. No one who had known the gentle disciple believed he had resisted, however, and all understood that Herod was using this method to destroy the followers of Jesus without a trial, which would reveal the lack of grounds for his actions.

"What of Peter?" Barnabas asked James.

"We expect to hear of his arrest hourly," the patriarch told them. "Herod has sworn to kill Peter, but he continues to preach everywhere that Jesus came to save Gentiles as well as Jews since his vision and conversion of the centurion Cornelius in Caesarea."

"Is this Cornelius of the Italian band?" Luke asked. The Italian band was a famous cohort, and Cornelius came from one of the greatest houses in the Empire.

"Yes, I believe he is," James said. "Do you know him, Luke?"

"There was a commander of the guard in Antioch many years ago named Cornelius who was also of the Italian band. It is probably the same."

Just then a young man came into the room. He broke into a glad cry at the sight of Barnabas, and the two embraced. Barnabas turned to Luke and the others. "This is John Mark, the son of my sister," he said proudly. "He serves as a scribe to Simon Peter."

Mark was young, about eighteen, Luke judged. He was a handsome youth, with dark hair, sparkling brown eyes, and a friendly manner. Shorter than Luke, he had small hands and feet and an infectious enthusiasm in his manner. "I have heard Peter speak of a youth called Luke," he said. "He carried the scroll containing the sayings of Jesus safely away from Saul when he killed Stephen."

"I am the same Luke," the young physician admitted.

None of them knew that Paul had come into the room until Luke heard his sharp intake of breath at Mark's words. He saw Paul staring at Mark with a strange expression, a look of both hurt and anger, as if he did not like having his part in the death of Stephen remarked upon. It only lasted a moment, however, then Barnabas introduced his nephew to Paul. Mark flushed when he realized that Paul must have overheard him, but before he could say anything in apology Paul turned abruptly to Luke. "I have promised my old friend Glaucus that you will attend him at once, Luke," he said. It was more an order than a point of information.

"Let me take you to Glaucus," Mark offered, and in the hall outside he mopped his forehead with the sleeve of his robe. "I am always saying the wrong things. Peter is often displeased with me because of it."

"You mentioned the scroll I took to Damascus," Luke said. "Do you know where it is now?"

"The scroll disappeared a few years ago," Mark told him, "when the Sanhedrin was especially busy trying to destroy the disciples. Some say a woman took it away, but Peter insists that when there is a need for the sayings the scroll will reappear."

"Does Peter know where it is?"

"I think he does," Mark admitted. "But I am babbling on as usual. You will be wanting to see Glaucus."

The room they entered was bright with sunlight that poured through a window opening upon the central garden around which the house was built. On a low couch lay a white-haired man with the features of a Greek patrician. His cheeks were pale from illness, and there were

135

dark shadows of sickness under his eyes. It was to the girl by the window that Luke's eyes were drawn irresistibly. She was looking out into the garden when they entered, and in the sunlight her profile was etched as cleanly as the head of a Greek goddess upon a gold coin. So startlingly beautiful was she that Luke involuntarily caught his breath at the sight of her. Her features were of classic Greek, her hair dark but wavy and bound with a simple white bandeau. Her eyes, dark and direct, met his as she turned her head. She was tall for a girl, almost as tall as Luke, and her body was as graceful as a Greek statue. Luke judged that she was about twenty years old. She was dressed in a simple silken stola of pale green color with long loose sleeves and girded at the waist with a narrow leather belt. The sandals upon her feet were also of leather.

All of this Luke took in with one quick glance before Mark said, "Glaucus, this is Luke, the physician, of whom Saul spoke."

Luke managed to take his eyes from the girl long enough to bow courteously to the older man. Then Mark said, "And this is Thecla."

The girl turned from the window and came across the room smiling, her hand extended in the Christian greeting. "Welcome to Jerusalem, Luke," she said, her handclasp firm and friendly. When their hands touched, Luke felt as if a warm current had suddenly flowed between them, a purely physical communion that was strange and new and infinitely exciting. Thecla's eyes were almost upon a level with his and, looking into them, he saw a sudden warmth spring up there as if she, too, experienced a similar feeling, then she colored slightly and withdrew her hand from his, going with Mark to the door before returning to the couch.

Glaucus appeared to be suffering from nothing more serious than a mild remittent fever, but Luke could not be sure without further study. The elderly man's pallor seemed more marked than he would have expected, and his body was thin, as if he might be suffering from some more deeply seated wasting disease as well. Luke did not wish to alarm father or daughter unduly, so he merely prescribed a light diet and a tonic and promised to visit the patient again later. Thecla followed Luke from the room and into the enclosed garden around which the house was built. There was a small pool filled by a pipe connected to the aqueduct that brought water from the hills. Thecla stopped beside it and turned to face him. "Do you think me unmaidenly, following you out here like this?" she asked, smiling. "After all, we just met."

"Did we?" he asked, looking into her eyes. "I felt in the room there as if I had known you for a long time."

"And I too." Then she laughed a little self-consciously. "You have been reading too much Greek philosophy, Luke. Surely you don't believe that we live over and over again, in different bodies, as some of the philosophers claimed?"

"Perhaps I can express it better another way," he said.

> *"The soul is immortal and 'tis no*
> *possession of thine own, but of Providence.*
> *And after the body is wasted away,*
> *like a swift horse freed from its traces,*
> *It lightly leaps forward and*
> *mingles itself with the light air,*
> *Loathing the spell of harsh and*
> *painful servitude which it has endured."*

"What a beautiful thought," Thecla cried, her eyes shining. "You are a poet, Luke, as well as a physician."

"The thought is not mine, although it is a favorite with me. The verse was written by Apollonius of Tyana, a philosopher."

"I know his writings," Thecla agreed. "But I never saw that particular verse before. Isn't it strange, Luke, that a pagan poet should express so exactly the way those of us who have accepted Jesus feel about his promise of life after death?"

"I am not a Christian, Thecla," he said. Then, moved by an impulse to be utterly frank with this beautiful girl, he told her of his association with the Christians at Antioch and of the things that went before it, his experiences here in Jerusalem and on the road to Damascus, the meetings with Saul and the cure of Apollonius. When he finished, her cheeks were flushed with excitement and her eyes shining. "It must be all a part of God's plan, as Paul says, Luke," she cried. "And think how wonderful it is that you were chosen!"

"But chosen for what, Thecla?"

"Perhaps to do some great deed which will make your name famous for ages."

Luke smiled at her enthusiasm. "For the time being I shall concentrate on being as good a physician as I can."

"Do you think Father is going to be all right?" Thecla asked.

"I found nothing serious," Luke said. "But he is very thin."

"I know," Thecla said with a worried frown. "He has been losing weight for a year. I would hate for him to become an invalid; he is so wrapped up in his work."

"His work?" Luke echoed in surprise. The frail man on the couch hardly seemed able to do any manual labor.

"We have a school for Greek children in Iconium," she explained. "Father thinks that the modern Greeks are drifting too far away from the noble principles of the old philosophers, so he teaches them Socrates and Plato and Aristotle, while I try to help them learn weaving and other things they will need to know to make a living."

"How did you happen to take up the Christian faith?" Luke asked.

"We had gone to Tarsus to visit relatives and I heard Saul—or Paul, as you call him—preaching on the streets. What he said impressed me so much that I brought Father to hear him. Before we left Tarsus both of us decided to follow Jesus."

Luke had a sudden inspiration. "If you are going back to Iconium, why not go as far as Antioch with us?" he asked. "We will be returning in about a week, and I could look after your father on the way." He did not add that it would give him an extra few days with Thecla while the boat moved along the coast from port to port, and perhaps some additional days in Antioch as well, until they could take ship for Tarsus.

"I would like that, Luke," Thecla said warmly. "And so would Father, I am sure." Just then Paul came from the house into the garden and Thecla called to him. "Luke wants Father and me to travel as far as Antioch with your party, Paul. Then he can look after Father on the way."

Luke saw an odd look in Paul's eyes for just a moment, almost as if the idea displeased him. But when he spoke he said, "How fortunate for both of you. I am going to the house of Mary, the sister of Barnabas, Thecla, to leave word for Peter to join us here this evening. Would you like to go with me?"

"Oh, I would," she said warmly. "I have not been out of the house for days."

Paul turned to Luke, his manner almost peremptory. "Manaen is going to the palace now to try to get an audience with Herod, Luke. You will remember that he and Herod were boys together. Herod is always fearful of his health, and if you and Probus go with Manaen, you may be able to influence Herod on behalf of Peter and the elders and perhaps persuade him not to continue the persecution."

"I will do what I can," Luke promised. "Good-by, Thecla."

"Good-by, Luke," she said, smiling. "I will see you at the evening meal."

iv

As Luke, Manaen, and Probus were approaching the gate of Herod's magnificent palace a strange figure emerged from a shack close to the gate. It was an old man, skinny and tall, with a long beard and fiery eyes. "Whither goest thou, my brethren?" he inquired, peering at them.

"You are Agabus, the prophet," Manaen cried, "I saw you once before on the shores of Galilee."

"He who speaks the warnings of God goes whithersoever his feet are directed," Agabus intoned. "Now I bring warning from the Most High to Agrippa, but he gives it no heed, so he will perish."

"Agabus is the last of the old-time prophets of God," Manaen explained while they waited to learn whether Herod would grant an audience to his childhood playmate and the physician and apothecary from Antioch.

"He looks more like one possessed by a devil," Probus observed, but Manaen shook his head. "Agabus has never failed to be right in his prophecies. If he foretold my death, as he has Herod's, I would start to set my house in order."

A slave came to the gate then to escort them to the presence of the King. The Emperor Tiberius had hated this sniveling grandson of Herod the Great and had kept him in prison to keep him from plotting discontent among the Jews. But Agrippa had been a close friend of dissolute Caligula, and when that most perverted of all the Romans came to the throne at the death of Tiberius, the Jewish prince was haled forth from prison in triumph and given the crown, not only of the tetrarchies of his uncles Philip and Antipas, but of Judea as well. Once more a king, Herod Agrippa I, reigned over all the Jews, but when Caligula tried to force this proud people to worship him as divine, a rebellion had flamed even before the new king could take his throne. The death of Caligula suddenly removed this source of discontent, and Agrippa was elevated to the kingship in Judea under the protection of the Emperor Claudius.

The new king had not been long in showing the cruelty and perversion characteristic of his family. When the followers of Jesus began to admit Gentiles to this new branch of the Jewish faith, he found most of the orthodox Jews strongly behind him in his plan to persecute and destroy the new faith. Only the sickliness of the King, his dalliance with a succession of women who pleased his fickle desires, and his love of feasting and drinking had kept him from turning all of his evil energy against the Christians. Lately, however, the murder of James had emboldened the most vicious of the Herods to redouble his efforts against the fledgling sect.

Luke was shocked by his first sight of the Jewish King. Agrippa reclined on a couch in a magnificent apartment, as elaborately decorated as anything Luke had seen in Antioch, although the Jews abhorred ostentation. The monarch was short, his legs spindly, and his body bloated, his face swollen with dissipation and plethora. His skin was unhealthy in appearance, his ankles swollen, and he breathed with a rasping wheeze that was notably unpleasant in sound.

On a cushion at Herod's feet a beautiful young woman reclined, dressed in the diaphanous pantaloons and circular golden breastplates of the Eastern dancing girls. Her mouth was sulky and her hair unconfined. She had been dancing strenuously, for her breasts still rose and fell quickly, and the musicians in the corner held their instruments in their hands. A dozen slaves waited for the King's nod to carry out his every wish.

Agrippa hardly bothered to acknowledge the introduction of the three. "Come to the point, Manaen," he said contemptuously. "For what favor do you remind me that we were boys together? And expect none, for you well know that I hated you as a child and see no reason to alter my feelings now."

The King of the Jews seemed to regard himself as above all niceties of ordinary conduct. He tousled the hair of the dancing girl with a heavily ringed hand whose fingers were as puffy as his ankles and stared at them truculently with bloodshot eyes. Luke could make the diagnosis in one quick glance: plethora, brought about by an overabundance of blood from gluttony, drunkenness, and debauchery. Herod's body was obviously beginning to break under the strain of the overloaded blood vessels, as shown by the puffy skin and the rasping wheeze. He might live ten more years, or he might die tomorrow.

"Well, speak up, Manaen," Herod snapped. "Who are these people with you?"

Manaen found words then, having recovered from his shock at the condition of his boyhood playmate. "I bring Luke, a physician of Antioch, who is also the son of Theophilus, deputy governor of Syria. And Probus Maximus, an apothecary and historian."

Agrippa's manner moderated a little. "I met the noble Theophilus in Rome," he acknowledged. "His son is welcome to the court of Herod."

Luke bowed low. "What do you do?" Herod barked at Probus.

"I mix medicines according to the secrets of the Egyptians," Probus said smoothly. "Potions which can kill or cure, according to your desires."

"Are you a poisoner?" Herod laughed unpleasantly.

"Only in the service of so great a king as yourself, noble Herod, since kings can do no wrong."

Agrippa stared at him for a moment, then laughed loudly. "You are a droll fellow and an impudent one." He leaned forward, suddenly malevolent again. "Give me one reason why I should not have your tongue torn from your mouth?"

"Because I control strange powers which might better be used in your service," Probus said urbanely. "Such as this, for example." He whisked the amber *elektron* from his robe and, quickly rubbing it with the woolen cloth, held it above the dancing girl's head. Instinctively she recoiled, but as her head moved, her hair rose stiffly under the strange power of the *elektron,* so that it appeared suddenly to be standing on end.

"By the tents of Israel!" Agrippa exclaimed. "What devil's work is this?"

"No devil's work," Probus assured him, beginning to rub the *elektron* again. "Merely a harnessing of the forces of nature. It is even said," he continued, "that this stone has the power to stimulate the growth of hair. If Your Majesty wishes . . ." He held the *elektron* out toward Agrippa's own balding head, but the King recoiled in obvious fright. "Later, perhaps," he stammered, "not now." He turned back to Manaen then. "What do you want?" he barked unpleasantly.

Manaen was nervous in the face of Herod's obvious antagonism. "I—I have come to beg that you lessen your zeal in persecuting those who follow Jesus of Nazareth."

"Are you a follower of the Nazarene?"

"Yes."

Herod's face purpled, and his fingers in the girl's hair clenched, so that she squealed with pain. "You, a Jew, admit to believing in one who threatened to destroy the temple built by my grandfather?" he shouted. "How dare you show your face before me?"

Manaen cringed before the King's murderous rage. "I am sure that Jesus was speaking in parables," he tried to explain, but Herod cut him short.

"Say no more! Go while I let you have your life!"

"But——" Manaen tried to protest.

"Go! Go!" the King screamed in fury. Realizing that he would only damage the cause he had come to plead by staying, Manaen quickly left the room. When Probus and Luke started to follow, Agrippa called them back. "Wait, you two. I would speak with the physician."

Not knowing what treatment they would find at the uncertain temper of the King, Luke and Probus turned reluctantly back to the royal presence. "Are you followers of Jesus too?" Agrippa snapped.

"We believe in your God," Luke told him, "and we work with those who follow him. But we have not been baptized."

"You are Greeks, are you not?"

"Yes," Probus said. "And citizens of Rome. I am a graduate of the University of Alexandria and other schools. Luke possesses the certificate of a physician from the Temple of Asklepios at Pergamum and was at one time the surgeon to the Roman commander, Sergius Paulus."

Agrippa's manner became less truculent. From his long residence at Rome he knew what such qualifications meant. Realizing this, Probus had listed them in order to impress him. "I heard of your success with Sergius Paulus," the King admitted. "Have you any other important cases?"

Luke hesitated, but Probus said, "Naturally a physician is not allowed to boast of his cures, but it was Luke who cured Gallio recently in Antioch."

Agrippa's face darkened once more with anger. "A curse on Junius Gallio," he almost screamed. "He is supporting these Nazarenes by recommending to the Emperor that they not be persecuted. But I will break up this sect," he shouted angrily, "or die in the attempt."

Then with an effort the King calmed himself and wiped his face with a perfumed cloth which a slave sprang to hand him. "Come closer, Luke," he ordered, "and tell me whence come this swelling of my ankles and hands and this accursed wheeze in my breathing?"

Luke knelt beside the couch and examined Agrippa briefly. He found nothing that the first quick glance had not told him. His fingertips sank into the puffy flesh of the monarch's ankles to the depth of the nails, and when he put his ear to the pallid skin of the King's chest a bubbling wheeze was plainly audible, as described by Hippocrates in such cases. The veins everywhere were so distended that they stood out from the flesh, a sure sign of severe plethora.

"What is your opinion?" Agrippa demanded.

"Less food and wine would do you no harm," Luke said frankly.

"Others have told me that," the King growled. "But I refuse to starve myself and die of thirst to please physicians. What medicine will cure me?"

"None," Luke told him. "Your body is clogged with blood from too much food and drink."

Luke's calm appraisal of his condition evidently impressed the torpid monarch, for a look of apprehension came into his eyes. "Am I going to die?" he demanded.

"You could die at any moment," Luke warned, "especially if you let yourself become angry or excited. But with proper diet and abstention from all drink except a little wine, you could live many years."

"I choose to go on eating and drinking as I please," Herod stated positively. "Have you no treatment to relieve me?"

Luke shrugged. "I could open your veins and remove some blood. It would relieve the congestion for a short while."

"Open the veins!" Herod recoiled, blanching. "I am not committing suicide." Luke remembered then that in Rome those who incurred the displeasure of the Emperor were allowed to open their veins, thus bleeding to death.

"Only a small opening is made," Luke explained. "And when the required amount of blood has been let, the cut is closed with a tight bandage."

Herod rubbed his chin. "This is a strange practice indeed, but if it will help the swelling and wheezing, I would try it." He looked keenly at Luke. "How do I know that you would not let me bleed to death? After all, you are allied with these Nazarenes, and they would like nothing better than to have me die."

"I have sworn an oath as a physician," Luke reminded him quietly. "Besides, your guards can stand by to see that I take no more than a full goblet measure of blood."

"I must think about this," Herod said. "Visit me again tomorrow and I will give you my decision."

Probus said, "We will need a safe-conduct so that we may visit Your Majesty. There are tablets in the corner; I will write one for you to sign." Before Herod could object, he picked up a tablet and wrote quickly upon it with a stylus:

The physician, Luke, and the apothecary, Probus, with their assistants are to be admitted to my presence at any time.

Agrippa, Rex

Herod scrawled his name, but as he was dismissing them he began to laugh. "It would be better if I were to send you to care for that old crow of a prophet, Agabus, that lives by my gate, Luke," he chortled. "A soothsayer has told me that I shall not die so long as Agabus lives, so I keep him constantly under my protection, although he reviles me. See if he needs any pills or concoctions as you go out."

Agabus was eating his daily meal at the palace kitchen, the guard informed Luke and Probus, so they did not disturb him. As they walked back to James's house Luke asked, "Why did you ask for that safe-conduct, Probus?"

The apothecary smiled knowingly. "Everything I know about Herod Agrippa tells me he would murder his own mother, and probably did. You never know when something like this may be valuable."

v

Manaen had brought word of Agrippa's resolve to destroy the followers of Jesus to James and the others, and it was an anxious group

143

who waited for the return of Luke and Probus. Peter was there, and Luke saw that he had changed little in the past six years. The big disciple's face was lined more deeply, but he had the same look of peace and the same kindly majesty was in his eyes. "We meet again, Luke of Antioch," Peter said warmly in greeting, "according to God's purpose."

Thecla and John Mark were sitting at the back of the now crowded room. She beckoned to Luke, and he went to sit beside her. The purpose of the meeting, it seemed, was to give Barnabas, Paul, and the others an opportunity to hear Peter's story of his vision and the conversion of Cornelius, the centurion of the Italian band at Caesarea. Peter told the story simply: "I saw the heavens open, and a vessel descended looking like a great sheet with knots at the four corners. In the sheet were all manner of four-footed beasts of the earth, even wild beasts. And there were creeping things and fowls of the air. Then a voice said to me, *'Rise, Peter; kill, and eat.'*"

"Were there swine among these animals, Peter?" Paul inquired. "And fish without scales?" These were unclean foods according to Jewish law.

"Yes, there were swine," Peter replied. "And many other unclean foods. But when I said, 'Not so, Lord; for I have never eaten anything common or unclean!' the voice replied, *'What God hath cleansed, that call not thou common.'*"

"There can be no doubt, then," Paul cried; "God means for all men to be cleansed through the blood of Christ, even as he made the food clean that was unclean."

"God did mean that, I am sure," Peter agreed. "For the same words were repeated three times before the vessel was raised up to heaven. And when I preached to Cornelius and the Gentiles in Caesarea, I found them filled with the Holy Spirit."

"It is the answer we have been seeking, Barnabas," Paul cried. "The Lord has truly given us the charge to preach to the Gentiles and bring them to Jesus."

There was a chorus of agreement, but one voice was lifted in objection. It was the patriarch James, the brother of Jesus. "Are you sure, Peter," he asked doubtfully, "that the Lord really meant for you to go in with the uncircumcised and to eat unclean foods with them, contrary to the laws of Moses?"

"The Lord God has spoken to us through Peter," Paul said sharply. "Remember his words, *'What God hath cleansed, that call not thou common.'*" In his annoyance Paul was perhaps more curt than he had intended, Luke realized. But his tone seemed disrespectful toward the brother of Jesus.

144

"It is something we have never done before," James still demurred. "Perhaps there is some way we can be sure . . ."

"To compromise would be to defeat the very purpose of Jesus in coming to earth and dying on the cross," Paul argued hotly. "God has said: *'Through his name whosoever believeth in him shall receive remission of sins.'*"

James did not object further, but it was plain that he was not entirely satisfied by Paul's explanation. Just then the evening meal was brought in, however, and there was no more opportunity to discuss it. Thecla helped to serve the meal and afterward to clean up the dishes and utensils. While the older men talked Luke slipped out into the garden, for he wanted solitude to think.

Paul's concept of the sinfulness of all men troubled him, for it seemed to give no credit to those who tried to live according to the words of Jesus, *"As ye would that men should do to you, do ye also to them likewise."* Nor did it seem to agree with what Barnabas had told him Jehovah had said through the prophet Micah many years ago, *"What doth the Lord require of thee, but to do justly, and to love mercy, and to walk humbly with thy God?"* Why should man then be automatically condemned, no matter how well he tried to live, if he did not believe that Jesus was the son of God?

A shadow appeared on the surface of the pool beside him, and he looked up to see Thecla there, her white stola shining in the moonlight. "I saw you come out, Luke," she said quietly. "If I am intruding upon your thoughts, send me away."

"I could imagine no more lovely or welcome an intruder," he told her, taking her hands. With her he felt his doubts slipping away and a deep sense of peace and a quiet happiness flowing into his soul.

"I saw that you were worried in there tonight," she said. "Can I help you?"

"Perhaps I need the one thing you seem to have, Thecla—faith. Tell me, what is it that you believe about God and about Jesus Christ?"

"I am sure that God is good, and wise, and eternal," she said thoughtfully. "And that men could be like him if they could only give up any concern for self and let their spirits rise above the limits of their bodies to some higher place of peace and real happiness. And I believe, too, that God sent his son Jesus to suffer and die that all men might know the extent of his love for them."

It was a simple and eloquent profession of faith, and Luke found himself moved strongly by it. "Where is this higher place of peace and happiness? In heaven?"

"In heaven, yes," she agreed. "Certainly there. But those who live according to the principles of Jesus and who believe that he died for

145

them should be so proud and happy that wherever they live there will always be happiness and peace."

"Bithynia," Luke whispered. "Peaceful land."

"What did you say, Luke?" Thecla asked.

He told her about Bithynia then, describing what he had seen with Silvanus that morning in the glen, with the lacy veil of the fog drifting aside to reveal the fertile valley, the meandering course of the river, the geometric arrangement of green fields and pastures, the stone pattern of the fences, and the cloud-girdled mountain ranges encircling the fertile valleys.

"How beautiful it must be, Luke," she said softly. "When are you going there?"

"When my work is done, I suppose."

"But there is always sickness," she protested. "Your job would never be finished."

"Silvanus believed, as Peter seems to do, that God has a special task for me," he explained.

"Why could your work not be to tell the people of Bithynia about Jesus?"

It could be the answer, he thought. Why had he not thought of it before? And if that were true, he could go on to Bithynia now, as soon as they returned to Antioch. Bithynia! With someone like Thecla beside him! The thought set his pulses racing. The picture would not be complete without her, he realized. That was the meaning of the strange feeling he had experienced when he had first met her, a sense of the rightness of their coming together, as if that, too, were part of some divine plan.

He took her hands and drew her close. She did not resist, as if she, too, understood. "Will you go with me, Thecla?" he asked. "Will you go with me to Bithynia?"

She caught her breath, and he could see the glory suddenly spring into being in her eyes. Then she was clinging to him, laughing and sobbing with joy. "Of course I will go with you, Luke," she cried. "When I first saw you I knew I would go with you to the very ends of the earth if you wanted me."

Neither of them heard the door leading from the house into the garden open, but a faint sound, like a man's exclamation of surprise and displeasure, warned Luke they were no longer alone. He turned in time to see a short, stocky figure momentarily silhouetted in the partly open door as it closed. There was no doubting the identity of the man nor that he must certainly have seen them standing in each other's arms beside the pool. It was Paul.

vi

In the morning Luke asked John Mark to take him where his medical services would be needed most, and in a few hours they had a small surgery in operation in one of the poorest sections of the city. As soon as word spread that a Greek physician was treating all who came without charge, patients flocked to him from all directions. With Probus to help, Luke worked without stopping through the morning, and when Thecla came at noon, bringing bread and cheese and some dried figs, they took only a few minutes to eat before going on with their work. Thecla stayed awhile to help them, but late in the afternoon she heard that Peter was preaching in the street not far away and went to give him a message from James. Luke and Probus were preparing to close the surgery for the day when a beggar came hopping to them, shouting, "I seek the physician! Where is the physician?"

Seeing that the man did not appear to be ill, Probus said, "Come tomorrow, my friend. The physician has exhausted his supply of medicines."

"I want no medicine," the beggar shouted. "The girl needs help."

"What girl?" Luke asked quickly.

"The beautiful Greek who was working with you here."

"Thecla!" Luke cried in alarm. "What is it, man? What is wrong?"

"She was distributing alms to the poor, and there was a riot. The Romans are arresting her, and she sent me to tell you."

Guided by the beggar, Luke and Probus found the location of the riot quickly. A mob of people were milling about, shouting angrily at two Roman soldiers who were guarding Thecla between them with drawn swords. When Luke pushed his way through the crowds to them, Thecla threw herself into his arms, sobbing hysterically.

"What stirred up the crowd so?" Luke asked.

Thecla quickly regained her composure in his arms. "I—I saw some beggars and felt sorry for them," she told him, "so I opened my purse to give them a coin. It contained all the money we have, and when they saw the gold, the beggars became excited and tried to take it from me. A crowd gathered and the soldiers came; they were going to arrest me for causing a disturbance."

"I will be responsible for her," Luke told the soldiers. "May we go now?"

"You will need a guard," one of the soldiers said. "The sight of gold would drive these beggars to murder. Wait until they disperse and we will accompany you."

147

The crowd was slow in scattering, and there was still a considerable press of people about them when trumpets sounded in the street and a voice shouted, "Make way for the King. Make way for King Herod Agrippa."

Luke felt a sudden dismay. Herod was an unpleasant enough customer to meet at any time, for one could never predict what he would do. He searched for some way to escape, but the crowd only pressed closer about them in the rush to clear the street. Someone tried to snatch Thecla's purse, and when Probus struck him a little circle of excitement and angry voices again boiled up about them. Into this confusion marched a dozen soldiers guarding the sedan chair in which sat the pudgy King of the Jews. His eyes darted over the crowd and he shouted angrily, "Disperse this rabble, guards! How dare they impede the passage of the King!"

The members of the royal guard began to beat about them with their swords, unmindful of how many heads they cracked, while Herod sat up in his chair and laughed in glee when the heavy blades brought blood and howls of pain. Suddenly he spied Thecla with Luke and Probus, huddled against the wall of a building to escape notice. "Hold!" the King cried. When the tumult subsided a little he shouted, "Luke, the physician. What are you doing in this crowd?"

Luke tried to answer, but the hubbub drowned out his voice. "Bring me those two men and the girl," Herod ordered the guard. Seeing that they were to be taken to the royal presence whether they wished it or not, Luke guided Thecla through the crowd until they stood beside Herod's chair. The King leaned out and stared at Thecla with open admiration. "What a lovely thing," he exclaimed. "Who are you, child?" His small eyes darted over her lovely young body greedily.

"I am Thecla of Iconium," she said with quiet dignity. "The daughter of Glaucus. We are on a pilgrimage to your city."

"She is a Greek," Luke reminded Herod pointedly. "And a Roman citizen."

The King seemed to be in high good humor today. "Our girls could do well to copy your dress and appearance, my dear. You must visit my court." He turned to Luke. "I sent a message to you a few hours ago, physician. I would have you bleed me this evening as you suggested."

"I have been treating the sick here in the Lower City and received no message," Luke explained. "But I shall be glad to wait upon you when I have escorted Thecla to her lodging."

Herod smirked. "Is your lodging in the same place?"

Luke took an angry step toward the fat tyrant, but Probus's warning hand on his arm stopped him. Controlling his anger, Luke said, "Thecla and I are betrothed. We plan soon to be wed."

148

Agrippa lifted his eyebrows. "Then this is a festive occasion. Bring your betrothed and we will have a supper in your honor tonight after you have finished the blood drawing. I see that you carry your tools with you, so we can all go on to the palace now."

Luke wanted to object, for he instinctively distrusted the King. But he could see the wisdom of not stirring up the uncertain temper of Herod Agrippa. "As you wish," he said, bowing to his better judgment.

Since it was only a short distance to the palace, they walked in the van of Herod's chair. "Keep him in a good humor, Luke," Probus warned in a whisper. "He could clap us into a dungeon tonight and we would never be heard from again."

"I don't like the way he looked at Thecla," Luke protested.

"Nor I. But stirring him up will only make it worse."

"Probus is right, Luke," Thecla agreed. "I am not afraid so long as you are with me."

As Herod was being lifted from the sedan chair at the gate, Agabus, the prophet, appeared from the shadows. Luke was surprised at the fear in Herod's eyes and the way he backed away from the old man's bony admonishing finger. "Beware thy sins, O King!" Agabus thundered. "The people cry out for bread and sickness gnaws their vitals because their ruler is evil. The Lord will cast thee out and the worms shall eat thy body."

Herod giggled nervously. "Behold the voice of my sins," he said. "I let him live so that none may say I have no conscience. See how healthy Agabus is under the dirt. I shall not die so long as my conscience lives by my gate."

The bloodletting did not take long. Herod lay down on a couch in his apartment, and while Probus squeezed his arm to distend the veins, Luke plunged a small scalpel-lancet through skin and blood-vessel wall to release a spurt of dark, impounded blood. Agrippa turned a little pale when the stream spattered into the goblet Luke held to catch it, but by the time the vessel was full he was so much relieved that the wheeze had disappeared and he laughed and joked while Probus applied the bandage.

"The relief will be only temporary," Luke warned the King, "unless you restrict your diet and abhor wine."

Herod shrugged. "You can always remove the excess blood. Perhaps I shall make you my personal physician, Luke. Then the lovely Thecla could grace my court always."

The feast Herod had promised them was a lavish affair, with rich viands of all sorts, many of them, Luke observed, belonging to the group which orthodox Jews labeled "unclean." Herod seemed far more Roman than Jew but apparently gave lip service to the religious law of his people in order to maintain his hold over the hierarchy of priests in the Sanhedrin, through whom he controlled the country. There was music during the feast, and the sulky dancing girl whirled and stamped in a provocative dance before the King, obviously angry that another woman occupied the place of honor at Herod's right hand. More than once Luke saw Herod's pudgy fingers stray toward Thecla, but each time she managed to escape his touch gracefully without offending the bloated monarch.

When finally Thecla pleaded the lateness of the hour and her father's illness as a reason for retiring, Herod let them go without protest. "I must go to Caesarea in a few days for a celebration at the theater," he told Luke as they were leaving. "But I will want you to examine me again upon my return."

"I plan to return to Antioch soon," Luke protested.

"Your plans can wait," Herod said airily. "I will pay you well, so you have nothing to lose by staying in Jerusalem." As they were going out, the *atriensis,* who had charge of the slaves, handed Luke a small box, and when they opened it outside the gate, they saw that it was filled with gold. On top of the coins lay a beautiful emerald necklace, obviously for Thecla.

"Taint not your fingers with the riches of Mammon, my brothers," a deep voice said beside them, and they looked up to see the prophet Agabus standing there. "Give the cursed gold of Agrippa to the poor he starves that his coffers may be filled."

"We will do that, Agabus," Luke promised. Then, obeying an impulse, he asked, "When will this disaster to Herod that you predict take place?"

"Man knoweth not the day nor the hour," Agabus intoned, and they could get no further satisfaction from him.

When Luke was kissing Thecla good night outside her father's room she suddenly clung to him, trembling. "Take me away, Luke," she begged. "We can hire a carriage and leave tomorrow with Father for Joppa or some of the ports to the north. The others can catch up with us later."

He held her close, knowing the source of her fears. Naked desire and lust had burned in the eyes of Herod Agrippa tonight, and what the King desired in his own country he often took.

"Herod leaves within a few days, dearest," he assured her. "We should be safe while he is gone, and I will try to arrange for us to go before he returns. Remember, we are Roman citizens. He cannot trouble us so long as we claim the protection of Rome."

She shivered. "Agrippa and Claudius are friends. The Emperor would not stand in his way."

"I will speak to Barnabas," he promised. "Perhaps we can leave sooner."

Barnabas and Paul were in the outer room. Luke told them of his experiences with Agrippa that evening and of Thecla's fear of him. "What would you like to do, Luke?" Barnabas asked when he finished the account.

"Thecla and I would like to take Glaucus and leave for Antioch as soon as we can," Luke said.

"This is all Agrippa's kingdom," Paul objected. "He could order your arrest anywhere short of Antioch if he wished. Besides, your medical work is important here in Jerusalem, Luke. People are talking about it already, and if we can stay here a month or more, the Christians will become a powerful influence and our cause will be favored."

"But Agrippa has threatened to arrest Peter and destroy the Christians."

"Christ will guard us," Paul said calmly. "It could not be the will of God that his Church should be destroyed here when it has such a glorious opportunity." Paul's tone was confident, almost as if he believed he could speak for God himself.

"I still think we should leave Jerusalem, Paul," Barnabas said quietly. "God has called us to work among the Gentiles, while Peter and James have been given the Jews as their province. We should leave this region to them."

"But they move so slowly," Paul said in a tone of exasperation. "And James has not yet accepted God's word that the old laws of circumcision and cleanliness have been set aside by him."

"Nevertheless, Thecla and Luke must be protected," Barnabas insisted. "I will ask James to call a meeting of the elders to discuss this whole question."

"The work of Jesus is more important than what happens to one or even two persons, Barnabas," Paul said sharply. "If Thecla and Luke must suffer so that the word is spread more widely, they must accept it. After all, Christ suffered and died on the cross."

When Barnabas left the room shortly, Luke and Paul were left alone together for the first time since they had come to Jerusalem. Paul's manner tonight had been different, almost as if he were nursing a grudge, and yet Luke could not imagine how he had become offended unless it had something to do with last night, when Paul had seen Thecla in Luke's arms. "Is anything wrong, Paul?" Luke asked, breaking the silence.

"What could be wrong, Luke?"

"I don't know. You seem angry at me. Is it because Thecla and I became betrothed without asking your blessing?"

151

"Why should you ask my blessing?" Paul demanded. "You are both of age."

"Thecla and I are both very devoted to you, Paul. And it was through you that she and Glaucus became Christians."

"Are you going back to Iconium with Thecla and Glaucus?" Paul asked suddenly.

"For a short while. Then she and I hope to go into Bithynia to teach about Jesus and care for the sick."

Paul went to the window and stood looking out for a moment. Then he turned to face the younger man. "Barnabas and I have hopes of great things for Christ from you, Luke," he said. "You are well educated, a Greek, and you have influence and command respect by virtue of being the foster son of Theophilus. But if you go to Bithynia, you will be burying yourself where you can be of no help to us."

"We would be teaching the Way of Jesus," Luke protested.

"It is not right for a woman to preach," Paul said positively. "And you could not enter the synagogues. Besides," he added, "how could you preach about Jesus when you do not accept him?"

"I believe his teachings; it is just that I am not yet ready to accept him as the son of God, as you do."

"Christ died to atone for man's sins," Paul stated flatly. "Only through him can man hope for eternal life. If you do not believe that, your teachings would be worthless."

Luke did not argue the point since Paul was so adamant about it. He did not want to break with Paul over a question of theology, for he recognized that there was a bond between them, a bond cemented by the strange way in which their lives had become entwined in the past six years. Yet Paul's manner toward him these past few days had been notably different, straining that bond.

"Is it my plan to marry Thecla that you object to, Paul?" he asked.

"If you would serve Jesus as I do," Paul said, "there can be no thought of marrying and giving in marriage. We must all labor to prepare for his return and his kingdom."

"But when do you think that will be?"

"I know not," Paul admitted. "But I was called to preach the word and prepare men for his coming. Nothing else matters. Good night, Luke," he added abruptly, and left the room.

vii

Barnabas had requested a meeting of the elders of the Church the next evening at the home of his sister Mary, the mother of Mark. Late in the afternoon Luke and Probus were working in the surgery, to which patients now came in droves, when John Mark came running, his face pale, his hands shaking. "Herod has arrested Peter and Thecla," he gasped. "I saw the soldiers taking them away and ran to tell you."

The forceps Luke was holding dropped from suddenly nerveless fingers. They had been expecting the arrest of Peter at any moment, but it seemed unbelievable that Thecla had been taken too. Then he remembered Agrippa's manner during the feast and Thecla's fear when Luke had held her in his arms later. Why had he listened to Paul? He could have taken a carriage that morning as reason had urged him, removing Thecla and Glaucus from the reach of Herod. But now it was too late. A disaster worse than anything he had envisioned had already struck.

"How did it happen, Mark?" Probus asked.

Mark managed to control himself enough to talk coherently. "Peter was preaching in the street, and Thecla and I were with him. Suddenly the soldiers came and arrested Peter and Thecla. I tried to go with them, but Peter sent me to you."

"Why was Thecla arrested?"

"The soldiers refused to explain, but I heard the captain say he was glad he had found her with Peter, so they were seeking her too. They will kill Peter this time." His voice broke again. "And Thecla too. What can we do? What can we do?"

The same question was throbbing in Luke's brain. What could they do against the power of Herod? And Thecla's fate would be worse than Peter's, for the King's actions last night left no doubt of his desire for her.

"It will take a miracle to save them," Mark groaned, and Luke echoed the thought. But whence would come the miracle? For the moment he was too stunned to think logically.

A sad group gathered soon at the house of Mary. With Peter in prison, they naturally looked to James for guidance, but the gentle brother of Jesus could only suggest that they pray and hope for deliverance through God's will. Paul, too, seemed dazed, as if he could not yet believe what had happened. "We must pray God to deliver them," he said. "It is the only way."

"Do you believe it was God's will that they should be taken?" Probus asked a little acidly.

Paul stared at him dully. "It must have been."

"Then what shall we gain by asking God to release them?"

For a moment Paul did not speak, then some of his old fire kindled again in his eyes. "Are you then of so little faith, Probus, that you doubt the pattern of God's will?" he asked, but his voice was gentler than it had been in other discussions. "Who knows? By letting them be taken and then setting them free, God may plan to show the multitudes that he can deliver men even from the power of kings and emperors."

Probus beckoned to Luke to follow him into the garden. "We will get nothing done, Luke," he said in disgust, "so long as Paul dominates them and believes as he does. As far as I am concerned, God helps those who help themselves. We must figure out a way to release Peter and Thecla and hide them somewhere from Herod."

"But how, Probus?" Luke asked hopelessly, remembering how he had held Thecla in his arms in this very spot. "How shall we do it?"

"There must be a way. If it came to a bribe, I still have the emerald from the Temple of Asklepios in Pergamum."

John Mark came into the garden and hurried over to them. "Have you thought of anything?" he asked eagerly.

Luke shook his head, and Mark groaned, "Why did it happen today? I had persuaded Peter to leave tomorrow for Joppa, where he would have been safe."

"Why Joppa?" Probus asked. "It is also ruled by Herod."

"Peter had a letter from Cornelius, the centurion he converted in Caesarea a few months ago, asking him to meet him in Joppa and preach to some of his friends there."

For the first time Luke felt a faint hope stirring within him. "Cornelius might help us. He is well liked by the soldiers, and his connection with the Italian band makes him an important person in the Roman Army."

"What could he do?" Mark asked dubiously.

"Herod goes to Caesarea within the next few days, and I am sure that he will not do anything to Peter before he returns——"

"How can you be sure, Luke?" Probus interrupted. "Herod is absolutely unpredictable."

"He will want to make an example of Peter," Luke explained. "And he can do that best by letting him be tried by the Sanhedrin and stoned to death or crucified. Then Herod can claim that Jesus is powerless to help even those who believe in him. While Herod is gone, Cornelius might be able to help."

"It sounds logical," Probus admitted. "But what about Thecla?"

"I must go to Agrippa and try to find out something about her. He may listen to reason when I threaten to ask Theophilus and Junius Gallio to intervene through the Emperor."

All of them realized that Luke's hope of influencing Herod had little chance of success, but no one could suggest anything better. He had no trouble gaining entrance to the palace when he presented the safe-conduct Probus had cleverly obtained. While the *nomenclator* was conducting him to the presence of the King he carefully replaced the tablet in his cloak, for no one knew when he might need it again.

Herod looked up from his couch when Luke was ushered into the audience chamber, and his face grew dark with anger. "How did you get into the palace?" he demanded. "Speak up, or you will feel the mercy of my faithful Geta." A squat man with bulging muscles and an incredibly evil face stood beside the couch. He smirked now, and Luke realized that he was the infamous torturer whose name was a synonym for cruelty throughout Judea, a fit servant of an evil master.

"I am your physician," Luke reminded Herod. "You gave orders that I was to be admitted at all times."

"You will be admitted no more. What do you want?"

"I came to ask you to release Simon Peter and the girl Thecla who was here with me yesterday."

"Has something happened to the lovely Thecla?" Herod inquired with an exaggerated concern.

"She was arrested this afternoon with Simon Peter, on your orders," Luke said bluntly.

"My orders?" Agrippa lifted his eyebrows in an elaborate gesture of disavowal. "I know nothing of it. You told me yourself that the lovely Thecla is a Lycaonian and a Roman citizen. Surely you don't believe that I would arrest her." Beside him Geta guffawed at his master's jest, and the slaves grinned.

"Then you deny that you have hidden her away somewhere?"

Herod's cheeks suddenly purpled with anger. "Beware that you do not tempt me too far, Luke of Antioch," he growled. "I might forget who your father is. Or should I say your foster father," he added cunningly, "for I understand that you are really the brat of a common freedman."

Luke curbed his anger, for he saw now that his only hope of getting any information about Peter and Thecla from the pudgy King lay in trapping him into revealing his plans unwittingly. "What about Simon Peter?" he asked then. "He has broken no Roman law."

Herod shrugged. "Peter has created a disturbance by preaching an alien faith, but I will not argue the point with you. As soon as I return from Caesarea he will be tried according to Jewish law for consorting with the uncircumcised and eating unclean food."

"His blood will be on your hands," Luke warned, "as the blood of Jesus was on those of Pontius Pilate."

Herod's face suffused again with unhealthy color, and he pushed himself up from the couch to a sitting position. "I have sworn to destroy this Nazarene sect," he screamed. "And neither you nor Junius Gallio nor anyone else will stay my hand. Now leave the palace before I have you clapped in prison."

Luke was dejected as he left the palace, for his mission had been a failure. He had learned nothing of Thecla, except that Agrippa obviously did not intend to publicize her arrest, but to keep her for purposes of his own. And of Simon Peter he knew only that the big disciple would not die before Herod's return. Then he thought of Agabus and went to the shack beside the gate. The old prophet was lying on a pallet, but he was not asleep. "You seek word of Peter and the girl, Luke of Antioch," he said before Luke could question him. "They were taken to the dungeons of Herod not four hours ago."

"Can you tell me what will be their fate?"

"Peter is the anointed of the Lord, and his time is not yet," the old man said. "But the girl will bear you no sons."

Luke turned away, his head bowed. There could be only one interpretation of the prophet's words. Peter would somehow escape Herod this time. But Thecla was lost to him, just when they had discovered their love and were planning such a wonderful life together. And Manaen had said that the prophecies of Agabus always proved true.

viii

Luke's despondency over Thecla's fate did not keep him from working actively for Peter's release; he and Mark rode to Joppa that very night to seek Cornelius. The sun was high the next morning when they guided their horses across the plain before the seaport city.

Cornelius greeted them warmly. He was a commanding figure in his early fifties, with dark hair and the clean-cut features of the northern Italians, the highest type of Roman officer.

"Luke of Antioch," the centurion repeated when Luke was presented. "I knew a boy once by that name." Then his face broke into a smile. "Of course I remember your face now; you are the foster son of Theophilus. What of Peter?" he asked, turning to Mark. "I wrote asking him to come here if he could."

"That is why we came," Mark explained. "Peter is imprisoned and we need your help."

"Agrippa has also taken my betrothed, Thecla of Iconium," Luke added.

"So Herod finally dared lay hands on Peter." Cornelius's fists clenched until the marks of his nails showed in the palms. "I have been afraid this would happen, for Agrippa believes he can gain anything he wishes from the Emperor Claudius. Perhaps he is right," he continued. "Tiberius was harsh, but just. Caligula was a monster, and this Claudius is little better. He and Agrippa were very close in Rome."

"We were hoping you could help us," Mark said. "But with such strong forces against us——"

Cornelius interrupted him: "When does Herod go to Caesarea for the celebration in his honor?"

"Within a few days," Luke said. "He told me yesterday that he would not do anything to Peter until his return."

"Then we have a chance. Galba, the chief captain of the prison in Jerusalem, is my friend. He hates both Herod and Geta. But we will need money for bribes."

Luke told him of the chest of gold which Herod had given him and the emeralds for Thecla. "Excellent." Cornelius applauded. "We will use Herod's own gold to thwart his purpose. You and Mark must rest now, Luke, while I make some preparations and order a chariot for tonight. We can be in Jerusalem in the morning, but I shall have to hide in the hills until Herod is gone, for he hates me. If he knew I was in the city he might even take Peter and the girl to Caesarea with him to make sport for the crowd at the games."

"But Jewish law forbids such things as games," Mark protested. "Would he dare to defy Moses?"

"Herod is a Jew only because he was born one, and it is convenient to give lip service to your religion," Cornelius pointed out. "Underneath he is as cruel as Caligula or Claudius. He even revived the old Roman sport of lashing condemned political prisoners to young bulls and turning the lions upon them. And I am sorry to say that Caesarea, being a Roman rather than a Jewish city, approves of the sport." Then, seeing the despair on Luke's face, he put an arm about the young man's shoulder. "But cheer up, Luke. We may be able to save your betrothed yet."

ix

Cornelius hid in the hills outside the city while Luke and Mark made their way into Jerusalem on foot. There was no further news of Peter and Thecla, who had been swallowed up in the prison as completely as if buried alive. To keep from thinking of what might be happening to Thecla, Luke threw himself into the work at the surgery, which had accumulated during his absence. Dead tired at the end of the day, he slept through the night. Shortly after sunrise the news came that Herod Agrippa had departed for Caesarea and the great festival which he was staging there a few days later in honor of the return of the Emperor

Claudius from his victorious campaign in Britain. When Luke learned that neither Thecla nor Peter had been in the train of the King his hopes began to rise a little. Mark went immediately for Cornelius, and everyone was full of hope again, but Luke could not get out of his mind the warning of Agabus that Thecla would bear him no sons.

When Cornelius returned that night, his face drawn with weariness, there was a look of satisfaction in his eyes. "It is arranged," he told them quietly. "Galba will assign special men to guard Peter tomorrow. At midnight he will walk out of the prison. All the guards will be so occupied as not to see him and therefore will be able to swear that they had nothing to do with his escape."

"And Thecla," Luke urged. "What of her?"

Cornelius turned to him, his face grave. "Thecla is not in the prison, Luke."

"But she was taken there! Agabus saw her enter."

"Herod has taken Agabus with him to Caesarea, but I learned that he told you the truth. Thecla was taken to prison with Peter, but she defied Herod when he had her brought to his apartment. The soldiers told me he was so angry that he sent her back to the prison, vowing to kill her by torture. Geta and a special group of guards took her away from the prison, but Galba did not know where they went."

Stunned by the terrible news that Thecla was in the hands of Herod's infamous torturer, Luke could only sit dumbly, unable to think, until Cornelius's hand on his shoulder brought him from the momentary stupor. "All is not lost, Luke," he said kindly. "Peter and Thecla were in the same part of the prison. Galba told me that. And when Peter is released tomorrow night, he may be able to tell us something more of the girl."

"But what can we do?" Luke asked hopelessly.

"If we can find out where she is I will use some of Galba's men and take your betrothed from Geta by force. Herod will be occupied in Caesarea, and before he can stop us, you and Thecla can escape by way of Joppa and a fishing vessel."

With that small solace Luke had to be content, but the ominous words of Agabus still kept running through his mind, dimming any hope he might have had.

It was a grave but optimistic group who waited the next night at the home of John Mark for news of Peter's release. Barnabas and Paul were filled with a quiet satisfaction, for they had finally gotten from James and the elders a decision approving the admission of Gentiles to the Christian faith. Now that there could be no preaching in Jerusalem until Agrippa ceased his persecution, Paul and Barnabas were anxious to return to Antioch and begin their missionary journey, while John Mark was to take Peter into the hills of Galilee after his release, where he would be safe from Herod's soldiers.

Cornelius was at the prison, waiting to spirit Peter away as soon as he emerged from the gate, and John Mark had a cart ready to take the big disciple into the hills. But an hour before midnight a girl who had been helping Mary serve rushed into the house, crying, "Peter is at the gate."

"That is impossible," Mark said. "He will not be released for another hour."

"It is Peter," the girl insisted. "I know his voice." And when Luke went out to see, it was indeed Peter who stood there, calmly smiling.

Pandemonium filled the small house then. Everyone hurried to embrace Peter, and there were alternate weeping and laughing over his safe delivery from the hands of Herod Agrippa. In the excitement Luke was not able to ask about Thecla. Then there was a knock on the outer door, and he went to open it. Cornelius came in, his face grave. "A strange thing has happened, Luke," he said. "Peter came out of the prison by another entrance about half an hour ago. Galba discovered it and came to tell me. But no one knows where he went."

"Peter is here," Luke told him.

"Thank God! I was afraid he had been spirited away somewhere."

"How did he escape, then?" Luke asked.

"No one knows, and I could not inquire closely. It may be that our plans miscarried and those inside the prison released him earlier than we had planned. I must question Peter about it."

But Peter could not help, for to him the escape was a true miracle. His fetters had been removed earlier by the guards, and when he pushed the door of his cell it had opened, as had the other gates between him and freedom. Peter had simply walked out of the prison as if there had been no locks or bars.

"It is a true miracle!" Paul cried. "God has set you free, Peter, to show his power over Herod." And not even Probus, who usually doubted miracles, offered to disagree. As Cornelius had said, a miscarriage of their plans could have released Peter earlier, or a miracle could really have happened. No one would ever know for certain.

When the hubbub finally quieted enough for Luke and Cornelius to ask about Thecla, Peter did have some news. "The girl was brought before Herod," he told them. "He offered to make her his concubine, but she spurned him. Our cells were close together, and she told me about it when she was brought back. Herod was so angry that he swore he would have her killed." He hesitated, as if there were more that he did not want to tell.

"Go on, Peter," Luke urged. "I want to know the worst."

"I heard the guards talking when the torturer came for her," Peter said then. "Thecla will be thrown to the beasts during the celebration at Caesarea. She was spirited away so that none here would know of Herod's plans for her."

Not even Luke's worst fears had conjured up anything like this. His thoughts went back to that day in the amphitheater at Antioch, to the young man and girl standing there proudly facing death. Then he had been filled with horror, although the victims had been strangers. And Herod had even more barbarous ways of executing those he condemned, such as lashing them to bulls before turning the lions into the arena, so that the spectators could enjoy a greater thrill as the fear-crazed animal fought for its life with a helpless human victim upon its back. Suddenly he could control himself no longer. "If God is just and all-powerful, as you claim him to be," he burst out, "how could he let Thecla be thrown to the lions?"

"Question not the will of God, Luke!" Paul shouted angrily. But Peter came over and took Luke by the shoulders. "I can understand your bewilderment, Luke," he said gently. "But the ways of God are often beyond the comprehension of man, and we must simply trust that his will is best. If it be the will of God, your Thecla will be saved."

Luke clung to Peter for a moment, like a child seeking assurance and protection from a parent. And as he did so he felt a new strength of purpose come into being within him. He raised his head then, his gaze clear and determined. "I am going to Caesarea tonight," he told them.

"I will go with you," Probus said at once.

"And I," Cornelius affirmed quietly.

"What can you do, Luke?" Mark cried. "You would be helpless against Herod and the power of Rome."

"If it is possible to save Thecla from Herod, I shall do it," Luke said quietly. "And if not, then I hope to die with her."

His determination heartened them all. Barnabas, Paul, Peter, and Mark all offered to go, but it was decided that Peter should flee at once to the hills of Galilee with John Mark as they had planned, the same hills from which many another rebel against injustice had defied the Herods and Rome. Cornelius, Probus, and Luke, traveling by military chariot, could reach Caesarea before the games when Herod planned to satiate his blood lust. Barnabas and Paul would travel the same road more slowly with Glaucus, who was still weak. "If you are successful, Luke," Barnabas said as he was leaving the house, "go to the house of Philip near the water. He is one of the Seven and respected by all in that city. And if you fail"—the red-haired man's voice broke—"I commend you to God."

It was early morning before Cornelius could obtain a large chariot for them and two swift horses to pull it. As they left the city the sun was already gilding the tops of the mountains to the east. Travelers bound from Jerusalem to Caesarea sometimes went to Joppa by land and thence by water to the capital of the Roman province. More often they took the Central Highway leading northwestward from the Holy City to Antipatris, thence along the Via Maris, the ancient Way of the Sea between Egypt and Mesopotamia, as far as Pirathon, and again westward to Caesarea on the coastal road. It was customary for land travelers to spend the night at Antipatris, but since they reached that city before nightfall, Luke, Probus, and Cornelius pushed on along the Via Maris to Pirathon.

At Pirathon they found quarters at an inn, and Luke fell asleep as soon as he lay down, exhausted from the days of worry and traveling. All along the road they heard talk of the great festival which Herod Agrippa was holding in Caesarea. The games which would climax the celebration would be held on the day after the morrow, giving them about twenty-four hours after their arrival in Caesarea in which to try to help Thecla.

It was well after midnight when Luke was awakened suddenly by a strange sensation, a feeling as if a giant hand had lifted the floor beneath him and shaken it. The timbers of the building groaned, and somewhere in the inn a jar tumbled to the hard floor with a crash. Probus, who was sleeping beside Luke, sat up. "What is it?" he asked sleepily.

Again the shaking came, this time less severe. "It is nothing but an earthquake," Probus said in disgust, and lay down again. Antioch was often called "the city of earthquakes," and this whole coast was often subject to them. When there were no more tremors they fell quickly asleep again.

A dismal scene greeted them in the morning. As so often happened after earthquakes, rain was pouring in sheets outside, blotting out all vision more than a few yards away. While the innkeeper served breakfast he told them that the damage had been particularly great along the road between Pirathon and Caesarea. Already peasants were coming in to report that houses had been shaken down and stone fences broken apart by the tremors. Cornelius went out to the stables after the meal but returned, shaking his head. "We cannot travel in such a storm," he said gravely. "The horses would not be able to see the road, and we would go over the side of the mountains."

"But we must get there," Luke protested. "Tomorrow is the day of the games."

"The games will not be until the middle of the day, and we are little more than a half day's journey from Caesarea. If the rain lessens we can still get there before nightfall."

Through the morning Luke watched the water pouring down, and his spirits grew lower and lower. But shortly after noon the sky lightened a little, and by midafternoon Cornelius was able to order the horses hitched to the chariot and they set out toward Caesarea once more. Progress was slow, for the road was badly washed, and a broken chariot wheel now would mean disaster. Besides, the road was clogged with travelers, on horses, in carts and carriages, and on foot, for the games tomorrow were attracting a great crowd. It was rumored that Herod would scatter a vast sum in gold for the crowd in token of his pleasure at the return of his friend, Emperor Claudius, from the fabulously successful campaign in Britain, where elephants had carried archers and spearmen to break the ranks of the Britons and send them reeling to their deaths. And some said a beautiful young girl would be bound naked to a bull and sent to die under the claws of the lions.

Hourly the press of people on the road became greater. Finally there was no moving, and word was passed back that the road was blocked. Cornelius went ahead on foot, his uniform and commanding presence opening a way for him when the others would have been held fast by the crowd. When he returned his face was glum. "The earthquake shook a mass of rock and dirt into the pass," he reported. "Not even foot travelers can get through now."

"When will the road be opened again?" Luke asked anxiously.

"They will work all night, but it will be at least early morning before we could get through."

"Then we are beaten," Probus said hopelessly. "God must indeed be working against us this time. Even if we got to Caesarea, it would be too late to work out any way to help Thecla."

"I am afraid you are right," Cornelius agreed. "If there were only some other road."

"There must be paths across the mountains." Luke was grasping at anything which seemed to offer a shred of hope.

Cornelius looked up at the towering crags. "I have lived in Caesarea many years," he said, "and have traveled this way a number of times, but I never heard of another road."

"But there must be," Luke said stubbornly. "Someone in the crowd may know of it." He climbed up on the rim of the chariot. A hundred or more people were milling about on the road immediately ahead and behind them, cursing, grumbling, or merely waiting patiently for the road to be opened again. "Does any among you know a way over the mountain?" he shouted. "I must reach Caesarea by morning on a matter of life or death."

There was no answer, nothing except shaken heads from the crowd.

"A hundred sesterces to any man who can lead me over the mountain and set me on the road to Caesarea," he shouted in desperation.

There were murmurs of interest from the crowd, nothing more. Then Luke saw an old man on a mule prodding his animal through the crowd. "Can you help me, good father?" he called.

"I know a way," the old man mumbled. "But it is narrow and can be traversed only on foot."

"Can I get horses on the other side?" Luke asked, his hopes soaring at this unexpected aid.

"Y-yes," the old man said. "My son has mules at his farm on the other side of the mountain."

Luke jumped down from the chariot and opened his purse. "Here are twenty sesterces," he said. "The rest is yours when I reach your son's house and the mules."

"The way is rough," the old man warned, "and you will need the feet of a mountain goat."

"I will chance that," Luke told him, and turned to the others. "You two can wait and come on through when the road is cleared. If I fail to make the city, you will find me somewhere along the road beyond the mountain range."

"Two will have a better chance of getting over the mountain pass than one," Probus urged. "Cornelius can come through in the morning with the chariot."

"Probus is right, Luke," the centurion agreed. "Only one of us can drive the horses; the difficult job is going to be climbing the mountain paths."

And so Luke and Probus followed the old peasant off the road and along a path that wound up the mountainside. Sometimes it was little more than a narrow ledge, with yawning depths below them and only the bare rock wall of the crags to cling to. The going was hard, even for Luke and Probus, and the old man had to stop frequently to get his breath. During one of those rest periods Probus asked, "Have you formed any plan of action, Luke, once you get to Caesarea?"

"Nothing except to find Thecla and go with her into the arena. When Agrippa sees me there I hope he will stop the execution for fear of setting Theophilus and Petronius against him. If not, Thecla and I can die together."

"It is a forlorn hope," Probus said dourly. "Herod is swollen with power, and with Claudius back in Rome I believe he would dare almost anything."

"Can you think of anything better?"

"Nothing very practical," Probus admitted. "Herod will certainly not be expecting us, and the element of surprise will be in our favor, small as it is. I am sure we can both get into the amphitheater with the safe-conduct, and I might even get close enough to the throne to stab him in the back with this." He took from his belt a long, narrow dagger.

"But you would be killed by the guards."

"Perhaps so, perhaps not. There would be quite a commotion." Probus smiled wryly. "Having been in a few riots, I have learned to take care of myself."

Luke shook his head. "I am resigned to dying with Thecla, Probus, but you must not endanger your own life because of me. You saved me once on the cliffs above Bithynia. That is enough to ask of any man."

"God will give me what I deserve," the apothecary said philosophically. "How better can a man deserve life than by trying to save another?"

Darkness caught them less than halfway across the mountain range, and the old man stopped on a small plateau, flatly refusing to go on until the moon rose about midnight. He insisted that they would only fall in the darkness and lose their lives, since the way was even more dangerous ahead of them than behind. They had no choice but to agree when their guide lay down and began snoring. Luke and Probus propped their backs against the rocks and waited for the moon to rise.

Luke did not mean to sleep, but weariness overcame him. It could have been the similarity of the small plateau to the glen where he and Apollonius had buried Silvanus that brought on the dream. Or perhaps it was another force, one watching over them there close to the mountaintop. In the dream he stood at the edge of the glen where Probus had driven the chariot over the cliff, with the small cairn of stones marking the grave of Silvanus at his back. As plainly as if he were really there he could see Bithynia and the distant road winding along the face of the mountains from the heights to the valley below. Two small figures were walking down that road hand and hand.

And now, as if his eyes had been given the power of extra vision, the figures grew nearer until he could distinguish their faces. The girl was Thecla, and he recognized the man as himself. They walked down the road happily, eyes fixed eagerly upon the plain of Bithynia, their feet hardly touching the path. In the dream Luke could even read their thoughts, the happiness they shared at the prospect of reaching the beautiful land below them at the foot of the mountain and the realization of their dreams of the future.

Then with a sudden horror he saw the road begin to crumble ahead of the two lovers and tried to call out to them, to warn them against the danger. But no words came, and he could only watch, unable to warn them while they continued down the road, oblivious of the danger. When at last he found his voice to shout, "Thecla! Thecla!" it was too late, and she slipped from the road to go plummeting down to the rocks below while he watched, frozen with horror.

"Luke! Luke!" At first he thought it was Thecla calling to him, then he opened his eyes and saw Probus bending over him, shaking him. "Wake up, Luke," Probus cried. "You were having a nightmare."

Luke sat up. The moon was already up, but the old man still snored on the grass. "It is late," he said in sudden apprehension. "Look how high the moon is."

"It was a lucky thing for us that you had a nightmare," Probus said as he went to wake up their guide. "Your groaning awakened me, or we would have slept here until morning and never made Caesarea in time."

The dream was still vivid in Luke's thoughts as they continued their climb in the bright moonlight. Had God chosen this way to reassure him that he and Thecla would still take the road to Bithynia? he wondered. But if so, why had Thecla fallen from the road, leaving him to go on alone? Or had some higher force than their own weary minds sent the dream to awaken them before they lost all chance of helping Thecla? Then the way became steeper and more perilous, forcing him to keep his thoughts upon the job at hand.

x

Herod the Great, builder of the magnificent temple at Jerusalem, had also reconstructed the old city of Samaria and renamed it Sebaste, Greek for Augustus. Within sight of Sebaste on the coast he built a new city which he named Caesarea. It was the military headquarters for the Roman government of the district. The first Herod had also transformed the shallow harbor into a safe anchorage by building a giant stone mole reaching in a half-mile crescent out into the waters of the sea. Upon the hills close to the water he had erected a great amphitheater, and nearby a palace and a citadel similar to the grim fortress of Antonia in Jerusalem.

As Luke and Probus rode down from the foothills on the mules they had purchased from their guide's son, the sun was bright upon the stone seats, great columns, and splendid façade of the amphitheater. Long lines of people converged upon the huge stadium from all parts of the city, and already the seats were half filled.

The roads were crowded, as were the streets, and it was more than an hour before they were able to make their way to the theater itself.

Long before they reached it, the roars of the crowd told them the games had begun. As they rode into the city they rehearsed once more their plan of action. Luke would try to reach the lower levels where Thecla would be confined before her appearance in the arena, while Probus would use the safe-conduct to make his way to the first level above the arena, where the boxes of the rich stood and the shining, golden throne prepared for Herod Agrippa. At some tense moment in the games, when attention would be drawn upon the arena, he would try to get close enough to the King to thrust the sharp stiletto he carried inside his cloak into Herod's body, hoping in the resulting confusion to make his escape. Somehow, in the tumult over Herod's murder, Luke would try to save Thecla. Both realized that theirs was a stratagem of desperation, far more likely to result in failure than success, with death at the hands of Herod's guards for both of them.

"Look!" Probus cried suddenly. "There is Agabus."

The old prophet stood beside the gate, as gaunt as ever in his dingy robe and sandals. "Beware the vengeance of the Lord," he shouted to the laughing throng entering the theater. "This day death will strike. Repent and seek God before his wrath is upon you."

Probus's eyes gleamed suddenly. "We may be able to use Agabus," he told Luke in a low voice. "Remember that Herod fears him. If we can make the prophet denounce the King before the crowd for abducting Thecla at the same time Herod sees that you are ready to die with her, he may relent for fear of both Roman justice and his God."

When Luke touched Agabus's arm the old prophet turned burning eyes upon him. "The girl you seek still lives, Luke of Antioch," he said at once. "But this day Herod will throw her to the beasts."

"Will you help us, Agabus?" Luke begged. "Will you go to Herod and denounce him for what he has done?"

The prophet gathered up his long robe. "The wicked shall perish and the righteous shall triumph," he intoned. "The Lord God has spoken, this day Herod shall die and the worms shall eat his body."

Luke hurriedly purchased tickets for them, counting out the gold with trembling fingers. Inside the amphitheater, Probus took Agabus and the tablet with the safe-conduct, for he would need it to reach the box where the King was directing the games. Luke must find his way to Thecla as best he could. The ticket seller told him that the gladiators were fighting now, whipping up the blood lust of the crowd in preparation for the *venatio,* when Thecla would be thrown to the lions.

With a pounding heart Luke made his way through the corridors that ran beneath the building, past the rooms where the gladiators awaited their turns. He could hear the roaring of the lions held ready at the very side of the arena itself, the barred doors of their cages operated by a huge lever so that the beasts could be released directly into the arena at the proper moment. Farther along he crossed the broad rutted corridor leading to the "Death Gate" and saw the death wagon itself waiting patiently for its load, the bridle of the horse secured to a ring in the wall while the driver enjoyed the games before hauling away his load of mutilated flesh. Luke carefully mapped in his mind the location of the various passages so that if by some miracle he and Thecla did escape he would not become lost here in the maze and be recaptured.

Where a narrow side corridor opened into the main one he came upon a guard, the first he had seen, and judged that Thecla must be confined nearby. "I am a physician," he announced in an authoritative tone. "King Herod has sent me to watch the girl and make certain that she does not strangle herself or take poison to cheat the King of his pleasure."

The man bowed respectfully before the King's physician and led him to a cell that opened on the side corridor. He unlocked the door and, when Luke entered, locked it again. Thecla was standing before a small barred window in the wall of the cell, the sun shining on her hair so that her head seemed ringed by a bright halo. Her face was uplifted to the rays while her lips moved in prayer. When she turned, a glad cry broke from her lips and she threw herself into Luke's arms. For a long moment neither of them could speak. Tears of joy were streaming down her cheeks and Luke's own eyes were wet. "Oh, my darling," she whispered. "I thought I would never see you again."

"Then you know——" He stopped.

"That I am to be thrown to the wild beasts? Yes, but I am not afraid. When people see through me how Jesus gives strength to those who believe in him, my death will not have been in vain. But how did you get here, Luke?"

He told her of Peter's release from prison, his dismay at learning that she had been taken away, and how he had fought to reach her. She touched his face then with loving fingers. "Surely in all the world there was never a love so great as ours, Luke," she said softly.

He kissed her fingers gently and went on to tell her of the plan he and Probus had evolved. It seemed more futile and hopeless now than ever, but the thought brought no despair. If it was necessary for him to die, too, he was ready, secure in the knowledge of their love. Then a new thought struck him and he told her of the dream last night on the mountain, when he had seen the two of them descending the road to Bithynia. "It must be an omen that we will escape," he said, but he did not tell her how the dream had ended.

"Bithynia," Thecla repeated softly. "I have been thinking a great deal about it these last few days, Luke. No matter what happens to me, you must go on with your plans. And when I am gone——"

"Don't say it," he begged. "There is still a chance of help."

"Then it can come only from God, Luke," she said. "Let us pray to him on our knees." Her hand in his, they dropped to their knees on the stone floor of the cell and prayed, Thecla for strength during the coming ordeal, and Luke for some miracle to save her. And as he prayed Luke felt a great peace begin to fill his soul. It was almost as if a quiet voice had spoken to him telling him not to be afraid.

When they rose from their knees Thecla said gently, "I could go out there happy, Luke, if I knew that you had found Jesus here in this cell with me."

He took both her hands and drew her gently to him. "I think I was very near to him just now, my dearest. Nearer than I have ever been before."

The tramp of marching feet in the corridor outside the cell warned them that Thecla's time had come, and they could only embrace hurriedly before the key of the guard grated in the lock and the door was flung open. The officer in charge of the guards took a tablet from beneath his arm and began to read:

"'Thecla of Iconium, having appeared before the presence of Herod Agrippa I, King of Judea, Samaria, and Galilee by the grace of the Emperor Claudius, you have been judged guilty of heinous crimes, as well as of being a follower of the pretender, Jesus of Nazareth. It is therefore the will of King Herod and the Emperor Claudius that you shall die this day by being lashed to a bull and sent among the lions.'"

He put down the tablet and, stepping quickly up to Thecla, seized the collar of her stola and ripped it completely from her body, leaving her nude save for a small apron covering her loins. Instinctively the girl cringed before the gaze of the soldiers, covering her breasts with her hands and bowing her head while her cheeks crimsoned with shame.

The rude violation of Thecla's virginal beauty was more than Luke could stand. With a strangled cry he launched himself upon the officer. Taken by surprise, the man crashed back against the wall of the cell. Then one of the soldiers brought the butt of his sword sharply against Luke's temple, felling him. As he sank into dark oblivion he heard a single cry of anguish from Thecla, then knew no more.

Luke struggled from a painful haze in which the walls of the cell seemed to throb with a mighty force. Dazedly he wiped away the blood which was trickling down across his face from a cut in his scalp. Slowly, then, memory of the recent past returned, the stripping of Thecla before the soldiers, his own futile attack, and the blow which had rendered him unconscious. Putting his fingers to his temple and finding only a shallow cut, Luke realized that he owed his life to the fact that the soldier had used the butt of the sword instead of the blade, else his skull would have been split. But he would far rather have died with Thecla than to have been left lying there, unable to help while she was clawed to death by the lions.

But had she been killed yet? The blood around the cut was still fluid when he touched it; no clot had formed, as would have occurred if more than a few minutes had elapsed. There might still be time to reach Thecla.

Luke pushed himself to his feet and staggered to the gate, clinging to the bars when the room dipped and swayed about him. The gate was not locked now, and he pushed it open and stumbled out into the corridor, leaning against the wall until his head cleared enough so that he could stand upright. Some instinctive reasoning made him turn toward the waves of sound rocketing through the corridors from the arena. There was no time to look for a weapon, but when he stumbled over something and fell to his knees, he saw that it was the handle of a battle-ax dropped by a wounded gladiator being borne from the arena. Picking up the ax, he thrust it under his cloak where it would not be seen.

The sound of cheering grew louder, and Luke knew that he was near the entrance to the arena itself. He moved faster now, urged on by the need to discover what had happened to Thecla. Only one man was at the entrance to the arena when he reached it, a burly fellow whose duty it was to operate the long lever by which the doors of the animal cages were opened, letting the roaring and growling beasts out upon the field. The man did not try to stop him, however, when he moved out into the bright sunshine of the white-sanded arena.

No one noticed Luke, for all eyes were upon the throne of Herod. He saw Thecla, hardly fifty feet away from him at the side of the arena, her nearly nude body lashed to the back of a young bull which was tethered by ropes in the hands of three slaves. Neither the crowd nor the slaves holding the bull were watching the girl, however. All eyes were directed to the golden throne of Herod Agrippa which occupied the largest box and was fully visible from where Luke was standing near the arena entrance.

"People of Israel." Herod's voice rang out over the amphitheater. "I bring you this great spectacle in honor of the safe return of the Emperor to Rome."

A roar of applause rocketed upward to the topmost seat of the great theater, and for a moment Herod could not continue. Luke could see him standing upon the dais that supported the throne, his rich purple robe shining in the sun only a little less brilliantly than the crown upon his head and the jeweled scepter in his hand.

"Soon I will order the lions released," Herod shouted, "and a cursed Nazarene will be sent to death under the claws of the beasts. But first I would give my people a small token of the generosity of your King." At his words a hundred slaves in different parts of the amphitheater began to scatter gold pieces to the crowd as a sower would scatter seeds. Some of the coins fell into the arena, and Luke saw the slaves holding the bull to which Thecla was bound picking them up surreptitiously.

Then a stentorian voice sounded: *"It is the voice of a god and not a man."* Luke saw that the words had been shouted by Geta, the torturer, who stood at the far side of the arena evidently for just this purpose. And as if they had been waiting for this signal, hundreds of well-rehearsed voices took up the cry, until the crowd joined in chanting, *"It is the voice of a god and not a man!"* over and over in a swelling torrent of sound.

The railing before which Herod stood was not more than a dozen feet over Luke's head. He could even see a fatuous smile break over Herod's face at this far from spontaneous tribute. Then another figure appeared suddenly on the dais beside the magnificently garbed King. With his height, his long beard, the flapping gray robe, and the bony forefinger lifted like a pillar of warning, Agabus was the very personification of doom. Luke saw the King turn startled eyes upon the old prophet, then the voice of Agabus boomed out over the hum of the crowd:

"Repent, ye children of Israel. Follow not this false King who has led you into idolatry, for this day God shall smite him for his sins."

Herod's face purpled with rage and he took a step toward the old prophet, raising the golden scepter in his right hand. Luke could see the maniacal rage in the King's face, as could everyone in the great theater, when he struck Agabus with the jeweled symbol of his authority, bludgeoning him viciously again and again.

The prophet's upraised arms dropped to his sides, and he collapsed upon the dais at Herod's feet, a crumpled pile of dirty gray robe and matted hair from which blood was already seeping where his scalp had been torn by the jewels of the scepter. For a moment Herod stood with the bloody scepter in his hand, staring in horror at the body of the old prophet with whose life his own had been tied by the soothsayer. Something of the terror that gripped the King was transmitted to the crowd, too, for a sudden hush fell over the entire theater. In that silence Herod's strangled cry could be plainly heard, and the crash as the scepter dropped from powerless fingers. The King groped for the rail before him with one hand, while the other clutched at his throat. Then as death seized him his body collapsed across the railing and fell to the white sand of the arena below, the royal robes making a splash of brilliant purple against the snowy sand in the bright sunlight.

Stunned by the shock of the King's death, the whole theater was gripped by some of the fear which had been in the King's face those last few seconds. The bull to which Thecla was tied sensed the terror, as animals do, and, rearing up suddenly, tore the tethering rope from the hand of one of the slaves. Then, wheeling, it plunged toward the entrance to the arena, jerking the ropes from the hands of the other two slaves. Free except for the helpless girl lashed to its back, the bull plunged instinctively for the passage through which it had been led into the arena.

Luke was almost bowled over by the rush of the bull, but, still clutching the battle-ax he had picked up in the corridor, he managed to seize one of the ropes that bound Thecla to the animal. At the gate leading from the arena the bull swerved away from the crumpled figure of the King lying on the sand, striking its shoulder against one of the pillars supporting the gate, close to where the lever hung which opened the cages. The man who controlled the lever turned and ran, while the crazed animal stopped uncertainly, quivering with terror.

The momentary stopping of the bull gave Luke the opportunity he needed. Swinging the bloody battle-ax in both hands, knowing that the animal must be felled with one blow if he were to make full use of the momentary advantage which had been given him, Luke drove the blade with all his force into the bull's skull between the horns, splitting the bony case. The animal crashed to the sand, and while the body still quivered in death, Luke worked desperately with the blade of the ax, slashing the ropes that bound Thecla.

Thecla had fainted, and with her body limp against the ropes, it was only a few seconds' work to free her. Dropping the ax, Luke lifted her in his arms. Already, however, the slaves had recovered their wits and, with the guards, were converging upon him. Desperately Luke glanced around for something to hold them back, to give him time enough to escape through the corridors with Thecla.

Then his eye struck the lever that controlled the cages and, seizing it with one hand, he let his own weight and that of Thecla bear upon the lever. Hinges groaned as the barred gates of the cages were lifted, freeing the animals. Then the lions plunged from the cages, some to rush upon the body of Herod Agrippa, some to tear at the still quivering body of the bull, while the screams of the guards and slaves fleeing in terror filled the arena.

Luke wasted no time watching the effects of his quick thinking.

With Thecla's limp body across his shoulder he raced through the corridor toward where the death cart waited, the horse still tethered to a ring in the wall. Placing Thecla in the cart and covering her with his cloak, Luke quickly untied the reins and leaped upon the seat, urging animal and cart toward the Death Gate.

No one blocked their way as the cart rumbled from the amphitheater into the bright sunshine, for the gate was unguarded. In the street outside Luke slowed the cart to a more sedate pace so as not to attract attention. But he had little fear now, for the streets were almost deserted and the pandemonium back in the arena would keep the guards busy for a while trying to prevent a riot.

Thecla was already beginning to stir and warm color was returning to her cheeks. Luke had time now to feel a surge of elation, for with Herod dead and Thecla safely out of the hands of Geta and his soldiers, Cornelius could protect them and smuggle them out of the province, perhaps by means of a coastal vessel, as he had suggested. One thing only marred his happiness, the uncertainty about what had happened to Probus and Agabus.

They were almost to the house of Philip when Luke saw a chariot being driven furiously through the streets behind the cart. For a moment he feared it might be pursuing them, but when the vehicle came nearer he could distinguish the tall figure of Cornelius at the reins and beside him the familiar form of the apothecary. When the chariot pulled up beside the cart he saw the old prophet sitting on the floor with a bloody bandage wound about his head, apparently little the worse for his experience at the hands of Herod Agrippa. Death had cheated Herod in the end, for it had been his own body, not Thecla's, which had been mangled by the lions in the arena.

xi

Paul, Barnabas, and Glaucus arrived from Jerusalem the next day, and there was much rejoicing at the house of Philip when they found that Thecla had been saved—miraculously, it seemed—from the horrible fate to which Herod had condemned her. The death of Herod forced the Roman authorities to assume the reins of government until the Emperor could name a new king for the Jews, and with Cornelius in charge of the Roman guard at Caesarea, there was no longer any danger to the Christians. Paul immediately began to preach, and soon great crowds were following him to hear him speak of Jesus and the imminence of his return to earth.

Paul seemed to take the dramatic death of Herod Agrippa almost as a personal triumph, a sign from God that the new venture of carrying the teachings of Jesus to the Gentiles had divine approval. Luke did not object, but Paul's bland assumption of credit to divine interference irked Probus, and during one of the evening discussions at the home of Philip the controversy flared into angry words. "Herod's death was not a miracle, Paul," Probus insisted. "It occurred from natural causes."

"Mock not God's work, Probus," Paul snapped. "You might suffer the same fate as Agrippa."

"Agrippa died from plethora," Probus said wearily. "Luke warned him in Jerusalem that it might happen at any time."

Barnabas, always a peacemaker between Paul and those who were antagonized by his positiveness, stepped into the breach. "Let us hear what Luke has to say about it," he suggested.

"Herod was suffering from a severe plethora," Luke said, "and I did warn him in Jerusalem that he might die suddenly at any time."

"But you bled him and removed the danger," Paul objected.

"Relief by bleeding is only temporary," Probus countered promptly. "Thecla heard Luke tell Herod that too."

"Yes," Thecla agreed. "Luke did warn Herod that the condition would return."

"But why would Herod die at just that moment?" Paul demanded, "unless it was the hand of God which struck him down?" He turned to Luke. "Can you prove that Herod's death was from a natural cause, Luke?"

"No," Luke admitted. The question was unfair, of course, for such a thing could not be proved, but there was no use in prolonging the argument.

"Then I shall go on preaching that God struck Herod down for his sins," Paul said. "Those who stand against Jesus will always fail."

"You give in too much to Paul, Luke," the apothecary complained when Paul had left the room with Barnabas. "First it was your bleeding that saved Apollonius at Tarsus, but you let Paul claim the credit. And now he is taking the death of Herod as a personal triumph. What right does Paul have to consider himself the personal representative of God on earth? You know that what he experienced on the road to Damascus was nothing but a hallucination."

"I don't think I understand, Luke," Thecla said, frowning. "Didn't Paul really see and hear Jesus on the road that day?"

"We have no way of knowing for certain, dear," Luke explained. "As Probus says, people sometimes imagine things like that so vividly that for them it becomes a reality."

"And the death of Herod? Do you really think it just happened?"

"You saw Herod's face after he struck Agabus, Luke," Probus said. "It was stark fear that killed him, or rather an attack of apoplexy brought on by fear for his own life when he thought Agabus was dead."

"Herod did say he could not die as long as Agabus lived," Thecla agreed thoughtfully. "But that means Paul could be wrong, that we all could be wrong, even about Jesus." The agony of doubt was in her voice.

Luke took her hands in his. "You must not lose your faith, Thecla," he said gently. "Probus and I see things differently from people like Paul. Sometimes I think God puts these doubts in our minds so that our convictions will be stronger when we have overcome them."

"How would you explain what happened?" she asked.

"I have been thinking about this whole question of miracles," Luke said. "And I am beginning to believe that God works more often through the hands and minds of men to accomplish his purposes than he does by direct intervention."

"Just as he used you to save the scroll when Stephen was stoned?" Thecla suggested.

"Yes. And as he used Cornelius to effect Peter's release from prison."

"But Paul acts as if he had caused the death of Herod himself," Probus said.

"Does it make any difference who gets the credit?" Luke asked gently. "The important thing is that we were able to save Thecla. And you were just as much responsible for that as I was."

Probus threw up his hands. "You have one fault, Luke. You think too much of other people and not enough of yourself."

"Thecla answered that for me in Jerusalem, Probus. She said that only by giving up concern for self and self-pride can the spirits of men rise above the limits of their bodies to a higher plane of peace and happiness."

"You can carry humility too far," Probus grumbled. "But I will at least promise not to argue with Paul any more about it."

"I knew you would," Luke said warmly. "For all his faults, Paul is very important to the world because he has the gift of making men believe the things he believes in. And the way of Jesus can certainly never hurt mankind, no matter who teaches it."

Since the threat of Herod no longer hung over the Christians in Jerusalem, Peter returned there immediately from Galilee. Mark came on to Caesarea, for he was very anxious to go with his uncle Barnabas and the others back to the new church at Antioch, where such great things were being accomplished.

They reached Antioch without event, and Luke took Thecla and Glaucus with him to the palace of Theophilus, where they were received warmly by the Roman jurist. Neither Thecla nor Mark had spent much time in Antioch before, and there was much for Luke to show them in his home city while they waited for the ship which would take Luke, Thecla, and Glaucus another step on their journey to Iconium.

As usual, Paul worked during the day at his trade of tentmaking and spent the evenings going from house to house, preaching to small groups. Against Luke's advice he continued to drive himself mercilessly, so eager was he to tell the story of what had happened to him on the road to Damascus and the dramatic events in Jerusalem and Caesarea.

If Paul's spirit was strong, however, his fever-weakened body was not. Two days before Luke was to sail Paul was carried to the house of Barnabas from one of his evening sermons in the grip of a terrible rigor and half unconscious. His teeth were chattering and his body was blue with cold in spite of the blankets and warm stones with which Luke immediately surrounded his body in the bed.

"Is it the old fever?" Barnabas asked anxiously.

"I think so," Luke agreed. "But it may be several days before we can tell."

The next day Paul was still seriously ill, and although Luke was fairly certain that he was merely suffering from a severe recurrence of his old fever, there was no way to be sure that something more serious had not occurred. Thecla herself raised the question which was troubling Luke that evening. "You cannot leave him, Luke," she said, "if he is still this sick tomorrow."

"Perhaps Thecla and Glaucus could delay sailing until Paul is better," Barnabas suggested. "Then you could go with them, Luke."

Luke shook his head. "The storms will be coming soon. This may be the last ship leaving for Perga in several months. Thecla and Glaucus will have to go on, regardless."

Thecla put her hand on Luke's arm. "We all know how important Paul is to the work of Christ, Luke, and you are the only physician whom everyone trusts." Her voice broke. "I—I want us to be together as much as you do. But Christ's work is more important even than our love. You must stay here and look after Paul."

Luke somehow managed to smile, although his heart was heavy with the thought that it might be months before he saw Thecla again. "We are young, dear," he agreed. "And I can always come on to Iconium by land when Paul is out of danger."

But as he watched the carriage bear Thecla and Glaucus away to

Seleucia and their ship, Luke could not help remembering the dream on the mountaintop that night when he had watched two figures walking happily down the road toward Bithynia, only to see the way crumble before them and Thecla's body go plummeting down to the rocks below. Almost echoing this scene was the warning voice of Agabus, "The girl will bear you no sons, Luke of Antioch."

Book Four: THE TRAVELERS

*And a vision appeared to Paul in the night;
There stood a man of Macedonia, and prayed
him, saying, Come over into Macedonia and
help us.*

The Acts 16:9

PAUL RECOVERED slowly from the attack of fever which had come so near to ending his life upon his return from Jerusalem. The apostle was not a willing patient, and if Luke had not held a tight rein over him he would have overtaxed his strength again and again, as he had done on other occasions.

Some of the loneliness Luke felt for Thecla was alleviated by the strong bond of companionship which grew up between him and John Mark. They were more nearly of the same age than most of the others who were active in the church at Antioch, and both were intelligent, sincere, devoted to the teachings of Jesus, and eager to show others the Way. From Mark, Luke learned many things which had not been in the scroll. He heard again the story which Peter had told in Jerusalem, how he had denied Christ on that night of agony. And he heard, too, the story of the crucifixion of Jesus as witnessed by Peter and the others and how Mary Magdalene, Joanna, and Mary, the mother of James, had found the tomb empty on the third day. Mark knew nothing of the present whereabouts of the women who had come to the tomb except that Mary was said to have returned to her home in Magdala at the time of the first persecution of the Christians in Jerusalem and the stoning of Stephen.

When Paul was finally strong enough to travel they decided, upon Luke's advice, to go only a short distance on the first missionary journey. And since Barnabas had come from Cyprus, which lay some

177

eighty miles off the coast of Syria, that large island was selected as their first goal. They were influenced in this decision by the fact that Luke's old friend, Sergius Paulus, was now proconsul of Cyprus.

The trip was uneventful, and they came in time to the city of Paphos, where the headquarters of the Roman government for Cyprus was located. From the start Paul had been noticeably cool toward Mark. Nor was there any longer the close bond between Paul and Luke which had existed prior to the trip to Jerusalem and his betrothal to Thecla. Instead Paul seemed to have withdrawn into himself. Barnabas attributed it to his illness, but Luke was fairly certain that the change was closely related to his betrothal to Thecla and their plan to marry in Iconium.

Paphos was a flourishing city and an important center for the worship of the pagan goddess Aphrodite. Here, as in many other places in the Empire, the Romans had found it expedient to work in close co-operation with the hierarchy of priests who controlled the temple and through the worship of the goddess exerted a strong influence upon the people. There were, however, many Jews in Paphos and several synagogues. And since a brother of Barnabas was influential in one of these, Paul first began to preach there. As usual, after preaching to the Jews he went out into the streets, and soon great crowds of Gentiles followed him everywhere, moved by this new faith and its promises of eternal life through belief in Jesus and the resurrection.

Soon after their arrival in Paphos, Luke and Probus went to the palace of the proconsul to pay their respects. Sergius welcomed them warmly and asked them about their mission to the island. "I remember your speaking of the Nazarene, Luke," he said when they mentioned Jesus. "Tell me more of him."

"You should talk to Paul," Luke said. "He is far more eloquent than I."

"An intelligent man is moved more by simple truths than by eloquence," Sergius reminded him. "Leave the orators to those who are guided by their emotions rather than by their minds." Then his face grew more serious. "But be careful how you teach a new religion here in Paphos. Aphrodite is very strong, and the priests do not encourage other beliefs. Even Mithras has never gained a strong foothold on this island."

A slave brought refreshment and they talked of other things, of the near disastrous expedition to the border of Bithynia and the miracle which had saved Apollonius in Tarsus. Presently there was a knock on the door of the audience chamber and a strange figure entered. The man was tall, his height accentuated startlingly by a high conical cap and a robe that fell to the floor around shoes pointed up at the ends in the manner of Persian magicians. Both robe and cap were ornamented with astrologer's symbols and signs of the zodiac. These, plus a swarthy face, beaked nose, and pale blue eyes, gave the visitor an oddly macabre appearance.

"My astrologer, Elymas," Sergius introduced the newcomer. "This is Luke of Antioch, a physician, and Probus, an apothecary."

Elymas bowed. "The stars control the health of men," he said in deep tones. "So physicians, apothecaries, and astrologers have much in common."

"Except that horoscopes never cured gout, and even magicians sometimes need the healing knife of the surgeon," Probus reminded him.

The magician shrugged and turned to the proconsul. "Forgive me for interrupting, O noble Sergius. I must bring a matter of grave importance to your attention. Certain proselyte Jews arrived yesterday from Antioch and have been creating a disturbance by preaching an alien faith, the worship of one Christos."

"Do you mean the sect of the Nazarene, Jesus?"

"It is the same," Elymas admitted. "The leading Jews of the synagogues have requested me to ask that you refuse these people the right to speak here."

Sergius lifted his eyebrows. "Rome guarantees freedom of speech to its subjects so long as they introduce no new religions and do not seek to overthrow the Empire. It is my impression that Jesus advocated neither."

"But one of these newcomers, a man named Paul, preaches that Jesus will return from the dead and reign as King of the Jews."

Sergius turned to Luke. "Is Paul preaching such things?" he asked.

"The confusion is over the meaning of Jesus when he spoke of his kingdom," Luke explained. "It is of the spirit and not of the body."

Sergius turned back to the astrologer. "Tell the Jews that I will examine this man Paul and see if he speaks contrary to Roman law," he directed.

"Are these men of the group from Antioch?" Elymas asked.

"The stars should tell you that," Probus said sarcastically. "Why not consult them?"

The long fingers of the magician curled as if he were wishing them at the apothecary's throat. "The priests of Aphrodite complain against these men too, noble Sergius," he said. "This Paul is preaching that Aphrodite is a mockery and that Jesus will triumph over her."

Sergius frowned. From his viewpoint this was a more serious matter, for while the Jews were small in number, the priests were very powerful. According to tradition, the divine beauty had risen from the sea on the very shores of the older city some two miles away, where the great Temple of Aphrodite was located. Poets since Homer had sung of the worship of Aphrodite at Paphos, and models in silver of the mysterious goddess were almost as much in demand here as were the images of Artemis produced by the silversmiths of Ephesus. The opinions of the powerful priests of Aphrodite could not long be ignored by a Roman governor who wished to keep peace in his district.

"You may assure the priests that I will personally examine this Paul at once," Sergius told the astrologer again. "If he is breaking the law, he will be restrained."

The summons for Paul to appear before the proconsul came the next day, and he departed for the palace in high spirits, confident that he would be able to turn Sergius Paulus to Christ. The interview was a long one, and Paul returned with the news that Sergius had received him well, had listened intently, and been favorably impressed. The proconsul had not committed himself, however, and that evening a message came asking Luke to come to the palace. Sergius was having a mild flare-up of his gout, and while Luke was relieving some of the pain by applying leeches the Roman official said, "I was much impressed by Paul this morning, Luke. In fact, I am strongly tempted to believe in Jesus myself."

"His Way is the best rule of life for all men," Luke said. "I am sure of that."

"I think you are right. But I find it hard to accept Paul's belief in the resurrection of Jesus. Tell me something of your own experience with this faith, Luke."

Luke recounted to him the now familiar story, including the seemingly miraculous series of events which had culminated in the death of Herod Agrippa at Caesarea.

"Do you believe that Jesus is the son of God?" Sergius asked.

"At first I did not," Luke admitted, "although I have always believed in his Way. Now, however, I am not so sure." And he went on to tell Sergius about what he had learned from Mark and Peter concerning the resurrection of Jesus.

"The evidence is strong," the Roman admitted. "Still, one thing worries me. Paul seems to believe that Jesus will actually return to earth in the flesh to rule over the Jews and all who believe in him."

"He does," Luke agreed. "Although I think he is wrong."

"I am first of all an official of Rome, Luke," Sergius pointed out. "If I did not believe as you do that the kingdom of Jesus is within man's soul, I would have to order Paul to leave Cyprus. Will you talk to him and warn him that so long as he preaches such a doctrine there is going to be trouble?"

"I can try," Luke promised, but he was already certain that the attempt would fail, for Paul rarely ever listened to him any more.

When Luke told Paul and Barnabas of his conversation with Sergius, Paul's eyes began to burn with the same stubborn light that had been in them often lately where Luke was concerned. "Sergius is sincere, Paul," Luke pleaded in conclusion. "He is very near to Jesus and is thinking of your welfare. Besides, what good will you accomplish if you force the Romans to arrest you?"

"Luke is right, Paul," Barnabas urged. "Try to see his point of view."

"The kingdom of Christ is at stake," Paul said flatly. "I must preach what I believe, nothing more, nothing less."

"But Jesus could have meant a kingdom of the spirit," Luke protested. "His words can be interpreted just as easily that way as any other."

"Who are you to interpret the words of Jesus, Luke?" Paul asked sharply. "Has God spoken to you as he did to me? Have you been singled out to spread the truth abroad?"

Slowly Luke shook his head. "No, Paul. I have not."

"Do not set yourself up then as a spokesman for Jesus. Only those called by him personally are his representatives on earth." Paul turned abruptly and left the room, putting an end to the discussion.

Barnabas saw the hurt in Luke's eyes. "Do not think too hard of Paul," he begged. "There will be times when we will all be hurt in our hearts and perhaps in our bodies, for Paul's sake. But he is the pillar of fire which will lead men everywhere to Christ, Luke. You and I and the rest must keep that fire burning, at no matter what cost to ourselves."

ii

The proconsul's prediction of trouble for Paul became reality much sooner than any of them expected. Probus brought word of it to Luke and Mark a few days later. "Elymas has challenged Paul to a public test of the power of Jehovah over Aphrodite," he reported.

"Surely Paul didn't accept," Luke said. "It is a trap."

"Of course it is a trap," Probus agreed. "But Paul fell into it, nevertheless. And they planned it carefully. Elymas is a magician, and the priests are accomplished at all sorts of deceptions. They set the time for tomorrow, when there is a feast day at the temple and a large crowd will be present. Thousands of people will see them make a fool of Paul."

"Perhaps God will give them a real miracle," Mark suggested.

Probus shook his head. "We can't wait for that. We must do something ourselves."

"Perhaps Barnabas could persuade Paul not to go through with it," Luke suggested.

"He has to do it," Probus stated flatly, "or be driven from the city. Sergius agreed to watch the test after Paul accepted the challenge."

"But why would Paul get into such a mess?" Luke asked.

Probus shrugged. "Paul is so certain he is the personal representative of God on earth that he really believes he can do anything. If he fails tomorrow, it will be the end of Paul with the pagans, for word of this will spread throughout the Empire."

Suddenly Luke had an inspiration. "Why not fight fire with fire, Probus?" he cried. "You are something of a magician yourself. Can't you work feats of deception equal to those of the priests?"

The apothecary's eyes began to gleam. "That may be the answer," he said thoughtfully. "The ground would be of their own choosing, but it would still be worth a trial. And I would like to best that charlatan Elymas in a battle of wits."

Early in the morning long lines of people were moving along the road leading from the city to the great white Temple of Aphrodite some two miles back from the seashore. An hour before the zenith, when the test was to take place, a great crowd had gathered before the temple. The proconsul was present, in a box built for him on the steps of the temple, and a guard of Roman soldiers escorted the Christians through the crowd. Paul paid no attention to the curses yelled at him by both Jews and pagans as he walked between two brawny soldiers, his eyes straight ahead, with Probus just behind him. The apothecary carried no equipment, but Luke noticed that instead of his usual toga and cloak Probus now wore a loose robe, belted at the waist, similar to the ones affected by Persian magicians and conjurers. His eyes were red, as if he had not slept, and Luke knew that he had spent the night watching the temple and the preparations of the priests. He seemed quite confident of the outcome, a feeling that Luke was far from sharing.

A surge of interest went through the crowd as the Christians were ushered up to one of the lower landings in front of the sacred buildings of the goddess. Shrewdly realizing that the crowd would be far too large to be accommodated inside the temple, the priests had chosen to accomplish their expected triumph in the open where everyone could see. Here, close to the box of Sergius, they had built a small altar, around which a square was roped off. The Christians were ushered into this reserved space, and the guards deployed around it, obviously to protect them from the crowd.

Luke studied the altar, seeking some clue to its use. It stood about waist-high and was some two feet square at the top, which appeared to have been made of two sheets of metal, with a narrow crack where they joined. The metal shone like gold in the sun, and he recognized it as copper. The mines along the north shore of the island supplied this metal to much of the Roman world. Upon the copper plates of the altar a small pile of kindlings and wood shavings had been placed, as if awaiting the application of a ritual torch.

Suddenly the sound of flutes and cymbals floated from the temple itself, heralding the beginning of the test, and from one of the side doors a colorful procession emerged. The great golden gate remained closed, but down the steps before it marched the musicians, followed by a procession of the famed temple dancing girls. Their nearly nude bodies were revealed rather than concealed by their diaphanous garments, and a great "Ahh" of appreciation went up from the crowd as they deployed upon the broad marble landing before the small altar and began a sensuous dance of adoration to a glittering silver image of the goddess borne by white-robed priests. When the dance was finished the girls sank to the marble steps in a semicircle of graceful human statues around the image of the goddess and the altar before her.

Trumpets blared once more, and a file of priests descended the steps to the altar, wearing richly jeweled robes and carrying the golden instruments of worship. Beside the chief priest was the magician Elymas in his tall conical cap and elaborately decorated robe. Both Elymas and the chief priest carried themselves arrogantly, as if sure of their triumph. And indeed the little band of Christians did look impotent before all this splendor.

Elymas raised his hands and a hush fell over the crowd. "People of Cyprus"—his voice boomed out over the crowd—"men have come among you preaching false gods, saying that another will rule, setting aside the power of Rome, to which we give our allegiance."

A roar of displeasure went up from the crowd, for the Romans had been kind to the island, furnishing a ready market for copper from the mines and building roads so that the inhabitants could move easily from place to place.

"The city of Paphos and the island of Cyprus owe much to the benevolence of the divine goddess Aphrodite, before whose glorious temple we now stand," Elymas continued. "Now these men come preaching that a false god they call Christos will destroy the goddess."

A louder roar of displeasure rose from the crowd. The worship of

Aphrodite, most dissolute of divinities, was attended with all manner of vice, and the city profited hugely from the many pilgrims who came to witness the sensuous rites of the temple.

"Fear not, people of Paphos," Elymas's voice continued. "For the guardians of the divine goddess will not let these usurpers go unmasked. These priests of a false god have been challenged to show their power here on the very steps of the Temple of Aphrodite. I demand, in the name of the divine goddess, that they equal the feats which her priest will perform here in her honor or be driven from the land with whips."

The sorcerer now turned to the small altar with its shining top of copper and the pile of tinder and shavings resting upon it. The sun was shining brightly, and in his tall cap and gaudily decorated robe Elymas was the very personification of evil. The fat chief priest moved closer to the altar and began to chant in a deep voice: "O Divine Aphrodite! Most beautiful of goddesses! Grant us a sign of thy favor this day that we may know thou art powerful over all false gods." At the same time the dancing girls began their sensuous weaving before the altar.

"Keep your eyes on Elymas," Probus warned in a whisper. "The crowd will be watching the priest and the dancers."

Luke saw the sorcerer unobtrusively take a small flask from his robe. It was an exquisite sample of the glass blower's art, filled with water or some liquid so clear that as Elymas held the flask cupped in his hands only those close to him could see it. Luke knew that fires could be lighted with a bit of glass, but he had never seen a flask of liquid so used before. Beside him Probus whispered, "The flask will concentrate the rays of the sun; watch how he does it."

Elymas held the flask in his hands, moving it about until the burning rays of the midday sun were concentrated upon the pile of shavings. Few in the crowd were watching him, however, for their attention was centered upon the priests as they went through the ritual of adoration to the silver image of Aphrodite and upon the semi-nude temple girls winding about the altar in sinuous rhythm. Suddenly, where the tiny spot of the sun's rays was centered upon the inflammable tinder, a tiny curl of smoke arose in the still air. And as the priests finished their chant and the dancing girls sank to the marble pavement, a small flame appeared. Consuming the tinder greedily, it leaped up in a crackling burst of fiery tongues.

A deep roar of astonishment came from the crowd at the seemingly miraculous lighting of the fire. Elymas raised his hands and boomed out in triumph, "The goddess has spoken! Death to the priests of the false god!"

In the excitement no one noticed when Probus took something from his loose robe and cupped it in his hands, as Elymas had done the flask. But when a spot of deepest green light appeared on the sorcerer's tall cap, Luke recognized the great emerald from the temple at Pergamum which Probus had carried with him since their departure. The strange green light with its glowing center, appearing suddenly and seemingly by supernatural means upon the tall hat of the sorcerer as Probus concentrated the sun's rays there, caught the attention of those in the crowd near the altar, and a ripple of uneasiness went through them at this new phenomenon.

Exulting in the triumph of his stratagem, Elymas did not realize that anything was amiss until the change in tenor of the crowd's attention brought him back to the present. Meanwhile the intense heat of the sun concentrated upon the cap by the emerald charred the fabric covering. In the center of the smoking cloth a tiny flame appeared as the rolled-up cone of parchment inside it was ignited. Still not realizing what was happening, Elymas stared about him perplexedly until the heat from the burning cap reached his head. Then in sudden fear he tore it off and stamped upon the flaming parchment.

The crowd found its voice again now, but not in approval. Instead a roar of laughter shook the very stones of the temple, partly at the ludicrous figure of the now much shortened sorcerer stamping upon the flaming cap, and partly in relief from the fear which had gripped them at the sight of the strange green light. Elymas was bested, Luke realized with a surge of exultation, bested at his own game. Beside him John Mark was jumping up and down excitedly, slapping Probus on the back.

But their triumph was short-lived, for a sudden "Ahh!" of interest from the crowd warned that something else had happened. In common with the crowd Luke's eyes were drawn to the great golden gates of the temple. They had been closed throughout the dramatic scene upon the steps, but now they were opening slowly, moved by no visible agent. The faces of the crowd reflected awe and fear, and the momentary triumph of the Christians was forgotten in the face of this new revelation of the power of Aphrodite.

"Hail, Aphrodite!" the chief priest shouted, recovering his composure. The crowd took up the cry in a rousing cheer that thundered against the temple and echoed through the vale in which it stood.

"Hail, Aphrodite! Queen of the gods!" The shout rose again and again.

"Remember the Mithraeum at Antioch, Luke?" Probus whispered quickly. "There is a pig's bladder filled with air beneath the copper bottom of the altar. The flames have expanded the air and moved a set of levers which opened the gates."

Luke nodded, but the knowledge brought no assurance. He wondered if he could move quickly enough to push against the altar and possibly turn it over, revealing the mechanism inside it. But it seemed strongly built, and he was sure that the priests would be able to restrain him before he accomplished his aim.

"Aphrodite defies all false gods!" the chief priest boomed out over the crowd. "If your god is strong, ye false priests, let him now close the gates and we will fall down and worship him."

Paul had remained immobile through the exciting happenings, as if waiting for something. Now he stepped upon the marble platform and faced the sorcerer and the chief priest. "O full of all subtlety and all mischief," he shouted angrily. "Thou children of the devil! Thou enemies of righteousness! When will you cease to pervert the ways of the living God whom we serve? If God wills, he can smite yonder gates so that they will close at his will!"

Elymas was quick to seize the opportunity afforded by Paul's words. "Let your god close the gates!" he shouted exultantly. "It is a test of strength between Aphrodite and the false god."

Luke saw Probus step quickly to the altar. Just before it he seemed to stumble and fell against it, scattering the coals upon Elymas and the priests, who jumped back instinctively. In the confusion Luke saw the apothecary flick from his sleeve the long thin knife which he had carried in Caesarea when he had set out to kill Herod Agrippa. As he half lay across the altar Probus slipped the blade between the copper plates that formed the top of the altar. There was an audible popping sound as it pricked the distended pig's bladder activating the mechanism of the gates. Elymas struck angrily at Probus, but the apothecary easily dodged the blow and quickly hid the knife in his flowing sleeve. A deep groan of stark fear came from the crowd then as the huge gates, no longer controlled by the bladder, began to swing slowly shut. While thousands watched in awe, they creaked together and once more closed the entrance to the temple.

Gibbering with terror, the fat chief priest fell to his knees before Paul, and the sorcerer reeled backward from the shock of this sudden reversal in their fortunes. "Elymas has been blinded by God!" Probus shouted, and Paul took up the cry also. "Behold, the hand of the Lord is upon him."

Whether from the shock of this unexpected turning of his plans against him, or because in his disturbed state his mind was temporarily controlled by the suggestion of Probus that he was blind—or indeed he may have been stricken blind from above—Elymas did indeed

186

totter and would have fallen had not John Mark taken him by the hand and led him a few steps away from the now useless altar.

The crowd heard Paul's words and saw the sorcerer's gropings. When Mark led him away they believed Elymas to be truly blind, and a moan of fear soughed through the vale. Those at the front fell on their knees before Paul, while others, terror-stricken, tried to force their way through the crowd in the hope of escaping from this powerful new god who had so dramatically vanquished the famous Aphrodite. A serious riot could have developed in a few seconds, but Paul now stepped into the breach, turning the full force of his eloquence upon the thousands who had gathered to see Aphrodite triumph over the false god but had instead seen evidence of a power never before dreamed of. His voice held them, calming their fears while in simple telling phrases he used the events they had just witnessed as evidence of the power of God. For more than an hour Paul continued to talk, and when he finished hundreds were kneeling and praying before him. Afterward the streets around the house of Barnabas's brother were jammed with people who came to hear and believe the new faith. Most prominent of all the many converts made in Paphos was Sergius Paulus, the Roman proconsul.

iii

With their mission in Cyprus accomplished and a strong Christian church established at Paphos, the missionary party sailed from that city to Perga, the nearest port on the mainland of Lesser Asia to Cyprus and the shortest and safest voyage in these days of subsiding winter storms. Past the bold promontories of Drepanum and Acamas their small vessel moved across the quiet waters of the Pamphylian Sea toward the great bay of Attaleia. Into this deep depression in the coast line emptied the waters of the river Catarrhactes—so named because it tumbled over high sea cliffs to fall into the bay itself—as well as the more conventionally ending Cestrus and Eurymedon. Some sixty stadia—a little more than seven Roman miles—up the river Cestrus, they came upon the city of Perga and docked in the very shadow of the great Temple of Diana for which the seaport city was famous.

One member of the party, however, was far from happy. John Mark had come on the expedition with great enthusiasm, seeing in it an opportunity for a far greater service than merely acting as secretary to Peter and the elders at Jerusalem. But Paul's antagonism toward him had increased rather than lessened on the journey. In fact, after their dramatic experience at Paphos, Paul's relationship with the entire party had somehow changed. At first big, patient, and generous Barnabas had been the leader of their mission, as he had been the leader of the church at Antioch. But Paul had raised the conflict in Paphos by accepting the challenge of Elymas and, as he had done in Caesarea after the dramatic death of Herod Agrippa, seemed to interpret the blinding of Elymas as a personal accolade from God, ignoring the part which Probus had played. Gradually he became more authoritative in his manner and speech, and rather than bring dissension once more into the group when it was achieving such marked success, Barnabas allowed himself to be pushed into the background, until Paul was now the acknowledged leader of the missionary group.

Matters came to a head when Mark found a letter from Peter waiting for him at the synagogue in Perga. Peter, the letter stated, was now active in the work of the Church once more and was planning to visit Antioch and several other cities, to see for himself the great work which was being accomplished for the Way of Christ. He asked that Mark return to join him in Antioch and resume the duties of his secretary in order to set down the messages which he was bringing to the new churches outside Jerusalem.

Peter had every right to inspect the activities of the Church anywhere, for Jesus had delegated to him the leadership of the disciples, but when Mark read the letter to them Paul's face took on an angry cast. "Why should Peter come to Antioch, Barnabas?" he demanded peremptorily.

"It is his right, Paul. We all know that the mantle of Jesus descended upon him."

"It was agreed in Jerusalem that we should preach to the Gentiles and Peter to the Jews."

"There are many Jews in Antioch," Barnabas pointed out reasonably. "And you and I are Jews, Paul. Don't forget that."

"I am neither Jew nor Gentile," Paul said sharply. "When God picked me for his work I gave up everything else."

"Why does it make any difference if Peter visits Antioch?" Barnabas said. "We are all engaged in God's work."

Paul made a gesture of impatience. "I will not have Peter nor anyone else interfering with my mission. He is not the only one called by God."

Watching the conflict between the two, Luke wondered why Paul was so disturbed. Could it be that he envied Peter the fact that he had walked with Jesus and had been chosen leader of the disciples after the crucifixion? Certainly Paul's anger now and his hostility toward Mark, who had been so close to Peter, fitted such a pattern. But Paul had no real right to envy Peter, for he had never seen the Master himself.

Paul wheeled suddenly upon Mark. "Why did Peter write you?" he demanded. "Why not me? Or Barnabas?"

"Peter wrote because he wants Mark to join him again," Barnabas pointed out reasonably. "After all, Mark was with Peter for a long time."

"Then let Mark join him again," Paul said curtly. "We can go on without him."

Mark's cheeks crimsoned with humiliation and his mouth quivered from the hurt, for he was very sensitive. Remembering his own feeling when Paul had lashed out at him after his visit to Sergius Paulus, Luke instinctively put out his hand to comfort him. But another voice broke the awkward silence. "I will return to Antioch with Mark," Probus said, "since Paul has no appreciation for the efforts of others."

Paul wheeled upon him angrily. "Did God call you——" He was starting on the now familiar tirade, when Luke interrupted. "Even Jesus called disciples to help him with his work, Paul," he said. "Do you set yourself above the Master, that none but you can serve him well?"

Paul stiffened as if he had been slapped in the face, and the color slowly drained from his cheeks. For a long moment he did not speak, and Luke was almost sorry he had spoken, for he saw the agony in Paul's eyes. When Paul did speak his voice was humble. "You are right, Luke," he said. "No one of us who serves Jesus can be puffed up over the others, for he humiliated himself so far as to die the most shameful of deaths for our sake. Forgive me, my brothers, if in my zeal I have been impatient. We will all go on together."

"Let Mark go back to Antioch," Barnabas suggested. "Peter needs him and Mark can carry word of the great victories we have achieved for Christ in Cyprus, so that all who serve him will be encouraged to labor on."

Mark and Probus departed a few days later. Paul wished to remain in Perga for a while, but with summer coming on Luke was afraid the heat of the lowlands might bring on Paul's fever again and suggested that they should do as the people of that region did in the spring and journey to the uplands where the air was cool and sweet. In the end Paul agreed when Luke pointed out that if the apostle became sick for several months from the recurring fever, as had happened on his return from Jerusalem, their cause would be crippled.

The travelers reached Antioch-in-Pisidia, their immediate destination in the Galatian uplands, on the day before the Jewish Sabbath and found lodging at an inn. Looking over this city through which he had passed twice before, Luke found little change. Although the

Camp of Mars outside the city itself was now deserted, the eagles of Rome were still prominently displayed, for this Roman *colonia* sat astride the great trade routes between the East and the West and was in contact with both. As in all cities ruled directly from Rome, there was freedom of religious worship to established religions, and the synagogue of the Jews in this smaller Antioch stood just off the Augusta Platea in the center of the city. On the morning of the Sabbath, Paul and Barnabas attended the services in this synagogue, as was their custom in all cities they visited. And although not a Jew, Luke went with them, for Gentile believers in the Jewish God were welcome in the synagogues, and he was curious to see how the travelers would be received in this Roman city.

The arrangements were generally the same in all Jewish houses of worship, the men sitting upon benches on the main floor of the building, the women restricted to a gallery protected by a wooden latticing. A pulpit stood in the center, and on one side of the building, toward the Holy City of Jerusalem, was the closed ark in which were kept the manuscripts of the law, the Torah. Some few benches were placed at a higher level, making a place of honor for the "rulers of the synagogue," men who by learning, age, or unusual piety had earned the respect of the congregation.

When they entered the synagogue Paul and Barnabas placed over their shoulders the scarf-like embroidered *tallith* which marked them as Jews and gave them the right to speak before the assembly. The building was almost filled, and shortly the service began.

First prayers were recited in Hebrew by an old man, the "apostle" of the congregation. Next the scrolls of the law were handed to the "reader" by the *chazan* and a long reading began in Hebrew, followed by a translation into Greek, for many of the younger Jews in these Greek cities had never seen Judea and the Temple. Several centuries before, the books of Jewish law and the teachings of the prophets had been translated into everyday Greek as the Septuagint. Then with great ceremony the scrolls were rolled up again and returned to the ark.

Throughout the ceremony Luke had noticed the eyes of the congregation turning frequently to Paul and Barnabas, but there was nothing unusual in that. With his great size and red beard, the majestic Barnabas was always a center of attention, and Paul's godlike head and the play of emotions upon his mobile features also set him apart. Now, having returned the scrolls to the ark, the *chazan* came over to where they sat and said courteously, "Brothers, if you have any message of encouragement for the people, you may speak."

By consent between Paul and Barnabas it was Paul who rose on such occasions. He went to the pulpit where all might see him and, standing there in the center of the congregation, turned slowly, facing them all in turn, his eyes glowing with the fervor which always gripped him when he spoke of the Way. Then he lifted his hands, almost as if he were welcoming the people to his embrace, and began to speak. The audience was spellbound from the very first words, for here in the essence was what Paul believed and taught, the truths which he was firmly convinced were revealed to him first on the road to Damascus and with which he hoped to bring all men to belief in Jesus and his Way:

"Fellow Israelites and you who reverence God, listen! The God of this people of Israel chose our forefathers, and made this people important during their stay in Egypt, and then with an uplifted arm he led them out of it. Then after he had fed them forty years in the desert, he destroyed several nations in Canaan and gave them their land as an inheritance for about four hundred and fifty years. And after that he gave them judges until the time of Samuel, the prophet."

This was a story the Jews of the congregation had all heard many times, for the history of their people was read to them frequently. But there was not an impatient move in all of the synagogue, so great was the force of Paul's vibrant voice and personality.

"Then they demanded a king and for forty years God gave them Saul, the son of Cis, a man of the tribe of Benjamin. Then he deposed him and raised up for them David to be King, to whom he bore this testimony, *'I have found David the son of Jesse, a man after mine own heart, which shall fulfil all my will.'* It is from this man's descendants that God, as he promised, has brought Israel a Saviour in the person of Jesus, as John, before his coming, had already preached baptism as an expression of repentance for all the people of Israel. As John was closing his career he said, 'What do you take me to be? I am not the Christ; no, but he is coming after me, and I am not fit to untie the shoes on his feet.'"

A rustle of interest passed through the congregation, and Luke understood now Paul's purpose in this account of what was to his listeners an old, old story. He was specifically identifying Jesus as the Saviour and Messiah promised by God to the Jews.

"Brothers," Paul continued, "descendants of the race of Abraham, and all among you who reverence God, it is to us that this message of salvation has been sent. For the people of Jerusalem and their leaders, because they were ignorant of him, by condemning him have actually fulfilled the utterances of the prophets which are read every Sabbath, and although they could not find him guilty of a capital offense, they begged Pilate to have him put to death. When they had carried out everything which had been written in the Scriptures about him, they took him down from the cross and laid him in a tomb."

The speaker stopped for a moment and looked around, watching the intent faces looking up at him. When he spoke again his words pounded at them, driving the truths home.

"But God raised him from the dead, and for many days he appeared to those who had come up with him from Galilee to Jerusalem, and they are now witnesses for him to the people. So now we are bringing you the good news about the promise that was made to our forefathers, that God has fulfilled it to us, their children, by raising Jesus to life. Just as the Scripture says in the second Psalm, *'Thou art my Son; this day have I begotten thee.'* So, my brothers, you must understand that through him the forgiveness of your sins is now proclaimed to you, and that through union with him every one of you who believes is given right standing with God and freed from every charge from which you could not be freed by the law of Moses."

For a long moment after Paul finished speaking there was no sound in the synagogue. Then the *chazan* asked, "What is your name, brother?"

"I am called Paul." And then he added proudly, "But once I was called Saul of Tarsus, until Jesus spoke to me on the road to Damascus and I was blinded by him so that when I regained my sight I knew that I had seen the glory of the Lord."

The speech brought a low rustle of words from the congregation as neighbor whispered to neighbor that this was indeed the same Saul who had persecuted the Nazarene sect but had then turned his coat and joined them. When the service was over they left the synagogue, but so great was the press of people following them that Paul was forced to stop in the street outside to speak to them again. Climbing upon a cart, he continued to lecture the crowd, amplifying the simple truths of the Christian faith which he had expounded in the temple.

As on previous occasions in Antioch and Paphos, Paul's teaching appealed greatly to the people, and a great crowd followed him and Barnabas as they moved about the city, speaking from street corners, by the pools where the women went to get water from the Roman aqueduct, in the eating places, and everywhere that people gathered. Luke, as usual, devoted himself to healing the sick, giving unstintingly of his knowledge and skill to the poor of the city, and buying medicines with money from his own purse for those who could not pay.

On the following Sabbath, Paul was eager to return to the synagogue and continue his address to the Jews there, but as they approached the building a great crowd barred all entrance to it, until Paul was recognized and a path made for him to the door. "Behold!" the *chazan* said to Paul accusingly. "The house of God is filled with Gentiles and proselytes, so that the chosen people of the Most High cannot enter."

This was a bad situation, Luke recognized, for the Jews were very jealous of the exclusiveness of their God, keeping themselves aloof from the Gentiles in their worship. And for the hated "unclean and uncircumcised" to push their way into the synagogue to hear Paul, denying the Jews their own place of worship, was especially humiliating to a proud people.

"Since so many Gentiles have come to hear you," the *chazan* suggested, "why do you not leave the synagogue to the Jews and address these unclean ones outside?"

The familiar stubborn light began to glow in Paul's eyes as he took the *tallith* he carried and draped it over his shoulders. "I am a Jew," he said proudly. "It is my right under the law to speak in the synagogue."

"It is as you say," the *chazan* admitted reluctantly. "The law gives you the right to speak."

Paul turned to the crowd. "Be patient a little while, my brothers," he called to them. "When I have worshiped in the manner of my people, I will come again and speak to you."

Inside the synagogue the atmosphere was far different from the previous Sabbath. Now the faces occupying the elevated benches reserved for the "rulers of the synagogue" were hostile, and a murmur of anger ran through the congregation as Paul took his place and the service began. A week ago when he had spoken of the coming of the Messiah promised by God to the Jews, these people had listened with willing hearts, but now there was no welcome for him. Upon the street corners and in other public places throughout the city Paul had preached that Jesus died as much for Gentiles as for Jews. But the Jews for centuries had prided themselves upon the favor of their God, Jehovah, and upon their role as his chosen people even through times of persecution and dispersion. When Paul promised the same benefits to others, even to the "unclean," the inherited pride of the Jewish people in regard to their religion had triumphed and turned them against the newcomers.

When the Torah was put away in the ark and the time came for the congregation to be addressed by any visitors who wished to speak, it became evident that the *chazan* did not intend to offer that privilege to Paul. He had begun to dismiss the congregation with the customary benediction, but Paul leaped to his feet. "Ye Jews of Antioch," he cried, "I would speak to you again of that which I mentioned on the previous Sabbath——"

He was cut short by an old man who stood up among the rulers. "We want not your opinions, turncoat Jew," he shouted angrily. "Go to the Gentiles." And from all parts of the synagogue similar cries arose, some accusing Paul of blaspheming, others of defiling the synagogue by bringing Gentiles into it. Luke saw a look of stunned disbelief appear on Paul's face. He seemed to falter a moment and put his hand upon the bench for support. For Paul, who prided himself upon his strict Jewish upbringing and his strict observance of the law, it was a terrible shock to be reviled in a Jewish synagogue with the ceremonial *tallith* upon his shoulders, and Luke could understand what a blow this must have been.

Fortunately Barnabas took command and saved Paul from bodily injury at the hands of the angry Jews. With his commanding presence Barnabas turned the attention of the congregation upon himself when he said in a loud voice, "God's message had to be spoken to you Jews first, but since you continue to thrust it from you and since you show yourselves unworthy to receive eternal life, now and here we return to the heathen. For here are the orders which the Lord has given us, *'I will also give thee for a light to the Gentiles, that thou mayest be my salvation unto the end of the earth.'*"

A hush fell over the congregation, for Barnabas was quoting from the prophet Isaiah, and they were familiar with the passage from frequent readings in the synagogues. Taking Paul by the arm, Barnabas urged him from the building; and, apparently stunned by the hostile reception from his own people, the apostle allowed himself to be led away.

The Gentiles who had been in the synagogue now rushed out, joining those outside in beseeching Paul to speak to them of Jesus. At this evidence of approval and interest the color began to come back into the apostle's face and his eyes lit with something of their old fervor. When he began to speak, his voice soon regained its old dynamic magnetism.

The disapproval of the Jewish congregation was soon overshadowed by Paul's tremendous appeal to the Gentiles. Crowds followed him everywhere, and hardly a day passed that many were not baptized. But as Luke continued his work among the poor he soon began to hear rumors of a plot to drive Paul and Barnabas from the city.

When Luke told Paul and Barnabas what he had heard, Paul was inclined to laugh it off. He was meeting with great success in Pisidian Antioch, and a huge mass meeting was planned at the old site of the Camp of Mars for the following evening, when he would address thousands of people. The Jews, he argued, were only trying to scare him away; they would not dare to attack Roman citizens in a Roman *colonia*.

But Luke and Barnabas were not so certain as Paul of his safety and decided that Paul must never be without one or both of them at night, when any attack would almost certainly come. The next evening the three of them left the inn where they were staying, bound for the Camp of Mars, where the crowd was already beginning to gather. Many people were on the road that led by the river from the city to the camp, so they felt safe. Later, when they would be returning after the crowd had dispersed, the danger might become real.

The three of them were therefore taken completely by surprise while passing through a grove of trees when a dozen men in dark robes moved suddenly from the shadows. Before they could cry out for help, dark cloaks were thrown over their heads and they were carried back into the shadows, away from the road. There they were bound and gagged expertly, thrown into a waiting cart, their bodies covered with loose straw. As the vehicle moved along a connecting path toward the woods outside the city no one would have taken it for anything but a farmer's cart.

Luke had heard of the Jewish punishment of whipping. Restricted by law to not more than forty lashes, it was customary to stop at the count of thirty-nine so as not to chance breaking the ancient rule. But thirty-nine lashes administered by angry men could be grievous torture, and more than one had died from them.

When the cart was well away from the city rough hands dragged them from it and lashed them to trees. Then their garments were ripped to the waists, leaving their backs bare. Luke braced himself at the whistle of a rawhide thong through the air and clenched his jaws tight to keep from screaming when the whip cut through his skin and brought blood on the first stroke. In waves of searing pain the agony increased, rising to a peak beyond which there seemed to be no bearing. Vaguely he realized that the warm fluid trickling down his back and pooling at the waist where his robe was girdled was his own blood. The torture seemed endless and his senses swam so that he lost all track of time, and the only reality was a hell of almost unbearable pain.

Finally the lashing stopped and Luke was dimly conscious of the dark forms melting into the woods and the cart being driven away. For a long time his body sagged against the ropes while he floated in and out of consciousness. The burning pain rippled through his back with every movement, but at last the strength of his young body began to overcome the shock and he was able to fumble at the cords which bound him to the tree. They were slippery with blood from his cruelly lacerated back, but he finally managed to loosen the ropes and step free.

In the darkness he could barely make out the figures of Paul and Barnabas lashed to other trees. Barnabas groaned and moved slightly, but Paul's body was limp against the ropes. As leader of the expedition and target for the displeasure of the Jews, he had naturally taken the full fury of the beating. Sure that Paul must be dead, Luke felt for his pulse, but to his surprise the beat was perceptible, although faint. Gently he released the ropes that held Paul to the tree and eased his body to the ground. Barnabas had regained consciousness now. "Is Paul dead, Luke?" he asked anxiously.

"He still lives," Luke reported as he started to work on the cords that held Barnabas, "but his wounds are grievous."

"Thank God! All is not lost then."

"We must get Paul to a place of safety where his wounds can be dressed."

"But where can we go?" Barnabas asked.

Luke felt for his purse and breathed a silent prayer of thanksgiving when he found it still at his belt. "I can go into the city and buy a mule and cart," he said. "Then we can take Paul down by the lake somewhere; surely there will be a farmhouse where we can stay until his wounds are healed."

All of this took time, and it was after dawn before they drove the rough cart Luke had purchased into the yard of a farmhouse and found that the owner had heard Paul's preaching in Antioch and was glad to take them in. Paul was conscious by now, but still dazed, and badly in need of warmth and rest. Luke dressed his wounds with a soothing balm he had purchased in the city and administered a potion to bring on sleep. Then he treated the injuries of Barnabas and cared for his own wounds as best he could with the help of the farmer's wife.

Luke was young and strong and his wounds healed quickly, as did those of Barnabas. But Paul was inclined to be sickly, his body constantly drained of its vigor by the demands of the intense spirit which burned within him as well as the recurring bouts of fever, and it was weeks before he was able to travel. Being a Greek, Luke was least likely to attract attention in a Greek city, so he was able to enter Antioch freely and talk to the leaders of the Gentiles who had been converted by Paul and instruct them to set up a church, elect officers, and go about spreading the gospel of Christ. So in spite of their ill treatment at the hands of the Jews, they at least had the satisfaction of seeing a strong group of Christians develop in Pisidian Antioch.

As was to be expected after such a terrible experience, Paul was listless and depressed. He did some work for the farmer, mending tents and weaving bags on the crude loom of the household, and in the evening the neighbors often gathered around while Paul spoke to them of Jesus. But the fire seemed to have gone out of Paul, and Luke worried more and more about it as the apostle's visible wounds healed without any sign of healing for the grievous wound he had sustained in his spirit.

Thinking perhaps to stir Paul's interest, Luke suggested that they go to the governor in the city and demand their rights as Roman citizens by insisting that those who had persecuted them be punished. But Paul only shook his head. "It is only right that we should suffer for Christ's sake," he said. "Remember what he said in the scroll? *'Blessed are ye, when men shall revile you, and persecute you, and shall say all manner of evil against you falsely, for my sake.'*" Then he put his hand upon Luke's shoulder. "Why do you follow me, Luke? When I revile you and let you suffer punishments you do not deserve?"

"It is my duty as a physician and a friend," Luke said simply.

Paul smiled, and his face came alive again. "Jesus said, *'Greater love hath no man than this, that a man lay down his life for his friends.'* But no one could ask of a physician that he share the dangers of those he treats. To me you will always be *'the beloved physician,'* Luke, one who stood by me even at the risk of his own life."

iv

Never had Luke seen a more bare and dreary region than the vast central plain of Galatia across which they traveled from Antioch to Iconium. Now, as they came down from the higher land to the northwest, their eyes were drawn to the startling mass of stone, which the natives called the "Black Mount," rising precipitately from the plain as a rock might jut from the ocean, and silhouetted against the snowy tops of the mountains in the distance.

Iconium was a fairly large city, Luke saw as they rode through it, following the directions which Thecla had given him in Antioch for finding her home. His heart beat fast at the thought of seeing his beloved again, but when they reached the house they were told by the neighbors that Thecla and Glaucus had gone to Lystra, some fifty miles away, because of the illness of Thecla's aunt. Paul wished to stay a few days in Iconium and preach in the synagogue on the Sabbath, but Luke was anxious to go on, so he joined a passing caravan, with the understanding that Paul and Barnabas would follow him a few days later.

He had been directed how to find the house of Eunice, Thecla's aunt, by the neighbors in Iconium, and as he came along the dusty street beside it he saw Thecla cutting flowers in a low walled garden beside the house. Soundlessly he vaulted over the low wall and came up behind her before he spoke her name.

The girl stiffened, recognizing his voice, then turned, and with a cry of joy threw herself into his arms, heedless of anyone who might be passing on the street. When he kissed her lips they were salty with her tears. For a long moment of utter rapture he held her in his arms without speaking, reveling in the thrill of having her close to him again.

"Why did you not come sooner, darling?" she asked after a while. "I have been watching for you for months, it seems."

"It will take days to tell you all that has happened," he said. "Tell me about yourself and Glaucus."

A shadow crossed her face. "Father is not well, Luke. He tries to keep on teaching, but he is so weak that I am worried about him."

Glaucus had indeed changed for the worse, Luke saw when they entered the house. There was the same gentle dignity and quiet intelligence in his face, but his skin was as pale as alabaster except for the faint flush of fever, as if the frail body were being consumed by a slow fire. As he watched Glaucus's rapid breathing, the hacking cough, and the red stain upon the handkerchief that he put to his mouth, Luke's trained senses made the diagnosis. An advanced phthisis, burning away the frail body as it consumed the lungs, was written there as plainly as in the works of Hippocrates.

While Luke was giving an account of his travels since Thecla and Glaucus had left him in Antioch, a boy of perhaps fourteen came into the room. He stopped shyly, and Thecla reached out to draw him to her. "This is Timotheus, usually called Timothy," she told Luke. "He is the son of my aunt Eunice, whose house this is."

Timothy smiled shyly and bowed courteously. He was a handsome lad. Thecla had told Luke in Jerusalem that her aunt Eunice had married a well-to-do merchant of Lystra, only to be widowed when her son was about ten years old. Timothy sat on the floor at Luke's feet while he continued his story, and when he told how they had bested the magician Elymas at Paphos, the boy's eyes glowed with excitement. "Thecla has been telling me about Paul," he said eagerly. "Is he coming here?"

When Luke said, "Yes, Timothy, Paul and Barnabas will be here in a few days," the child's face lit up as if he had received a gift.

Eunice had recovered from the illness which had brought Glaucus and Thecla from Iconium, and the girl and her father had been on the point of returning home when Luke arrived, but they decided now to wait for Paul and Barnabas. The evening meal was in the nature of a feast of thanksgiving, both for Eunice's recovery and for Luke's arrival. There was much talk, and Luke and Thecla had no chance to be alone, but Luke's heart was at peace just from being with Thecla again and feeling her love encompass him like a protecting garment. Afterward, when they did go into the garden for a few minutes to say good night, Thecla said, "Father is not going to be able to travel for a long time, dearest, if he ever does. After Antioch and Jerusalem, do you think you could be happy staying in Iconium until—until we know what is going to happen to him?"

Luke drew her to him. "Is that what is worrying you? I thought I saw a frown on that lovely forehead."

"Then you wouldn't mind?" she asked anxiously.

"Do you have any idea how lonely and dull Antioch was after you left?" he asked. "A sheepherder's hut would be heaven with you, and Rome a desert without you."

She sighed then with utter happiness. "How foolish I was not to know that, Luke! I should have listened to my heart and not to reason."

"We will both listen to our hearts from now on," he promised.

Life was pleasant in Lystra; it was summer, the flowers were blooming in the garden, and Luke and Thecla were together. Eunice, Timothy's mother, was a beautiful woman in her late fifties. Upon little Timothy had been centered all of the devotion of Eunice and her mother, Lois, who lived in the household, yet the boy remained remarkably unspoiled. Timothy took Luke in charge while Thecla helped with the duties of the house. Proudly he pointed out the attractions of the small city, the Temple of Diana outside the gates, where by looking through a forbidden window one could see fat priests gorging themselves on meat from the sacrifices; the shops where sweetmeats were sold; the glowing forges of the silversmiths casting silver images of Diana to be sold during the ceremonies of pagan worship; the caves in the hills where the boys played at being robbers.

The people of Lystra were simple folk, peasants for the most part, as well as weavers, smiths, food and wine sellers, carpenters, builders, and a small number of scribes and clerks who were servants of Rome. There was none of the sophistication here that characterized the larger cities and little of the vice to be found in Rome, Alexandria, Antioch, Ephesus, and the other great population centers of the Empire. The town contained no physicians of any competence, and so Luke was at first regarded with suspicion when he offered to treat the sick, since he healed in no one's name except the science of medicine. But people quickly gained confidence in his kindness and skill, flocking to him daily for treatment.

Timothy had heard Luke say that Paul and Barnabas were coming to Lystra in a few days, and every afternoon he went to the outskirts of the city to look for them where the road from Iconium passed the

Temple of Diana. It was almost a week later, however, that the boy came running to the small surgery where Luke was treating the sick, shouting that the expected visitors had arrived.

Luke put down the scalpel with which he had been incising a boil. "Where are they?" he asked. "At your house?"

"No. They stopped at the big rock near the temple to preach. Now the people are preparing to worship them. I heard a man say that it was Jupiter and Mercury who had come to Lystra."

Paul and Barnabas mistaken for heathen gods! It was a natural thing for these rude and unlettered people to do. Farmers often looked for the gods to visit them in person to favor their crops, and many brought sick to the temple, hoping the gods would appear in person and heal them. But the same ignorance which could lead the people to mistake Paul and Barnabas for divine beings could also cause trouble when they were found to be mortal.

A crowd had gathered before the temple by the time Luke and Timothy reached it, and people were streaming from the city as word passed swiftly of the divine visit. Pushing through the crowd, Luke saw Paul standing on the big rock Timothy had mentioned, speaking to the crowd. From the Temple of Diana across the road a procession of priests was just emerging, carrying with them a silver image of Diana and trays laden high with offerings. Obviously it was their intention to ask the divine visitors to favor the city by dwelling for a while at least in the temple of their sister goddess.

Carried away as usual by the fervor of his preaching, Paul had not noticed the priestly procession, and Barnabas, standing on the ground at a lower level, was not able to see it. Luke tried to shout and attract Paul's attention as he worked his way through the crowd with Timothy following close in his wake, but the noise of those about him drowned out his voice.

When finally Paul noticed the commotion before him, Luke was close enough to see him frown in bewilderment as the priests prostrated themselves before the rock, offering their gifts. "Sirs," Paul asked. "Why do ye these things?"

The leading priest rose and held up his arms in supplication. "O Chief of Gods and Heavenly Messenger," he intoned. "Come into the Temple of Diana that we may honor thee with a worthy sacrifice."

Paul stared at him in amazement. "Who do you think we are?"

"Thou art Mercury," the priest said promptly. "And he whose beard flames like the sun can be none other than Jupiter, mightiest of all the gods."

For a moment Paul was aghast at this identification with a pagan deity, then his face suffused with anger and shame and he tore his robe in a typically Hebrew gesture of sorrow and disavowal. "Men!" he shouted. "Why are you doing this? We are merely men with natures like your own. We have come to tell you the good news so that you may turn from these foolish things to the living God who made heaven and earth and sea and all they contain."

The chief priest looked befuddled. "Are you not Jupiter and Hermes, his messenger?"

"Nay, we are men like yourselves, by name Paul and Barnabas, Jews who preach the words of the living God and his son, Jesus Christ."

By this time the priest had begun to realize the error into which he had fallen. Being human, he turned his anger not against himself for his stupidity, nor the crowd for being fickle, but upon the men whom, a few minutes before, he had been ready to acclaim as gods. "Jews!" He spat the word out as an insult. "Dare you to call the goddess Diana a vain idol before her very temple? Retract or I call upon the goddess to smite you from that rock."

Paul lifted his head defiantly. "Invoke your pagan idol," he told the priest. "If she be indeed divine, let her smite me with lightning and hurl me from this rock as an evidence of her power."

Nothing happened, and the priest, defeated but still haughtily defiant, led his procession back to the temple. Now that the visitors were proved mere men and not gods, most of the crowd turned away, too, but a number still remained. To them Paul preached eloquently. Luke could see that something, perhaps the altercation with the priest, had kindled again in Paul the fire which had been subdued after his experience in Antioch, for the Paul who spoke now was more nearly the same one who had dared the sorcerer Elymas on the steps of the temple at Paphos and held the crowd spellbound in the synagogue at Pisidian Antioch.

v

Fired with enthusiasm, Paul went out that very evening to speak in the streets of Lystra to all who would stop to hear him. Barnabas, however, remained behind, and Luke saw that his friend was worried. "What is it, Barnabas?" he asked as they sat talking after the evening meal. "You are troubled about something."

"Paul does not know of this yet," Barnabas said, "but I had disquieting news from Antioch through a caravan we met on the way here."

"What is wrong?"

"Some of the elders in Jerusalem have been urging that all who follow Jesus obey the Jewish laws of diet and be circumcised. They have even sent out representatives who teach that Gentiles cannot be accepted into the Church without first obeying these rules."

"But that would wreck the whole program of carrying the word to the Gentiles," Luke cried, aghast.

"That is not the worst," Barnabas continued dourly. "The proselyters have already come to Antioch and caused a split in the church there."

"How could Peter let a thing like this happen?" Luke asked. "It was his vision at Joppa that authorized you to preach to the Gentiles."

"Peter is easily swayed," Barnabas explained. "The Judaizers are even claiming that Peter himself supports this new rule."

Here was disquieting news indeed, for if Paul were to learn that his work among the Gentiles was being jeopardized by the very people who had been given the task of spreading Christ's gospel on earth, the shock might bring on again the depression which had worried Luke so much after their painful experience at Pisidian Antioch. And yet it was not fair to keep the news from him much longer.

"I have tried to persuade Paul that we should return to Antioch," Barnabas said, "without telling him about this until we get there and can see what the situation really is. But he wants to go on with this work, since he has met with some success in Galatia."

In the end they decided to say nothing to Paul for a few days, hoping that some other expedient would come to mind. Paul continued his preaching, and on the Sabbath he went to the *proseucha,* a temporary building which served the small Jewish congregation of the city as a place of worship in lieu of a synagogue. The Jews received him rather coldly, for they had been warned about him from Antioch, so he turned his efforts more and more to the Gentiles, with considerable success.

Luke was becoming adept at learning the sentiments of a city from the idle talk of his patients, and as he worked in his small surgery he soon detected evidence of a strong undercurrent of resentment in Lystra against Paul. As usual, it was fanned both by the priests of Diana, who had ample reason to hate the apostle, and the Jews, who objected to the freedom with which Paul invited Gentiles to share the favors of Jehovah.

This time, however, disaster struck before Luke had a chance to make any preparations. He was setting a fracture late one afternoon when Thecla came running into the surgery, sobbing hysterically that Paul was dead. When Luke calmed her enough so she could talk intelligibly, he was able to get the story of the tragedy.

Paul had been preaching in the streets, as usual. This time those who sought to destroy him had skillfully infiltrated the crowds, saying that he was really a practitioner of black magic and sorcery and was in league with devils. One told of seeing him at midnight conferring with evil spirits. And another professed to have seen him robbing a grave. To a people as ignorant and superstitious as these, little more than a rumor was necessary, and this spread rapidly through the crowd. When Paul had finished his address and started homeward, a threatening group followed after him, accusing him of all manner of evil.

Paul had tried to argue them out of the foolish charges, for he was afraid of nothing when it came to spreading the beloved word. But the crowd was in no mood to listen and began to pelt him with balls of clay mixed with spittle, so that in a matter of minutes his robe was spattered with mud. Then the ringleaders, judging correctly the temper of the crowd, began to pelt him with stones, and soon a veritable avalanche was pouring upon his head. Buffeted with stones, half blinded, Paul had still tried to reason with his persecutors, but a large stone had struck him on the temple, felling him and leaving him senseless. When someone in the crowd shouted that he was dead, they had ceased the stoning and dragged his inert body to the refuse heap just outside the gates of the city.

"Did you touch him?" Luke asked Thecla. "Could you be sure that he is dead?"

"I didn't see him closely," she said. "But I heard them screaming that he was dead."

"Go to the house," Luke directed, "and tell Barnabas to bring a cart to the rubbish heap. I will see whether Paul is really beyond help. Sometimes victims of stonings are knocked senseless but can be saved by a physician."

A crowd of people stood at the gate, watching the inert and battered form lying on the refuse heap. Some were weeping, some mildly curious, but there seemed little animosity left in them now. Luke pushed his way through and went to kneel beside Paul's body. His fingers automatically sought the pulse, and his heart leaped when he detected a slow, even beat. Quickly Luke ran his fingers over the apostle's skull, seeking some evidence of a dangerous fracture, but found none. There was a rounded bluish swelling over the temple which could account for the unconsciousness, since blows in that region brought stupor more quickly than in any other part of the head. The very location of the blow might have saved Paul's life, Luke realized, by bringing on unconsciousness before he could be battered to death by the stones.

There was a well close to the gate, and Luke tore off part of Paul's now tattered robe and moistened it in water. As gently as he could he began to sponge away the blood which had run down the apostle's face from a half dozen superficial cuts, in addition to the wound which had felled him. The coolness of the water served to revive Paul, and he opened his eyes and stared at Luke. "They stoned me as they did Stephen," he whispered. "Why am I alive?"

"You were knocked unconscious and the crowd thought you were dead."

"Then God must have guided the stone that felled me." He moved his head a little and saw the crowd waiting at the gate. "Are they waiting to stone me again?"

"No. Those who did it ran away. Many of the crowd there are believers; they were weeping for you when I came through the gate."

"Then I must show them that God keeps watch over his servants."

"Thecla has gone for Barnabas and a cart. You must lie still until they can come."

"We who have faith in Christ can triumph over evil men and stones," Paul insisted. "If I rise and walk into the city, all will know the power of Jesus."

"You will be endangering your life," Luke warned.

Paul smiled. "God saved me from the stones, Luke. It does not seem to be his will that I die here in Lystra. Help me up, please." At first the apostle swayed so from dizziness at the change of position that Luke was forced to support him or he would have fallen. But when his head cleared a little, they began a slow progress toward the city.

A cry of amazement went up from the crowd when the man who they had been told was dead began to walk, and people all around them fell to their knees, some praying, some shouting with joy at the seeming miracle which had brought Paul back to life. Others pushed forward to touch the apostle's robe in the hope that some of the power which had raised him might spread to them. What had been an ignominious defeat had now become a triumphal procession, more impressive to these simple-minded people than any preaching could have been, for here was visual evidence of the power of God which Paul had been telling them had raised Christ from the tomb.

They met Thecla, Barnabas, and Timothy bringing the cart, but Paul refused to ride, and so the triumphal procession continued through the city to Eunice's house. That night all of Lystra hummed with the news of the miracle which had been wrought that day, and crowds gathered around the house demanding that Paul come out and speak to them. Even in his weakened condition he continued to do so, until shortly before midnight he fainted and Barnabas sent them away.

In the morning Paul seemed to be all right, but Luke was worried about him, and after a conference it was decided that they should all return to Iconium, Paul and Glaucus riding in the carriage which had brought Thecla and her father to Lystra, the others following in carts, including Timothy and his mother and grandmother. At Iconium, Luke hoped that Paul could rest and heal the injuries from the stoning.

When Paul became feverish shortly after their arrival in Iconium, Luke thought at first that the effects of the stoning had brought on another recurrence of the intermittent fever which was the apostle's particular nemesis. But Paul soon fell into a stupor, alternating with periods of delirium, and Luke was certain that the trouble was coming from the injury which had rendered him unconscious at the stoning.

The fever continued to burn Paul's body and his delirium increased; Luke remained at his bedside most of the time, as he always did when charged with the care of a seriously ill patient. And when he had exhausted his meager supply of drugs with no appreciable effect upon Paul's condition, his hopes for his friend's life grew lower and lower.

Glaucus was now so weak that he was unable to teach, and the entire burden of the school fell on Thecla's shoulders. Luke helped her when he could, but they could snatch only an occasional moment to be alone together. In spite of the work and his worries about Paul, Luke was experiencing a quiet happiness here in Iconium with Thecla that he had never known before.

Barnabas was working steadily to build up a strong church in Iconium and meeting with considerable success, but Luke knew that he was worried about the things he had heard from Antioch regarding the change of policy toward Gentile converts on the part of James and Peter in Jerusalem. Then they learned that proselyting Christians had actually appeared in Pisidian Antioch and Lystra, announcing that Paul and Barnabas were no longer authorized to accept Gentile converts freely upon the profession of their belief in Jesus and the resurrection from the dead. Barnabas and Luke both realized now that they could not remain aloof from the controversy much longer, but neither felt that he could leave Paul and go to Antioch and Jerusalem.

So the months passed, one and then two, before Paul began to show definite signs of recovery. Even when he was able to sit up in bed there were long weeks before he was well enough to travel again. In this period of enforced rest, so galling to one of Paul's temperament, Timothy helped him most. Whenever he was not busy with his schooling or with the chores of the household, the boy was always with Paul, his eyes glowing with interest and excitement as he listened to stories of other cities and other lands. And as strength returned to his hands, Paul taught Timothy how to cut the tough *cilicium* and sew it into tents and other useful articles of cloth.

The warmth of spring was already beginning to filter from the seacoast up into the mountains before Paul was able to attend services with the congregation at Iconium. And on his first visit he learned of the activities of the proselyters who had come behind him to undo his work, when one of them, lately come from Jerusalem, rose in the synagogue and spoke against Paul, telling of the new decisions of the elders at Jerusalem.

Luke had expected trouble when Paul first learned of this new complication, but he was surprised by the calmness with which the apostle received the bad news. Instead of reacting with anger, Paul rose after the proselyter and talked at length, recounting how Peter had received the vision at Joppa in which he had been instructed to kill and eat the animals let down from heaven in a sheet. Then he went on to interpret how Peter had taken this as a sign that he should preach to the Gentiles and how, when he reached the house of Cornelius at Caesarea, the Holy Spirit had descended upon the converts there, proving that the vision of Peter had indeed come from God. The crowd listened eagerly, for they had been troubled by the words of the proselyter, and at the end of the service hundreds gathered around Paul to hear more.

Afterward, at the home of Glaucus, Paul asked, "How long have you known of the work of these Judaizers, Barnabas?"

"Several months," Barnabas admitted.

"Why did you not go to Antioch and Jerusalem if necessary?"

"Luke was not certain that you would live, Paul," Barnabas explained. "I stayed to help in any way that I could."

"The welfare of no one person is worth more than the Church of Christ," Paul insisted. "We must lose no time in getting to Antioch at once."

"Suppose Peter and the elders will not relent in their decision about the Gentiles?" Luke asked. "What will you do?"

For a moment Paul did not speak, as if he were considering such an eventuality for the first time. Then he said decisively, "The Church of Jesus can never grow among the heathen if it is hemmed in with senseless restrictions. Before I would let them destroy my work I would break with Peter and the elders and start a new church." Then he added briskly, "But we will not consider such an eventuality. When I talk to the others in Antioch and Jerusalem I am sure I can convince them that God intends for the Gentiles to be accepted without restrictions."

"You are going with Paul to Antioch, aren't you, Luke?" Thecla asked as he held her in his arms for the few precious moments they tried to find for each other each day.

"What else can I do, dearest?" he said resignedly. "Paul is in trouble and he still does not have his strength. He will need all the help his friends can give him."

206

"You and Paul are more than just friends, Luke," Thecla said. "Both of you are a part of some great purpose of God's."

"But when are we to think of ourselves, Thecla?"

"God's plan for you comes first, Luke. We both belong to Jesus before we do to each other."

"It will not be long," he promised. "And when I come back to you nothing will ever separate us again."

vi

They arrived in Syrian Antioch in the middle of an afternoon, and Luke went immediately to the apothecary shop where Probus ministered to the sick and poor along the Street of the River. A long line of people waited outside the shop. Probus was applying a dressing of balsam to an ulcer on the leg of an old man, but when he saw Luke his eyes kindled with pleasure and he engulfed the young physician in a hearty embrace. For a moment both were too filled with emotion to speak.

Probus held Luke by the shoulders and searched his face keenly. "You have matured since I left you in Perga," he said then.

"Perhaps it was the whips," Luke said, smiling.

"Surely you did not let them whip you too," Probus said quickly. "You, a Roman and the son of Theophilus."

"How did you know about it?"

"These cursed proselyters who have come here to wreck our work told of it. They used the whipping as evidence that neither the Gentiles nor the Jews had accepted Paul in Galatia."

"But the whipping was by Jews. Our mission was an outstanding success among the Gentiles everywhere."

"We need good news," Probus said. "The Judaizers have nearly wrecked the church here at Antioch."

"But how? Gentiles were first accepted here."

"As soon as these agents appeared here with their story that Gentiles must be circumcised and adhere to Jewish rules of eating in order to be accepted by Jesus, many in the Church seized upon this new idea to set themselves above the Gentiles. Now each side spends its time fighting the other for fear it will get ahead, and nothing is accomplished."

This was bad news indeed, for the church at Antioch was the pattern for all others, the example given by Paul and Barnabas everywhere to show how Jew and Gentile, black and white, rich and poor could work together for the teachings of Jesus.

"What about Thecla?" Probus asked. "Is it still the same with you?"

"We are to be married when I return to Iconium in a few months."

"Good," Probus said approvingly. "Perhaps I can go back with you. The highlands of Galatia and Lycaonia have always appealed to me."

The situation in Antioch was so bad that Paul decided he could accomplish more to heal the dangerous rift in the Church by going at once to Jerusalem. Since Paul was now in good health and much stronger after the sea voyage from Perga, Luke decided to remain in Antioch and again took up residence at the palace of his foster father on the *insula*. Theophilus was away, but he returned a few days later and welcomed Luke warmly. "There is much we need to talk about, Luke," he said.

"Tell me about Apollonius and Mariamne," Luke urged.

Theophilus smiled. "I visited them in Ephesus a few months ago. Mariamne thinks she is going to have a baby. They both said they wished you could be there. After Apollonius was saved, they seem to think you have some miraculous power."

Luke shook his head. "I am not even certain that I helped him at all."

Theophilus looked startled. "You don't believe it was really a miracle, do you, Luke? Those things are all right for the simple, but intelligent Greeks long ago disproved divine intervention."

"Paul performs real miracles. Miracles of faith."

Theophilus frowned. "I am afraid I don't understand you."

"I am not sure I understand myself, sir," Luke admitted. "But strange cures do happen just the same."

"Do you mean that people can be cured of a real disease simply by having faith that they will be cured?"

"Something like that," Luke admitted. "For example, at Pisidian Antioch when I first came with the armies, there was a serious epidemic of dysentery when men drank water polluted from bathing and the discharges of the city. That disease, I am sure, was caused by something in the water that poisoned or damaged their bodies."

"The animalcules of Marcus Terrentius Varro," Theophilus agreed. "I remember your mentioning them when you came back from the war. But do you think all disease originates from such a cause?"

Luke shook his head. "Some illness comes, I am sure, from somewhere inside ourselves, probably from a state of unhealth in the soul."

Theophilus smiled. "Remember Plato's warning against trying to separate the body from the soul."

Luke nodded. "That is why I think a disorder of the soul always brings on a disorder of the body, as when a man who is sick in his soul dies from the sheer loss of desire to live."

"But what brings on a sickness of the soul? The daimonion of Socrates?"

"Perhaps, if you want to call it that. I do believe that man is controlled at all times by one of two forces within him and that the health of his soul depends upon how well the good forces control the bad."

"Do you believe, then, that the Nazarene appeals to and strengthens the good forces in man? And that the miracles he performed can be explained in this way?"

"Yes, I do," Luke said.

"But what about the supernatural being the Jews call Satan or the devil? Does he control the evil in men?"

"The more I read the ancient scrolls of the Jews," Luke explained, "the more I realize that they wrote in terms of symbols. Many people believe in an actual evil force, concentrated in the person of a supernatural being, but I am sure the devil that troubles man lies within his own being."

"That is the Socratic philosophy," Theophilus agreed. "But why is it there? What is its purpose?"

"The demon or daimonion in man," Luke said earnestly, "I believe to be the love of self or the urge to self-importance. When a man yields to the impulse to be more important than his fellows, the demon gains control."

"Would you have all men give up self-esteem?" Theophilus demanded. "Even the Nazarene prided himself upon being the son of God."

"Nothing should give a man more pride than that he was created, as the Jewish poets wrote, 'in the image of God.' But when he feeds his demon of self upon greed, lust, and the desire for gain and high position, he encourages the daimonion to gain control. Unless he then nourishes the good part of his soul with humility, helping others, kindness, and pride and dignity in himself as the image of God, there will be a constant battle. And conflict in the soul brings on conflict in the body and disease."

"I am beginning to see the connection," Theophilus admitted.

"When self gains the ascendancy in men's souls," Luke continued, "it damages their bodies just as surely as it damages their outlook on life, their relationships toward others, and their real stature as human beings. And those damages produce disease just as surely as do the animalcules of Marcus Terrentius Varro."

"Ingenious," Theophilus said admiringly. "And very logical. But what about these miracles of faith?"

"Anything which enables man to control and gain advantage over his private demon of self—such as the principles of Jesus and the Christian faith—stops the damage to both soul and body and stops the disease."

"But what about an acute illness, such as the pneumonia that almost killed Apollonius?"

"Probus claims that it was my bleeding him that brought about the cure."

"And you?"

For a moment Luke did not speak, then he said slowly, "I don't know. Sometimes I believe that it was a direct intervention by the hand of God in order to influence someone to believe in him."

"But who?" Theophilus asked, frowning.

"Perhaps to show me there is a true God," Luke said. "Although I don't know why. But I am sure that I first started to believe in him then."

Paul and Barnabas did not remain long in Jerusalem, returning in less than two months. With them were John Mark and two new workers, Judas and Silas. Accustomed as he was to Paul's changes in temperament, Luke was still startled by the change in him during so short a time. The Paul who went to Jerusalem had been quietly determined to plead his cause and induce the elders and the patriarch James and Peter to retract their insistence upon the adherence to Judaic laws by Gentile converts. But the Paul who returned was the triumphant apostle, now unquestionably the leader of all those who sought to forward Christ's kingdom outside Jerusalem and Judea, and next in authority to James himself.

Mark told Probus and Luke how it had all come about, painting for them the dramatic scene when Paul had faced a hostile congregation that was determined it was doing the right thing in forcing Jewish customs upon Gentile converts, and had come out with his every desire approved. The Judaizers, mostly Pharisees who had come to believe in Jesus but were too steeped in the traditional religious laws of the Jewish people to accept Gentiles freely into the Church, had argued their case. Then Paul told how Gentiles and Jews alike had flocked to hear him and Barnabas on their travels. He described the conversion of Sergius Paulus and the dramatic scene when the sorcerer Elymas had been vanquished, going on then to their troubles at Pisidian Antioch and how the church there had been stronger after their whipping than before, largely because of Luke's efforts in organizing it while Paul was recovering from his wounds. He turned next to Lystra and his miraculous escape from death by stoning and the effect that his rising from the rubbish heap and walking into the city had exerted upon Jew and Gentile alike. And he told, too, of the strong church at Iconium, largely developed by Barnabas while Paul had lain in a delirium from the effects of the stoning at Lystra. Each success, each seemingly miraculous delivery from death, was interpreted by Paul as further evidence that God approved the carrying of the Word to the Gentiles. Paul had been fighting for the very existence of his own great mission, and Luke well knew how eloquent he could be on such occasions. It was no surprise that he was able to convince James and the elders that his mission to the Gentiles was approved by God.

"What about Peter?" Luke asked. "We heard that even he had sided with the Judaizers."

"Peter did not entirely support them," Mark explained. "Since he denied Christ, Peter often hesitates to make a sharp decision, for fear that he might be wrong in some part of it. We Jews are bound to see things differently from others, Luke, and Peter is as proud of the heritage of the Jews as any of us. But when he heard Paul's arguments he was the first to support him."

"I am glad," Luke said sincerely. In his mind he could see the big disciple standing majestically before the crowd and speaking in the simple tone and language of a Galilean fisherman, which was so different from Paul's impassioned and sometimes mystical utterances. Peter's approval would have almost as much effect upon the congregation as Paul's arguments, for Peter's sincerity always radiated from him like a perceptible aura.

"James gave his approval to Paul's work," Mark told them; "there is no more question about admitting the Gentiles freely."

"I hope that means the end of discord in the Church," Luke said.

Probus shook his head. "Those who want to believe Paul right will do so, but there are many who dislike him. So long as people continue to be guided by human motives, Jews are going to resent Gentiles and there will be trouble. Paul should have gotten something in writing from James and the elders to prove that they endorse his work."

"But he did," Mark said. "Silas and Judas came along as witnesses, and James wrote a letter which I copied with my own hand. Here is what it says:

"The apostles and the elders as brothers send greeting to the brothers from among the heathen in Antioch, Syria, and Cilicia. As we have heard that some of our number have disturbed you by their teaching, by continuing to unsettle your minds, we have passed a unanimous resolution to select and send messengers to you with our beloved brothers Barnabas and Paul, who have risked their lives for the sake of our Lord Jesus Christ. So we send Judas and Silas to you, to bring you the same message by word of mouth. For the Holy Spirit and we have decided not to lay upon you any burden but these essential requirements, that you abstain from everything that is offered to idols, from tasting blood from the meat of animals

211

that have been strangled, and from sexual immorality. If you keep yourselves free from these things you will prosper. Good-by."

vii

Healing the split in the church at Antioch proved not quite so simple a task as Paul had anticipated when he returned from Jerusalem with the letter from James. Cloaked in his new authority, he was inclined to be intolerant of everyone who did not immediately agree with him, and there was a constant tension in the church, with tempers ready to explode at any time. In such a situation Luke's own calmness was an asset, and Barnabas prevailed on him to delay returning to Thecla at Iconium until the situation could gradually be righted.

And so month after month dragged on. Luke poured out his heart to Thecla in regular letters which went northward along the caravan routes, then westward by the "Old Way" to Iconium. Slow but definite progress was being made in unifying the church, and when word came that Peter was coming from Jerusalem for a visit, Luke began to look forward to seeing his majestic friend once more.

Peter's arrival, unfortunately, brought more trouble, for a group of Jewish Christians accompanied him from Jerusalem. At first everyone was busy proudly showing Peter and the visitors the great things which had been accomplished in Antioch. But as the days passed, Luke noticed that those who had accompanied Peter were associating with a small clique who had been recalcitrant about accepting the instructions of James and the elders. When Peter, too, began to associate more with this group and to shun the Gentiles in the common meals and the rituals of the church, it was soon apparent that the rift was rapidly widening again, this time stimulated by Peter himself.

Paul reacted as he would have been expected and indeed as he had every right to do, with a deep anger against Peter. Only a few months before Peter had espoused the acceptance of Gentiles upon equal terms into the Church, now he was going against his own pronouncements. Luke and Barnabas argued that Peter had vacillated before and that he must soon see the error into which he was being led. But Paul insisted that Peter must be publicly rebuked if the rift which was already widening again were to be permanently healed.

Fire was in Paul's eyes as he stood up to speak before the congregation on the following Sabbath. As he watched him defy those who stood against him, Luke's thoughts went back to the day on which he had first seen Paul, as prosecutor for the Sanhedrin at the trial of Stephen. The years and the recurrent bouts of fever, plus his injuries at the hands of his enemies, had not dealt lightly with the apostle. Their weight had bowed his shoulders, and his rather short body was less erect. But his head still had its leonine cast, and his eyes—for all that he suffered from a persistent inflammation which sometimes made it almost impossible for him to see—still burned with the hot fire of his spirit. He had become more bald through the years, and his beard was thinner and tinged with gray. But the long flexible fingers of the artisan had lost none of their grace and dexterity, for he had worked continually at his trade of tentmaker, even in Antioch. As Paul talked now, his hands moved constantly, almost as an artist would use a brush, painting in gestures as well as words the thoughts he wished to express.

Peter sat quietly in the elevated space where, as was customary in Jewish synagogues, the "rulers of the synagogue" had their places. Among the new ecclesiae, or congregations, however, they were called "elders" and "deacons." For all his size and exuberant good health, Peter's complexion had always been sallow and pale. His hair, only just now beginning to be shot through with gray, was rich and full, and his beard curled about a chin which may have been weak, since Peter was not a strong and dominant character, although he had been given a position of leadership by Jesus. But there was something about the big apostle that inspired love just the same, a quiet dignity and majesty and a light of kindness and tolerance shining in his eyes. Peter could understand the vacillations and indecisions of others because he had suffered such things himself.

When Paul began to speak his voice lashed the congregation like a whip, bringing people sharply upright with surprise. Everyone could see that he was burning with a deep anger, an emotion more powerful than the usual dynamic fire which motivated him. "Men and brethren," he said, "I speak to you today because the Church is in danger. Certain people have come among you and seek to unsettle your faith, the same faith which I have taught you and through which you have placed your trust in me. I say to you that if anyone is preaching a doctrine to you which is contrary to the one which you received from God through me, a curse be upon him."

These were strong words, and a deep murmur ran through the congregation, for everyone in the building knew that it was Peter to whom this public condemnation was directed.

"You all know," Paul continued, "that not long ago Barnabas and myself journeyed to Jerusalem because then, as now, false prophets had come among you, preaching that men could not be saved as God revealed to me merely by believing in the Lord Jesus Christ and his resurrection, but must needs be circumcised and keep the laws of Moses. At Jerusalem I laid before James and the elders the way to salvation which I have preached unto you and to the brethren in Galatia, Cyprus, and Cilicia, and which all of you have believed. And when the leaders saw that I had been entrusted with the charge of taking the truths of Christ to the Gentiles and the heathen, just as Peter was entrusted to take it to the Jews—for the same Spirit of Christ which had been at work in Peter for his apostleship to the Jews had been at work in me, too, for the apostleship to the heathen—these same leaders gave to Barnabas and me the right hand of fellowship, with the understanding that we should go to the heathen and they to the Jews. They asked us only to remember the poor, which we were eager to do.

"Now Peter knew this, and when he first came to Antioch he ate and associated with everyone, whether Jew or not, whether circumcised or not. Recently other false prophets have come from Jerusalem, saying that the Jews should not eat with the uncircumcised, and Peter has joined them. So I say to him now, before this congregation: If you are living like a heathen and not like a Jew, although you are a Jew yourself, why do you try to make the heathen live like Jews?"

Paul paused for a moment, then went on: "We ourselves are Jews by birth, and yet we know that a man does not come into right standing with God by doing what the law commands, but by simple trust in Christ. Through the law I have myself become dead to the law, even as you who have accepted Christ with me have done, so that I may live for God. I have been crucified with Christ, and I myself no longer live, but Christ is living in me; the life I now live as a mortal man I live by faith in the son of God, who loved me and gave himself for me. And if right standing with God came only through the law, as the false prophets have told you, then Christ died for nothing.

"But Christ did not die in vain, for all of you are the sons of God through faith in him. And all of you who have been baptized into union with Christ have clothed yourselves with him. There is no room for Jew or Greek, no room for slave or freeman, no room for male or female, for you are all one through union with Jesus Christ. In union with Christ Jesus neither circumcision nor the lack of it counts for anything; but only faith that is spurred on to action by love. The whole law of Christ is summed up in one saying, *'You must love your neighbor as you do yourself.'* If then you continue to bite and eat one another, beware lest you be destroyed by one another.

"Practice living by the Spirit, for the products of the Spirit are love, joy, peace, patience, kindness, goodness, faithfulness, gentleness, and self-control. There is no law against such things. If we live by the Spirit, let us also walk where the Spirit leads. Let us stop being ambitious for honors, so challenging one another and envying one another. For if anybody thinks he is somebody when really he is nobody, he is deceiving himself. Everyone should test his own work until it stands the test, then he will have grounds for boasting with reference to himself alone, and not with reference to someone else. For everyone must carry his own load."

Now Paul's voice rang out over the hushed crowd in a veritable paean of triumph. "But may it never be mine to boast of anything but the cross of our Lord Jesus Christ by which the world has been crucified to me and I to the world! Now peace and mercy be on all who walk by this rule; that is, on the true Israel of God. Let nobody trouble me after this, for I carry on my body the scars that mark me as Jesus's slave. The spiritual blessing of our Lord Jesus Christ be with your spirit, brothers. Amen."

Paul sat down, but there was still no sound from the congregation. All of them knew that his words had been directed to Peter, and they waited for Peter to answer. What they did not seem to realize was that they had just heard a truly inspired description of the Way they were all pledged to follow, a way of life given to the world by the gentle man who had died on the cross upon the hill of Calvary before Jerusalem.

Peter remained silent, however, and the service was soon over. People gathered around Paul, praising his words and congratulating him, but Luke did not see Peter in the crowd. Then he spied the tall form of the older apostle leaving the church and hurried after him. Peter was halfway down the street when Luke caught up with him and touched his arm gently to attract his attention. "What is it, Luke?" Peter asked kindly.

"I want you to know," Luke said earnestly, "that I think Paul did wrong in rebuking you before the congregation."

Peter smiled and took Luke's arm. "Come walk with me by the river, Luke," he said. "I need a keen mind like yours to help me think." Peter did not speak until they reached the stone parapet at the end of the street where the brown flood of the Orontes flowed below them on its way to the sea. "I will tell you a story, Luke," he said gently. "Once when I was with Jesus a controversy sprang up among the disciples as to which of them might be greatest. I have always tried to remember what the Master said then, Luke: *'The one who is lowliest among you all is really great.'*"

"But you were the one Jesus chose to lead the disciples. Everyone loves you, Peter, and we all know that you meant no harm when——" He stopped in some confusion, for to go on would have meant admitting that Paul's rebuke was justified.

"Yes, Luke," Peter said gently. "Paul was right in rebuking me, and so I had no right to speak against him. To deny any man the right to believe in Jesus and come to him is to deny the Saviour." Peter bowed his head, and when he spoke again his voice was muffled, as if his throat were filled with emotion. "I denied him once, Luke, and I should get down on my knees and thank Paul for showing me that I was about to deny him again.

"Paul has been chosen by God for a great work," Peter continued, "perhaps greater than my own. If I had answered him publicly it would have been to justify myself by humbling him. And Jesus told us we should humble self, as he did."

"What are you going to do then?" Luke asked.

"Do?" Peter smiled. "The Lord's work, of course. I am still the apostle to the Jews. There are many of our people in the cities of the Decapolis and even as far as Babylon and Rome who have not heard of Jesus. I shall carry the message to them."

Impulsively Luke said, "Let me go with you, Peter. Thecla could travel with us; she would be a comfort to your wife."

"Do not tempt me to think of my own wishes, Luke," Peter said with a smile. "We all know that only your medical skill has made it possible for Paul to carry his message to the Gentiles. He needs you far more than I do. Remember the words of Jesus, Luke, 'The one who is lowliest among you all is really great.' Your humility and devotion to the Way will be properly rewarded someday, if not on earth, then in heaven with Jesus."

When Luke returned to Barnabas's house he found Paul and Barnabas facing each other angrily. Barnabas's first words betrayed the source of his resentment. "Why did you reprimand Peter before the congregation, Paul?" he demanded. "You had no right to do that."

Paul's color rose. "By what right do you censure me, Barnabas?" he snapped.

"Any follower of Jesus has a right to protest an insult to the one upon whom the mantle of the Lord fell."

"When Peter tried to drive a wedge between Jew and Gentile he forfeited any right to wear that mantle."

"Upon whom is it to descend, then?" Barnabas asked with biting sarcasm. "You?"

"Why not?" Paul demanded, his face set in an angry cast. "Did not the Lord speak to me from the heavens and call me to do his work? Has he done more for Peter?"

"Do you dare set yourself above Peter?" Barnabas asked incredulously.

"Peter denied Christ. He himself admits it."

"But that was God's will. Jesus himself foretold it. And no one has been more faithful since the resurrection than Peter."

"Has Peter risked his life to carry God's message to the heathen?" Paul demanded. "Has he been whipped with thirty-nine lashes or felt the stones upon his body?"

"Peter never shirks danger," Barnabas argued. "He remained in Jerusalem when Herod had sworn to imprison him. And God recognized his courage and zeal by releasing him from prison. Has he done as much for you, Paul?"

The words were spoken, and Luke realized from the sudden look of horror on Barnabas's face that he had not meant them as they sounded. But in his angry state Paul took them as an accusation that God had withheld approval of his work when he had failed to stay the lashes at Pisidian Antioch or the stones at Lystra. "I yield to no man in serving God," Paul said coldly. "If the Lord does not support my mission, let him deny me by some sign." He turned and left the room, slamming the door with a finality which left no doubt in either of their minds that he was terminating his partnership with Barnabas.

"I never meant to imply that God did not support Paul," Barnabas said miserably. "He should know that."

"Paul was angry, Barnabas. He may feel different later."

Barnabas shook his head. "I have hurt Paul in his most vulnerable spot, Luke, his pride in being called directly by Jesus to carry the message to the Gentiles. There can be no healing the breach now. One thing I wish you would do for me, Luke. Ask Paul to let Mark go with you on the next visit to Galatia; there is much that he could learn from Paul."

But Paul flatly refused to let John Mark go along with them. The reason he gave was that Mark could not be trusted on so important an expedition because he had given up and returned from Perga on the previous one. But Luke was sure that what rankled in Paul's mind was the suspicion that Mark would be a spy for Peter. Now he realized just how deep a schism had developed in the Church of Jesus, a breach whose widening might prove the undoing of all their work.

viii

Luke sadly bade farewell to Barnabas and Mark when they departed a week later for Cyprus, where Barnabas planned to spend several months strengthening the churches. Paul's party, consisting of Luke, Probus, Silas, and the apostle, left Antioch a few days later, taking the land route so that Paul could visit Tarsus and the cities on the way where the Christians from Antioch had set up small churches. Paul was jubilant over the new venture and the opportunity to see and reaffirm the faith of those who believed throughout Cilicia and Galatia, unhampered by the work of the Judaizers who had so nearly wrecked the infant Church. At first Luke was saddened by the absence of Barnabas and Mark, but his spirits rose as the miles passed beneath their sandals along the coastal road to the north, shortening the distance between him and Thecla. And it was pleasant to have Probus as a traveling companion once more.

In Tarsus, Luke learned of the death of Glaucus some months before. The realization that Thecla was free to come to him when they reached Iconium set his heart beating faster in eager anticipation of the time when he would see her again and hold her in his arms, this time for always. Word of the action by the Church at Jerusalem in regard to the Gentile Christians had gone ahead of them, and as they reached the highlands their progress became in every sense a triumphal procession. There were stops at Derbe and Lystra while Paul preached and helped perfect the organization of the churches in those cities. Great crowds gathered all the way, and hundreds of converts were baptized in every village where they stopped.

Finally, however, they came to Iconium, and Thecla met them at the outskirts of the city with Timothy and his mother. To Luke the girl seemed more beautiful than ever. Sorrow over the death of Glaucus, whom she had loved deeply, had mellowed her girlish loveliness, and in the period of almost a year since he had seen her Thecla had matured into a beautiful young woman. Out of consideration for Thecla's grief for her father Luke did not urge their immediate marriage but was content to take up again their life where they had dropped it here in Iconium. He worked in his small surgery by day to help the sick and held Thecla's warm hand in his while they sat on cushions in the large common room in the evening listening to Paul, or stole a few moments together late at night in the garden before retiring.

Luke was happy with his work and his nearness to his beloved, until one day Probus asked, "Have you noticed how much time Paul spends talking to Thecla lately, Luke?"

Surprised, Luke said, "There is nothing wrong with that; it was Paul who converted her."

"He loves her; you know that, don't you?"

Luke smiled. "Don't you? I thought we all did."

"Not in the way I mean," Probus insisted. "I noticed it first in Jerusalem when you and Thecla became betrothed. And now it is even more apparent."

Luke was silent, for he remembered his own observations in Jerusalem and afterward. Now that he thought of it again, he could remember many small things which seemed to fit in with Probus's statement about Paul's loving Thecla.

"When are you and Thecla to be married?" Probus asked.

"We haven't agreed on a date. Why?"

"Paul has been talking to her about marriage; I overheard them once or twice. And you know his views about it."

"Vaguely," Luke admitted. "I have been busy with the sick and haven't listened to him preach lately."

"He states flatly now that people should no longer marry because the return of Jesus is so near. I have never heard him so emphatic before. If I were you," Probus continued, "I would talk to Thecla right away, before Paul convinces her that she should not marry you."

"But Paul wouldn't do that," Luke protested. "He knew we were planning to be married on my return to Iconium."

"Ask Thecla," Probus warned darkly. "It may already be too late."

Luke could not believe that Probus could be anything but mistaken. But when he held Thecla in his arms that night with perhaps more than his usual hunger for her, she pushed him away and said, "Please don't, Luke."

Luke felt a sudden chill. Could Probus be right, after all? He took Thecla's chin in his hands and turned her face up to him. In the moonlight he saw that her eyes were troubled and her chin quivering, as if she were about to cry. "What is it, dearest?" he asked. "You haven't changed your feelings about me, have you?"

For answer she threw herself into his arms and held him as if she never wanted to let him go. But he felt her tears dampen his tunic and her shoulders jerk from the sobs she could not repress. "What is wrong, dear?" he asked anxiously. "Anything that troubles you is my concern too."

She raised her face then. "Have you spoken to Paul about our marrying, Luke?"

"To Paul? No. But he knew our plans. Anyway, what does he have to do with our marrying?"

"Don't be angry, Luke," Thecla pleaded. "I only want to do what Jesus would wish for me to do. And Paul says——"

"Then Probus was right," Luke exploded.

"Probus? I don't understand."

"Probus believes Paul is in love with you himself, Thecla, and that he is trying to delay our marriage by convincing you that the coming of Jesus is so close that people should not marry."

She flinched as if he had struck her. "But he couldn't, Luke," she cried, and the pain in her voice went through him so that he wanted to take her in his arms again and comfort her. But she stiffened in his embrace, and he let his arm drop to his side. "What a terrible thing to say. Paul thinks only of Jesus, you know that."

When Luke did not answer at once, she begged piteously. "You couldn't believe anything like that, Luke. You couldn't."

"Paul is a man, Thecla," he said then, "and you are a very beautiful woman, more so now than ever before. I never told you before, but Paul came into the garden that night at the house of James in Jerusalem and saw me kiss you when we became betrothed. Afterward he was so angry with me that he refused to bless our marriage." Then he added with a smile, "But I don't blame anyone for falling in love with you, darling. Remember how quickly it happened to me?"

"But Paul is above such things as—as what marriage means. He loves everyone in the way Jesus did."

"I don't think there is anything wrong in the way I love you, Thecla," Luke said quietly. "Has Paul been telling you that there is?"

She did not answer but turned suddenly and ran into the house. Luke remained in the garden for some time before going to his own couch, but when finally he did, he had made his decision. There was only one answer: he must have it out with Paul as soon as possible.

Leaving Probus to finish the work in the surgery, the next day Luke returned early to the house of Eunice. He found Timothy there, fairly jumping with excitement. "Paul is taking me with him when he starts on his journeys again, Luke," the boy reported. "I am to be his clerk."

"But what of your studies, Timothy?"

"Thecla will teach me."

"Is she going too?" Luke asked.

"Why, yes. Hasn't she told you? I heard them speaking of it this afternoon."

"I haven't seen Thecla since morning."

"She must plan to tell you about it tonight," Timothy said. "I heard her begging Paul to let both of you go along, and he agreed."

Luke's heart leaped. Could it be that Thecla had talked Paul into approving their marriage? He started to ask Timothy, then did not, for the boy had revealed accidentally what Thecla had been discussing with Paul. To ask any more questions would be the same as eavesdropping upon her.

Thecla and Paul came in a little later. The girl was radiant. "Paul has promised to let me go with the rest of you on your journey to other cities, Luke," she cried. "I talked him into it."

"Are we to be married before we start?" Luke asked. "People might talk unless we were."

"I am Thecla's spiritual father now that Glaucus is dead," Paul said quickly. "Timothy is going, too, and Thecla could travel with the

220

group as his governess. There could be no possible cause for anyone to object."

Probus was right, Luke realized. Paul had already talked the impressionable girl into his own way of thought. And with the realization came a rising anger that he no longer tried to control.

"I have cause to object," he said flatly. "Thecla and I are betrothed, Paul. Why have you tried to talk Thecla out of marrying me?"

Paul was momentarily taken aback by the direct question, but he recovered his composure quickly. "Both of you know my feelings about marriage, Luke," he said reasonably. "The coming of the Lord Jesus is near, when there will be no marrying or giving in marriage. People should be thinking of other things besides themselves."

"You said Jesus was coming soon last year," Luke pointed out. "And he has not returned to earth yet."

"These are the words of Jesus," Paul said. "*'Be ye therefore ready also: for the Son of man cometh at an hour when ye think not.'* Actually I wish all men were like to myself, so busy with the Lord's work that there is no time for worldly things."

"Is it a sin for people to love each other and have children?" Luke demanded.

"A sin? No. But it would be a fine thing for them to remain single as I am." Paul turned to Thecla. "I know you are conscious that your body is a temple of the Holy Spirit, my dear. Furthermore, you are not your own, since you have given yourself to Jesus. You have been bought and actually paid for, so you should honor God with your body."

"Why this talk of bodies and dishonor?" Luke demanded angrily. "Thecla and I propose to be married legally and spiritually. There is nothing either dishonorable or sinful about that."

"You and Thecla are of age, Luke," Paul said reasonably. "I could not forbid you. But the time has been cut short until Jesus shall come, and therefore men who have wives should live as though they had none, for the outward order of the world is passing away. An unmarried man is concerned about the affairs of the Lord, but a married man is concerned about the affairs of the world and how he can please his wife, so his devotion is divided. An unmarried woman or a girl is concerned about the affairs of the Lord so as to be consecrated in body and spirit, but a married woman is concerned about affairs of the world and how she can please her husband. It is for the welfare of both of you that I say this, not to put restraint upon you, but to foster good order and to help you to an undivided devotion to the Lord. In my opinion, Thecla will be happier if she remains as she is, a virgin, and I think I have God's spirit in what I say."

Luke could see by the way Thecla was drinking in every word and the exalted look in her eyes that she was completely under Paul's magnetic spell. He had seen others so affected by the apostle's dynamic personality. Believing in Paul as she did and in his right to speak directly for Christ, Paul's arguments, his commanding presence, and his sonorous voice had entranced her, until she was no longer capable of exercising her own will in his presence. It was similar to the trancelike state in which the priest-physicians of Asklepios sometimes seemed to accomplish miraculous cures and which he had seen Probus evoke by letting impressionable people gaze at the great emerald from Pergamum.

"While I cannot approve of your marrying"—Paul's voice broke into Luke's thoughts—"I have thought of a way to please you both and reward you for keeping your bodies inviolate for Christ. When we leave here we will all go into Bithynia together."

"Oh, Paul!" Thecla cried. "How wonderful!" She turned to Luke eagerly. "Your dreams will be realized then, dear."

Luke nodded dully, but there was no joy in his heart. Bithynia had first meant a place of peace and withdrawal from the troubles of the world. Lately, however, he had seen a richer and fuller picture, a home where he and Thecla would live a life of their own together, bringing children into the world and watching them grow up, teaching them to revere the past because of its lessons for the present and to think for themselves; and, most important, showing those around them how true happiness comes from living the Way of Jesus.

But now everything was changed, and even with Thecla beside him there was no lure to Bithynia, because there would be no children, no real home together. Paul would control Thecla by convincing her that the way he described was the way Jesus would want her to be.

Ironically enough, Luke could understand Paul's reasoning and the motives behind it and could even sympathize with him. Believing as he did that people should remain in the state in which they had been called to the service of Christ, Paul could not marry, and so his love for Thecla must have tormented him in a bitter conflict between Paul, the man, and Paul, the apostle to the Gentiles. When he saw her betrothed and about to be married to another, his convictions had then come to the rescue of his conscience, for he could logically discourage Luke and Thecla from marrying, feeling that in using his power over the girl he was really serving the best interests of the faith he believed in, while at the same time keeping her inviolate and firmly bound to himself.

Luke was faced with a hopeless impasse, for if he gave in, Thecla must gradually be drawn closer to Paul and his way of thinking and so would be lost to him. While if he forced it to an issue now, Paul's in-

222

fluence over Thecla was so great that she might forswear marriage forever and be equally lost to him.

Suddenly he saw an answer to his problem. It was so simple that he wondered why it had not come to him before. Many of the new converts in Galatia and elsewhere, fired by Paul's convictions of the hourly coming of Jesus, had taken virgins as their espoused wives, living with them as man and wife but without the physical relations of the married state. Paul had gone on record as approving these odd relationships, and to a girl in such a state of religious ecstasy as the apostle had induced in Thecla, such a mystical union would seem an ideal way of serving God and keeping herself inviolate of any sin. Married under such conditions, Luke could keep Thecla close to him always. And sometime, he was sure, Thecla would come to her senses and realize that such a half marriage, without children or a home of their own, was the mockery which Luke firmly believed it to be.

Luke turned to Thecla and took her hands in his. Under his calm, loving gaze her eyes lost some of their rapt expression and an answering warmth kindled in them. "You love me, don't you, Thecla?" he asked tenderly.

"Oh, I do, Luke," she said in a rush as the soft color poured into her cheeks. "You know I do. Are we not betrothed?"

"I want you to be my virgin," Luke said then. "To live with me as man and wife, except that I promise to hold you inviolate as long as you wish."

"Oh, Luke," she cried, her eyes suddenly glowing. "Could we?" She turned quickly to Paul. "Would that be all right, Paul?"

Before Paul could answer or object, Luke said, "You have publicly approved such marriages, Paul. All of us have heard you."

Luke saw the animation die out in the apostle's eyes, and in its place came a look almost of hopelessness and defeat, such as had been there after the whipping at Pisidian Antioch. Luke suddenly felt a sense of pity toward Paul, for he wondered if in the same situation he would have had the strength and courage to adhere to his principles and deny himself the woman he loved. Impulsively he put out his hand. "I am sorry, Paul," he said sincerely. "Really sorry."

For a long moment Paul stared at him, and Luke knew that the apostle realized and understood his own thoughts. Then Paul gave him his hand and smiled with something of the old feeling of comradeship which had been theirs. "God bless the both of you," he said, "and give you strength to keep your vows."

When Paul had left the room Thecla came into Luke's arms, and this time there was no reluctance. "See how wrong you were about Paul, darling?" she cried. "He has approved our marriage, and now we can be together always. And if Jesus is coming back soon, it will be better if we"—her cheeks crimsoned suddenly and she hid her face against his breast—"if we stay as we are."

"I love you enough to want to be with you on your own terms, Thecla," he said, holding her close to him. But to himself he added, "If that is the only way."

When Probus heard about the arrangement he was forthright in his condemnation. "You are a fool to let yourself be tricked into any such unnatural relationship," he told Luke. "Paul would not dare take Thecla for himself; now he has talked you out of having her as your wife."

"What else could I do?"

"Women need to be handled firmly, like children," Probus said. "You should have told her the truth."

"But that would have meant an open break with Paul," Luke protested.

"Why not? You cannot go on giving up your whole life for him. You have yourself and your place as a physician to think of."

"Peter and Barnabas think my place as a physician is with Paul. Why do you follow him, Probus? Sometimes I believe you hate him."

The apothecary smiled wryly. "Sometimes I do," he admitted. "I know I am a fool to be traveling on foot through a barbarous country when I could make a fortune treating bald heads in Antioch. Still, there is something about a man battling the world for a principle he believes in that makes you want to help him. And somehow I always manage to get on the side of the fellow who is sure to lose."

Luke smiled. "This time you will not lose, Probus. The Way of Jesus will go down through history as a guide for men to live by."

Probus shrugged. "Perhaps. But even if it does, who will remember Luke and Paul and Barnabas and Peter and the rest of you who are giving your lives to it?"

ix

Nothing was changed outwardly by the marriage of Luke and Thecla, for they did not live together, except in the same house as they had before. And yet when he heard Thecla singing as she worked, or saw her coming down the street toward his surgery on her way to the market place, Luke's throat filled with pride that she was his wife, even though only in name. If the love that he and Thecla felt for each other could of itself bring such happiness to marriage, Luke sometimes thought, what must be the ecstasy of a bodily union which produced another being? But such thoughts only brought on the old torment that still came when he held Thecla in his arms. And somehow he could not rid himself of the idea that such a relationship as theirs, denying to them as it did the complete fulfillment of their love, was innately sinful.

So the months passed busily, for churches were springing up in all the towns along the trade route and in the Lycaonian highlands. "It must be nearly time for Mariamne to have her baby," Luke suggested to Thecla one day. "Theophilus said she and Apollonius wished I could be there when it happens."

Thecla's face lit up. "Why couldn't we go on to Ephesus and meet Paul later? I heard him telling Silas yesterday that they must be making plans soon to go on to Thyatira and then north into Bithynia."

Luke's heart warmed at the thought of having Thecla to himself for a while, although he hoped for no change in their relationship yet, for she was still under the spell of Paul and his rather mystical beliefs about the coming of Jesus. "We will speak to Paul about it tonight," he promised. "Mariamne was a favorite of his, so I am sure he would not object."

Paul gave his blessing to the trip without objection, and they set out a few days later on the Old Way with Probus, bound for the city of Ephesus.

"There is a saying that 'all roads lead to Ephesus,'" Probus told Luke and Thecla when they paused at the top of a hill a week later to look down upon the famous city of the Greeks spread out before them in the shallow basin of the Meander and Cayster rivers, where they joined before emptying into the Aegean Sea. Over the low-lying hills to the east from which they had come an endless file of dromedaries moved along the caravan route from the cities of Asia and beyond, their backs piled high with bales of rare fabric from Mesopotamia, silver and steel from the forges of Damascus, and spices and condiments for the tables of the Romans and rich Greeks.

Up the shallow channel of the Cayster, dredged to permit small vessels to come right into the city, a few cargo smacks were beating slowly cityward against the wind, and in the distance a galley moved gracefully along, the banked oars flashing in the sunlight as they were lifted dripping from the water. Three miles away the sea itself was visible only as a bluish haze on the horizon to the west. Larger ships, cargo vessels from Alexandria and the Syrian ports, and the great triremes with which Rome used to move military forces from place to place did not essay the shallow channel of the Cayster but docked at the fine port of Miletus some thirty miles to the south. A stone-paved highway, built by the Romans, connected busy and prosperous Ephesus with its sea terminal.

The great Temple of Artemis or Diana, for which Ephesus was famous throughout the world, lay about a mile and a half northeast of the city, and a broad thoroughfare paved in marble, a continuation of one of the main streets of the city, ran to it. Over this marble road thousands passed each year to worship at the shrine of Artemis and to witness the vice-ridden ceremonies honoring this most dissolute of the goddesses. The patrons of divine Artemis were wealthy, and her priests occupied a high place in the life of the city.

Descending the hill, Luke, Thecla, and Probus turned into the ancient road that ran from Smyrna to Ephesus. Where the road to the Temple of Artemis joined their route they mingled with the vast throng moving into the city from the morning worship at the temple. Many of the faithful carried small silver statues of the goddess or replicas of the famous temple which were sold everywhere. Inside the city itself the shops of the silversmiths were crowded with these emblems rather than the silver plate, engraved fruit baskets, bracelets, earrings, and medallions sold by the workers of silver of other cities.

"The Ephesians seem devoted to their goddess," Thecla observed. "Do they know nothing of Jesus?"

"Ephesus has good reason to be content with Artemis," Probus explained. "Her temple is one of the seven wonders of the world, and the silversmiths make a fortune from these little idols you see everywhere. Ephesus without Artemis would be like a Roman without his toga." Then he grinned. "I will make a prophecy. When Ephesus loses faith in Artemis, the silversmiths will starve."

Along the broad street they were traveling marble statues of many gods had been set in niches between the shops. Prominent among them were the Roman emperors who had been declared divine by official order. "It must be a wicked city," Thecla said, "to worship so many gods."

"All cities are wicked," Probus agreed. "When men leave the fields and move to the cities they lose part of their souls. Let me see. The Roman headquarters should be over on the west side of the city, if I remember correctly."

Apollonius engulfed Luke in a massive embrace, then stood back to look at him, as if still unable to believe his own eyes. "I thought you were still in Antioch, Luke," he said. "Mariamne and I have wished for you more than once these last few days."

"Is anything wrong?" Luke asked quickly.

"It is past her time, a week at least, perhaps more. The baby seems to be so large, and Mariamne is so slight."

"Women have been having babies safely for thousands of years," he reassured Apollonius. "Mariamne will come through all right." These

226

were common fears from expectant fathers, and there were always errors in calculating the date of confinement.

"That isn't the only worry I have," Apollonius said. "My legion has been ordered to leave for Britain in a few weeks. There is a shortage of experienced officers for this expedition, and I see no way of getting out of it." Then his face brightened. "But I will not worry with you here, little brother."

Luke looked at Thecla and knew that her thought was the same as his. Must they give up their cherished plan to go to Bithynia now that they were actually on the way? He took Thecla by the hand and introduced her to his brother as his wife.

Apollonius's mouth dropped open with amazement. "I didn't even know you were married, Luke," he said, but added gallantly, "You picked a beautiful girl, though." He took them by the hand. "We must go to Mariamne at once; she will want to know that you are here. And you too, Probus," he told the apothecary. "I shall not soon forget that you saved my life when we were attacked near the grave of Silvanus."

Apollonius and Mariamne dwelt near the Roman headquarters in a small but comfortable villa built around a garden. When Luke first saw Mariamne he was shocked. He remembered her slender loveliness, and now her body was grossly distorted far beyond what he would have expected from her pregnancy. Her face was swollen and her ankles puffy and large, until her appearance was almost a caricature of her former beauty. At the sight of them she burst into sobs, and Luke realized it was as much at realizing how she must look as from joy and relief at seeing them. With immediate understanding Thecla went to Mariamne and put her arms about the weeping young woman, comforting her while she led her to a couch. They sat there together while Luke told Apollonius and Mariamne about their experiences since they had seen each other and gave them messages from Theophilus in Antioch and Ananias in Tarsus.

Apollonius would not hear of their staying anywhere except at the villa. When he returned to Roman headquarters Probus went with him to look over the city, leaving Luke and Thecla with Mariamne. Luke made a thorough examination of the pregnant girl and when he had finished gave her a draught to quiet her nerves. Thecla came out into the atrium where he was reading a short time later and sat on a cushion, resting her head against his knee. "I am worried about Mariamne, Luke," she said.

"She is not well," he admitted.

"The baby seems so large."

"Much of that is swelling," he explained. "Did you notice how her ankles and the rest of her body are puffed?"

She shivered. "Is pregnancy always like this?"

Luke put his arm about her. "Of course not. Most women have very little trouble, and they forget even that as soon as they see their babies."

"Mariamne told me how glad she and Apollonius are that you are here, Luke. Doesn't it scare you sometimes to have so many people dependent upon you?"

"That is part of being a physician."

"But you are more than just a physician. People seem to trust you the very moment they see you. I—I guess it is because the light of your soul shines in your eyes."

"Now you are flattering me," Luke told her, smiling. "I think everybody would like to be kind and thoughtful of others, but they are afraid of being rebuffed and hurt."

"Aren't you ever afraid of that, Luke?"

"No, dear. I decided long ago that what anyone says about me or thinks of me cannot hurt me so long as I know I have done right inside myself."

"Jesus was that way, so you must be right." Then soft color stole into her cheeks. "If Paul is wrong about his coming so soon, Luke, do you suppose we could have a baby of our own someday? I would want a boy just like you."

"Of course, dear," he told her. "Whenever you wish. And I would be perfectly happy with another Thecla."

Thecla reached for his hand with a sigh of pleasure. They were closer than they had been at any time since his return to Iconium, Luke realized. Perhaps it might even be best for them both if they stayed here in Ephesus with Mariamne and the baby for a while as Apollonius had suggested, letting Paul go on without them. But he did not believe that Paul would immediately agree to any such arrangement.

The next morning Mariamne complained of a severe headache, and when Luke examined her again, he saw that the swelling in her body tissues had increased. The baby was in a normal position and apparently healthy, for it kicked strongly as he felt its outlines through the young mother's abdomen. But there was no sign as yet of the contractions of the womb which would have meant the onset of the birth pains. Something else worried him, too, a strange look about Mariamne's eyes, with a dulling of their normally clear gaze that he was unable to explain.

Through the day Mariamne was no better. Luke had never seen a case like this, where the baby seemed to poison the mother, but he had heard of them. All authorities agreed that only an early onset of labor and delivery of the baby could stop the lethal process. Talking the case

228

over with Probus at the evening meal, Luke said, "If there were only some way of removing the baby from the mother's body."

"The ancient Jews claimed to have removed a living baby by cutting through the walls of the body into the womb. It is described in old Jewish scrolls, and I have run across it in the writings of some Persian poets."

"But did they ever save both mother and child?"

"I found no record that they did," Probus admitted. "And you would hardly want to try such a hazardous procedure when Mariamne will probably get rapidly better after the baby is born."

Perhaps an hour later Thecla called urgently to Luke from the room where Mariamne lay. One glance told him what was happening. Mariamne's head was thrown back until her body seemed to be arched upon head and heels, and her limbs were jerking spasmodically. It was the convulsions of childbirth, the most dreaded of all complications, and the one most universally fatal!

The initial convulsion lasted less than a minute, then Mariamne's racked body fell back on the couch. Apparently unconscious, she breathed stertorously with her eyes closed, but a few seconds later she moaned in her coma and put her hand to her abdomen. When Luke felt for the womb through her abdominal wall he found the muscles hard under his fingers for fully a quarter of a minute. "The pains have begun," he reported to Thecla and Probus. "There is some hope now."

"But how can she stand such spasms?" Thecla asked fearfully. "I thought that one would twist her body in two." As if to echo her words, Mariamne was racked by another convulsion, one so severe that she was unable to breathe while the muscles were contracted, and her lips and ears turned blue before they finally relaxed and her body fell back inert upon the couch.

None of them knew Apollonius had come in until they heard his gasp of horror. White as marble, he swayed and would have fallen in a faint had not Probus seized him and led him to a chair. "Is she dying, Luke?" he asked piteously.

"No," Luke told him, "but she is gravely ill. We must try to get the baby delivered before the spasms take all of her strength."

"But how can you do it?" Thecla asked. "The pains have just begun."

"Get me several pitchers of hot water," Luke directed. "And bring blankets and cloths. Sometimes wrapping in hot cloths makes convulsions less severe."

Thecla and the servants returned in a few minutes, bringing basins of hot water and blankets. Together they wrapped Mariamne's body in a steaming cocoon, but even with the heat another terrible spasm racked her body.

229

"If you dared to cut into the womb," Probus said thoughtfully. "But then she could hardly stand it now."

Luke nodded agreement. "There is nothing to do but wait—and hope."

Luke and Probus and Thecla worked all through the night giving Mariamne what little help they could by easing her body during the spasms, replacing the hot cloths and blankets, and praying when there was time. But as the hours wore on they could see that the battle was being lost. Slowly at first Mariamne's pulse grew weaker, then more rapidly as the end approached. Finally there came a time when the bluish color of her lips, ears, and skin no longer lightened between the spasms, and Luke knew that death was only a few minutes away at most. There had been no sign of movement from the baby for the past several hours, and Luke was sure that it had died, poisoned perhaps by the same agent which was killing Mariamne, if indeed it had not been killed by the powerful contractions of the mother's womb upon its tender body.

Depressed by their inability to help or to comfort Apollonius, they watched death take Mariamne. When at last there was no sign of breath or flutter of the pulse Luke reached down to draw the sheet up over the face of the dead girl. But as his hand passed over her now relaxed abdomen he felt a sudden faint movement, as if something had kicked feebly against his palm. Instantly he realized that the baby was still alive.

"Probus!" he cried. "My instrument case. The baby still lives."

The quick-witted apothecary divined his intention at once and ran for the case of scalpels, tearing it open as he came back and holding one out to Luke.

"What are you going to do?" Apollonius cried. "Don't cut her now."

But Luke was already tearing the covers away, exposing the dead girl's body with the tremendously enlarged womb containing the baby inside it. "He is going to open the body and try to save the child before it suffocates," Probus explained as Luke drew the knife down the rounded eminence of Mariamne's abdomen, slitting open the skin and the thinned-out muscles beneath in one quick stroke.

Apollonius started to object, but Probus said quickly, "The *Lex Caesaris* demands that a physician open the body of the mother to save the child if he thinks it still lives." Actually, as Probus well knew, there was really no "Law of the Caesars" to that effect on the statute books. But custom dating back into antiquity decreed that the physician attending a woman who died in childbirth should open the body and deliver the still living child if possible.

The explanation stopped any objection from Apollonius, half crazed

230

as he was, and Luke worked swiftly on, slitting the thin membrane lining the abdomen and exposing the bluish-red mass of the womb. An awkward stroke now might cut through the muscle and plunge the knife into the baby inside the uterus. And yet he must work fast, for only seconds remained to reach the child before it suffocated.

Stroking carefully, he cut through the muscular wall of the womb and saw the almost black blood ooze from cut vessels. With his sleeve he wiped it away—there was no time to reach for a cloth—and cut again, ever deeper. Suddenly the entire muscle wall parted, weakened as it was from the strain of the convulsions, and a gush of yellow fluid poured out over Mariamne's body and drenched Luke from the waist down. He could see the baby now, however, and felt it kick feebly against his hand.

"The baby lives," he cried exultantly. "We are in time."

Quickly he slipped two fingers into the opening he had made in the womb and, using them to protect the baby, cut down through the wall until a space was opened up through which he could lift the baby from its mother's body. It was a boy, large and heavy. He held it up by the feet with the head down and slapped the child sharply on the buttock. Its chest jerked convulsively once, twice, then expanded as air rushed in for the first breath. An initial wail of protest was followed by another, and in a few seconds the boy was crying lustily, the blue tint of its lips and skin fading quickly into a healthy pink.

Apollonius stared at the baby as if unable to believe the miracle he had witnessed, while Thecla sobbed with relief after the almost unbearable tension. "Wonderful, Luke," Probus said admiringly. "I never saw anything like that before."

Luke breathed a silent prayer of relief and thanksgiving at having felt the initial kick through Mariamne's body which had told him the baby was alive. Otherwise, he knew, the child would have died with its mother. Quickly now he tied the gelatinous cord connecting the child to its mother's body and cut it across. Thecla had gained control of herself now, and when Luke held out the baby to her she wrapped it in a blanket and took it into her arms, cradling it to her breast and crooning softly to it. As if it realized that all danger was over, the child stopped crying. Seeing the glory in Thecla's eyes, Luke thought that it would indeed be a sin to deny her children of her own, as Paul wished.

x

Apollonius was so distraught over the death of Mariamne that Luke and Thecla were forced to take over the entire operation of his household. Thecla gladly assumed the care of the infant, who was given the name Apollos Lucanus. The strapping wife of a Roman soldier was hired as a wet nurse, and the household quickly settled down to the happy sort of existence that surrounds a growing child. Luke gave of his medical skill unstintingly to those who came to consult him, but Ephesus was a busy city of workers, and so a considerable portion of his practice could afford to pay. The fact that he had at one time been military physician to Sergius Paulus, who was highly respected in Roman military circles, also brought him many patients from the governing class.

The eagerness with which Thecla assumed the care of the baby betrayed her strong maternal instincts and, listening to her crooning to the child, Luke found himself dreading the day when he would have to tear her away from it. Preparations for the sailing of the Ephesian guard for Gaul and Britain went on apace, and the day of Apollonius's departure drew nearer. A letter had been dispatched to Theophilus in Antioch and to Ananias in Tarsus telling them of the death of Mariamne and the almost miraculous birth of the child, but it would be several months at least before Theophilus could come from Antioch for the baby. And even then the child should not make such a long and difficult voyage until it was at least six months old.

One night as Luke and Thecla stood beside the cradle she said, "Why can't we stay here until the baby leaves for Antioch, Luke, and go to Bithynia later? After what happened to Mariamne, we owe it to her to see that her baby is well cared for."

"Probus has been trying to convince me that we should stay in Ephesus, at least for a while," Luke admitted. "But what can we do about Paul?"

"He would understand," she said. "There must be many places he has not visited in Galatia and here along the coast. Then we could all go to Bithynia later on."

"We certainly can't leave the baby until Theophilus comes," Luke agreed. "I will ask Probus to meet Paul at Thyatira—he should be there any day now—and explain all this to him. Then if Paul wants to go on anyway, Probus can go with him. He knows everything that I do for Paul when he is sick."

Probus departed the next day in a chariot placed at his disposal by Apollonius. They had figured that it would not take more than three or four days for him to drive the fifty-odd miles to Thyatira, talk to Paul and return, but a week passed before the chariot drove into the courtyard of the villa. To his surprise, Luke saw that Paul was with the apothecary.

Paul was in high spirits, and both Thecla and Luke were glad to see him, so the meeting was a happy one. "I would have returned sooner," Probus explained to Luke, "but when I got to Thyatira, Paul had already gone through to Troas, so I followed him." Troas, the ancient Troy of the famous Trojan Wars, was some fifty miles northwest of the city of Thyatira, where the road branched northward across the Olympian range to Bithynia.

Paul took up the account then. "I stopped at Thyatira, Luke, because I had promised you that we would go into Bithynia, but a warning from God told me to go on to Troas instead. And it was here that the call came to Macedonia."

"Macedonia? You had not planned to go there, had you?"

"*I* had not planned it," Paul said, "but God had. A man came to me by night in a dream and said, 'Come over into Macedonia and help us.' And when I pleaded that there was work to be done in Galatia and Bithynia, he still remained, saying the same words. So I could only conclude that God's will was being revealed to me."

Luke glanced at Probus, but the apothecary only shrugged. Whether it had been Paul's desire to move to new territories which had brought on the dream, or whether God had really called him to a new field, no one would ever know. But Paul's eagerness and enthusiasm left no doubt that the suggestion was welcome to him. And it might be a good move, Luke realized. The cities of Macedonia, the province lying northward on the Greek mainland around the upper coast of the Aegean Sea, across from Ephesus and Troas, were largely Greek with a few Jews. For the most part their level of culture and education was higher than that of the rude peasant people of the Galatian highlands, whose shifting moods they all had ample reason to fear. In Grecian cities Paul might not be believed at once, but he would be accorded a courteous hearing, for the Greeks welcomed anyone with a new concept in the field of philosophy.

"Macedonia is a fertile field," Luke agreed. And Probus added, "Certainly more so than Galatia. And the teachings of Christ have always appealed to Greek thought."

"Exactly what I told Silas and Timothy," Paul said enthusiastically. "They are as eager to go on as I am."

Thecla had gone to the nursery and now she came in, carrying the baby in her arms for Paul to see. A less observant man than Paul could not have failed to see how happy she was in her maternal role. Luke saw the apostle glance at her sharply, and a frown, as if of displeasure, momentarily creased his forehead. He tousled the child's dark hair for a moment, then turned back to Luke. "Probus tells me you and Thecla would like to stay on in Ephesus for a while, Luke."

"At least until Theophilus is able to take the child back to Antioch with him," Luke explained. "There is no one else to keep him."

"Apollonius is worrying about the baby," Thecla added. "And since he is going so far away, the least that Luke can do is see that Apollos Lucanus is safe."

"We can talk more of this later," Paul said. "I would like to rest awhile now."

Probus took Paul to his quarters, leaving Luke and Thecla alone with the baby. "What was wrong with Paul, Luke?" she asked. "Why should he mind our staying in Ephesus with the baby when he is not going to Bithynia after all?"

"I don't think it pleased him to see you with the child," Luke told her.

"But why, Luke?"

"Have you looked at yourself when you have him in your arms, darling? Anyone could see that God intended you to have children of your own."

Slowly the animation faded from her face. "You think Paul is afraid I might want a child so badly that I would break my vow of—of chastity?"

"I have always been perfectly honest with you, Thecla," Luke said. "It seems obvious to me, and Probus agrees, that Paul has loved you for a long time, probably since your conversion in Tarsus. And in the way that I love you, the love of a man for the woman he takes as his wife, to bear his children."

"But I am *your* wife."

For a moment Luke did not speak, then he stooped and kissed her. "Are you, dear?" he asked gently. "It is for you to say."

He saw the unhappiness fill her eyes until the tears started and her chin began to quiver. Then with a muffled sob she ran from the room, holding the baby so close against her breast that he set up a wail of protest.

That night at the evening meal Paul said abruptly, "Luke, I want you to go into Macedonia with me."

"Why do you want Luke?" Thecla asked.

"Luke's work as a physician creates much good will everywhere we go," Paul explained. "Besides, you must have learned a great deal about the region around the Aegean Sea, Luke, when you were at the Temple of Asklepios in Pergamum."

"Yes," Luke admitted. "We often treated sick from Philippi and Corinth who had not been cured in the temples at Athens and Cos."

"Then you can be a great help to me," Paul said. He turned to Thecla. "It should only be a few months, my dear, and meanwhile I

234

can see how happy it will make you to stay here and look after Luke's namesake."

"What about Bithynia?" Thecla asked. "You told me you would go there with us."

"I go where God directs me," Paul explained. "So I may not ever see Bithynia. But I have another reason for wanting you with me," he told Luke. "Lately I have had a feeling that my fever may be coming back."

"Macedonia is highly populated," Probus reminded him. "You would always be able to find competent physicians."

"None so competent as Luke," Paul said, smiling. "But I am thinking more of the value of his medical work in fostering good will among those we visit than of my own welfare."

"Suppose Luke wants to have a life of his own," Probus argued. "He is well liked here in Ephesus and is doing much good, not only in healing the sick but in showing how to live in Christ. And Thecla is happy here too. Why not leave them alone when they are doing good work?"

Paul flushed with exasperation. "Must I remind you, Probus," he said sharply, "that I am the leader of our party, called by God and designated by James and the elders at Jerusalem to carry the gospel of Jesus to the Gentiles? If I feel that Luke can best serve Christ by helping carry the Way to those in Macedonia, it is his duty to obey me unless he wishes to sever his connection with us."

Probus stood up. "You are clever, Paul," he said bitterly. "But you are fighting a losing battle when you use religious teachings to keep Luke and Thecla from being what they rightfully should be, man and wife. One day they will come to their senses." With a snort of disgust the apothecary left the room.

Paul was not even taken aback by the objections of Probus, and the thought came to Luke that he might even have been expecting some such argument and had prepared himself for it. "I am afraid Probus has not yet experienced the true baptism of the spirit of Jesus," Paul said in tones of regret. "Else he would not be so suspicious of those who must do the Lord's work even at the sacrifice of their own desires."

"But Probus is good and kind," Thecla protested. "Look how he gave up his business in Antioch to work with the poor. And I have heard Luke say he could have been chief minister to Sergius Paulus in Cyprus if he had wished."

"Jesus accepts no halfway service," Paul said a little sternly. "Remember his words, *'If anyone chooses to become my disciple, he must say No to self, put the cross on his shoulders daily, and continue to follow me.'* Will you go into Macedonia with me, Luke?"

Luke turned to Thecla. "It is for you to decide, dear."

For a moment she did not speak. And then her voice was so low that it was barely a whisper. "We serve Christ, Luke, so we must put his cross on our shoulders daily. You will have to go."

"God will reward you both for this sacrifice," Paul said briskly. "Be sure of that."

Later, when Luke was bidding Thecla good night, she clung to him, sobbing. "I do love you, darling," she whispered, "more than anything else in the world except"—her voice broke—"except Jesus."

When Luke told Probus of his decision the apothecary said angrily, "You are a fool, Luke. Paul said nothing about your going to Macedonia when we were returning from Troas. In fact, he was very much interested when I told him of the work you had been doing here in Ephesus. But when he got here and saw what being with the baby is doing to Thecla, he realized he was losing his hold over her. Now he is determined to separate you."

It all fitted the facts, Luke realized, and in spite of his desire to be entirely fair to Paul, he was more than halfway sure Probus was right. "It may be better this way, though," he said. "As it is, Thecla and I can never have children of our own until she realizes what you and I know, that Paul is wrong about the immediate coming of Jesus."

Probus threw up his hands in disgust. "Anybody but Paul could see it, but he is so certain that he will be the chief minister when Christ comes that he can't understand anything but an earthly kingdom. As long as you let Thecla stay under his influence there will be no real life together for the two of you."

Luke smiled. "I am not entirely without method, Probus. Apollos Lucanus is pleading my case with Thecla far more eloquently than I could do myself. But I am going to ask a favor of you. Will you stay in Ephesus and look after Thecla and the child until Theophilus comes?"

"Would you trust me with your wife and the baby? Paul insists that I am not even a real Christian."

Luke smiled and gripped the thin man's shoulder. "I would trust you with my life," he said simply. "Our friendship is a rock to which I have returned for shelter again and again."

"And I would do the same for you, Luke. Only my loyalty to you has kept me from deserting Paul and his mystical ideas a long time ago."

As they were preparing to depart Paul said to Luke before the others, "I am not unmindful of the sacrifice you are making in going with us, Luke. And therefore I am designating you not only as our physician but as a teacher also, with full authority to represent me and the Church before the Macedonians." While this might have seemed a lightly placed honor, in view of his long associations with the Christians Luke knew that it was much more, for Paul did not easily relinquish any of the authority granted to him as apostle to the Gentiles. Only Barnabas and now Silas, who had become Paul's closest traveling companion, could claim such a right.

xi

"So we sailed from Troas and struck a straight course for Samothrace," Luke wrote Thecla a few weeks after their departure from Ephesus. "And from there we went on to Philippi, a Roman colony, the leading town in this part of Macedonia. This is a very interesting place, for it was before this city that Mark Antony defeated the murderers of Julius Caesar."

Luke put down the stylus with which he had been writing upon a wax tablet and went to the window. From the elevation on which the house stood his gaze encompassed the plain of Philippi lying between Mount Haemas and Mount Pangaeus, with roses already blooming on the Pangaean foothills. The plain was green, and in the bright afternoon sunlight Luke could almost imagine himself looking at the very ridge upon which Brutus and Cassius had camped on their flight from Rome after the assassination of the greatest of the Caesars. Left of the open space of the plain lay the marsh across which Mark Antony had led his forces to attack the hill where Cassius had died. Augustus had named the city a Roman *colonia* with the title of Colonia Julia Philippensis, and before its very gates Antony and Cleopatra had been forced to bow to the power of Augustus, the first Emperor of Rome to be deified. Luke and his companions had entered Philippi along the Egnatian Way, through the magnificent archway which marked the *pomerium,* the line inside which foreign gods were not permitted to be worshiped and where the divine Emperor himself held sway with the other Olympians.

Luke turned back from the window and picked up the stylus once more and continued to write:

We have been in this town some days, and on the Sabbath we went outside the gate, to the bank of the river, where we supposed there was a place of prayer, and we sat down and began to talk to the women who had met there. Among them was a woman named Lydia, a dealer in purple goods from the town of Thyatira, and she stayed to listen to us. She was already a worshiper of God, and the Lord so moved upon her heart that she accepted the message spoken by Paul. When she and her household were baptized, she begged us, "If you have made up your mind that I am a real believer in the Lord, come and stay at my house." And since she continued to insist that we do so, it is from her house that I write you now.

We have met with great success here, but a strange thing has happened about which I am somewhat troubled. As we were on our way to a place of prayer a slave girl met us who is subject to fits in which she speaks with tongues and has the gift of fortunetelling, by which her owners make great profits. This girl kept following Paul and the rest of us, shrieking, "These men are slaves of the Most High God, and they are proclaiming to you a way of salvation." After which she would fall down in a fit. When she continued to do this Paul became much annoyed at her and said to the evil spirit within her, if in truth it was such and not some other disease which caused the fits, "In the name of Jesus Christ I order you to come out of her."

It was like a scene from a Greek drama. The girl was lying on the ground, jerking and shrieking that Paul and the others were servants of the Most High God, and a considerable crowd had gathered as a result of the commotion. When Paul adjured the evil spirit to come out of her, the girl at once got up off the ground, so that the crowd murmured with a great wonder at what they had seen, and many followed to listen to us. Her owners were very angry at Paul's interference, and I believe that they are going to try to make trouble for him, since this happened inside the *pomerium,* where the Roman authorities have forbidden anyone to preach or worship any but their own gods.

But you are not to worry about us, my darling, for this is a Roman colony and, being Romans by birth, we are safe. If Theophilus has already come, tell him that I have just heard that Junius Gallio, of whom you have heard me speak, is lately come to Corinth as proconsul of that province, and I hope to see him later when we reach that city. I pray daily that our mission may meet with success so that I may return to you in a short time. Give Probus my greeting in Christ and kiss the baby Apollos Lucanus for me.

Your loving husband,
LUKE

The letter finished, Luke put down the stylus and blew away the shavings of wax from the tablet. Travel by ship from Philippi and other Greek cities to Ephesus was frequent, and there were also frequent caravans traveling along the Egnatian Way to Troas and the cities of the eastern coast of the Aegean, so he knew the letter would reach Thecla within two weeks at most. And by that time he hoped that their mission in Philippi would be finished and they could move on, bringing nearer his return to Thecla.

As Luke was leaving the house to dispatch his letter in the market place where the caravans stopped, he saw a group of Lydia's servants moving toward it, carrying someone on a litter. Thinking that Paul had gotten in trouble, he hurried to meet them, but when he came closer he saw that it was the slave girl from whom the apostle had released the evil spirit just the day before. She was unconscious now, and there were bruises about her head and on her face. Lydia herself was following the litter. "Thank God you are here, Luke," she said. "The owners of this girl have beaten her until she is almost dead, all because she listened to Paul and refused to tell fortunes for them."

"Where did you find her?"

"On the street; she had run away from them and fallen in a faint."

While Luke was looking at the girl her body began to jerk, but only the right arm and leg seemed to be involved. This spasm was much more severe than the one she had exhibited yesterday, so that he was forced to restrain her else she would have fallen from the litter.

"Take her into the house," he directed the servants. "I will come and take care of her."

By the time they had transferred the slave girl to a couch the spasm had stopped, but the girl still remained unconscious. Luke examined her carefully. There was an egg-shaped swelling over her left temple, apparently where she had been struck an especially hard blow in the beating.

"What do you think happened to her?" Lydia asked.

Luke pointed to the egg-shaped swelling. "She must have been struck on the head hard enough to bring on unconsciousness. But there is a strange thing here. I have never seen a convulsion before involving only one side."

"She was having one of the fits when I found her in the street," Lydia said. "Many people have gone to listen to Paul speak because they heard how he cured this girl yesterday. Now her owners will claim that she is not cured and they will not believe him."

The same thought was in Luke's mind. Paul's apparent cure of the girl had created a great impression, and if it became known now that the cure was only temporary, the good effects of their visit here might be greatly lessened. And then he had a thought. "Was there a crowd around her when you found her, Lydia?" he asked.

The shopkeeper shook her head. "She had just fallen. I know that, for I saw her stagger and sink to the ground."

"Perhaps no one else knows of this, then. Caution your servants not to speak of it, and I will see what I can find out about her injuries. We still may be able to cure her."

There was a fine library at Philippi, near the great forum that occupied a central position in the city. Vaguely Luke remembered a description of injuries such as this in the writings of Hippocrates, and since all large cities contained scrolls of the writings of the father of medicine in their libraries, he hoped to find the answer he sought there. Nor did he have to search very long. Of injuries to the head the great Hippocrates had written five hundred years before:

When a person has sustained a mortal wound of the head . . . for the most part convulsions seize the other part of the body; for if the wound is situated on the left side, the convulsions will seize the right side of the body; or if the wound be on the right side of the head, the convulsion attacks the left side of the body.

Luke put down the scroll and rubbed his chin thoughtfully. The girl did show convulsions on the right side of the body, and the injury did seem to be in the region of the left temple. But Hippocrates had spoken of mortal wounds, and the girl's injury did not seem that severe. Then he remembered the soldier injured by the kick of a horse in the Camp of Mars outside Pisidian Antioch. He had shown just these one-sided convulsions, and when Luke had drilled this skull with a trepan in about the same area of the temple as the swelling on the slave girl's head, he had found an accumulation of blood. As soon as it was released the man had gotten dramatically well. Could this be a similar case? he wondered.

Luke picked up the scroll he had been reading and unwound it until he came to the section where Hippocrates described the indications for drilling the skull with the trepan:

Of these modes of fracture, the following require trepanning: the contusion, whether the bone be laid bare or not; and the fissure, whether apparent or not. . . . But if the bone is laid bare of flesh, one must attend and try to find out what even is not obvious to the sight, and discover whether the bone be broken and contused, or only contused; and if, when there is an indentation in the bone, whether contusion or fracture, or both be joined to it; and if the bone has sustained any of these injuries, we must give issue to the blood by perforating the bone with a small trepan.

That might be the answer, he thought. And if he were able to relieve the girl by letting out an accumulation of blood inside her skull, he would not only be saving her from death but would be cementing Paul's position in Philippi. It was worth trying, he decided, but first he would have to talk to Paul and Silas about it. Fortunately he knew where they were preaching, and as he approached the crowd around Paul he saw Silas and Timothy at the edge of it and went up to them.

Silas was an older man, even older than Paul, quiet in manner, but intelligent and capable, and well suited to balance the mercurial temperament of the apostle. He had taken the place of Barnabas in many ways, although he was not so nearly the equal of Paul as Barnabas had been. As he came up to Silas and touched him on the arm Luke heard Paul saying to the crowd, "Many of you saw yesterday how the power of Jesus drove out the devil from the slave girl who told fortunes. Even so he has power to drive the evil of sin from your hearts if you will listen and believe in him."

"Is anything wrong, Luke?" Silas asked. "You seem disturbed."

"The slave girl was not cured," Luke reported in a low voice. "Her owners beat her and the convulsions returned."

"Could it be the beating that brought them back?"

"I think so," Luke admitted. "But the people would never believe that Paul cured her if they knew of it."

Silas looked at him keenly. "This is serious," he said. "Is there anything you can do for her?"

"I might be able to cure her," Luke said, "by drilling a small hole into her skull with a trepan to let out any blood which may have accumulated there."

"The girl is a slave," Silas reminded him. "Could you do anything to her without her owners' permission?"

"The law recognizes the right of a physician to treat slaves in order to save life," Luke explained. "And with the injury from the beating, her life is definitely in danger."

"We must speak to Paul," Silas said then. "He will be finished in a short while."

When Paul was free they all went to the house of Lydia. The slave girl was in an almost continual convulsion now; her condition had definitely grown worse in the past few hours.

"The evil spirit has returned and taken possession of her again," Paul said promptly. "There is no other explanation."

Luke pointed to the swelling over the girl's temple. "The spasms can be explained by this injury."

"Jesus healed the woman of Magdala who had fits and was possessed of seven evil spirits," Paul reminded him. "It could be the same with this poor girl."

"Then order the spirit to leave her again," Luke said impatiently. "And if it does not, admit that I am right."

"Whether the spirit leaves her or not will be according to God's will, not mine, Luke. And man does not challenge the will of God."

"But if you are not able to cure her," Luke insisted, "will you give me leave to try my methods?"

Paul smiled. "Christ has said we should not shun the physician. Perhaps in this instance God has chosen to release the evil spirit through the agency of your hands and not mine, Luke. You may try your plan."

"Then I must hasten," Luke said somberly, "for she is worse than she was when I saw her first." He looked around. "Timothy, you can help me, and Silas will direct the slaves who will hold her."

The preparations did not take long. A table was brought in from the kitchen, and Luke showed the slaves how to hold the girl upon it, with her head turned to one side so that he could work in the region of the left temple. He shaved a wide circle of hair from her head and washed the scalp carefully. Then he arranged the instruments he would use on a small table beside her head. A freshly honed scalpel went first, then the trepans, small, rounded, burrlike drills turned by a short handle that fitted into the palm of his hand. Beside these Luke placed pads of the washed wool which Hippocrates recommended for dressing wounds, a mixture of wine and oil for washing the wound, and a bowl of hot tar with which to fill it when he was finished. Military surgeons had long recognized the value of the wine-oil mixture and also the tar in treating war wounds, and Luke judged that they would be equally effective in those made with the scalpel. In a brazier beside the table two irons soon glowed red-hot, with tongs beside them by which they could be handled to sear the wound in case bleeding could not be controlled.

Timothy's face was white, but his mouth was set in determination, and Luke felt sure he would come through all right. To put him at ease Luke began to talk about the opinions of Hippocrates on the treatment of wounds.

"Did Hippocrates perform surgery?" Timothy asked in surprise. "I thought he lived five hundred years ago."

"People have been trepanning skulls for many thousands of years," Luke explained. "There was a royal skull opener in Egypt before the time of your Jewish prophet Moses. It was his duty to trepan the skull of Pharaoh when he lay dying to let his soul escape. Men have drilled the skull for epilepsy and injuries, and sometimes to let out what they thought were devils."

"Then maybe Paul is right." Timothy was unwilling to admit that his idol could ever be wrong. "Perhaps the devil inside her may escape through the opening you plan to make."

Luke smiled. "I think you will soon see the nature of the devil which causes her trouble, Timothy." He picked up the scalpel. "Are you ready?"

Timothy nodded. His fingers gripped tightly the pad of washed wool which Luke had shown him how to use in sponging the blood away from the wound. Luke set the blade on the swollen skin and cut through the scalp for about two inches, forcing the blade down until he felt it strike the bone. The girl moaned and tried to twist away from the pain, but the slaves held her in position. Removing the blade, Luke pressed the washed wool tightly into the wound in order to close the cut blood vessels by pressure until the clotting of the blood could stop them from bleeding.

Timothy's eyes were wide with interest now. "Why does she not bleed to death?" he asked.

"The pressure will control bleeding," Luke explained. When he removed the wool pad a few minutes later, he was pleased to see that there was only a slight flow of blood from the wound.

"Will you use the iron?"

"No, I think not."

Timothy drew a long breath of relief.

"I am going to use the trepan now," Luke told him, "so keep the wound clear of blood for me."

Timothy pressed the wool gingerly against the wound, flinching visibly as the warm blood soaking it touched his fingers. When he drew the pad away Luke studied the bone revealed in the depth of the wound. He could see a jagged line crossing the bone in the wound now and realized that he was right about the injury. There appeared to be what Hippocrates called a "fissure" of the bone here, and undoubtedly a severe contusion or bruise of the tissues both inside and outside the skull, ample reason for the hemorrhage he felt sure was lying just under this bony layer.

Luke took the smallest trepan now and, settling the handle in his hand, pressed the cutting end against the skull just over the fissure. With a steady twisting stroke he turned the instrument and felt it bite into the bone. The faint odor of bone dust rose from the wound, and Luke saw the beads of sweat start out on Timothy's forehead. But the boy kept his feet and cleared the wound of blood every time Luke removed the trepan.

For a while there was no sound except the faint rasp of the instrument cutting through the skull. Then Luke perceived a slight change in the resistance of the bone to the trepan, warning him that he was entering the open space underneath. He removed the instrument and studied the wound for a moment, then, replacing it, turned the handle carefully until an opening had been made completely through the bony layer. Then he removed the trepan and washed the wound out very carefully with water and wine.

A dark red fluid, half clotted and half liquid, was oozing through the trepan opening. "What is that?" Timothy asked.

"It is blood which has accumulated here from the injury," Luke explained.

"Then you were right, Luke."

"Most natural phenomena have natural causes, Timothy. Aristotle and the old Greeks knew that, but we have lost sight of many of their teachings."

"She has stopped jerking already," Silas reported.

Luke had been so intent upon the wound that he had not been watching the girl. Now he saw that Silas was right. When the dark blood had begun to ooze through the trepan opening, the girl's arm and leg had stopped jerking almost immediately, definite evidence that he had located the cause of the trouble.

Working as gently as he could with the blunt end of the scalpel, Luke removed the clotted blood from beneath the skull around the opening and allowed the fresh bleeding to escape. When it had died away to only a slight ooze of blood-tinged fluid, he washed the wound out once more with oil and wine. Then he applied a dressing of the washed wool and bandaged it snugly into place.

"She is conscious, Luke," Silas reported with awe in his voice.

The slave girl's eyes were open, and she stared at him with a look of perplexity, as if she could not understand what had happened to her. "How do you feel?" Luke asked her.

The girl's lips moved in a low whisper. "They beat me."

"Yes, I know," he told her. "But Lydia found you and brought you here."

Her hand went up and touched the bandage. "I feel different, like a weight was gone. What did you do to me?"

"Your head had been injured. I am a physician, so I treated you."

Suddenly she seized his hand. "Will I be all right now?"

"Yes," he told her. "But you may still have the spasms that you had before."

"I don't mind that," the girl said. "My mother and sister had them too."

It was as Luke had suspected, a simple case of epilepsy.

"My masters taught me fortunetelling," she added. "They would beat me if I didn't say the right thing."

As they were taking the girl to her couch Lydia came in, her face concerned. "The owners of this girl have gone to the magistrates," she told Luke. "They are demanding that all of you be arrested."

"But she is going to be well," Luke said confidently. "They will have no case against us when I tell how they beat her."

xii

Trouble from the owners of the slave girl came quickly. Late that afternoon there was a tremendous hammering on the gate outside

Lydia's house, and a frightened slave returned crying that the Roman lictors demanded at once the persons of Paul, Silas, and Luke, having with them an order for their arrest issued by the Roman magistrate. There was no choice but to obey, and the three were taken into custody by four brawny lictors bearing the fasces, the ax surrounded by rods, which was the emblem of Roman civil authority. The rods, tied in a bundle around the long-handled ax that formed the center, were for the very practical purpose of beating those condemned by the court to be punished in that way, while the ax, freed in an instant by loosening the thongs which held the rods around the handle, was a formidable weapon in case of resistance.

"With what are we charged?" Luke asked the chief lictor as they were being taken away.

The man shrugged. "The warrant is issued by Aureliano, the magistrate, but I can tell you that it is in the matter of the slave girl who tells fortunes. Come along now and make no trouble."

Aureliano was a fat bored Greek in an obvious hurry to get away to his evening feast. He looked at the prisoners with evident distaste. "Are you Jews?" he demanded scornfully. Now that the Emperor Claudius had ordered all Jews out of Rome, lesser servants of the Empire lost no opportunity to revile them.

"Yes, we are Jews," Paul said proudly, ignoring the fact that Luke was not a Jew. Luke could have claimed his own Greek nationality and his Roman citizenship as a bar to whatever unpleasantness Aureliano had in mind for the despised Jews. Or he could have pointed out his relationship to Theophilus and his friendship with Junius Gallio, now proconsul at Corinth. But he had never sought to escape any of the tribulations which had come to them on their journeys and he did not do so now.

Aureliano spat into the cuspidor beside his desk. "Who speaks against these Jews?" he demanded.

One of the owners of the slave girl stepped forward. "I do, most noble Aureliano. These men continue to make a great disturbance in our town. And they worship other gods and advocate practices which it is against the law for us Romans to accept or observe."

"Name your charges," Aureliano ordered. "What law have they broken?"

"This one"—he pointed to Paul—"took away a valuable slave girl belonging to me. And he cast a spell upon her so that she no longer has the power of soothsaying."

"Is it true that you stole this slave?" Aureliano demanded of Paul.

"The girl proclaimed us as what we are," Paul said defiantly. "Servants of the Most High God. And when I cast out the devil which

245

tormented her in the name of Jesus Christ, she followed us in gratitude."

"See!" the accuser cried. "He admits worshiping foreign gods, and inside the *pomerium,* too." Paul had been trapped neatly. The worship of foreign gods inside the line where it was prohibited by imperial edict was a serious offense for which they could, at the very least, be beaten with rods by the lictors. Unless Luke could show that the girl's healing had not been a religious matter but a medical one, it might go badly with them.

Before Paul or the magistrate could speak, Luke stepped forward and said in flawless Greek, "I am a physician, noble Aureliano. The owner of the slave girl lies. He beat her, and she would have died had I not treated her by drilling the skull. You can see the girl and the wound from her treatment at the house of Lydia."

"You lie, Jewish dog!" the girl's owner shrieked. "Many people saw this man"—he pointed to Paul—"cast a spell over the girl." Several of those with them spoke up and confirmed the statement.

Aureliano yawned. "I weary of all this. You Jews are always causing trouble; no wonder the Emperor has expelled you from Rome. Take them away," he barked to the chief lictor, "and beat them with rods. Then confine them to the jail, and if I find in the morning that these charges are true, they shall be beaten again."

"But you have only to go to the house of Lydia, the seller of purple," Luke protested. "You will see there that I speak the truth."

"Take them away," the magistrate ordered. "Let me hear no more of this."

To be beaten with rods before a crowd was the greatest possible humiliation for a Roman citizen. Luke could have saved himself from it still, as could Paul, by claiming their citizenship. But when Paul said nothing, Luke also remained silent, even when the lictors stripped them to the waist in the courtyard of the prison and began to lay on with the rods. Actually the beating was not so painful as the whipping by the Jews at Pisidian Antioch, for although the rods bruised and caused pain, they did not send flames of agony through the body as did the whips in the hands of angry men. The three of them endured the pain stolidly, then were hustled into the jail and secured, Luke in one cell and Paul and Silas in another.

No one brought them even a jar of water, and the cell was cold and damp. Shivering upon the hard bench against the wall that served also as a bed, Luke asked himself bleakly why he let these tortures be inflicted upon him when he could have stayed with Thecla in Ephesus. Glorying that he could suffer some of the things that Christ himself had suffered, Paul had done nothing to prevent their sentencing and punishment. It was almost, Luke thought, as if Paul were himself playing the role of a messiah, the second great leader who would be next to Christ himself if the earthly kingdom which he hourly expected to be established came to pass. He realized now just how right Probus had been in his shrewd estimation of Paul's character. The apostle's deliberate refusal to admit anything but a supernatural role in the death of Herod Agrippa, the besting of Elymas at Paphos, and now the healing of the slave girl, all fitted such a concept.

Luke remembered, too, the day in Antioch when Paul had as much as admitted the belief in his greater right to wear the mantle of Jesus than Peter, after the apostle to the Jews had encouraged the split in the Church by siding for a short time with the Judaizers against Paul on circumcision and dietary laws. Was Paul really setting himself upon a high place where no true follower of the meek and lowly Nazarene should be? If Paul had indeed developed a conviction of his own role as a messiah, then Luke could no longer follow him, for he was deeply convinced that Jesus meant nothing like that for himself.

In spite of the hard couch, Luke finally fell asleep. Some time later the light of a torch shining in his eyes brought him awake. The jailer stood outside in the corridor, and with him a fat man who seemed very much disturbed. It was Aureliano, the magistrate, sweating and pale, although the night was cool. With his hands on the bars of the door he peered in at Luke. "Lydia, the seller of purple, has come to me," he said. "She tells me you are a Roman citizen and the son of Theophilus."

"That is true."

The magistrate looked as if he were going to faint. "Why did you not tell me you were Roman citizens?"

"You gave us no opportunity," Luke reminded him, "in your haste to get the whole thing over with."

"And did you really cure the slave girl of fits by drilling her skull?"

"Yes. I tried to tell you that yesterday."

"Unlock the cell," Aureliano ordered the jailer. "Then go and let the other two out."

Here, Luke realized, was an excellent opportunity to impress upon the magistrate of an important city of Macedonia their rights as Romans. Word of it would be carried to other centers, and they would be less liable to summary arrest in the future. "Release them yourself," he told Aureliano, "else I will report this matter to the Roman governor."

Aureliano started to puff up, then collapsed like a pricked wineskin. He took the keys from the jailer and went to unlock the other cell.

It was a triumphant procession that marched through the streets to

Lydia's house, and a considerable crowd followed, so that Paul had to remain outside and preach to them. Luke found the slave girl in excellent condition, her wound already beginning to heal. That night it was decided that they should move on to another city, now that the nucleus of a strong church was established in Philippi. But before he left, Luke had the satisfaction of knowing that the slave girl had been purchased by Lydia and would no more be injured by beating.

When they joined a caravan the next day bound for Thessalonica, Paul and Silas traveled with the leader at the head of the party, while Luke, as usual, went to the rear to treat anyone who might fall out because of injured feet or illness. Shortly Timothy dropped back and joined him. Luke saw by the concern on the handsome youth's face that there was something on his mind, but he did not question him until Timothy spoke of it of his own accord.

"I have been talking to Paul," Timothy said finally. "He insists that it was a real miracle that healed the slave girl, in spite of what you did."

Luke smiled. "It may have been. I have often suspected that God works through the hands of physicians to heal the sick."

"But why, when God can do anything himself?"

"God made the laws by which the world and the sun and the stars operate, Timothy," Luke said earnestly. "I am sure he expects man to use those laws to help him live the best life it is possible for him to live. If sometimes natural events seem to fit into the pattern of our lives, while at other times they do not, it may be that God's will is working according to a plan we do not understand, or that we are not living our lives in conformity with his laws."

"But Paul says we must only believe, not try to understand, God's purpose."

Luke nodded. "I know Paul believes that we should have faith and believe there is a God and that Jesus is his son, without asking for proof. But some, like you and me and millions who will come after us, are not satisfied with simple faith. We must seek the cause of what we see and convince ourselves that it is all simply an expression of the laws of God. In the end, however, I believe we are stronger than those who accept simply on faith, because we have found the ultimate truth that all things come from God and are produced at his will."

"But where do you find this proof, Luke?"

"In the simple things, such as the hemorrhage which caused the convulsions of the slave girl. Or the triangles by which Aristarchus was able to measure the relative distances of the sun and the moon from the earth, and Eratosthenes to determine the size of the earth and prove that it is a globe. One advantage of my kind of faith is that it cannot flag, for it is based upon discernible truth and not subject to human fallibility."

"How can you explain a life after death?" Timothy asked. "Is there any proof other than in faith?"

Luke rubbed his chin. "I never really tried to put it into words before," he admitted, "but I think there is. I suppose I would say that we give a part of ourselves to those we love and receive in return some of the soul of those who love us. Thus we can become immortal through the portion of our love that enriches the lives of others and lives on in them. I suppose you could call that the immortality of love, and I am sure that Jesus would be immortal in the hearts of those who receive his love through his teachings and who love him, even if he were not the son of God."

"Sometimes I think you understand Jesus and his way better than any of us, Luke," Timothy said impulsively. "Better even than Paul and Peter and the others."

"I have tried," Luke admitted. "And I think I do understand what he meant to teach us through his life."

"And through his death too?"

Luke shook his head gently. "Not yet, Timothy. I can only see the meaning of his death now as Paul said once, as 'a dim reflection in a looking glass!' Someday, though, I hope to see it clearly. Then I shall know the whole answer to the question of why he came to earth."

xiii

Luke had written to Thecla concerning their adventure in Philippi and had told her of their plans to go on to Corinth, one of the largest and most influential cities of Macedonia. At Philippi he had also learned the good news that his old friend, Junius Annaeus Gallio, had recently assumed the governorship at Corinth and had instructed Thecla to write him there in care of the governor.

Gallio welcomed him warmly when they arrived in Corinth several weeks later, but even more welcome was a letter from Thecla:

My DEAREST LUKE,

After your painful experience in Philippi I was almost afraid to hear from you again, lest it bring news of more disaster. But now that you say you may soon be with me again my heart is filled with happiness and I pray daily to God for your safe return before much longer.

Theophilus is here and plans to take the baby back to Antioch with him as soon as the weather becomes more favorable. He assures me that, with Junius Gallio as proconsul in Corinth, you and Paul and the others will be in no danger of mistreatment such as you have already suffered in Philippi and the other cities. Theophilus would like for both of us to return with him and the baby to Antioch when you leave Macedonia, but I would not want to influence you in any way, for I know how you have longed to go into Bithynia. Still, Apollos Lucanus does need care, and if perchance you feel that we might remain with your foster father until he is a little larger, I would not feel that we were remiss in our duty, for Christ has told us to care for and cherish the little ones.

Probus has fallen in love with the daughter of a respected apothecary here, and they are to be married within the next few weeks. They are very happy, and he plans to make his home here in Ephesus, where there is a good opportunity in that field.

Being with little Apollos Lucanus, darling, and watching him grow, and especially seeing how much he is like your brother Apollonius, has made me realize something I never knew before, what a privilege it must be for a woman to become a vessel through which the things she loves in her husband can be preserved in their children. I have prayed God to show me what is right, and I am sure now that the love and happiness the baby has brought to me are indeed a sign that there would be no sin in bearing your children. And since we know not the day nor the hour when Jesus will come, or indeed if he will actually come in person, to reign over the earth, I wonder if we should delay any longer making a home together for ourselves and our children and showing others by our example the Way of Jesus.

Do what you think is right, Luke, and what God tells you in your prayers you should do. But if you feel that you are no longer needed in Macedonia, come back to me. My arms ache to hold you and to feel you close to me.

Your wife,
THECLA

Thecla's letter filled Luke with joy. His immediate impulse was to leave Corinth by the next boat crossing the narrow neck of the Aegean Sea to join her in Ephesus. It would be better, he realized, to do as Thecla obviously wished to do, join Theophilus in the voyage to Antioch when he took the baby home with him. And if they were going to have children of their own, Thecla would have servants in Antioch to help care for Apollos Lucanus and their own child when it came. Bithynia must wait for a more opportune time, and yet he did not postpone their going into the beautiful land which he had seen only once, from the glen where Silvanus was buried, without a twinge of regret. In Antioch there would be controversy, for he knew that the split between the Jews and the Gentiles had never been completely healed, while in the country on the shores of the Pontus Euxinus there would be peace. But when it came to a matter of Thecla's welfare, his own wishes must always be thrust into the background.

Luke's first impulse was to speak to Paul immediately about leaving Corinth, but when he mentioned it to Silas, the older man looked glum. "I would not want to interfere with your plans, Luke," he said, "but I am afraid the same forces are at work here that have caused trouble for us in Philippi and in Thessalonica."

"There are not many Jews in Corinth," Luke protested.

"No, but they have a powerful advocate now. Sosthenes, the most influential Jew in all of Macedonia, has come to fight the battle against us."

"They have already driven Paul from the synagogue," Luke pointed out. "Why are they not satisfied with that?"

"The Corinthians have accepted the truths of Jesus more readily than most of the people we have visited," Silas explained. "The Jews are afraid that the Christian Church will become more powerful here than they are, but this time I hear they are not trying to get Paul into disfavor with Rome through the usual charge that he preaches Jesus as a king. They will accuse Paul before Gallio of breaking the Jewish law and thus try to convict him as a criminal against the Empire for inciting a religious disturbance."

Luke frowned. "Have you spoken of this to Paul?"

Silas shook his head. "Paul is riding the crest of success here in Corinth, so he would not hear to any suggestion that we leave. Corinth is one of the crossroads of the Greek world," Silas continued. "If Paul develops a great church here, the effects will eventually be felt not only throughout Macedonia but into Mysia and perhaps into Italy itself."

"But what can I do?" Luke asked. "I could use my influence with Junius Gallio, but he is entirely honest, and I could not influence him against his better judgment."

"Suppose Paul is arrested at the request of this Sosthenes?" Silas said. "Could you go to Gallio and explain the facts of the case?"

"Of course," Luke agreed. "But Paul would not like it. He would want to argue his own case."

"Stay a little longer, Luke," Silas begged. "You have helped us out of trouble so many times that I will feel better with you here."

Reluctantly Luke agreed, for he knew that Silas spoke the truth.

Paul had such a penchant for getting into trouble that cool heads would be needed if the Jews made trouble for him.

Luke received a message only a few days later, asking him to call upon the proconsul, Junius Gallio, that evening. He had no way of knowing whether the call was a medical one or not, but he tucked his medical case under his arm before he left for the palace of the governor.

The sun was setting over the Gulf of Corinth as Luke walked through the city. Guardian of the isthmus between Macedonia and the Peloponnesus, Corinth stood securely upon a rock almost in the center of the narrow "bridge of the sea," as the isthmus was often called. Alexander the Great and Julius Caesar had both projected a canal across the narrowest point of the land bridge, a distance of only a little more than four miles. And in Rome the project was still mentioned frequently in the imperial councils. The geographer Strabo had summed up the reasons for Corinth's importance when he said that the city "is called wealthy because of its commerce, since it is situated on the isthmus and is master of two harbors, one of which leads straight to Asia, and the other to Italy; and it makes easy the exchange of merchandise from both countries that are so far distant from each other."

The shadows of evening were creating their nightly patterns upon the city as Luke climbed from the lower terrace to the upper, an elevation of roughly a hundred feet. In the background to the southwest, the towering mountain called Acro-Corinth pushed fifteen hundred feet above the city and more than eighteen hundred above the sea itself. Here, in the very center of the city, was the agora, the market place found in all Greek cities. All day long it was filled with the hum of commerce, the muted obbligato of voices, rumbling vehicles, and animal sounds, which made up the music of a great city's living. Now the noise of the market was stilled with evening, and instead, queues of pleasure-loving Greeks were already entering the drinking houses, while others moved toward the magnificent Temple of Apollo, rivaling in splendor but in no way equaling the gleaming white Temple of Aphrodite which stood at the very summit of the Acro-Corinth, close beside the Roman citadel dominating the city and protecting it from attack.

Crossing the agora, Luke passed the elevated platform or *rostra,* from which the governor was accustomed to hear complaints and even to try serious matters in public, so that the people might see the justice of Rome and realize its fairness and efficiency. Gallio had just come from the bath and was in a pleasantly philosophical mood before his dinner. "I sent for you," he told Luke, "because this Jew Sosthenes has demanded that I arrest your friend Paul for preaching a new religion."

"The Jews have caused us a great deal of trouble in almost every city we have visited," Luke admitted.

"But why?" Gallio asked. "Paul is a Jew and the Nazarene he follows was a Jew. There are many Jewish sects, such as the Pharisees, the Sadducees, and the Essenes, but none of them cause much trouble among the Jews. Yet everywhere you Christians go, trouble explodes."

"I think it is a matter of interpretation, sir," Luke explained. "Paul and the Christians among the Jews believe that Christ was the Messiah promised by the Jewish prophets for thousands of years and the true son of God. But the Jews believed the Messiah would be a great leader or king who would lead them in earthly conquest, so they will not accept so lowly a person as Jesus. They fight Paul because he preaches that Jesus came for a different purpose, to save them through his death."

"I have been studying this Christian faith," Gallio admitted, "since you first explained it to me in Antioch, Luke. But frankly, I still do not understand this talk about the Nazarene's dying to save others. It sounds very much like the metaphysical concepts of the Mithraeans and the followers of Dionysius."

"It is an interpretation which Paul has put upon the life of Jesus himself," Luke explained. "He teaches that those who believe Jesus to be the son of God and that he was resurrected from the dead will be freed from sin and given eternal life, and that the blood of Jesus, like the blood of the bull in the taurobolium of the Mithraeans, cleanses them of sin. But it is only a belief. As you say, the Jewish religion has long been divided into sects, so the Christian faith, as far as Jews are concerned, is no new religion, but merely a different form of the ordinary Jewish worship of Jehovah."

Gallio looked at the young physician keenly. "One thing I have never been able to understand fully, Luke. You are a Greek and a member of one of the most powerful families in the Empire. Why do you follow Jesus?"

"I follow him because his principles seem to me to be the only way through which men can find peace and a real purpose in life," Luke said simply.

"But you have been whipped and beaten with rods. Surely you cannot call that peace."

Luke smiled then. "Paul calls it the 'peace which passeth all understanding.' Actually it is an inner feeling of purpose, a pride in what you are doing even in the face of adversity, which comes only to those who follow in the Way of Jesus."

253

"What shall I do about Paul then?" Gallio asked. "They are making a continual howl for his arrest."

"I think you should arrest him, sir."

Gallio stared at him. "But why?"

"Are you satisfied now that the controversy is merely one of opinion between different sects in the worship of Jehovah?"

"Yes," Gallio admitted. "Actually I had arrived at that conclusion before I talked to you, but I see it much more clearly now."

"Your opinion carries great weight throughout the Empire," Luke pointed out. "If Paul is arrested and you rule that the Christian faith is a sect within the Jewish religion, the way would be made clear for Paul to keep on with his teachings without being haled into the Roman courts by Jews in every city he visits."

"Most of our law codes are based on just such decisions," Gallio agreed. "Very well then. I will let your friend be taken. And if ever I am in the toils of the law, Luke," he added with a smile, "I hope I have an advocate who is half as eloquent as you are."

Paul's arrest came the next day as Gallio had promised. Luke had said nothing to Paul of his summons by Gallio, and Paul made no objection to the arrest. In fact, Luke suspected that the apostle welcomed an opportunity to defend himself before this most famous of Roman judges.

The trial was held a few days later, and a vast crowd filled the agora long before it was to take place. The Jews in Corinth were relatively small in number and not well liked by the Greeks, so there was little sentiment against Paul. Most of the people came out of curiosity to see this fellow who caused such a commotion wherever he went and to hear the decision of their new proconsul in regard to him.

Luke stood close to the *rostra,* with Silas and Timothy beside him. Trumpets announced the coming of the governor, and a lane was made through the crowd to let him reach the *rostra.* A dozen brawny legionnaires came first, clearing the way. Junius Gallio rode in a sedan chair, for his gout did not permit much walking, with the petty officials of the court and the lictors with their fasces bringing up the rear. Paul walked among the lictors, unmanacled, his head lifted proudly and his eyes burning with an exalted light. When Gallio mounted the platform and took his seat on the thronelike chair of the judge, Paul was directed to stand one step below him, about ten feet away from Luke and the others.

A clerk stepped forward, unrolling a scroll from which he read in a pompous voice: " 'Tiberius Claudius Caesar Augustus Germanicus, Pontifex Maximus, of Tribunitian authority for the twelfth time, Imperator the twenty-sixth time, Father of the Country, Consul for the fifth time, honorable, greets the city of Corinth through his friend, Junius Gallio, Governor of the Province of Achaia. In order that justice may be given freely to all, Junius Gallio this day holds court in the agora of Corinth, to hear complaints against those said to have broken the laws of the Empire.'"

The clerk put down the first scroll and took up a second. "'Sosthenes, of the synagogue of the Jews in this city, speaks this day against one Paul, lately of Tarsus, saying that he breaks the laws of Rome by inducing people to worship foreign gods forbidden by Roman law. He claims further that this same Paul leads people to worship the God of the Jews in a manner which violates their own law.'"

Junius Gallio said, "Let Sosthenes come forward and explain these charges so that we may decide of what, if anything, the prisoner Paul is guilty."

A plump Jew stepped upon the lower platform of the *rostra* where Paul stood, and bowed. "Most noble Proconsul," he began, "we know how the reputation of the judge, Junius Gallio, has spread throughout the Empire of Rome and that in all countries who give allegiance to the Emperor none is so revered in the administration of justice."

"My qualifications are not in question," Gallio cut him off sharply. "With what crime do you charge this man?"

Sosthenes was obviously taken aback by the jurist's manner, and a murmur of amusement ran through the crowd at his discomfiture. But he quickly recovered his dignity. "This man Paul teaches that the ancient laws of the Jewish people concerning diet and circumcision should be put aside."

"Are there other sects among the Jews who have given up these laws?" Gallio asked.

"Some no longer follow the rules of clean and unclean foods," Sosthenes admitted. "But all Jews must be circumcised."

"Does this Paul urge Jews to do away with their laws in this respect?" Gallio asked.

"He has never been heard to do so," Sosthenes admitted. "But he does advocate such for Gentiles."

"Would you force all Gentiles to be circumcised?" Gallio demanded sarcastically. "I have talked to your high priests in Jerusalem, but I never heard of such a thing."

"N-no," Sosthenes stammered. "We do not advocate that."

"Paul invites those not of Jewish blood to worship one whom you Jews consider your private God," Gallio said severely, "so you seek to have him imprisoned by Rome. Yet you claim your God to be above others. Would you refuse everyone else the right to worship him?"

255

Sosthenes, seeing that the case was going badly against him, tried another tack. "Paul claims that Jesus of Nazareth is the promised Messiah of the Jewish people," he argued. "A fact which is disputed by the high priest in Jerusalem."

Gallio shrugged. "Is this the Messiah promised to the Jews in your ancient writings?"

Sosthenes admitted that this was true.

"What rule is there to determine when he has come, or who he is when he does come?"

"He will come as a king to rule over the Jewish people," Sosthenes stated. "When Paul says that Jesus of Nazareth is the Messiah and will one day come to rule over the Jews, he breaks the laws of Rome."

"I am the judge of who breaks the laws of Rome," Gallio reminded the Jewish leader. "Do you assure me that this Jesus was not the Messiah promised by your ancient writings?"

"The Sanhedrin at Jerusalem has ruled that he is not," Sosthenes declared triumphantly.

Gallio smiled, and too late Sosthenes realized the trap into which he had been led. "Then since Jesus has officially been declared not to be the Messiah, no Roman law has been broken. Paul merely states his own beliefs, which you deny. I will admit that there is a quarrel between you, but there is none with the authority of Rome."

"B-but when he preaches that the Nazarene will return as king——"

"Has he returned?" Gallio demanded. "Does Paul claim that he lives now on earth?"

"N-no."

"Then you have no case." Gallio struck the arm of his chair with the jeweled miniature of the fasces which he carried as a token of his office. "If it were some misdemeanor or underhanded rascality, O Jews, with which you charge this man Paul, I would in reason listen to you. But as it is a question about words and titles and your own law, you will have to see to it yourselves. I refuse to act as judge in these matters." He pounded again on the arm of his chair with the fasces. "The prisoner may go free, and henceforth let no man accuse him unjustly for crimes he has not done."

A mighty roar of approval rose from the crowd. The Greeks, who had witnessed with high glee the discomfiture of the Jewish prosecutor, began to crowd around Sosthenes, pummeling him with their fists, but Gallio paid no attention to them. "You are free," he said kindly to Paul. "Go your way henceforth in peace. The Jews will trouble you no more by accusing you of breaking Roman law."

Paul seemed unable to understand that the trial was over. "But my defense," he started to say.

"You needed no defense," Gallio told him. "Luke has already informed me about the truth of these matters. I would have released you at once, but it seemed best to have a public hearing and dispel for all times these things of which the Jews accuse you."

Luke heard Gallio's words and saw the color slowly drain from Paul's face. Suddenly he turned away. He had intended for Paul to be vindicated and his mission given the seal of approval by Rome's most famous judge. Those things had happened, but Paul had looked upon the trial as a heaven-sent opportunity to lecture the Greeks upon his beliefs and his position as apostle to the Gentiles. Instead, Paul's pride had been wounded, and Luke knew from previous occasions what that meant. Such a wound had caused the break with Peter and with Barnabas and had sent John Mark away from them.

And yet Luke could not see how he had acted wrongly. The decision of Gallio would almost certainly go down in history as an endorsement of the right of Paul to preach his beliefs without opposition from the Roman Empire itself, relegating the controversy between him and the Jewish hierarchy at Jerusalem to the status of a conflict within the scope of the Jewish religion. That in itself was an important step for the Christian faith, unshackling, as it were, one of the fetters which had restrained its free spread before.

Luke was almost certain, too, that this important purpose could not have been accomplished had Paul spoken in his own defense. For Paul's often mystical concepts of Jesus and his place on earth could easily have been construed, as they had been again and again, as the ambition to set up another earthly ruler with divine powers. Since the Roman emperors considered themselves divine, to advocate such a king was a serious crime, one for which Paul might easily have been executed by Rome.

It was an hour or more before Luke returned to the house beside the synagogue where they were staying, but he found a tense group awaiting him. Silas and Timothy sat in one corner of the room, looking very unhappy. Paul was pacing up and down, his face flushed and his eyes fiery. Hardly had Luke come into the room when he lashed out at him. "By what right did you speak to Gallio before the trial, Luke?" he demanded.

"I have known Junius Gallio for a long time," Luke said patiently. "When the Jews demanded that he arrest you, Gallio sent for me to talk about their charges."

"*I* was on trial," Paul said hotly. "*I* was suffering imprisonment for the sake of Jesus. It was my place to speak to the judge and to the crowd and tell them the truth."

"Would you have told them that Jesus is coming soon to reign over the Jews and all who believe in him?"

"Of course," Paul said sharply. "It is the truth."

"Then Gallio would have been forced to imprison you and perhaps even to execute you as a traitor to Rome."

"I would die gladly for Christ's sake," Paul said. "My courage has never been questioned."

"No one questions it now, but I do question your judgment of what is best for the cause of Jesus. How could you help advance his Church when you were shut up in prison? What proof do you have that he is really coming back to earth while you and I, and even generations to follow us, are alive?"

Paul made an impatient gesture. "I have told you before, Luke, that the things are revealed to me from God."

"But he speaks also to Peter and the others who walked with him on earth," Luke reminded Paul. "And he tells them no such thing. Do you hear what God speaks to you, Paul, or what you wish to hear?"

Paul's color rose and his mouth set angrily. "God singled me out on the road to Damascus, Luke! How many times must I tell you that?"

"Jesus of Nazareth is the Messiah, Paul," Luke said evenly. "Not you. But I am afraid that in your own mind you have set yourself up as equal to Jesus or only slightly below him. The decision of Gallio in your favor is far more important than the wound you imagine you have received to your pride, for from now on the Way of Jesus can be preached wherever you go without opposition from Rome. You should get down on your knees and thank God that Gallio sent for me to learn the truth."

But Paul did not relent; instead, his face grew more set. "Who are you to determine what is truth and not truth about Jesus, Luke?" he asked with biting sarcasm.

"I am a physician, an ordinary man," Luke told him quietly. "God has never spoken directly to me, Paul, but in my heart I am sure that I know the Way of Jesus better than you do. What you preach is not Christ, but Paul. I pray that before it is too late you may see the difference. Good-by."

The apostle stared at him as if he did not understand the word. "What do you mean, Luke?" he asked a little hesitantly.

"I stayed here in Corinth because I saw that trouble was coming," Luke explained. "Now that you are free to preach wherever you please, you need me no longer. Thecla and I are going to Antioch, where we can rear our children and live as Jesus meant us to live. . . .

You will always be welcome in our home, Paul, for it was through you that I went to Jerusalem and found Thecla."

He turned and left the room then, but the picture he left behind was to be engraved forever in his mind: Silas, obviously unhappy, but loyal to Paul; Timothy, his chin working piteously to keep from weeping. And Paul with a look in his eyes which Luke had seen there only a few times before, when he had been whipped at Pisidian Antioch and when he had been stoned at Lystra, a look of utter defeat. And even though they were parting in anger, Luke was genuinely sorry that he had been the one to inflict upon Paul what he was certain was the worst blow the apostle had ever received.

Book Five: THE WRITING

The former treatise have I made, O Theophilus, of all that Jesus began both to do and teach.

The Acts 1:1

LUKE was at work in his old surgery in Iconium when the letter came from Ephesus, carried by one of the caravans which passed through this way station on the Via Augusta almost every day. Thecla brought it to him and they read it together:

To Luke and Thecla, my beloved brother and sister in Christ, from Probus Maximus at Ephesus, Greetings:

Theophilus stopped at Ephesus with the lad Apollos Lucanus on his way to Rome and told me of your decision to return to Iconium before going into Bithynia. I have not written you before, trusting that I might be able to pay you a visit ere this. However, conditions here at Ephesus are such that I shall not be able to leave for some time, so I write to tell you some of the things that are troubling me and to ask your advice.

To begin: you both know how Paul, after Luke left him in Corinth, achieved great success in Macedonia and established strong churches there during a stay of several years. When he came to Ephesus, Paul went into the synagogue and had a discussion with the Jews. They asked him to stay longer, but he would not consent; as he bade them good-by he promised, "I will come back to you again, if it is God's will!" Then he set sail from Ephesus and when he reached Caesarea went up to Jerusalem and greeted the Church there.

When Paul returned to Ephesus he went to the synagogue here and for three months spoke courageously, keeping up his discussions and continuing to persuade them about the kingdom of God. But some of them grew

261

harder and harder and refused to believe, actually criticizing the Way before the people, so he withdrew his disciples and continued his discussions in the lecture hall of Tyrannus. This went on for several years, so that everyone living in the province of Asia, Greeks as well as Jews, heard the Lord's message.

Paul then decided to pass through Macedonia and Greece on his way to Jerusalem, saying, "After I have gone there, I must see Rome too." So he sent Timothy and several others off to Macedonia while he stayed on for a while in Asia. Now a great commotion has arisen about the Way. As you know from your visits to Ephesus, the silversmiths made a great profit from the statues of Artemis, and in fact it is the first industry of the city. Since Paul had been preaching here, so many have taken up the Way of Christ that the sale of statues has fallen off markedly and some of the workmen in silver have nothing to do.

Because of these happenings I am sorely afraid that an attempt will be made by the silversmiths and others to cause trouble for Paul, in the hope of driving him from Ephesus, as he has been driven from other cities. Paul had planned to go to Macedonia, but now he insists upon remaining here, although I think that much of the difficulty could be resolved if he were to go away for a little while. We should then be able to keep up the work with far less opposition from those who speak against Paul.

When you wrote me of your departure from Antioch for Iconium you mentioned that you hoped yet to go into Bithynia. And I remember that Paul planned to go there many years ago but went to Macedonia instead. If you are planning soon to go to Bithynia and could come by way of Ephesus, it might be that Paul could be persuaded to go in that direction for a little while, at least until the turmoil here subsides. In any event, we would be overjoyed to see you both and perhaps you would be able to reason with Paul. Unless we can manage to quiet the conflict here somehow, I am afraid that it may become serious, for the silversmiths are a very powerful group and dominate the life of Ephesus.

Before he left for Macedonia, Timothy asked me to greet you in Christ for him when next I wrote you. My wife and two sons wish you good health with me, and hope to see you both before much longer,

> The blessings of God be upon you,
>
> PROBUS

Luke put down the letter. "It hardly seems eight years since we saw Probus," he observed. "The time has passed swiftly."

"That is because they were good years," Thecla said, "even with the disappointments." Luke knew what she meant, for it had been a bitter blow to her that she had not been able to bear him the child they both wished for so deeply. Understanding her thought, he put his arm about her. "No man could want for more than you have given me, darling," he said. "Since we have been together I have realized how unfruitful life was without you."

Thecla smiled and laid her hand upon his cheek. "Why don't we go on to Bithynia, Luke? It might be the best medicine I could have."

"We will talk about it tonight," he promised. "I must visit some of my patients before dark."

"And I must stop in the agora for some cooking oil," Thecla said happily, "or you will have no supper tonight."

Luke finished his work and closed the surgery. When his calls were finished he turned his steps toward the small building which served the Christians as a place of worship and, entering it, dropped upon his knees in the cool half darkness of that place of quiet and peace.

Kneeling there, Luke's thoughts went back over the eight years since they had departed from Ephesus for Antioch with Theophilus and the baby, Apollos Lucanus. There had been pleasant years in Antioch, working in the church with Barnabas and the others, serving the poor people in the district beside the river with his medical skill, and teaching the Way as much through the example of their own lives as through words spoken in the church. Thecla had been happy mothering the son of Apollonius and watching him grow from a lusty infant to a sturdy little boy.

But as the years passed, Luke had seen that Thecla's health was undergoing a gradual decline. At first he thought the change might be due to her disappointment at not bearing him a child, but later he was forced to admit that more serious forces were at work. One winter she was seriously ill for months with a cough and fever and a pain on breathing which only subsided when the warm summer sun returned to the mouth of the Orontes.

Glaucus had died of phthisis, the wasting disease of the lungs which sometimes dragged on for many years. Luke also knew that the families of phthisis victims often developed the same symptoms. Soon there was no longer any question that Thecla was suffering from the same disease which had killed her father, and with that knowledge Luke could understand why they had not been able to have a child. Women with phthisis were frequently childless, perhaps as a protection sent from God, Luke thought, for with pregnancy the disease often flared up and quickly became fatal.

Then, a little more than a year before, Theophilus had been called to preside over the law courts of Rome, a signal honor and recognition of his reputation as a jurist. Apollonius, too, had returned to Rome from Britain at about the same time, so it was natural that Theophilus should take the boy to Rome. Luke had been thinking for several months that he should take Thecla away from the low swampy region of the coast, known to be unfavorable to phthisis sufferers, perhaps going to the highlands of her own country of Galatia, where the crisp air was much more health-giving. Thecla had seized joyously upon the suggestion that they return to Iconium when Theophilus left Antioch, and it had proved a good move, for she had improved markedly. She had gained weight, her color was better, and she rarely complained of being tired any more.

With Thecla's seeming recovery the question had come up again of their going to Bithynia, taking up the plans which had been interrupted eight years ago when they had gone to Ephesus and found Mariamne in the terminal weeks of the pregnancy which had cost her life. Remembering the peaceful land of Bithynia, the tall mountains and the green and fertile valleys, the white sands of the shore which Silvanus had described, and the healthful climate, Luke felt again as he knelt in the church the tug which the memory always brought to his heart and the longing for the peace which it represented. But he was troubled by the thought that such a move might not be best for Thecla. It was this question for which he had come to seek an answer from above here in the cool shadows of the church.

He said no prayer but let his troubled thoughts speak themselves. And as he knelt there he felt a calmness come over him, a sense of certainty and purpose as reassuring as if God had actually spoken to him. When finally he got to his feet it was with the conviction that the path of God's purpose upon which he had set his feet so many years ago in Jerusalem still lay ahead, toward Ephesus, certainly, and perhaps to Bithynia, although something warned him that the road was still far longer than that shown on any map.

The evening meal was finished and Luke and Thecla were sitting upon their favorite bench in the garden beside the pool which burbled with the flow of water from the Roman aqueduct. Around them the hushed voices of the night brought the quiet contentment which they loved so well. He put his arm about Thecla, and she rested against him as she loved to do here in the garden in the evening, when they talked together or merely shared unspoken thoughts in the sweet communion that comes to those who are sure of their love.

"I went to the church to pray this afternoon," Luke said. "To ask God if we should go on to Ephesus or stay here."

"What did he tell you, Luke?"

"I am sure now it is God's will that we should go to Ephesus."

"And to Bithynia?"

Luke smiled. "Probus once said that Bithynia is a place of the mind more than of the world. I think I reached Bithynia years ago, darling,

264

when I first held you in my arms in the garden of James at Jerusalem. It would be selfish for any man to wish for more."

Thecla put her fingers to his cheek in a loving gesture. "And my Bithynia is here with you, Luke," she said. "But I have known for a long time that this is just an interlude before you must go on with whatever purpose it is that God has set for you. Sometimes I think I have almost grasped what it is that you are to do, Luke, but then it slips away and I cannot lay hold upon it. I am sure, though, that we will know the truth soon."

Luke remembered the odd feeling of certainty and purpose which had come over him that afternoon while he was praying in the church. And his thoughts went back to that day in Antioch when a strange restlessness had assailed him and sent him to the theater where he had seen the Christians torn by the lions and had first met Barnabas. He had experienced much the same feeling when he had stumbled from the theater into the bright sunshine that afternoon, as if he had wandered away from a road for a while but had found it once again.

Then he bent his head and kissed Thecla gently. "Few men ever come to understand the will of God, dearest," he said. "But whatever it is that I am to do, these years with you have been an important part of the preparation for it."

"Have I changed you much?" she asked. "I don't see that I have, for you were always kind and gentle and good—like Jesus."

"Your love has made me richer than I ever hoped to be," Luke told her. "Timothy and I once talked of immortality and decided that love might be the only thing that is really immortal."

"Then my love for you will live through eternity. It is a beautiful fancy, Luke."

"It may be more than fancy, dear," he said. "Whatever I am, whatever I do, will be increased beyond measure by the love you have given me. And whatever it is that God wishes me to give to the world will be more important because a part of both of us and the people who loved us—yes, even Jesus—will go with it."

Thecla sighed deeply. "Then the souls of those who die may even be nourished by the love of the ones they leave behind?"

"Yes, I think they may," he agreed.

For a long moment she did not speak, then she said, "If Jesus does take me before your work is finished, Luke, can I wait for you in Bithynia?"

He held her tightly then, and it was on his lips to protest that she must go with him now, as soon as they could set foot upon the road to Thyatira and then northward across the towering Olympian range to the shores of the Pontus Euxinus. But with the thought came the

265

memory of that dream upon the mountain when he and Probus had been hurrying to Caesarea, where Thecla was to be thrown to the wild beasts. As vividly as he had seen it that night came the picture of himself and Thecla walking gaily down the mountain road from the highlands to the plain of Bithynia, and the sudden crumbling of the road which had sent her body plummeting to the rocks below, leaving him alone. A sudden stark fear gripped him then, and he could only hold her tightly in his arms as if afraid she would be torn from him, for the constriction in his throat would not let him speak.

ii

Luke and Thecla were familiar with the residence of Probus from the time when they, too, had lived in Ephesus, before Luke had gone with Paul to Macedonia. Anna, the apothecary's plump Greek wife, bustled out to meet them with her two strong boys, but since it was only the middle of the afternoon and they had not been expected, Probus was still at his shop. While Thecla lay down to rest, Luke went through the city to where the apothecary shop was located in one of the busier sections, close to the agora.

It was hardly a week before the Feast of Artemision, as the spring games in honor of the Ephesian Diana were called, and the streets were already beginning to be crowded with people. May was renamed Artemision in the cities where her worship predominated, and in the first days of the month people poured into Ephesus from all parts of Asia for the games and celebrations which occupied most of the month, as well as the revelry which always characterized the worship of this most dissolute of goddesses. In order that riots and conflict should be kept at a minimum, it was the custom to elect wealthy men from each district of the province to supervise the games and aid in the entertainment of the crowds, giving them the title of Asiarchs, or, more colloquially, "Chiefs of Asia."

Normally the shops of the silversmiths would be crowded with statues of the many-breasted Artemis and replicas in silver of her temple, ready for the crowds which would be thronging the city. But now as Luke walked along the colonnaded street below the agora where the shops predominated he saw that many were closed; their forges were cold and the tapping of the tiny hammers of the artisans had been stilled. Even in the agora trading seemed to be dull for such a season.

The shop which Probus and his father-in-law operated in partnership was impressive in appearance, as befitted one who compounded medicines for the wealthy. Probus was at the back, dispensing medicines to the sick poor who came to him, as usual without any fee. The two friends embraced each other fervently, and Luke helped treat the patients who waited. Afterward Probus showed him through the complete apothecary shop. "I suppose some would think it odd that I compound medicines for the rich in the front of the shop and treat the poor in the back," he said. "Paul and some of the others here have criticized me for it."

"But Paul has always worked wherever he went."

"He still works daily at the shop of a tentmaker near the agora. Do you want to go and see him?"

Luke shook his head. "Not yet. I want to study the situation here first."

"You will find Paul changed," Probus warned. "Even his teachings are different."

As they were walking to Probus's home in the twilight, the apothecary said, "The people are crowding in for the games and the city looks prosperous now, but make no mistake about it, there is unrest and even want beneath it all. All the shopkeepers hate the Christians, but the silversmiths are the worst."

"But men can carry on commerce and still follow the Way of Jesus," Luke protested. "After all, he worked as a carpenter himself and he certainly must have been paid for his work."

"There is no real reason why commerce and the Christian faith should be in conflict," Probus agreed, "but they will be so long as men want to make a profit to which they are not entitled by the labor they contribute to the product. Jesus said, *'The laborer is worthy of his hire,'* but the employer seeks to pay him less than he is worth and the worker tries to get more."

"The answer is still simple," Luke pointed out. "When all men live according to the Way of Jesus, there will be no conflict, either in business or on the battlefield."

When the children had been put to bed, Probus and Anna, Luke and Thecla sat talking. "How is Paul?" Thecla asked the apothecary.

"His health has been exceptionally good," Probus said, "but his teachings have become steadily more mystical and unreal, although I must confess that they seem to appeal to people even more than before."

"I spoke of this to Barnabas in Antioch," Luke said. "He, too, feels that Paul has gone a long way from the teachings of Jesus."

"But Paul could be right," Thecla said. "How do we know what will happen when Jesus returns to earth?"

"We must remember what we know about Jesus and the things he did and taught on earth," Luke said. "If Jesus were to come again today, I believe he would be a simple carpenter or some such humble laborer as he was before. And I am sure he would go about again among the people, the poor as well as the rich, to remind them that all are equal in the sight of God, emperors with workmen, and princes with beggars." He turned to Probus. "What do you think men seek in Jesus today?"

"Paul says eternal life, but I doubt if so many of us are concerned right now with what is going to happen when we die. I see the Way as a method of finding happiness in life."

"And I," Luke agreed. "But I would go farther and try to find just how it brings us that happiness. For a long time I have wondered why so many people seem uncertain of themselves and go from one philosophy to another, even from one religion to another, searching for the answer to a question which they don't seem to be able to put into words, as if they were afraid of something they cannot understand."

"You can walk through the agora tomorrow and see that fear in a thousand faces," Probus agreed. "But what are they afraid of?"

"Perhaps they are afraid they are not as important to the world, to themselves, and maybe to God, as they would like to be. They may be searching for something to give them a sense of value in themselves and in their work, the things that breed confidence and self-esteem.

"But it is a poor form of self-confidence that comes from getting the best of others in business," Luke continued. "Or giving more to charity, and dressing in fine silks and linens. I remember, Probus, you once said that each of us is trying desperately to get ahead of the other so he can then try just as desperately to get ahead of the one over him."

Probus nodded. "If you need proof, I can show you plenty here in Ephesus, even among those who profess to be Christians."

"Then they are not true followers of Jesus," Luke said. "To me the simple teacher of Galilee has a message for the world which a Jesus who comes with power to rule over the earth could never have, but not through promising me that I shall live forever. As a lowly Nazarene, Jesus showed me that I am important in the sight of God as an individual, created in his image, and that I have a god of my own, whatever my station, not just the god of a people or a nation. Those who follow the real Way of Jesus will always have that confidence and can never be uncertain or afraid."

Thecla put her hand upon his. "No one has ever stated the Way of Jesus more clearly than that, Luke. Maybe God intends for you to teach such truths to the people."

"I am not eloquent like Paul," Luke protested. "I can think these things, but if I spoke them, people would not listen."

"Then you should write them down," Probus said. "Paul has become so preoccupied with his position as the divinely elected apostle to the Gentiles and the mystical instructions which he claims God has revealed to him that he has forgotten the real teachings of Jesus. Wait until you hear him on the Sabbath, Luke. You will see how far afield he has gone."

Looking around him on the following Sabbath at the crowd which filled the lecture hall of Tyrannus and spilled into the street outside, Luke could see that Ephesus had indeed proved one of Paul's most successful ventures. Watching Paul stand in the pulpit and wait for the crowd to settle down for his sermon, Luke decided that the years had not dealt lightly with the apostle, even though they had been a period of success and accomplishment during which he had seen the Christian faith spread from this great center of Ephesus throughout the province of Asia. Paul's face was lined and his shoulders drooped, as if from the weight of heavy responsibilities. His hair had thinned noticeably, but his head still had its leonine cast.

When Paul raised his hands it was with the same familiar gesture, as if he were taking them all into his embrace, that Luke had seen him use many times in Antioch. "Jesus Christ has made a covenant with us," Paul said, "promising that he will return in glory upon a cloud. When a will is made, it is necessary that the death of him who makes it be proved; a will is valid only after a man is dead, and has no force whatever while the one who made it is alive. Not even the first covenant between God and Israel was ratified without the use of blood, for after every regulation in the law had been spoken by Moses to all the people, he took the blood of calves and goats with water, crimson wool, and a bunch of hyssop, and sprinkled the book containing the law and all the people, saying, 'This is the blood that ratifies the covenant which God commanded me to make with you.' In fact, under the law, almost everything is purified with blood, and without the shedding of blood no forgiveness is granted.

"It is by the will of God that we are consecrated through the offering of Jesus's body once for all, as a sacrifice for sins. For by that one sacrifice he has made perfect for all time those who are consecrated to him."

The speaker paused in that dramatic way of his, as if waiting for the significance of this part of the message to sink in before going on. Then, seeing that his audience was listening raptly to his every word, he continued, "Since, my brothers, we then have free access to the real sanctuary through the blood of Jesus, let us continue to draw near to God with sincere hearts and perfect faith; with our hearts cleansed from the sense of sin and our bodies bathed in clean water. Let us, without ever wavering, keep on holding to the hope that we profess, for he is to be trusted who has made the promise. Let us continue so to consider one another as to stimulate one another to love and good deeds.

"For if we go on willfully sinning after we have received full knowledge of the truth, there is no sacrifice left to be offered for our sins, but only a terrifying prospect of judgment and that fiery indignation which is going to devour God's enemies. Anyone of Israel who broke the law of Moses paid the death penalty without any show of pity, on the evidence of two or three witnesses only. How much severer punishment do you suppose that one deserves who tramples the son of God underfoot and counts as a common thing the blood of the covenant by which he was consecrated? Therefore, if we would escape judgment for our many sins we must have faith in Jesus Christ and the power of his blood to free us from sin.

"Now faith is the assurance of the things we hope for, the proof of the reality of the things we cannot see. Therefore, let us throw off every impediment and the sin that easily entangles our feet, and run with endurance the race for which we are entered, keeping our eyes on Jesus, the perfect leader and example of faith, who, instead of the joy which lay before him, endured the cross with no regard for its shame, and since has taken his seat at the right hand of the throne of God.

"May God who gives us peace, who brought back from the dead our Lord Jesus, who through the blood by which he ratified the everlasting covenant is now the Great Shepherd of the sheep, perfectly fit you to do his will, he himself, through Jesus Christ, accomplishing through you what is pleasing to him. To him be glory forever and ever. Amen."

Luke and Thecla waited with Probus outside the lecture hall to speak to Paul. As usual, the apostle was surrounded by a crowd of people questioning him about points which he had emphasized in the sermon. Watching him at a closer distance, Luke saw still other changes since he had last seen Paul. Gone was the humility which had been his in Damascus after being stricken blind on the road and when Luke had helped him escape from the city in the weaver's basket. Nor was this the same Paul who had prayed for Apollonius to be healed in Tarsus. The air of authority which clothed the apostle now, an air bordering upon arrogance, was the same as he had worn when he reprimanded Peter before the congregation at Antioch, and when he had broken with Barnabas, and when Luke had left him at Corinth.

Finally Paul saw them waiting and hurried over to embrace them. "Thecla and Luke!" he cried joyously. "I did not know you were in Ephesus."

"We arrived only a few days ago," Luke said, "on the way to Bithynia."

"Bithynia?" Paul smiled. "It is a long time since we started there and the man of Macedonia spoke to me in the vision."

"Why not go with us now, Paul?" Thecla asked impulsively. "It is not too late."

"No, Thecla. The forces against Christ are too strong here in Ephesus. I must stay and fight them lest they triumph and lead others astray. You heard my sermon today, didn't you?"

"Yes," Luke told him. "You were never more eloquent."

"Then you know that the coming of Jesus grows nearer daily. It will require all my efforts to strengthen the faith of those who already believe, so that they will not be found wanting."

"How can you be so sure that he is coming soon?" Luke asked.

"It has been revealed to me. The time is at hand when he will come in all his glory, and those of us who have served him well will be with him in his kingdom." Paul's voice rose, as if he were addressing a congregation. "He will trample underfoot the temple of pagan gods and destroy those who dare stand against him and his kingdom. The first time he came to die for our sins that his blood might wash them away. But now he will reign in his rightful form as king over all those who believe in him, and destroy all earthly rulers who dare to stand against him."

"Careful!" Probus warned. "Or you will be in trouble with Rome again."

"Are you still of so little faith, Probus," Paul said sternly, "that you cannot see the truth?" Then he turned to Luke. "And you, Luke. Do you deny the truths I spoke to the congregation this morning?"

Luke shook his head. "I do not deny them, Paul. It is your right to teach what you believe. But they are not the things that Jesus taught his disciples. I think you have changed the simple faith he taught into something different, something he would not preach were he here today."

Paul's face flushed with annoyance. "I told you once that these things have been revealed to me from God, Luke. I gave you the title of teacher once, but if you do not believe what I teach, I cannot let you go abroad to Bithynia speaking as one who comes from me."

Luke remembered another occasion when he and Paul had quarreled over Paul's interpretation of the meanings of Jesus after Paul had talked to Sergius Paulus at Paphos. Then Barnabas had persuaded him to go on with Paul and swallow his pride. This time Paul had given him the choice of teaching his doctrines or none at all. But before he could speak, he felt Thecla's hand upon his arm and knew that she was begging him silently not to pursue a quarrel with Paul.

With one of those amazing changes of mood which he sometimes displayed, Paul smiled suddenly and embraced both Luke and Probus. "We are old friends and should not quarrel," he cried. "I am leaving soon to carry money to Jerusalem, which the churches have been collecting for the poor. Let us journey there together and see our comrades and talk over the things which we believe with James and the elders. I am not one to hold a grudge, Luke, when we are all concerned with the Way of Jesus and how we may serve him best."

Luke and Probus looked at each other uncertainly, surprised by the suggestion, but Thecla said, "We could go, Luke. It would be nice to see our friends in Caesarea again." Luke understood that there was more in her mind than just the desire to see the daughters of Philip in Caesarea, with whom she had become close friends while they were there after the death of Herod Agrippa. Luke's break with Paul at Corinth had made Thecla unhappy, for she loved them both. And he knew she had gone on hoping for a reconciliation between the two who had once been so close. Nor would he mind going back to Jerusalem, he thought, as long as Thecla was with him, for it would be pleasant to see Mark and Peter and the others again. Besides, he might learn something about the whereabouts of the scroll and read again, in the very words of the Master, the truth about the Way. Perhaps he might even be able to show Paul how he had departed from it.

"Take your time and think it over," Paul urged. "I know you cannot make such a decision quickly. I must go now and confer with the presbyters about the money for Jerusalem."

As they watched him stride away Thecla said, "You three were such close friends once, I would like to see you together again."

"It was Paul who broke up the friendship," Probus reminded her. "If he had not changed, we could have continued on together."

Luke reached out and squeezed Thecla's hand. "But then I might not have had Thecla, nor you Anna, Probus. So everything has happened for the best."

"You heard Paul preaching today," Probus said as they walked home. "Where did he get this idea of the blood of Christ washing away all sins?"

"He thinks that God revealed it to him," Luke pointed out. "How do we know that he did not?"

"Would Jesus teach one thing if he is the son of God, as we believe him to be, and then God tell Paul to preach another?" Probus demanded. "You know more about the life of Jesus than anyone else, Luke. Was there anything in the scroll about the way in which a person could be saved?"

272

Luke rubbed his chin thoughtfully. He was remembering those days on the road to the Sea of Galilee from Joppa, when he had read the scroll in the evenings in his tent and pondered its teachings while jogging on a placid mule at the end of the long Roman column. And now an incident from the scroll came to him as clearly as if the stained and torn roll of parchment were again unrolled before him.

"There is a passage I remember now," he said. "Jesus was asked by some Pharisees when the kingdom of God would come, and he answered, *'The kingdom of God is not coming with visible display, and so people will not say, Look! Here it is! Nor, There it is! For the kingdom of God is within you.'* "

"You see!" Probus cried. "He says nothing of covenants, sacrifices, or blood. We must go with Paul to Jerusalem, Luke. Peter and the others who heard Jesus speak will confirm these sayings, and then Paul will be forced to admit that he is wrong."

Luke smiled. "Paul believes too strongly that these things have been revealed to him, Probus. But at least we can know in our own minds what is the truth. Then I will know what to teach in Bithynia. What I can't understand," he added thoughtfully, "is why Paul has added these concepts to the simple Way of Jesus that we all lived those first years in Antioch."

"You and I are Greeks," Probus pointed out. "We admire logic and reason, so what appeals most to us in the teachings of Jesus is their simplicity. But Paul is a Jew and even more emotional than most of them are. Sheer logic and simplicity would not appeal to him as they do to us; he would naturally favor the mystical elements which he has added to the life and teachings of Jesus."

Luke nodded thoughtfully. "You may well be right, Probus. Do you suppose it has ever occurred to Paul that his idea of Christ's blood as a sacrifice that removes sin is almost identical with the taurobolium ritual of the Mithraeans?"

"He would deny it if you pointed out the obvious parallels," Probus said. "But what worries me is the dangers in these concepts Paul has added to the true Christian faith."

"Dangers?"

"Yes. Paul preaches that only belief in Jesus as the son of God and in his blood as a sacrifice for mankind can put men right with God. It will be easy for some to conclude that man is thereby absolved from living according to the Way of Jesus."

"But what can we do?"

"Nothing, unless James and the elders at Jerusalem can reason with Paul. You know Paul is always confident that a miracle will arrange for him to triumph over anyone who dares to stand against him, just

273

as he interprets his triumph at Paphos as an intervention by God. But one day he is going to get himself into a situation from which no lucky accident can extract him. It could happen right here in Ephesus, if the silversmiths managed to stir up the people as I know they are plotting to do. If we could make Paul see reason, we might be able to avert disaster for him."

"Whatever happens," Luke said, "we must protect him, Probus. Paul is the greatest teacher since Jesus, even if we can't wholly agree with what he teaches. Nothing must happen to him."

iii

The Temple of Diana at Ephesus was rightly called "the Temple of Asia," just as the city was the chief center of that large and populous province. The colonnades of the Ephesian temple represented the first maturing of the graceful feminine lines of the Ionic style, whose delicate beauty was preferred by Asiatic Greeks to the plainer Doric lines of Athens' own magnificent Parthenon and Propylaea. One of the largest shrines in the world devoted to the worship of the deity of the fountains, it was more than one hundred and twenty-five paces in length and seventy in breadth. Each of its hundred and twenty-seven columns was the gift of a king, and the women of Ephesus had con tributed their jewelry to restore the temple after the fire set by the fanatic Herostratus had almost destroyed it in the year of Alexander's birth. The Ephesians had continued to add adornments to the building, and when Alexander offered them the entire spoils of his conquests in the East in return for letting his name be inscribed upon it, the city fathers had proudly refused. This was the shrine of the goddess whose worship Paul's successful campaign in Asia was imperiling.

As people began to pour into the city for the traditional holiday season of Artemision, as much devoted to games, the theater, and other favorite pastimes of the Greeks as to the worship of Diana, Paul redoubled his work. Twice daily he spoke in the lecture hall of Tyrannus, and great crowds filled the building on every occasion. Even the Asiarchs, whose duty it was to furnish entertainment for the people and control them while in the city, came to listen, and some remained to believe.

Such a preoccupation with unworldly matters at a time ordinarily devoted to revelry inevitably had a further effect upon the business of the city, particularly the work of the silversmiths, already seriously threatened by the tremendous influence which the Christian faith had achieved over a large segment of the people. In such an inflammable situation trouble was not long in developing. The first word that Luke and Probus had of it was when Alexander, a Jewish coppersmith and a friend of Probus, came to the shop one morning very much disturbed. "Demetrius, the leader of the silversmiths, is exciting a crowd to riot against Paul," he reported. "I came to warn you before the mob gets out of control."

Probus lifted his eyebrows. "You Jews are against Paul too. Why not let Demetrius and his followers drive him out, as you would like to happen?"

"It is well known in Ephesus that Paul is also a Jew," Alexander explained. "A mob aroused against any Jew in these times may turn upon all of us." Since all Jews had been ordered to leave Rome by Claudius, unruly elements in other cities of the Empire had seized the opportunity to persecute this already much dispersed race.

"Paul absolutely refuses to leave Ephesus," Probus said.

"Then there will be serious trouble," Alexander said grimly. "A large crowd was forming when I left, and Demetrius is whipping them into a frenzy."

"Let me go with you to Demetrius," Luke suggested. "Perhaps I can reason with him."

Alexander shrugged hopelessly. "You will be wasting your time," he warned. "But I will take you to his shop."

Such a large crowd had gathered in the street before the establishment of Demetrius that they could not get near it. Looking around him, Luke found this crowd little different from others which had been stirred up by the visits of Paul. There was the same shouting but saying nothing, the same angry gestures, the same sporadic fights. This one, however, had the advantage of a forceful and skillful leader, which made it doubly dangerous.

Demetrius stood on a table which had been dragged from the shop. "Men of Ephesus," he shouted. "You know well that our prosperity depends upon this business of ours, and you see and hear that, not only in Ephesus but all over the province of Asia, this man Paul has led away a vast number of people by persuading them, telling them that gods made by human hands are not gods at all. Now the danger facing us is not only that our business will lose its reputation, but also that the temple of the great goddess Artemis will be brought into contempt and that she whom all Asia and all the world now worships will soon be dethroned from her majestic glory."

"Great Artemis of Ephesus!" someone shouted, and the crowd took up the cry so that Demetrius could not be heard. "Great Artemis of Ephesus!" The chant rose in waves of sound.

"Look!" Probus cried. "They have Gaius and Aristarchus." Two men were being dragged through the crowd toward the platform upon which Demetrius stood. The speaker looked down at the struggling knot of men who surrounded the two and asked in a loud voice, "Who are these two?"

"This must be prearranged," Probus observed. "Demetrius knows those two well. But why has he taken them instead of Paul?"

"Perhaps he hopes to lure Paul into his hands?" Luke said. "He is sure to come when he learns that they have captured Gaius and Aristarchus."

"They are companions of Paul," the men who had dragged the two through the crowd shouted in answer to Demetrius, at which the crowd began to howl once more. Some who were close to the platform struck at the victims with heavy staves which many of the crowd carried. "Hold your staves," Demetrius shouted. "We will take them to the theater so they may be judged."

The mob seized eagerly upon this idea and began to surge through the streets toward the great theater at the end of the colonnaded street leading from the Temple of Artemis, dragging Gaius and Aristarchus with them. At almost every street corner it gained in numbers as more and more people attached themselves, joining in the rhythmic chant of "Great Artemis of Ephesus!" The passions of such an excited group could be skillfully directed upon Paul and the Christians whenever Demetrius was ready, leading to a full-scale riot.

Into the great outdoor amphitheater they poured, spilling out into the lower rows of seats. Gaius and Aristarchus, half conscious from the buffeting they had received at the hands of the crowd, were dragged to the stage behind the tall figure of Demetrius. As Luke, Probus, and Alexander were swept into the theater with the crowd the apothecary seized their hands and drew them into a side passage. "Follow me," he directed. "I know a way to get close to the stage."

The narrow corridor led under the marble tiers of seats and emerged through one of the lower *vomitoria* only a little way from the stage, where they could see and hear whatever happened. "Stay close to the opening," Probus warned, "in case we need to get out quickly."

"Where is the Jew, Paul?" someone in the crowd shouted, and others took up the cry: "Death to Paul! Death to the Jews!" This was the thing which Alexander had feared, for in their present state the crowd might easily turn upon all the Jews of the city. Before Luke or Probus realized what Alexander intended, he vaulted over the low parapet in front of the seats and ran for the stage. Upon the lower steps he raised his hand to attract the attention of the crowd, for, being a coppersmith, he would be well known to many of the metalworkers in the mob.

One of the crowd shouted, "There is a Jew!" and others took up the cry. Alexander would have been killed then and there had not Demetrius shouted, "We have no quarrel with the Jews of Ephesus. Let us judge the Macedonians here, then we will go in search of Paul."

"If Paul learns that Gaius and Aristarchus have been taken by the mob, he may try to come here," Luke said with a worried frown.

"God help him if he does," Probus added.

"You and Alexander can go out through the corridor by which we entered, Probus," Luke said urgently. "Find Paul and see that he does not come here, even if you have to restrain him by force."

Probus nodded his understanding of the stratagem. "What about you?"

"I will stay here to help Gaius and Aristarchus if I can."

"Paul can go to my house," Probus said. "We may be able to hide him until this blows over."

While Probus and Alexander made their exit hurriedly through the *vomitoria* by which they had entered the theater, Luke turned his attention back to Demetrius. The silversmith was not even trying to quiet the crowd, and Luke was sure now that his strategy was to use Paul's disciples, Gaius and Aristarchus, as bait to lure the apostle into the hands of the mob, which, in its present temper, would mean his death.

Into this tense and inflammable situation a new sound now intruded itself, the blast of Roman trumpets. Luke saw Demetrius wheel in the direction of the sound, and a look of dismay came over his features at this unexpected complication. The Roman authorities were very strict about riots and put them down when they arose, sometimes with bloody results. The sound of the trumpets had a quieting effect upon the crowd, too, for they knew well upon whom the staves of the lictors and the swords of the soldiers would fall if the riot had to be put down by force.

Through the entrance to the theater marched a tall commanding figure in rich garments, followed by several men in the purple mantles and garlands of the Asiarchs, who were charged with maintaining order at this season. Guarding them was a squad of Roman soldiers with drawn short swords. A hush fell over the crowd as this impressive group marched up to the stage, and beside him Luke heard one of the Ephesians tell another, "It is Aristides, the city recorder and chief magistrate, with the Asiarchs."

Before Demetrius, the recorder stopped. "Who incited this riot?" he demanded sharply.

"A man named Paul, noble Aristides." Demetrius bowed respectfully. "He has defamed great Artemis of Ephesus."

THE ROAD TO BITHYNIA

The crowd started chanting again, but the recorder silenced them with a stern order. "Who are these men?" he asked, pointing to the two Greeks. "And why have you beaten them?"

"They are followers of Paul," Demetrius explained. "The crowd would have torn them to pieces. But I insisted that they be brought here to be judged."

The recorder turned to the crowd, and his voice rang out over the theater. "Men of Ephesus," he said sternly. "Who in the world does not know that the city of Ephesus is the guardian of the temple of the great Artemis and of the image that fell down from the heavens? So, as this cannot be denied, you must be quiet and do nothing rash. For you have brought these men here, although they are not guilty of sacrilege or of abusive speech against our goddess. If Demetrius and his fellow workmen have a charge against anybody, there are the courts and the judges; let them go to law. But if you require anything beyond this, it must be settled in the regular assembly. For we are in danger of being charged with rioting for today's assembly, as there is not a single reason we can give for it."

This was a cogent argument to the logic-loving Greeks. Certain times were set by law for the assizes, when the authorities met with the people in assembly to hear complaints and try wrongdoers. But this was no such orderly gathering and could well bring down upon the Ephesians the wrath of the Roman authorities, who abhorred riots. Nor could Demetrius afford to defy the recorder, for it was within the power of the city official to have him arrested there and then.

At a nod from Aristides the soldiers blew another blast on their trumpets to gain the attention of the crowd. "I declare this assembly dismissed," he shouted. "All must leave the theater at once or suffer arrest."

While the crowd was filtering out of the theater in the wake of the official party, Luke made his way to the stage, where the injured men were lying. A quick examination told him that their wounds were not mortal, and he was looking around for someone to send after a cart or litter when he heard Demetrius speaking to the men who had dragged Gaius and Aristarchus through the crowd at the beginning of the riot. Luke bent over the wounded men so that Demetrius would not realize that he was eavesdropping.

"If we go quickly to the house of Priscilla and Aquila," Demetrius was instructing his henchmen, "we can still find Paul. Put cloths over your faces so that you will not be recognized. We can kill him then and blame it on unruly elements from the mob."

Luke's mind worked rapidly, for he knew that there was no time to be lost if Paul were to be saved. The crowd would not find the apostle at the house of Priscilla and Aquila, but someone there might reveal that Probus had come for him. There was only one answer: Luke must reach Paul at the house of Probus and get him away from the city before the silversmiths got there.

By taking short cuts and less frequented streets Luke moved as quickly as he could, but it seemed hours before he stumbled into Probus's home. Paul and the apothecary were arguing spiritedly when he entered, and he heard Paul shout, "I am going to the theater. Don't try to stop me."

Thecla saw Luke enter and went to him at once, thinking that he was hurt, for he was panting from having run through the city. "Are you hurt, dear?" she asked.

"I am all right," Luke gasped. "But we must get Paul away immediately."

"I will go to the theater," Paul insisted stubbornly.

"The mob has been dismissed by the city recorder," Luke explained. "But Demetrius and his men have gone to the house of Priscilla and Aquila to look for you to kill you. They are sure to find out from someone that you came here with Probus and follow you."

"I will speak to them," Paul began, but Luke cut him off impatiently. "Why do you think they will listen? The whole riot this morning was stirred up so the crowd would kill you and Demetrius could escape responsibility. They even dragged Gaius and Aristarchus there because they thought you would come when you heard they had been taken."

"I would have come," Paul cried indignantly, "if Probus had not lied to me and brought me here."

"You should thank him for saving your life, then. This is no mere riot, Paul, which you can quiet by speaking to the crowd. Demetrius is on his way here now with a group of hired assassins. I heard them say they would put cloths over their faces and kill you so that the authorities would not know whom to blame. We must get you to a place of safety."

"Luke is right, Paul," Thecla pleaded. "It would not help anything for you to be killed by a group of murderers."

For the first time a look of doubt appeared in Paul's eyes. While he might welcome a martyr's death such as Jesus had suffered, nothing would be accomplished if he lost his life on a back street at the hands of assassins.

Seeing that Paul was wavering, Probus said, "Silas has taken Anna and the children to her father's home, Luke. You must take Paul and Thecla there at once."

279

Luke shook his head. "Demetrius and his henchmen are in the street. We might easily run into them."

"The river is only a short distance from here," Probus said. "Take the first boat you find and row downstream. Silas and I will come down-river for you later, when the crowd has dispersed."

"But how will you escape?" Luke protested.

"I am well known in the city," Probus assured him. "They will not bother me."

A new sound came from the street, the tramping of heavy feet, as if a band of men were approaching the house. All of them realized instantly what had happened; Demetrius had learned or surmised where his quarry had flown.

"Quick," Probus directed, pushing the three of them toward the back of the house. "Make for the river. I will try to hold them here until you can get a boat."

Paul hesitated, as if even now he could not realize that he was facing violent death, but Luke seized his hand and urged Thecla out through the door leading into the small garden that gave access to the back street, half dragging Paul with them. As they scuttled down the tree-lined lane that ran back of the house toward the river they could easily hear the angry shouts of Demetrius and his men before the house.

"I hope nothing happens to Probus," Thecla panted, running beside Luke.

"Let us hope God will protect him," Luke agreed soberly. Behind them there was a momentary lull in the sound of the crowd as they surged into the house, thinking they had run their prey to earth. But there was no time to stop and learn what had happened to Probus. They had been given a few minutes' respite; it would be all too short a time in which to make their escape.

All three of them were exhausted when they reached the stone parapet that guarded the channel of the Cayster here in the city, but there was no time for rest. Luke climbed upon the parapet and searched the brown flood of the river for one of the boats which were usually tethered all along the banks and in which they could float down the stream to safety. But this time no boats met his gaze, nothing except the stream itself and the stone walls that lined its banks. Too late he remembered that the owners of boats took them out of the water during the Feast of Artemision for fear they might be stolen or damaged by the crowds that filled the city.

"What will we do, Luke?" Thecla cried. "There are no boats."

A sudden burst of sound, like dogs baying upon the trail of a wounded animal, told them the mob had picked up their escape route and were again in pursuit. But with their backs to the river there seemed no means of escape. Luke glanced down at the water, then back at the other two. "Can you swim, Thecla?" he asked.

"A little," she admitted. "Perhaps enough to get across, no more."

"And you, Paul?"

Paul turned when Luke spoke, but slowly, as if he were in a daze, still unable to believe that he was really facing death with no apparent help from any source, not even the divine intervention which he believed had always come to his aid. "No," he said dully then. "I never learned to swim."

Quickly Luke searched the banks of the stream once more for something upon which they could float downstream to safety, but there was nothing that offered any hope. Then he noticed something which in his anguish he had overlooked before, a narrow stone ledge about three feet above the water level and some five feet below the top of the parapet against which they were leaning. He recognized it at once as the opening of one of the great cloacas, or sewers, which emptied into the river every hundred feet or so here. Lined with stone, the cloacas were about four feet in diameter, with the opening only partially submerged in water, except when the tide was high and the level of the river covered them. Now the tide was low and the water level only half covered the mouth of the sewer, leaving several feet of open space above the water inside the passage. It was an unpleasant haven in which to be forced to seek refuge, but he saw no other alternative.

"The cloaca is only partially submerged," he told Thecla and Paul hurriedly. "There is a chance that we can drop over the bank here and hide inside it."

Thecla shivered at the thought of entering the water and the filthy sewer, but she nodded bravely to show that she understood. Luke climbed over the parapet above the mouth of the sewer and stood on the narrow stone ledge which had shown it to him. The small platform was only about a foot wide and barely long enough for him to stand on with a good footing.

"You first, dear," he said to Thecla. She climbed over the parapet, and Luke helped her down on the stone ledge beside him with her back to the river. Then, taking her hands, he lowered her over the mouth of the cloaca. She shivered as the water touched her body, but her eyes were unafraid and she even managed to smile. "Feel with your feet for the mouth of the sewer," Luke instructed her.

She nodded and moved her legs, then shook her head, and he let her down a little deeper. "I am touching it now," she said then. "There seems to be a platform here at the sewer mouth."

"Good." Luke released her hands. "Now creep inside and stay there, no matter what happens."

"You will come?"

"Yes, we'll come." He turned to Paul, who was standing beside the parapet staring back toward Probus's house. Already the forms of running men could be seen through the trees as the mob converged upon the river. "Over the side quickly," Luke told the apostle. "We don't have much time."

Paul stared at him a moment, his eyes dull and uncomprehending, then at Luke's urging he climbed over the parapet. Because of Paul's short stature Luke had to lean far over the ledge in order to lower him into the mouth of the sewer. From her position inside the cloaca Thecla took Paul by the knees and helped him to the underwater platform that marked the mouth. When Paul was safely inside, Luke dropped over the edge and into the water, landing upon the stones with a jarring thud. By the time he, too, was safely hidden, the first of the crowd reached the riverbank.

Although it was May, the water was cool, for the excess from the Roman aqueducts bringing water from cold mountain springs spilled over into the sewers. The passage was not so foul as Luke had expected, however, because such a volume of water flowed through it, but the smell was still fetid enough almost to nauseate them as they crouched inside and listened to the shouts of the mob overhead. It apparently never occurred to any of the mob to look for them inside the cloaca, for no one clambered over the parapet. Had they done so, however, the three fugitives would still have been safe, for only a few yards inside it was too dark for them to be seen.

Demetrius and his henchmen did not stay near them long. Luke heard the leader order them to divide and search along the riverbank. But they could hear the voices of people passing along the street from time to time, so they were afraid to climb out of their dank refuge. At Luke's suggestion the three of them tried to keep the circulation stirring in their bodies by moving about in the water, but the chill gradually penetrated deeply through them. And as the hours passed, Luke was more and more worried about the danger of this exposure to Thecla. Once or twice they heard the creak of oarlocks and sails, but it was only fishermen moving along the river and, once, a cargo galley beating its way upstream.

As the tide began to rise, the level of water in the cloaca grew higher, and Luke knew they would have to leave soon or be drowned. Through all this Paul had said little. He seemed to be in the grip of a profound depression of spirit, similar to the one which had seized him following their near death at Pisidian Antioch. Luke could sympathize with his reaction. For knowing Paul and his fierce pride in being the apostle to the Gentiles, he understood what a shock it must have been to be forced to escape the fury of a mob through such an ignoble route as one of the cloacas of the city in which he had made his greatest success.

Shortly after dusk a boat came along the canal with a lantern in the bow casting a fitful circle of light before it. Luke crept to the mouth of the sewer and looked out. The boat was rowed by a single figure, and he considered attempting a sudden attack upon it when it came closer, hoping to commandeer a way of escape for them. But when the light came closer he recognized Silas straining at the oars against the incoming tide.

"Silas!" Luke called. "Over here."

"Luke? Where are you?" There was profound relief in Silas's tone.

"Here in the mouth of the cloaca. Paul is with us."

"Thank God!" Silas said fervently. "I was afraid that all of you had drowned."

"We would have been taken by the mob," Luke explained as he seized the bow of the boat and maneuvered it into position against the mouth of the cloaca, "but fortunately I found this sewer in time."

Thecla and Paul crept out, and Silas helped them overside. Luke came last. "How did you know where to look for us?" Luke asked when they were safely aboard.

"Probus told me you were going to try to escape in a rowboat down the river," Silas explained. "But I had to wait for darkness before coming to look for you."

"Has the mob quieted down?"

Silas nodded, his face grim. "After what happened at Probus's house, the recorder sent troops to arrest Demetrius and his henchmen."

Thecla voiced the question that was in all their minds. "What was it, Silas?"

"Probus tried to delay the mob, and in their anger they turned upon him."

None of them wanted to ask the next question, for Silas's manner left little doubt of the answer.

"Probus is dead," Silas said at last. "I got to him a few minutes before the end, long enough to learn that you three had escaped to the river."

Stunned by the news, none of them could speak. In the silence Silas took the oars and began to row downstream, away from the city. Finally Luke said, "He sacrificed himself to save us," and his voice broke in a sob, for he had loved Probus. Thecla put her hand into Luke's to comfort him, but strangely enough it was Paul who voiced the thought which gave them all the most solace in the loss of their friend.

"I heard John repeat these words of Jesus once," the apostle said simply, " *'Greater love hath no man than this, that a man lay down his life for his friends.'* "

iv

Thecla was sitting in the garden of Lydia's house in Philippi when Luke came in carrying a letter from Timothy. They had come here with Paul after the riot in Ephesus had resulted in the death of Probus and so nearly cost them their own lives. Luke had been worried that the long immersion in the cold water at Ephesus might bring on a recurrence of Thecla's illness, and so at Philippi he had asked Paul to let them stay behind so Thecla could rest in the warm sun of Lydia's garden. Paul had been gone for several months collecting contributions from the churches to be carried to Jerusalem to relieve the famine, which was reported as becoming more acute daily. In the meantime Luke resumed the work which he had left off at Philippi when they had been thrown in prison and beaten on orders of the Roman magistrate.

Thecla looked up and smiled when Luke came into the garden. He stooped to kiss her, and she put her hand to his face and pressed his cheek to hers in a little gesture of endearment which they both loved. Once or twice lately Luke had wondered if her cheeks were not pinker than they should have been but had told himself that it must be from the sun rather than a recurrence of the fever which he had come to fear as a warning of the trouble she had suffered in Antioch.

"Philippi agrees with you, dear," he said. "I have never seen you more beautiful."

"Lydia will not even let me lift a hand for myself," Thecla protested. "I shall grow fat with nothing to do."

"Perhaps we will be moving on soon," he told her. "This letter is from Timothy."

"Read it to me!" Thecla cried. The boy who had been with them in Lystra and Iconium was grown to manhood now and had become a strong staff upon which Paul leaned heavily. Timothy wrote:

"Paul has asked me to write you, for he is very busy gathering alms to be carried to Jerusalem. And indeed I should have written you before, thanking you both for saving Paul from the mob in Ephesus, as should all who love Jesus. He has told us what you did and how Probus died to save him.

"We have been in Greece for the past three months, but the Jews there plotted against Paul, as they have in other cities, so we are traveling now by way of Macedonia to Troas, where we hope that you and Thecla can join us to go on to Jerusalem. Paul has been very much disturbed by letters which have come from the churches in Galatia, telling that they have been visited again by the false prophets who claim to come from James in Jerusalem. In addition they tell of the visits of some Jews who have been sent out by the Sanhedrin in Jerusalem, seeking to weaken the faith of the Galatians. At first Paul thought of going by way of Galatia, in order to visit the churches, but now he has decided to write them a letter which I am copying, setting forth all that has happened in the controversy over circumcision and eating unclean foods, and how he was given the message from James and the elders to the Gentile brethren, of which you already know. He thinks now that more can be accomplished against those who seek to undermine his work if we go on to Jerusalem with the gifts for the poor which we have been collecting and which are now a considerable amount, hoping to convince the Jews there that we should all work together in the service of God.

"We plan to reach Troas about two weeks hence and hope that you both will join us there. Thence Paul wishes to go to Miletus, so that he can confer with the Ephesian elders before sailing for Syria. Paul is in good health and bids me give both of you his greeting and his love.

"Yours in the service of Jesus,

"TIMOTHY"

"Why do the Judaizers still try to hamper Paul's work?" Thecla cried indignantly.

"Some sincere people think Paul is wrong about many of the things he teaches," Luke explained. "Perhaps some of the confusion arises because nobody has gotten together in one form all that we know about Jesus and what he did and said."

"Why don't you do it, Luke?"

Luke smiled. "I am a physician, not a writer."

"I kept the letters you wrote to me when you were in Antioch and I was in Iconium," she said, smiling. "Don't ever tell me that you cannot write."

"But I was writing to the one I love," he reminded her. "That makes a difference."

"You love Jesus," she said seriously. "And you would be writing about him. Sometimes I think you love him more than any of us, Luke, even though you never knew him. And I am sure you come nearer than anyone to understanding what he means to the world."

"I will think about it," Luke promised. "Mark may be writing such

285

an account already; he knows the story well. Shall we join Paul in Troas or sit here in the sun at Philippi?"

"We will go to Troas, of course," Thecla said promptly. "I told you I was getting fat here."

At Neapolis, the Aegean port of Philippi, Luke and Thecla were fortunate in finding a ship sailing for Troas the next day, a journey of from three to five days across the upper part of the narrow sea. The day after sailing they raised the towering peak of Samothrace, the Monte Santos of the old Greek mariners, and a few hours later the larger island of Imbros. As the ship rounded this island, the mouth of what seemed to be a great river opened to the east and a strong current gripped the vessel, setting southward. "Do you recognize that?" Luke asked Thecla, pointing to the distant opening in the east.

"It should be the Hellespontus," Thecla said. "Am I right?"

"Yes. But what lies beyond it?"

"The Propontis and then the Pontus Euxinus. See how well I know my geography?" Then she grasped his meaning and her face sobered. "Bithynia," she said slowly then. "It is the water route to Bithynia, but the current of the Hellespontus is carrying us away from it."

"The current of our lives," he reminded her gently. "It is setting in another direction, or we might be going to Bithynia even now."

"Are you disappointed, Luke?"

"Disappointed?" For a moment he did not go on, then he said, "No, I think not. I wonder," he added thoughtfully, "how many people are lost fighting against the very current which eventually would take them where they wish to go, perhaps even to Bithynia."

"Then you think God is sending us to Jerusalem?"

"Do you?"

She nodded and drew close to him, seeking his hand with hers. "Does it scare you sometimes, Luke? I mean to think that something over which you have no control is guiding you, just as the current has taken control of the ship?"

Luke smiled. "When I was younger I sometimes felt as if I had to rebel," he admitted. "But now I am sure that God's purpose is best for us." He put his arm about her. "This is a new adventure, dear. We should be looking ahead, not backward."

"I know," she said. She clung to him, and as he held her close he felt her tears upon his cheek. And as he watched the mouth of the Hellespontus disappear behind the rocky outcropping of Cape Helles, his own throat filled, for he knew that Thecla was wondering if she would ever see Bithynia.

Paul and the rest of the party were already at Troas when Luke and Thecla reached the ancient capital of the Trojans. Luke was quick to see the change in Paul, for he was by no means the same man who had preached so forcefully to the crowds in the lecture hall of Tyrannus in Ephesus. Paul had been depressed, as had all of them, by the death of Probus and the ignominy of his forced escape from Ephesus. But this was something different, as if a sense of impending disaster had come over him since Luke had left him and the others at Philippi. As soon as he could Luke took Silas aside and spoke to him about it.

"I have noticed a change," Silas admitted. "I think now it came when we reached Corinth and Paul saw how the church there had been split by the Judaizers."

"Have they crossed over into Macedonia?" Luke asked in surprise. "I thought they were active in Galatia."

"There seem to be two distinct movements now," Silas said. "One is the same group which has fought us ever since Paul began his missions to the Gentiles, teaching that they cannot be accepted into the Church of Christ unless they obey the Jewish laws of diet and are circumcised. The others are from the Sanhedrin and teach that Jesus was not resurrected, but that his body was stolen from the tomb by his followers to make him appear divine."

"But surely the Christians in Macedonia would not believe them?"

"Only a few listened," Silas admitted. "But those who claimed before to have come from James now claim to come from Peter. Some of the Macedonian churches have split up into factions, one group calling themselves followers of Peter and the other of Paul."

This was bad news indeed, for with Paul going to Jerusalem, the old controversy between Paul and Peter might flare up again. When Luke told Thecla of it her eyes filled with tears. "It breaks my heart to look at Paul now," she said. "But it must be more than just the trouble with the churches. Do you suppose God has revealed to him that he will be killed in Jerusalem?"

"Jesus knew that he would be crucified," Luke said. "And the Sanhedrin would certainly welcome an opportunity to kill Paul. But we are probably overconcerned," he continued. "Paul has had troubles before and survived them."

"I am glad you are with him, Luke. He needs you."

"He needs us all, dear," Luke said. "Paul is fighting for the Way of Jesus, in which we all believe."

"Must men always fight over their beliefs? Even Socrates drank the hemlock rather than recant his convictions."

Luke smiled. "We can hope that all men will one day believe in Jesus, dear. Then there will be no need to fight *over* their beliefs. But when men are no longer willing to fight *for* them, the world will be lost."

287

v

During the long voyage to the Syrian coast Paul became more like himself. It was like the old days when Luke, Paul, Barnabas, Probus, and Mark, an eager group of evangelizing Christians, had sailed to Cyprus. Thecla, too, was enjoying the voyage. Watching her as she stood in the bow with the warm summer wind blowing through her hair, Luke found himself hoping that he was wrong in worrying because the flush in her cheeks seemed more than the sun alone would have caused.

At Tyre, where the ship put in to unload, the Christians warned Paul again about the enmity of the Sanhedrin in Jerusalem, but the apostle laughed it off and insisted upon going on. Talking privately to the leaders of the Church there, Luke and Silas learned in what a state of ferment the Jews in Jerusalem really were over Paul. They blamed him, more than anything else, for the decrease in attendance at the temple by Jews living in other cities of the Empire, as well as the resulting loss of revenue to the priests and the merchants of the city who profited by the visits of pilgrims to the great religious festivals. This bitter hate against Paul had prompted the sending of the proselyters who had been following him in Galatia, Macedonia, Greece, and Asia, trying to wreck the churches which he had established so successfully in those provinces.

Leaving Tyre, the party came at last to Caesarea, where they planned to stop for a short while before going on to Jerusalem. Luke and Thecla lodged with Paul and Timothy at the home of Philip, who had been one of the original Seven at the time of the persecution which had brought about the martyrdom of Stephen. His daughters and Thecla were fast friends from her former visit here, when she had escaped death at the hands of Herod Agrippa. Luke, as usual, went out to care for the sick. In the evening Thecla would come to his surgery and they would walk back to Philip's house along the seashore in the gathering shadows of evening, or sit upon the great stones of the mole which formed the harbor, watching the water surge endlessly against the barrier.

One afternoon, however, they took a route through the city and climbed the empty tiers of seats in the great amphitheater until they could look down upon the arena where Thecla, tied to the back of the young bull, had waited for death under the claws of the lions. "I wonder what would have happened to me that day if you had not been able to bribe the old man to guide you over the mountain, Luke."

"Herod might still have died," Luke pointed out. "Probus and I were sure his anger at Agabus actually killed him, but there must also have been a tremendous excitement for him in being called a god by the people. That might have helped to bring on the attack that killed him."

Thecla's hand crept into his. "I have faith," she said, "but just the same I am glad that you got there that day." She hesitated, then went on: "Would you mind much if I didn't go with you to Jerusalem, Luke?"

"I thought you wanted to go."

"If what Paul expects happens, I—I would just rather not be there. And I would feel safer if you were not there, darling."

"Paul will be safe," he reassured her. "The priests hate him, but Jerusalem is still under Rome, and the soldiers are obliged to protect Roman citizens."

"Roman citizenship did not save you from being beaten in Pisidian Antioch," she reminded him. "Or in Philippi."

"But only because Paul did not claim his right and I felt I should share the troubles of the others."

"Paul owes much to you, Luke," Thecla said. "You gave up your career as a physician to go with him."

He drew her closer to him. "But if Paul had not converted you in Tarsus, you would never have come with Glaucus to Jerusalem and I would never have found you and fallen in love with you."

She put her arm about his waist beneath his cloak. "I wonder if that may have been part of God's plan too. Our life and our happiness together, Luke, could be only a preparation for something greater, something more important than either of us."

"Eternity?"

"No. Something in life, but I don't know exactly what."

"Being with you has made me a better physician," he said, "and a better man. I have gained a new understanding of what life can really mean for two people who love each other."

"God has been good to both of us in giving us each other," she agreed. "I should not be selfish and want to hold you if it is his will that you go to Jerusalem with Paul."

As they came along the street in the shadows of dusk, Luke saw an odd figure trudging toward Philip's house. The matted gray hair and beard and the long robe and staff looked familiar, but only when they came close enough to see the man's face did recognition come to Luke. Then he seized the old man by the shoulders and embraced him. "Agabus!" he cried. "What brings you here?"

The old prophet peered at him in the dusk. "I have come from the mountains of Judea, Luke of Antioch," he said, "with a message for him who was once called Saul of Tarsus."

"Paul should be inside the house. It is almost time for the evening meal."

The house was already crowded, for Paul was to speak that evening, but at the sight of the old prophet a hush fell over them. Agabus was known in Caesarea and respected for his ability to prophesy. The old man walked up to Paul and silently removed the apostle's belt. Then, sitting on the floor, he looped the belt around his own wrists and ankles and drew the loop taut with his teeth. "This is what the Holy Spirit says," he pronounced solemnly, " *'The Jews at Jerusalem will bind the man who owns this belt and turn him over to the heathen.'* "

For a moment there was no sound as the old prophet sat there with his hands and feet bound, then as Luke stooped to help him loosen the belt, Thecla cried, "It is a sign, Paul! You must not go to Jerusalem." Others took up the cry, and some of the women began to weep. But Paul held up his hand for silence, and when they had quieted enough for him to be heard he opened his arms in that familiar gesture of his. "What do you mean by weeping and breaking my heart?" he asked, smiling. "Why, I am ready not only to be bound at Jerusalem, but to die for the sake of our Lord Jesus. Besides," he continued, "Agabus did not say I would be killed. And this would not be the first time I have been given into the custody of the heathen and lived to tell the story. Come, let us sing and rejoice that so many old friends are all here together, praising God and Jesus Christ."

When Paul and the party left a few days later for Jerusalem, Thecla did not go with them. And in truth, Luke was not unhappy that she had stayed behind in Caesarea where she would be safe with the family of Philip, for the prophecy of Agabus had increased his uneasiness about the results of their visit to the Holy City. When they arrived at Jerusalem, Luke went directly to the home of Mary, the mother of Mark, to inquire about Peter and Mark. They were absent, he learned, visiting some of the churches in the cities of the Decapolis beyond the Sea of Galilee and in Galilee itself, but Mary insisted that Luke remain at her house while in Jerusalem.

Paul was staying at the home of his sister, who had been living in Jerusalem now for several years, with her son Joseph, who was apprenticed to a money-changer in the temple. The day after their arrival Paul, Luke, and the others visited the patriarch James and the elders of the Christian Church in Jerusalem, and that same day Paul addressed the congregation in the former synagogue, which served them as a church. He had been welcomed warmly by the church leaders, and the congregation listened with interest as he gave an account of his work during the past several years, since his last visit to Jerusalem while Luke had been in Antioch with Thecla and the baby, Apollos Lucanus. As Paul told of his work and the thriving churches he had established, Luke thought he seemed more like himself than at any time since the tragedy at Ephesus.

It was an impressive list of accomplishments that the apostle gave. Churches had been established and nourished until they were strong, thousands had been brought to know the Way of Jesus, and a far-flung organization of congregations had been linked together and with the Church at Jerusalem throughout the eastern end of the Mediterranean. And as a tangible evidence of the reverence these churches gave to Paul and the mother church in Jerusalem, he had brought substantial sums of money which they had sent to relieve some of the famine and suffering which gripped the city.

Paul finished his account of the sums given by the various churches and put down the tablet upon which they had been written. He looked over the congregation before him. "Our brothers and sisters in Galatia and Asia, in Macedonia and Greece," he said, "ask nothing in return for these gifts which they make out of love for Jesus and for you here who first were given the opportunity to come together to worship him as a congregation. But let me beg that you return that love with good measure; as our Lord Jesus said, *'Practice giving to others and they will give to you; good measure, pressed down, shaken together, and running over, people will pour into your lap. For the measure you use with others, they in turn will use with you.'*"

It was not said as a rebuke, although Paul had ample reason to rebuke some elements of this church which had sent out the false prophets to create discord among the new churches on the questions of circumcision and diet. Rather it was a plea for tolerance, something of a new role for Paul. Then he took another tablet from a sheaf which was on the pulpit before him. "I have one other thing to read to you," he said then. "It is a part of a letter which I have written to the church at Corinth, but I would speak it to all who follow in the Way of Jesus, wherever they may be, for we sometimes forget what he taught us about love for each other." Then he read in his deep, moving voice:

> *"If I could speak the languages of men and of angels, too,*
> *And have no love,*
> *I am only a rattling pan or a clashing cymbal.*
> *If I should have the gift of prophecy,*
> *And know all secret truths, and knowledge in its every form,*
> *And have such perfect faith that I could move mountains,*
> *But have no love, I am nothing.*

If I should dole out everything I have for charity,
And give my body up to torture in mere boasting pride,
But have no love, I get from it no good at all.
Love is so patient and so kind;
Love never boils with jealousy;
It never boasts, is never puffed with pride;
It does not act with rudeness or insist upon its rights;
It never gets provoked, it never harbors evil thoughts;
Is never glad when wrong is done,
But always glad when truth prevails;
It bears up under anything,
It exercises faith in everything,
It keeps up hope in everything,
It gives us power to endure in anything.
And so these three, faith, hope and love endure,
But the greatest of them is love."

Paul gathered up his tablets and scrolls and descended from the pulpit. Looking around him at the congregation, Luke could see that Paul's appeal for tolerance and understanding had been well received. Remembering his former truculence with Peter, Luke realized again what a tremendous change had come over the dynamic apostle in the months since he had heard him speak in the lecture hall at Ephesus before the riot of the silversmiths.

James, the patriarch, now rose to speak, evidently very much pleased with Paul's more reasonable attitude and the approval manifested by the congregation. "You see, Brother Paul," he said, "how many thousand believers there are among the Jews, all of them zealous champions of the law. They had been repeatedly told about you that you continuously teach the Jews who live among the heathen to turn their backs on Moses, and that you continue to tell them to stop circumcising their children and to stop observing their cherished customs. What is your duty, then? They will certainly hear that you have come. Now you must do just what we tell you. We have here four men who are under a vow. Take them along with you, purify yourself with them, and bear the expense with them of having their heads shaved. Then everybody will know that none of the things they have been told about you are so, but that you yourself are living as a constant observer of the law. As for the heathen who have become believers, we have sent them our resolution that they must avoid anything which is contaminated by idols, the tasting of blood, the meat of strangled animals, and sexual immorality."

Luke waited for Paul's answer, as did the congregation. He could understand something of the struggle which must be going on in the apostle's mind. Paul had always prided himself upon being a Jew and on his strict upbringing in accordance with the law, and had, in fact, always kept the laws, even when he had gone out as apostle to the Gentiles. And yet if he went through the ritual purification of the temple for the seven days, while paying the expenses of four others, as James suggested, the Judaizers among the congregation might well noise it abroad that Paul was espousing the Jewish laws for Gentiles as a prerequisite to being accepted by the Church. That, of course, would be playing directly into the hands of those who had fought him so bitterly here in Jerusalem. And yet Luke could see that James had chosen the simplest and most sensible way by which to avoid criticism here in Jerusalem that Paul had broken the laws of Moses and thus was liable to death according to Jewish law.

Paul hesitated only a moment. "I will do as you ask, James," he said quietly, "for I have always been zealous of the law and have shown the proper reverence for it."

It was decided then that Paul and the four men should go to the temple the next day to begin the ritual period of purification. Luke could see that James and the elders were pleased at this solution to the problem of Paul's presence in Jerusalem. And even Paul was satisfied, for that evening he seemed in better spirits than he had at any time since coming to the Holy City.

vi

As Luke went about giving his services to the sick, he could see just how much Jerusalem had changed in the period of almost ten years since he had visited the city. Even now, at the season of Pentecost, when pilgrims usually flocked here from all parts of the world, Jerusalem was quite evidently a dying city. Everywhere he went there were disease, famine, and misery. More than anywhere else, the grim face of want was apparent in the drawn faces of the children, their bodies swollen from lack of proper food, and the beggars who crawled in the dust of the streets, no longer able even to stand erect. Yet even in these drawn faces hate showed for the Roman conquerors, and in the hills, particularly of Galilee, where there had long been open rebellion, bandits openly defied the Romans. A seething undercurrent of discontent was apparent everywhere, and a premonition of disaster which seemed as certain as the setting of the sun beyond the mountains to the west.

The large offering which Paul had brought to James and the elders helped relieve some of the suffering among the Christians and the Jews, with whom they freely shared their good fortune, but it was pitifully inadequate to remedy the need of a large city of starving people. Depending almost entirely upon the offerings and the business which pilgrims brought, Jerusalem could not live when those pilgrims no longer flocked to the city, anxious to give part of their wealth to the Temple of Jehovah and the priests. It was easy to see why the Jews blamed Paul for their troubles and why his name was the most hated one upon their lips, more despised even than the Romans. And while James and the leaders of the Church were praying that Paul's visit might be accomplished without a riot, Luke was certain that the fanatic Judaizers who had fought Paul for so many years were still busy trying to discredit him and might even have joined forces with the agents of the Sanhedrin to deliver Paul into their hands, hoping he would be arrested and perhaps executed upon the order of the high priest and his associates.

As the days passed with no untoward event, however, Luke began to hope that they would be able to finish the week required for the purification of those Paul was sponsoring in the temple and get safely back to Caesarea without event. But on the sixth day, in the afternoon, the storm broke. Luke was walking from his surgery to the home of Mark's mother when he heard a tumultuous shouting from the direction of the temple. Minor riots were not uncommon in Jerusalem in these days of inflamed tempers, but the thunder of voices continued, and with a sudden conviction of disaster Luke hurried across the Vale of Kedron toward the temple, from which the smoke of the day's sacrifices rose in the still afternoon air. Soon he began to encounter Jews hurrying in all directions toward the scene of the disturbance. When one of them bumped into him in the narrow street, Luke asked, "Can you tell me what has happened?"

"A man has blasphemed against Jehovah and the temple," the Jew panted. "The crowd is going to drag him away to stone him."

"How did he blaspheme?" Luke asked. "Blasphemy" was a term used loosely by the Jews to denote almost any infringement of their religious laws.

"He is said to have taken a Gentile into the holy place, where only Jews may enter."

Luke stopped. It could not be Paul, he decided, for Paul would never break the strict law that forbade taking Gentiles into the holy part of the temple. And the four he was sponsoring were all Jews, so there could be no conflict there.

Ahead of him Luke saw a man staggering down the street, with blood streaming from several cuts about his head. When he came nearer he recognized him as a Greek named Trophimus, one of the presbyters of the church at Ephesus who had come with them, bringing gifts from that congregation to Jerusalem. The Ephesian stumbled and fell into the street. He would have been trampled by the crowd surging toward the temple had not Luke seized him under the arms and dragged him to the safety of an abandoned shop. Trophimus opened his eyes. When he recognized Luke he pushed himself up on his elbows. "Get to Paul, Luke," he begged. "They will kill him."

Luke took the wounded man by the shoulders and eased him back upon the floor. "Where is Paul?" he asked. "And what happened?"

"I was with Paul on the lower level of the temple," Trophimus gasped, "where the money-changers sit and the scrolls and animals are sold for sacrifice. Some Jews had been following us, and suddenly they seized both Paul and me and dragged us up the steps. Then they started beating us and shouting that Paul had blasphemed against the temple by taking me to the upper level."

"It was a plot, then?"

"Yes. As soon as they started beating us I heard others taking up the cry all around the temple. They were trying to enrage the crowd against Paul."

Alone, Luke knew he could do nothing to help Paul; in fact, he would not be able even to reach him through the press of the crowd which would already be surging around the temple. Only one power could save the apostle now, outside of direct intervention by God: that was the Roman garrison. They were constantly on guard against disturbances in this city of easily inflamed passions, and if he could reach them, there was a chance of saving Paul.

Leaving Trophimus in the shop, Luke set out as fast as he could run through the streets toward the Antonia. The Jews would not dare stone Paul to death inside the city, he knew, for that in itself would be breaking their laws. He must reach the Roman guard and get help before the mob could drag Paul from the city to the place outside the gates where Stephen had been stoned.

Up the steeply climbing streets toward the towering walls of the Antonia Luke ran, his heart pounding with the unaccustomed effort and his fears for Paul. At the gate a sentry barred his way, but he gasped, "I am Luke of Antioch, son of Theophilus, who is chief magistrate at Rome. Take me to the captain of the guard."

The name of Theophilus was enough to impress the sentry, and he called to the officer who sat in the guard post beside the gate. Luke gasped out his story to the captain, who recognized its significance immediately. "I will call Claudius Lysias, the colonel," he said. "Wait here."

The colonel came at once, concern written upon his face. A riot in

Jerusalem could mean the lives of the garrison, either at the hands of the inflamed Jews or on order of the Emperor for letting it happen. The disturbances which had wrecked the career of Pontius Pilate were still fresh in the minds of the Roman officers.

Luke repeated his story quickly, but before he had finished, Claudius Lysias was snapping orders to his captains. A few minutes later a strong force of soldiers trotted out the gate with the colonel and two captains at their head, spears at the ready to push their way through the crowds. Winded as he was, Luke could barely keep up, but he stayed close to the soldiers, determined to be present when they found Paul.

By the time the Roman party descended to the Vale of Kedron from the eminence upon which the fortress of Antonia stood, a howling mob of Jews was pouring through the defile, moving toward the city gate, outside of which was the traditional place of execution. The soldiers plowed through the mass of angry men, leaving bruised shins and cracked heads in their wake. By staying between the last pair of legionnaires Luke managed to reach the center of the riot with them.

Now he was able to see Paul, lying half conscious upon the stones of the street but apparently not seriously injured, for he got slowly to his knees while the soldiers cleared a circle around him. On the order of the colonel, one of the captains bent over Paul and affixed chains to his ankles and wrists. A hush fell over the crowd at this exercise of Roman authority, and during it the colonel demanded, "What crime has this man committed that you would kill him without a trial?"

A babel of angry shouts answered him as the Jews screamed insults and false charges at Paul. Seeing that he could get no sense out of the mob, the colonel ordered two of the soldiers to support Paul between them, and the group marched slowly back through the streets to the steps leading up to the Antonia. The angry crowd followed upon their heels and surged up to the very gate before which the colonel now stopped to speak to them again. For the moment, however, the howls of the crowd for Paul's blood were so loud that even the Roman officer could not be heard.

Luke had stayed close beside the soldiers who were half carrying Paul. When they set the apostle on his feet before the gate of the fortress, he saw that, while still rather dazed, Paul seemed to have recovered from the rough handling. He looked down at the chains upon his ankles and wrists, then said in Greek to the colonel, "May I say something to you, sir?"

Claudius Lysias looked surprised. "Do you know Greek?" he asked.

Something of the old look of fearless pride came again into Paul's face, and he answered, "I am a Jew of Tarsus in Cilicia, a citizen of no insignificant city. Please let me speak to the people."

The colonel was obviously startled by Paul's cultured tones, his composure, and his air of authority. "You may speak to them if you wish," he said courteously.

Paul turned to the crowd. With a proud gesture he raised his arms before him, in spite of the chains. "Men and brothers," he said to them in Hebrew, "listen to what I have to say in my defense."

Luke knew enough Hebrew from his years of association with Paul to understand what the apostle was saying. And when the mob heard him speaking in their own language, they grew quiet and listened.

"I am a Jew," Paul told them, "born in Tarsus of Cilicia, but brought up here in the city and carefully educated under the teachings of Gamaliel in the law of our forefathers. I was zealous for God, as all of you are today. I persecuted this Way even unto the death and kept on binding both men and women and putting them in jail, as the high priest and the whole council will bear me witness. Indeed I had received letters from them to the brothers in Damascus and was on my way to bind those who were there and bring them back to Jerusalem to be punished. But on my way, just before I reached Damascus, suddenly about noon a blaze of light from heaven flashed around me, and I fell to the ground and heard a voice saying to me, 'Saul! Saul! Why are you persecuting me?' I answered, 'Who are you, sir?' Then he said to me, 'I am Jesus of Nazareth whom you are persecuting.' The men who were with me saw the light but did not hear the voice of him who was speaking. Then I asked, 'What am I to do, Lord?' And the Lord answered, 'Get up and go into Damascus and there it will be told you what you are destined to do.' Since I could not see because of the dazzling sheen of that light, I was led by the hand by my companions, and in this way I reached Damascus. There a man named Ananias, a man devout in strict accordance with the law, of good reputation among all the Jews who lived there, came to see me and, standing by my side, said to me, 'Saul, my brother, recover your sight.' Then I instantly did recover it and looked at him, and he said, 'The God of our forefathers has appointed you to learn his will and to see the Righteous One and to hear him speak, because you are to be his witness to all man of what you have seen and heard. And now why are you waiting? Get up and be baptized and wash your sins away by calling on his name.'

"After I had come back to Jerusalem," Paul went on, "one day while I was praying in the temple I fell into a trance and saw him saying to me, 'Make haste and at once get out of Jerusalem, because they will not accept your testimony about me.' So I said, 'Lord, they know for themselves that from one synagogue to another I used to imprison and flog those who believed in you, and when the blood of your martyr Stephen was being shed, I stood by and approved it and held the clothes of those who killed him.' Then he said to me, 'Go, because I am to send you out and far away among the heathen.'"

Until Paul said this, the Jews had listened quietly, but now they began to shout again, making such a clamor that he could not be heard. "Away with him!" some shouted. And others called, "Stone him! Crucify him!" Some of the crowd, worked up into a fury once more, began to push up the steps toward the Roman guard. Rather than be forced to repel them with naked spears and swords, the colonel ordered his guards and the prisoner inside the gates and shut them to keep out the crowd. In the confusion Luke managed to slip in beside Paul.

When the gates were shut Claudius Lysias turned to one of the captains. "Now maybe we can find out something about this troublemaker," he said curtly. "Let him be flogged until we get the truth." Before Luke could protest, he had turned on his heel and entered the fort.

Under the direction of the captain preparations went forward immediately for the flogging. Paul was jerked across the parade ground to where a post stood with iron rings set into the wood, two at the bottom near the ground, and two others a little higher than an average man's head. One of the soldiers looped short strands of rope around the chains that bound Paul's ankles and wrists, while another brought a whip of leather thongs from the armory. The rope attached to Paul's wrist chain was run through the rings and drawn tightly and the apostle was stretched against the pole. When the second rope was secured to the lower rings, the victim was securely lashed so that he could not jerk away from the whip.

Luke had seen such a Roman interrogation by flogging in Antioch and knew its dangers. More than one victim had died under the lash, and Paul was not robust. While the ropes were being tied he came close to Paul and said, "Let me tell them you are a Roman citizen, Paul. The law protects you from being bound and flogged. It is your right."

Paul shook his head, but Luke cast about in his mind for some way to influence him. Then he remembered Paul's second greatest love after the Way of Jesus, the churches he had established throughout the provinces. "Think of the churches in Galatia and Asia, and in Macedonia and Greece," he urged. "They need you now more than ever."

Paul hesitated, and before Luke could say more, the captain called, "You, there. Move if you would not feel the lash yourself."

Luke moved back, but as the soldier was raising the whip, Paul spoke. "Is it lawful for you to flog a Roman?" he asked. "And one who is not condemned at that?"

The captain stared at him in amazement. "Did you say you are a Roman? It is unlawful to bind and flog a Roman citizen without a trial before a magistrate."

"He is a Roman citizen, and so am I," Luke said, stepping between Paul and the whip, so that it would strike him first if it were used.

The captain looked nonplused. "Put down the lash," he ordered. "I must consult the colonel about this."

Claudius Lysias came back with him, both of them quite obviously perturbed. The laws governing the privileges of Roman citizenship were very strict, and not even the Emperor could abrogate them without danger of punishment. "Tell me," the colonel said to Paul. "Are you a Roman?"

"Yes, I am," Paul said proudly.

"I paid a large sum for this citizenship of mine," the colonel said, looking at Paul as if he could not believe that a Jew who wore garments of homespun and rough sandals on his feet could aspire to citizenship in the mighty Empire of Rome.

"I was born a citizen," Paul said calmly.

"You should have told me that before," the colonel said severely. "Remove his bonds at once," he ordered the captain, "and put him in prison under guard." As Paul was led away he turned to Luke. "How do you come to be with this man? The captain tells me you are the son of Theophilus."

Luke quickly explained the reasons for his presence in Jerusalem. "What will you do with Paul?" he asked then.

Claudius Lysias shrugged. "First I must find out what these Jews charge against him. I will ask the high priest to convene their council in the morning and take Paul before them."

"But you will not turn him over to them, will you?" Luke asked, remembering the fate of Jesus and Stephen.

"I have no desire to follow in the steps of Pontius Pilate," the Roman said shortly. "So long as your friend claims the protection of Roman citizenship he shall have it from me, even if he decides to carry his case to the Emperor in Rome, as is his right."

As he was leaving the Antonia, Luke noticed a youth whose face seemed to be familiar waiting near the gates. He stared at Luke for a moment, then came closer and spoke courteously. "Is your name Luke?" he asked.

"Yes, it is."

"Paul pointed you out to me once," the youth explained. "I am his nephew Joseph."

"Your uncle is in prison, Joseph," Luke said kindly. "But the Romans will protect him."

"I was in the temple when the riot started and saw it," Joseph said eagerly. "They have been planning this for several days."

"They?" Luke asked. "Whom do you mean?"

"Some men who work for the priests, and some people among the Christians who hate Paul. They hoped to stir up the crowd so that Paul would be stoned to death before the Romans could save him."

"Where did you learn all this, Joseph?" Luke asked.

"I am apprenticed to a money-changer in the lower level of the temple," Joseph explained. "I often hear people talking when they do not know I am listening."

"Do many people know that Paul is your uncle?"

"No, Paul is hated so here in Jerusalem that we have not spoken much about it."

"Then you can help us," Luke told him. "The Romans are bringing Paul before the Sanhedrin tomorrow. I want you to listen in the temple and tell me if you hear of any more plots against him."

Joseph nodded his understanding, and Luke left him near his home while he went on to the home of Mark, where he was staying. The Christians in Jerusalem were stunned by the news of Paul's arrest, and that night the congregation prayed long for his safety, led by the patriarch James. Luke wished that Peter or Barnabas were here now to advise him, but Peter and Mark were still away in the region of Galilee and Barnabas was at Antioch.

Jews were already thronging the streets leading to the temple when Luke started for the fortress of Antonia to see Paul the next morning. From them he learned that the city was afire with the news that Paul would be brought before the Sanhedrin shortly before noon. At the fortress Luke was recognized and admitted to the cell where Paul was kept. He found the apostle striding about the narrow room, a look of calm purpose on his face. This was a very different man from the dazed and dejected Paul whom Luke had been forced to goad into claiming his rights as a Roman citizen the day before. "What has happened, Paul?" he asked. "Have they told you something which has given you new hope?"

"Not the Romans, Luke. God has spoken to me."

"God!" Luke echoed. "But how?"

"It was as plain as I see you standing there now. Last night in a dream the Lord came into this very cell and said to me, 'Courage, Paul. For just as you have testified for me in Jerusalem, you must testify for me in Rome too.'"

"In Rome? What could that mean?"

"I am to be released, what else could it mean? Then I must go on to Rome, for few have heard the teachings of Jesus there. I am sure it is the Lord's will that I go; nothing can keep me away."

"Nothing but the fact that you are in prison," Luke pointed out logically. "And that today you are to appear before the council."

"I do not fear the council," Paul said confidently. "They will tell lies about me, but I shall brand them as untrue. And since I have placed myself under the protection of Rome, I must be tried before a Roman magistrate. Then these false charges will be cast aside."

"I hope you are right," Luke said soberly. "But I have never seen the city so aroused. If the Romans set you free now, the Jews would riot and kill you."

"Wait until I speak before the council," Paul insisted. "The priests are also servants of the Most High. They must realize that I serve God just as they do."

Privately Luke was doubtful. He remembered Stephen's defense when Paul had been prosecutor. It had been eloquent but futile, and Stephen had not been hated in Jerusalem with anything like the virulence which the people now felt toward Paul.

The guards came shortly to take Paul to the temple, and Luke followed the Roman party, knowing that unless he went in with them he would have little chance of being admitted to the council chamber. The crowd already filled the lower terrace and spilled down into the streets leading to the temple.

Looking around him at the familiar room, Luke could see little change in the years since he had first sat here with Silvanus and Apollonius at the trial of Stephen. There were new faces among the judges who flanked the high priest on either side. But the long beards, the black caps and robes, the phylacteries, and the look of hate which they had turned upon Stephen were the same, only this time more intense. It was as much folly to expect justice from such an obviously biased tribunal, Luke thought, as there had been in the case of the other two martyrs, Jesus and Stephen, who had been sentenced to death by the Sanhedrin.

Luke noted one sharp difference, however. In the trial of Stephen, Paul had stood beside the chief priest in his capacity as prosecutor, but now he stood before the council in the position of the accused. And yet Paul faced the council confidently, convinced by his dream the night before that it was not God's plan for his career to end here, but that he was to teach the Way of Jesus in the very citadel of the Empire itself, the capital city of Rome.

A new prosecutor, a tall Jew with burning eyes, stood beside the high priest. Now, as the council was formally opened, he read the list of charges against Paul. They were as vague as those against Stephen, alleging that Paul had blasphemed against the temple by bringing one who was unclean into the sacred confines, and that he had been known to teach that circumcision was unnecessary and that Jews and Gentiles could sit down to eat together. The prosecutor then brought

301

on the usual file of witnesses who parroted their prepared testimony, after which he harangued the council at some length. Everyone present understood that all of this was a mere concession to the tradition that every accused must be tried before the council for a capital offense. The verdict was all too obvious in the manner of the judges.

When finally it came Paul's turn to speak, he walked over until he stood only a few feet from the council table itself, facing his judges proudly. "Brothers!" he cried in that ringing voice of his. "I swear to you by the Most High with a clear conscience that I have done my duty to God up to this very day, as a man and as a Jew, like yourselves."

A roar of anger came from the crowd, and one of the council leaned over the table and struck Paul upon the mouth, bringing blood to his lips as teeth cut into flesh. Paul made no move toward the one who had struck him, but his voice lashed out contemptuously, like the cut of a whip. "You whitewashed wall! God will strike you! Do you sit as a judge to try me in accordance with the law of our forefathers, yet in violation of that law you strike me?"

"He insults God's high priest," the man who had struck Paul screamed.

"I spoke to you who struck," Paul said, "and not to the high priest, for God has written, *'You must not speak evil against any ruler of your people.'*"

Claudius Lysias stood up. "Is this man to be given his right before the law to defend himself?" he snapped. "Or am I to remove him from the council chamber?"

The Jews quieted down at this peremptory demand, and after a while Paul was able to be heard again. "Brothers," he said then, "I am a Pharisee, a Pharisee's son, and now I am on trial for the hope of the resurrection of the dead."

Knowing the Jews as he did from long association and study of their religion, Luke could see Paul's purpose in thus injecting the question of the resurrection of the dead into the proceedings. In any gathering such as this there would be both Pharisees and Sadducees. While the Pharisees stood upon the resurrection of the dead and the assurance that all who obeyed the law would live in heaven with Jehovah, the Sadducees vehemently refused to believe in the resurrection and even denied the existence of angels or the Spirit. By appealing to the Pharisees to support him against their traditional enemies, thus reviving an ancient controversy which still divided the Jewish faith, Paul was using the old military tactic of dividing the enemy in the midst of a battle.

The ruse was effective, for a great hubbub arose again in the chamber and in the crowd outside. In the midst of the clamor one of the Pharisees of the council itself shouted, "We find nothing wrong with this man. Suppose a spirit or an angel has really spoken to him."

At that the opposing faction set up such a din that no one could be heard. The crowd was rapidly whipping itself into a frenzy, as much against each other now as against Paul, but Luke knew from his previous experience with crowds that all of this fury could just as easily be turned suddenly against the apostle at any moment. In the midst of the uproar Claudius Lysias apparently began to fear for the safety not only of his prisoner but of himself and his soldiers, for he suddenly barked an order to his men. The soldiers moved quickly to form a square around Paul and, drawing their swords, began to move out of the chamber. The crowd had no choice except to give ground if they did not want to feel the blades themselves, so a way was quickly opened for the Roman party to leave. Luke followed close behind the soldiers until he was safely away from the temple, then he turned and hurried to bring this news of Paul's fortunes to James and the others.

vii

Throughout that day and the next the city continued in a ferment over Paul. Now that the immediate controversy between the Pharisees and the Sadducees had subsided, both parties realized how Paul had cleverly set them at each other's throats to save himself, and their anger at him was even greater. When he was able to learn nothing by inquiry about the further plans of the council, Luke decided to go in search of Joseph. The youthful money-changer might have heard something in the temple which would give them a clue as to the next event in the controversy.

Making his way to the temple, Luke walked idly along the lower terrace where he knew the money-changers were located, stopping to look at the wares of the scroll sellers and to sniff the rich scent of frankincense and myrrh offered by the vendors of precious oils and balms. When he saw Joseph sitting behind his small table among the money-changers, he approached idly in order not to attract attention, and stopped before the table. The youth looked up, and a quick gleam of intelligence showed in his eyes. "You have foreign coins, sir?" he asked. "I can change them for you."

Luke fumbled in his purse until he found a gold piece of Ephesus, with the many-columned façade of the Temple of Artemis stamped upon it. Joseph examined the coin, then looked up. "This is indeed from a far-off land," he said. "I will have to go to another part of the temple to learn the rate of exchange. If you will go with me," he added significantly, "you can be sure that I do not cheat you."

Asking another money-changer to watch his table, Joseph got up, and he and Luke walked along the terrace until they were out of earshot of the other changers. "I was coming to see you as soon as I could, Luke," Joseph said hurriedly, "but the man to whom I am apprenticed would not let me leave. There were many people in the temple today, but not all to sacrifice."

"Have you learned something?"

Joseph nodded. "Many have been going and coming from the upper levels where the priests are, and I overheard some of their talk. Forty Jews have taken a vow to kill Paul and have persuaded the council to ask that Paul be brought to the council chamber tonight secretly, on the excuse that the crowd must not be stirred up by knowing that he is here."

Luke nodded his understanding. "Go on."

"The forty men plan to set upon the Romans and Paul in the darkness outside the temple and kill him. Then before the colonel can do anything, it will all be over."

"Are you sure this is to happen tonight?"

"Yes. And a messenger has already been sent to Claudius Lysias from the high priest, asking that Paul be brought to the temple tonight."

"Can you go with me to the Romans?" Luke asked Joseph. "The colonel may not believe the story unless you give him the details."

Joseph hesitated. "If it is known that I have gone to the Antonia, the conspirators might be warned. I think they may suspect me, anyway. But in another hour I will be allowed to go home for the noonday meal. Wait for me at the gate of the Antonia and I will go to the colonel with you."

Luke and Joseph were forced to cool their heels in the quarters of Claudius Lysias until the Roman commander had finished his meal. When he came in and saw them waiting, his face hardened. "I have had enough trouble about this man Paul," he snapped irritably before they could speak. "If you have come to ask me to release him, you are wasting your time and mine."

"We do not want Paul released," Luke said. "He would be killed immediately by the crowd if he were. This young man is Paul's nephew Joseph; he has a story you should hear."

"Get on with it then," Claudius Lysias said curtly, but he listened attentively while Joseph told of the plot to kill Paul on the way to the council meeting that night.

When Joseph finished, Luke said, "The youth would have no reason to lie about this. He may be in trouble with his employer already because he came with me to tell you the story."

The colonel nodded slowly. "I am sure he does not lie," he said, and picked up a small wax tablet from the table before him. "I have here a request from the council that Paul be brought before them tonight. I wondered myself why they could not examine him again by day. Now I know."

"Then you will protect him?"

"My sworn duty as a Roman officer requires me to do so," Claudius said crisply. He shouted for the captain, who was in the adjoining room, and when the officer appeared gave him cryptic directions. "Get two hundred men ready to march to Caesarea with seventy mounted soldiers and two hundred armed with spears." He smiled then. "I hardly think the crowds would attack such a body. Have them ready to march by nightfall," he continued to the officer. "You will provide horses for Paul and Luke to ride. I want them safely out of Jerusalem as soon as it becomes dark. And send me a scribe," Claudius added. "I wish to write a letter to Felix, the governor of Caesarea.

"There," Claudius Lysias said when he finished the letter. "This should insure that your friend gets a fair trial, Luke. One thing I would like you to tell me. How is it that you, a Greek and an aristocrat, are so devoted to this Jew who is always getting into trouble?"

Luke smiled. "Paul is my friend. We both serve God and follow in the Way of Jesus."

Slowly the colonel shook his head. "I must learn more of this strange faith of yours if it can inspire such loyalty. What does it offer that is so precious?"

"The right to eternal life, for one thing."

"The Pharisees claim they can obtain that merely by obeying the laws of Moses."

"There is something else," Luke explained. "An inner sense of peace and contentment from living as Jesus did."

"The Jews and all of us could use that," Claudius said. "The world seems to be in a turmoil which grows steadily worse instead of better."

viii

Luke was happy to be away from Jerusalem and its troubles and back with Thecla in Caesarea, although his joy was tempered by the knowledge that Paul was still in prison. Felix, the governor, had confined Paul to Herod's palace, however, so his condition was much better than it might have been had he been put into a dungeon such as the one from which they had been released by the magistrate at Philippi.

It was five days before Paul was brought to trial before the Roman governor, but Luke made no attempt to get in touch with Felix during that time. He remembered well his quarrel with Paul after he had spoken to Gallio in Corinth, and in addition, he was not at all sure that he could accomplish anything with Felix, who was of a far different stature from Gallio. A favorite of the Emperor Claudius, himself one of the most dissolute in a line of Roman emperors more renowned for their cruelty and licentiousness than for their leadership, Felix had been elevated to the governorship of the province upon the urging of the Jewish high priest, Jonathan. But when Jonathan objected to the habits of the governor, Felix had hired assassins to kill him, and the more compliant Ananias had been installed in the place of Jonathan. Felix had also seduced his present wife, Drusilla, away from her husband with the aid of a notorious magician, Simon Magus, and it was well known that those prisoners able to offer the governor a sufficiently large bribe usually went free, while the less fortunate languished in prison.

This was the sorry specimen of Roman judicial authority before whom Paul was heard. Time had been allowed for Ananias to come from Jerusalem with his bill of complaints against Paul, and he brought with him the leading orator and expert in Jewish law in the capital, a lawyer named Tertullus. But this time, in spite of what he knew about the character of the judge, Luke felt that Paul had some chance of obtaining justice. For no screaming mob packed the room, and Felix showed no sign of enmity toward Paul; rather his mood was one of boredom with the whole affair. Luke had brought with him the Ephesian, Trophimus, in order to prove the charge false that Paul had taken a non-Jew into the sacred portion of the temple.

Tertullus opened the hearing, bowing deeply before the Roman judge. "Your Excellency, Felix," he said in an ingratiating tone, "since we are enjoying perfect peace through you and since reforms for this nation are being brought about through your foresight, we always and everywhere acknowledge it with profound gratitude. But, not to detain you too long, I beg you in your kindness to give us a brief hearing, for we have found this man a perfect pest and a disturber of the peace among the Jews throughout the world. He is a ringleader in the sect of the Nazarenes; once he tried to desecrate the temple, but we arrested him. And now by examining him yourself, you can find out exactly what charge we bring against him."

The tirade continued, a tissue of lies as obviously false as the accusation of desecrating the temple. Then Tertullus brought a procession of witnesses before the judge, all swearing to these fantastic charges. When they had finished, Felix said, "Is there anyone else who should be heard before Paul speaks in his defense?"

Luke stood up. "I have with me Trophimus, an Ephesian," he said. "He is the man whom Tertullus claims was taken into the temple by Paul."

Felix looked up alertly. "Bring him forward; perhaps we can learn the truth of this matter."

The Ephesian made a convincing witness, establishing without question that he had at no time been near the portion of the temple which was sacred to the Jews. He told of the conspiracy and how those who denounced Paul had actually seized both of them and carried them up the steps almost to the forbidden portion of the temple before raising the cry of blasphemy. Luke then told the story of how Joseph had overheard the plot to kill Paul on the way to the temple and how Claudius Lysias had believed it and sent Paul away for his protection. When he finished he turned to face the high priest, who sat beside Tertullus. "You may learn the truth of what I say from the high priest of the Jews, who knew of this plot," he said. "Since it is against the laws of the Jewish people to lie under oath, he must tell the truth."

Felix looked at Ananias, but the priest did not speak, and everyone there knew that Luke's statement had been verified. Then the governor turned to Paul and asked him to speak in his behalf.

Paul stood up and came forward confidently. "Since I know that for many years you have acted as judge for this nation, O Felix," he began, "I cheerfully make my defense, for you can verify the fact that not more than twelve days ago I went up to Jerusalem to worship, and they have never found me debating with anybody in the temple or making a disturbance in the synagogues or about the city, and they cannot prove the charges they have made against me. But I certainly admit this as a fact, that in accordance with the way that they call heresy I continue to worship the God of my forefathers. And yet I believe in everything taught in the law and written in the Prophets, and I have the same hope in God that they cherish for themselves, that there is to be a resurrection of the upright and the wicked. So I am always striving to have a conscience that is clear before God and men. After several years' absence I came to bring contributions to charity for my nation and to offer sacrifices. While I was performing these duties they found me just as I had completed the rites of purification in the temple; however, there was no crowd with me and no disturbance at all. Let these men themselves tell what wrong they found in me when I appeared before the council—unless it is for one thing that I shouted out as I stood among them. 'It is for the resurrection of the dead that I am on trial before you today.'"

Paul stopped, and Felix turned to Tertullus. "Do you have anything more to say?" he asked courteously.

The Jewish prosecutor launched into another diatribe, but when he finished he had established no charges which were not already disproved by the testimony of Luke and Trophimus. Felix listened courteously, however, then thanked Tertullus and Ananias for coming down from Jerusalem for the hearing. "I will take this matter under advisement," he promised, "and look into it again." Upon that the trial ended and Paul was returned to prison.

Luke gave Thecla an account of the hearing that night. "Why did Felix not release Paul then, Luke?" she asked. "He must know that the charges against him are false."

"I am sure he knows it," Luke agreed. "But Felix will want to avoid any more trouble among the Jews, which would certainly erupt again if he freed Paul now. My thought is that he will choose to keep Paul in prison for a while. If he were guided only by the justice of the case, he would have released him at the trial."

"And there is nothing you can do?"

"I am writing to Theophilus at Rome, but it will be months before he could do anything about it."

"Are we to stay here then?" she asked. "Just waiting?"

"What would you like to do?"

She did not answer at once, then she said softly, "Do you remember when you and I and Probus traveled from Iconium to Ephesus together before Apollos Lucanus was born?"

Luke smiled. "I remember how pleasant it was, taking our time and enjoying the country as we went along."

"Why can't we do that now, Luke? I have never seen the region around Galilee, and you could visit the places where Jesus taught and perhaps find out some more about him from those who heard him."

"Peter and Mark are in Galilee," Luke said eagerly. "We could see them too."

"Then if Mark is not writing down the life of Jesus, perhaps you could do it, Luke. You have always said that someone should set down the things he said and did while some of the people are still alive who saw and heard him."

Luke took her hands and looked deep into her eyes. "Tell me the truth," he said with mock severity. "That is really why you decided we should go to Galilee, isn't it?"

Her cheeks crimsoned at thus having her deception exposed. "I should know better than to push you into anything," she said contritely. "But it is a good suggestion."

"It is more than that," he agreed. "Since this last experience in Jerusalem I have realized that someone must write a really authoritative life of Jesus. Then when the world knows what he really stood for, there will be less controversy over his teachings."

Thecla threw her arms around him. "And you must do it, Luke," she said happily. "When do we leave for Galilee?"

"I must see Paul first," Luke said. "Unless he approves, I would not feel right about such an undertaking."

Luke found Paul in a room of Herod's palace, guarded by a single soldier who stood outside the door. Paul was dictating a letter to Timothy, but he stopped to embrace Luke. "I owe you much for testifying in my behalf yesterday, Luke," he said. "When Felix heard you and Trophimus, he saw at once how false were the charges against me. How long do you think Felix will keep me in prison, Luke?" he added.

Luke hesitated, but he would not lie, so he repeated to Paul what he had told Thecla about the chances of release for the apostle. When he finished, Paul said, "That is just what I was telling Timothy this morning. You find me writing to the churches, strengthening them during what is sure to be a long absence from them. I may even have to be judged in Rome, Luke, and that sometimes takes years. Still," he added thoughtfully, "it may be that God meant just this when he spoke to me in the dream of testifying in Rome." Paul turned and put his hands upon Luke's shoulders. "God has been good to me, Luke, to give me such stanch friends in times of peril. And I shall always owe you a debt of gratitude for showing me how near I came to sinning grievously by thinking of myself before Jesus when we were in Macedonia and Greece, and even in Asia. Only when you risked your life and Probus gave his for me in Ephesus did I realize how grievously I had sinned. I have asked God to forgive me and he has done so; I need only your forgiveness now, Luke."

"There is nothing to forgive, Paul," Luke said quietly. "Each of us was following Jesus in our own way." Then he smiled. "But I am glad our ways are the same once more."

"And I," Paul agreed. "We must never let anything threaten our friendship again." Then he changed the subject. "Have you thought of what you will do next? I could not ask you to remain here, when I do not know how long I will be imprisoned. And you have both wanted to go to Bithynia for so many years."

"Thecla and I have decided to spend a few weeks in Galilee," Luke said. "Both of us have wanted for a long time to find out more about the life of Jesus."

"You might even find the scroll again," Paul suggested.

"I hope so," Luke admitted. "Thecla wants me to write a life of Jesus, using what I remember from the scroll and what I can learn from Mark and the others, as well as by talking to people in Galilee, where he taught."

Paul's face lit up. "Of course!" he cried. "You are the very one who should do it, Luke."

"Mark has gathered a large amount of information. I was hoping that he would write it."

Paul shook his head vigorously. "Mark is too young, Luke. It needs a careful man, a philosopher and a broad thinker such as yourself, to understand what Jesus means to the world. No, you are the one to write the story of his life. Have you made any plans?"

"Not yet," Luke admitted. "We have only spoken of it once."

"If I were going to retrace the steps of Jesus," Paul said, "I would start at Jerusalem, at the tomb where Mary Magdalene and the other women first found that he had risen."

Luke rubbed his chin thoughtfully. "Perhaps that is the way to learn the real story of his life," he admitted.

"It is," Paul cried. "Only when you remember that he was resurrected do the other events of his life fall into their rightful place." Then he threw up his hands in that odd gesture of his, as if he were taking the world into his embrace. "How I envy you the privilege of following in the footsteps of Jesus, Luke." Then his manner changed again and a note of deepest humility came into his voice. "No. The sin of envying others whom Jesus favors in his work is my greatest weakness. We all have our tasks. Yours is to set down the truth about our Lord. Mine shall be to testify for him in Rome. May God show you the things you will need to know about Jesus, Luke."

ix

Luke and Thecla left Caesarea a few days later, happy to be on the way to the beautiful Sea of Galilee. They went first to Jerusalem, since it was there that the final act of the drama of Jesus had been played out. Mark and Peter had not yet returned from Galilee, but they stayed at the house of the patriarch James while they visited the hill of Calvary upon which the cross had stood and the tomb in the gardens of Joseph of Arimathea where the body of Jesus had been placed. Once again they heard from James the story of how Mary of

Magdala, Joanna, and that other Mary, the mother of another James, had come to the tomb on the third day and found it empty. Luke wished to talk to the three women, but no one knew anything about them, except that Mary Magdalene was said to have returned to her home city of Magdala.

In the evening Luke and Thecla went alone to the Garden of Gethsemane on the Mount of Olives to pray where Jesus had prayed before the soldiers had taken him. Kneeling there, with the dying city of the Jews spread out below him, Luke felt a sense of peace and certainty possess his spirit which he seemed never to have felt before. Thecla sensed it, too, for when they walked down the mountain hand in hand, she asked, "Do you remember once when I told you there was something concerning you that seemed just out of my grasp?"

"Yes. Why do you ask now, dear?"

"While we were on our knees just now, I had a strange feeling, almost as if someone had spoken to me and told me we are on the right path. I am sure now that God wants you to follow in the footsteps of Jesus and set down his story for the world."

"I had the same feeling," Luke admitted. "As if I were back on a road upon which I started a long time ago—perhaps when I received the scroll from Stephen—but went afield."

"You will find the scroll again somewhere on the way," Thecla said confidently. "I know you will."

The next day they left Jerusalem, bearing a letter from James to the churches in Galilee and Judea, so that they would be freely accepted by the Christians wherever they went. Luke had purchased a mule in Jerusalem for Thecla to ride, for she seemed more tired now at the end of the day than in the months before they had come to Caesarea. And as she rode he walked beside the animal, telling her what he remembered from the scroll about the trip Jesus had made along this very road to Jerusalem, the trip from which he had not returned.

"Do you think he had hope even then that he might be spared, Luke?" she asked.

"He must have. For even in Gethsemane he prayed that the cup should pass if it was God's will."

"And yet he loved us all enough to die that we might know the truth of his Way." She put her hand over Luke's upon the rough coat of the mule. "I remember that you still came to me in the theater at Caesarea, Luke, although there seemed to be no chance that you could save either me or yourself from the lions."

"Sacrifice is the privilege of love," he said. "The love of a man for the woman he takes as his wife or the love a father bears for his children is no different from the love that Jesus bore for the world. If Jesus were nothing else but a man, I would still follow his Way, because it is based upon love for one another."

"Do you think love can conquer everything, even death?"

"Love removes all fear from death," he told her gently, for he knew what she was thinking. "Even if there were no such thing as eternal life in heaven, we would still live on after death because the love we give to others lives on in their souls."

"Then we become immortal through those we love," Thecla said softly. "It is a beautiful thought, Luke." She leaned down to kiss him. "I shall live forever in you and your soul, my darling, for you have all my love."

"And I in yours," he said, putting his arm about her as he walked beside the mule.

It was about a week later that they came down from the wild mountain country that lay to the west of the deep cup in which was set the jewel of the lake. They had been traveling slowly because of a steadily increasing weakness in Thecla which disturbed Luke very much. On the fertile Plain of Gennesaret near the city of Capernaum, figs, olives, and walnut trees grew everywhere, a green carpet when seen from the trail that descended to the water level from the city of Magdala upon the heights. Along the trail and the shore flourished oleanders, papyri, blossoming shrubs, and myriad wild flowers which grew like a many-colored carpet, making this fertile oasis a veritable paradise.

At Capernaum Luke and Thecla lodged at an inn. Learning that Peter and Mark were somewhere in the vicinity, they left the mule in the stable and started out the next morning to walk along the shore of the lake in the hope of seeing their friends or getting some word of them, for Peter was well known in this region. The sun was shining and the air was warm as they walked along the shore, stopping to talk to the fishermen and watch them draw their nets from the water, filled with the multicolored fish for which the lake was famous. Peter had been a fisherman before Jesus had called him, and from one of the boats which had just returned loaded with fish they learned that the big disciple was teaching along the shore only a short distance away.

Soon they came to a place where many springs burst from a little glen among the basalt rocks, the water being gathered into a small reservoir. People were moving about among the springs, some bathing and some drinking water from the smaller ones. Most of them were lame or sick. Some were even carried in litters or on the backs of relatives and friends, for the waters were thought to possess great healing properties. A little way to the east of the springs was a second and smaller plain, but one equally fertile with that of Gennesaret. Here a small bay, almost in the form of a semicircle, was set into the shore, with the sides shelving up the rocky elevation to form a perfect amphitheater where hundreds of people could sit and listen to words spoken from the shore or even from a boat in the bay. The slopes were green with grass, and as they rounded the shore and came to the little bay, Luke and Thecla saw a group of people gathered upon the lower edge of the slope, listening to a tall man with a white beard and majestic countenance who was speaking to them from the water's edge.

"There is Peter," Thecla cried. "And Mark is with him."

It was indeed Peter who was speaking, and Luke and Thecla found a seat upon a flat rock where they could hear him. He was telling again the simple story that he told so well, of his discipleship with Jesus and the crucifixion and resurrection of the gentle carpenter from Nazareth. When he finished and the crowd began to disperse, Luke and Thecla made their way down across the rocks to the shore where Peter and Mark stood. The two welcomed them joyously.

"What brings you two here?" Mark asked. "We heard from a traveler that Paul had been taken from Jerusalem to Caesarea."

Luke told them the story of the near tragedy in Jerusalem and Paul's imprisonment in the palace of Herod in Caesarea. "Thecla had never seen the Sea of Galilee," he explained then. "And since I wanted to learn more about what Jesus did and said in this region, we decided to come now. James told us you were here."

"What of Paul?" Peter asked. "Is he well?"

"Very well. And busy writing letters to all the churches. He expects to be imprisoned a long time and perhaps to go to Rome."

Peter nodded. "There are many Christians in Rome now. It might be well for Paul to go there."

"Don't you feel harsh toward Paul for—for what he did to you in Antioch?" Thecla asked.

Peter smiled. "No, my daughter. Paul has done a great work for Jesus. There is no reason why we should be enemies." Then he looked at Luke keenly. "Is it only to see the lake again that you have come here, Luke?"

"No," Luke admitted. "I have been thinking of writing down the things that Jesus did and taught so that there would be a record of them in the future."

"You can use the stories I have been collecting," Mark offered.

"Why not write the story of his life yourself, Mark?" Luke asked.

Mark shook his head. "Peter and I have spoken of this often. We agree that I am too young still to set down the truth about Jesus in the way that it should be told. Peter has often said that you are the one who should do it, Luke."

Luke looked at Peter in surprise, but the big apostle only smiled, as if at something which only he knew. "How long have you felt that I should write the story of Jesus, Peter?" Luke asked.

"Who can tell when a thought first comes into the mind?" Peter said. "It could have been in a tent one night on the road between Jerusalem and Joppa, Luke. Or when you offered to leave Paul and follow me in Antioch years ago. There is a proverb of the Jewish people," he continued: "'Man's goings are of the Lord; how can a man then understand his own way?'"

"But how can I be sure that God wants me to write the life of Jesus?" Luke asked.

"Are you certain in your own heart?"

Luke remembered when he and Thecla had been praying in the Garden of Gethsemane a few nights ago how a voice had seemed to speak to him from the darkness, and the strange peace and assurance which had filled his soul. "Yes," he told Peter. "I am sure in my heart."

"Then the Lord has revealed his purpose to you," Peter said briskly. "You need doubt it no longer. Now we must be on the road to Magdala."

"Why Magdala?"

But Peter only shook his head. "I cannot tell you now, Luke. Soon you will know the reason."

x

Guardian of the pass leading from the wild and forbidding beauty of the Valley of the Doves and the Plain of Sharon to the serene and quiet beauty of the Sea of Galilee far below, the city of Magdala sat astride one of the main arteries connecting the populous cities around the lake with Jerusalem and the cities of the coast. It was late in the afternoon and Thecla was riding the mule, for they had stopped at the inn to gather their belongings and the patient animal upon which she had ridden from Jerusalem. Luke noticed again how tired she looked and how delicately etched was the loveliness of her face, as if she had been losing weight. Seeing his eyes upon her, she smiled and squeezed his hand, but he could see the weariness in her eyes and he put his arm about her as they climbed the winding road to the fortress city, so that she could lean against his shoulder and gather strength from him.

Peter seemed to know exactly where he was going, for he led them off the main road into a street that curved along the brow of the mountain. He stopped before a low, rambling house that sat close to the street, with a small garden in front where bright-colored flowers grew and bees hummed lazily. A little girl was playing in front of the door. When she saw the big apostle she squealed suddenly with delight and ran to throw herself into his arms. "Uncle Peter!" she cried. "And Mark! I am so glad you came to see me." She was a startlingly beautiful child, with a mass of lustrous red hair, a clear translucent skin, and great violet eyes.

Peter lifted the child with his great hands and put her upon his shoulder, where she screamed with delight and mock fear, setting her fingers in his hair to steady herself on that lofty perch. "This is Luke and Thecla, Mariamne," he said. "They are friends of mine." The child flashed them a smile and held out her hand as composedly as if she were a grown woman, greeting them graciously in turn from her lofty perch.

A woman opened the door of the house and stepped out into the yard now. When she saw Mark and Peter a smile came over her face and she hurried out to make them welcome. There was no doubting her relationship to the child, for both had the same glorious red hair, the same translucent skin. The mother was as lovely in her maturity as the child was in her childish beauty. Luke judged her to be about forty or forty-five, although her body was still as lithe and as graceful as that of a young girl.

"Peter," she cried happily, embracing the apostle fondly. "And Mark."

"This is Luke, of whom you have heard me speak, Mary," Peter said. "And Thecla, his wife."

The red-haired woman gave Luke her hand in smiling welcome and embraced Thecla. "How lovely you are, my dear," she said, "but you are tired. Come in and lie down before the evening meal."

"I am weary," Thecla admitted. "It has been a long day."

Luke lifted her down from the mule, and they all went into the house. Luke and Thecla had a room to themselves, and he made Thecla lie down on the couch while he bathed first her face and hands and then her feet with water from a large jar in the corner.

The room opened upon a terraced garden in which a fountain tinkled and flowers grew everywhere in a riot of color. The house stood upon a precipitous hillside overlooking the lake, with the next house below it hidden beneath the brow of the hill, so that it seemed suspended upon the edge of a cliff. Far below them the slanting rays of the sun caressed the blue oval of the lake. The fishermen's boats with their bright-colored sails seemed only toys from this elevation.

"I am a poor physician," Luke told Thecla contritely, "not to have seen how tired you were. We could have rested a day before going in search of Peter and Mark."

315

"We might have missed them, too," she said. "Why did Peter bring us here, Luke?"

"He will tell us when he is ready," Luke assured her.

"Who is Mariamne's mother, Luke? She certainly isn't just an ordinary person, but I never heard Peter call her anything but Mary. And did you ever see anyone as beautiful at her age? She is as lithe as a dancer."

"A dancer!" The pattern fell suddenly into place in Luke's mind. "Mary of Magdala. She was a dancer before she followed Jesus."

"Whom are you talking about?" Thecla asked, still mystified.

"Mary Magdalene. Don't you remember? When I asked James about the women who visited the tomb of Jesus, he said that Mary was said to be living in her old home at Magdala."

Mark came in then to ask about Thecla and confirmed their surmise. This was indeed the home of Mary of Magdala, or Mary Magdalene as she had been called in Jesus's company, when she had ministered to him during those last months before the end. "She can tell you much about the life of Jesus too," Mark went on. "Peter has always said Mary loved and understood the Master better than any of those who were with him during the last days."

Darkness had fallen by the time they gathered for the evening meal, but the air was warm and fragrant with the perfume of the flowers that grew everywhere. They ate upon the terrace overlooking the lake, and afterward the little girl, Mariamne, insisted upon dancing for them. Watching her as she moved about the room gracefully, blown like a bit of thistledown upon the rhythm of the harp played by her mother, Luke could understand how Mary of Magdala had fired the hearts of men long ago with her dancing.

After the child was put to bed Mary told them again of those last weeks with Jesus when he had come to Jerusalem, knowing fully that a price had been set upon his head, and had faced the shame of arrest, the mockery of the trial, and the agony of the cross. Finally she told of seeing his body laid in the tomb and returning three days later to find it gone. When she finished, Peter said, "I brought Luke here today, Mary, because he is going to write the story of Jesus and the things he did and said."

Mary looked at Peter, then back at Luke. Luke felt as if the lovely violet eyes were searching his soul, but she only nodded, as if in approval, and said, "He must be the one for whom I have been keeping it, Peter. You said the time would come when it would be needed again."

"Yes," Peter said. "He is the one."

Mary got up and left the room, but she was gone only a few mo-

316

ments. When she returned she carried something in her hands, handling it tenderly, as if it were a jewel or something equally precious. Luke recognized the object instantly.

It was the scroll of the sayings of Jesus.

After they had knelt beside the bed and prayed before going to sleep that night, Thecla took the scroll from the table where Luke had placed it, touching the stains made by the blood of Stephen which were still faintly visible, and the tears where the stones had struck it. "How did Mary get the scroll, Luke?" she asked. "She didn't tell us."

"I think Peter gave it to her to keep after Paul came back to Jerusalem and the persecution became severe," he explained. "It would have been safer here, for the Sanhedrin was seeking to destroy it."

"Then Peter must have known where it was all the time."

"I am sure he did. He once told Mark that when the scroll was really needed it would be found."

"Why didn't he tell you, Luke?"

"Was I ready for it before now?" Luke asked. "Only since we made this trip together have I begun to understand what I really want to write about Jesus."

Thecla put her hand upon his. "I am happy that you brought me. Luke. And that we have at last found the scroll." She touched it again. "No wonder men were willing to die for it."

Long after Thecla was asleep Luke lay awake, troubled by a fear whose reality he understood now only too well. He should have been more thoughtful of Thecla's welfare during the past weeks, he told himself in an agony of self-accusation. Had he been less engrossed in learning about Jesus, he would have paid more attention to her loss of weight, the occasional twinges of pain which she had not entirely managed to hide from him, her weariness at the end of the day. All of it now fitted a pattern which he would have denied if he could but whose certainty oppressed him now. As she lay close beside him, the hurried beating of her heart even in sleep, the dry warmth that fever had brought to her skin, and the quickened rhythm of her breathing warned him that the plague which had killed her father was once more at work in her body, seeking to consume it. And when he put his ear against her skin as she lay sleeping, he could hear those strange sounds which Hippocrates had identified with advanced phthisis five hundred years before.

The next day the flush of fever was still discernible in Thecla's cheeks, and Luke suggested that she rest at the home of Mary while he and Mark went around the lake, visiting the spots where Jesus had taught and talking to those who still remembered the words of the gentle man who had showed them the Way to a new life. At night he and Thecla and the others talked over the things he had learned, with Mary and Peter filling in the details from their own intimate contact with Jesus. In this way Luke was able to build in his mind a vivid picture of the ministry of Jesus in Capernaum and along the fertile shores of the mountain-girt Sea of Galilee.

Thecla seemed very happy at Mary's home, although Luke could see that the fires which were consuming her burned more brightly each day. He left the scroll with her and she read it through many times, each day calling to his attention some new facet of the sayings of Jesus which he had not appreciated before. Once when he came back in the evening and entered the house without making his presence known, he found her sitting on the terrace, looking out at the lake, the scroll cradled in her arms as she would have caressed the child they had never been granted. She and Mary had become fast friends, and little Mariamne spent hours chattering to Thecla, so Luke was sure that she was not lonesome while he was away.

Finally a day came when Luke knew there was nothing more for him to learn about Jesus here in the cities around the lake. The path along which Jesus had come to Galilee lay southward, to Nazareth, where he had lived as a boy and a young man before beginning his ministry. Luke knew that Thecla could not make the trip in her present condition and probably would never be able to do it, for he was already trying to reconcile himself to the obvious fact that she could not live many months longer. There remained only the task of visiting the place where Jesus had spent his early years to learn whatever facts he could, before beginning the actual writing of the story which was now so vividly etched in his mind. And yet he was reluctant to leave Thecla and go to Nazareth or wherever else the quest might take him.

When Luke and Mark did not go down into the cities around the lake as had been their custom, Thecla asked, "Have you found out all that you can discover here, Luke?" They were alone on the terrace overlooking the lake.

"Yes, I have," he admitted.

"You must go on to Nazareth then, where Jesus was born."

"We can inquire in Nazareth when we return to Caesarea," he said.

She touched his cheek with her fingers lovingly, but when she spoke her words surprised him. "I think Bithynia would have been like it is here by the lake, don't you, Luke?"

"I am sure it will be, dear," he assured her. "We will be going there soon."

Thecla shook her head slowly. "This is no time to deceive each other, Luke. We both know I will never return to Caesarea."

"But you were sick once before and improved."

318

"Not like this. I didn't tell you then, but I lost some blood in a fit of coughing a few days before we left Caesarea to come to Galilee. Father did that before he began to get so much worse."

Luke bowed his head. He could have upbraided her for not telling him, but he knew why she had done so. More than anything else she had wanted to see this beautiful country and the places where Jesus had lived and taught. And had she told him about the hemorrhage, he would not have come but would have kept her in Caesarea. Actually he knew it would have made little difference in the final outcome, and Thecla had been happy here by the lake.

"Do not grieve, Luke," Thecla said gently. "I have no regrets, except that I did not bear you the son we both wanted. But we had Apollos Lucanus for a while, and I have loved being here with Mary and little Mariamne." She put her head against his chest and rested there, with his heart beating against her cheek.

"How strong and steady your heartbeat is, Luke," she whispered. "Like your soul."

He held her close. "I told you our souls are nourished by love, dear. If my soul is strong, it is from you."

She sighed happily. "God *has* been good to me," she whispered, "in giving me these years with you. I could ask no greater gift of life when I leave it than knowing you are finishing the task he set for you so many years ago. Promise me you will finish it, Luke, no matter what happens."

"I will, dearest." His eyes were wet with tears. "You know I will."

"I want you to stay with Paul, too," she went on. "I know I caused a breach between you once, but it is healed now and it must stay healed. There is something between you that must never be broken."

"I will stay with Paul as long as he needs me," he promised.

"Somehow I think I knew I would never get to Bithynia in the flesh, Luke," Thecla said thoughtfully. "But soon there will be nothing to keep me and I can go to wait for you there."

"I will come," he promised, sobbing. "Someday I will meet you in Bithynia." She kissed the tears from his eyes while he clung to her, knowing that he needed her far more now than she needed him. Finally she said quietly, "Please go on to Nazareth tomorrow, Luke, and finish your work. There is not much time, and I want to know the whole story of Jesus before I—before I go to him."

xi

It was a week later that Luke came to Bethlehem. The trail had led there from Nazareth, where he had spent two fruitless days searching for any members of the family of Jesus who might still be living there. But all of them had been dispersed during the persecution by Herod. One old man did remember a gentle carpenter who had lived in Nazareth and performed miracles. From him Luke learned how, when Jesus was twelve years old, he had been found in the temple at Jerusalem, disputing the law with the scribes and teachers, and had confounded everyone with his learning. One other thing the old man knew, that Jesus was said to have been born in Bethlehem while his parents had been on the way to Jerusalem to be taxed.

And so Luke had hurried on to Bethlehem, torn between the fear of going so far away from Thecla and the feeling that here was a clue which might lead to the truth about the birth of Jesus. He had brought the mule in order to travel faster, and they pushed southward along the great central highway through Engannim, thence westward to join the Via Maris along which he had traveled from Joppa to Jerusalem so long ago. From thence the route led over the wild mountainous country around Jerusalem, past Shechem to Beeroth and, skirting the Holy City, to Bethlehem.

Now as he moved through the dingy little city of David, Luke began to think that his mission would end uncompleted, for he found no one among the town officials who had ever heard the story he had been told in Nazareth. Nor did anyone among the few Christians in Bethlehem know anything of Jesus's birth. Thinking that if a child had really been born on the journey to Bethlehem to be taxed it might have been at an inn, Luke started making the rounds of the hostels in the city of David. But over and over again he received only a negative answer to his questions.

It was almost dark and his fruitless search had used up three precious days when late in the afternoon he came to a miserable inn which was little more than a hovel. He was tempted to go on and seek shelter at one of the better hostels, so sure was he that this miserable place could yield no information. But obeying the prodding of his conscience that he must leave no source unchecked, Luke opened the door and walked in. The proprietor, a Jew of about Luke's own age, looked up and, seeing a possible customer, brightened and bowed in welcome. When Luke finished telling what he sought, the innkeeper asked, "Why do you seek information about the Nazarene?"

"I am one of his followers," Luke explained.

"But you are not a Jew."

"No. I am a Christian and a Greek. Do you know anything about Jesus?"

"My father always claimed that the man called Jesus of Nazareth who was crucified in Jerusalem was born here, in the stable of this inn. But he also told of strange things happening at the same time, and we thought his mind was wandering, for he is very old."

Luke's pulse quickened with the excitement of what he might find here. "Is your father alive?" he asked quickly.

"Yes. He sits close by the oven, for he is old and his bones ache from any coolness."

"I would like to talk to him," Luke said. "Of course I will need a bed for tonight," he added diplomatically, although he would have chosen more promising quarters otherwise.

At first the old Jew beside the oven did not understand what it was that Luke sought. The fact that he spoke only Hebrew made communication doubly difficult, since Luke understood Hebrew much better than he spoke it. But at the mention of Jesus the old man's eyes lit up and he began to tell a strange and wonderful story. Hardly had he begun when Luke realized with a surge of joy that he had found at last what he was seeking.

Luke was up at daylight the next morning, although he had talked with the old innkeeper for half the night. Bethlehem had given him what he sought and he was happy as he turned the patient mule toward the valley highway paralleling the banks of the Jordan and leading northward to the cities and the Lake of Galilee. Day after day he prodded the mule, filled with a desperate urgency to get back to Thecla and tell her of his wonderful discovery. Darkness fell on the last day of the journey while he was still in Tiberias, some six miles from Magdala, but this was familiar ground, and he led the mule through the darkness around the lake and up the steep road to Magdala. Tired as he was, his heart was singing now, for the worst of his work was done, that of ferreting out a true account of Jesus from his birth to his death. Tomorrow he would tell Thecla the whole thrilling story, and no later than the next day he would start writing it down.

But when he stopped in front of the house of Mary he knew at once that something was badly wrong. Lights shone in every window, and before he could reach the door Peter opened it, as if he had been standing just inside watching for Luke's arrival. "We have been praying that you would get here in time, Luke," he said. "Thank God you have come."

"Is Thecla . . . ?" Luke started to ask, then the words died in his throat, for the answer he dreaded to hear was written in Peter's eyes.

"Thecla is dying, Luke," Peter said gently. "Yesterday there was a sudden rush of blood from her throat. We thought she would die then, but she has clung to life, I think because God revealed to her that you were near."

Peter led Luke into the house, guiding his steps when he stumbled because his eyes were blind with tears. Thecla lay on a couch, and Mark and Mary were kneeling beside her, their lips moving in prayer. When Luke came in they got up and left the room.

Looking down at the marble-pale face of his beloved, Luke thought for a moment that she had already gone, but then he saw her breast lift faintly with breathing, and when his fingers touched her wrist he felt the faint beat of her pulse. His eyes wet with tears, Luke dropped to his knees beside the couch and kissed Thecla gently on the lips. Her eyes opened then, and when she tried to lift her hand and could not find the strength to do so, he picked it up and put her palm against his cheek in the tender gesture which both of them loved so much.

"I knew you would come, Luke," she whispered.

"I came as soon as I could, dearest."

"Did you find what you were seeking?"

"Yes. At Bethlehem."

"Tell it to me now," she begged, "just as you will write it down, just as it happened."

And so Luke told her the beautiful story of Jesus's birth, just as he had learned it from the old innkeeper at Bethlehem:

"And in the sixth month the angel Gabriel was sent from God unto a city of Galilee, named Nazareth,

"To a virgin espoused to a man whose name was Joseph, of the house of David; and the virgin's name was Mary.

"And the angel came in unto her, and said, Hail, thou that art highly favoured, the Lord is with thee: blessed art thou among women!

"And when she saw him, she was troubled at his saying, and cast in her mind what manner of salutation this should be.

"And the angel said unto her, Fear not, Mary: for thou hast found favour with God.

"And, behold, thou shalt conceive in thy womb, and bring forth a son, and shalt call his name Jesus.

"He shall be great, and shall be called the Son of the Highest: and the Lord God shall give unto him the throne of his father David:

"And he shall reign over the house of Jacob for ever; and of his kingdom there shall be no end.

322

"Then said Mary unto the angel, How shall this be, seeing I know not a man?

"And the angel answered and said unto her, The Holy Ghost shall come upon thee, and the power of the Highest shall overshadow thee: therefore also that holy thing which shall be born of thee shall be called the Son of God . . . .

"For with God nothing shall be impossible.

"And Mary said, Behold the handmaid of the Lord; be it unto me according to thy word. . . .

"And it came to pass in those days, that there went out a decree from Caesar Augustus, that all the world should be taxed. . . .

"And all went to be taxed, every one into his own city.

"And Joseph also went up from Galilee, out of the city of Nazareth, into Judea, unto the city of David, which is called Bethlehem; (because he was of the house and lineage of David:)

"To be taxed with Mary his espoused wife, being great with child.

"And so it was, that, while they were there, the days were accomplished that she should be delivered.

"And she brought forth her first-born son, and wrapped him in swaddling clothes, and laid him in a manger; because there was no room for them in the inn.

"And there were in the same country shepherds abiding in the field, keeping watch over their flock by night.

"And, lo, the angel of the Lord came upon them, and the glory of the Lord shone round about them: and they were sore afraid.

"And the angel said unto them, Fear not: for, behold, I bring you good tidings of great joy, which shall be to all people.

"For unto you is born this day in the city of David a Saviour, which is Christ the Lord.

"And this shall be a sign unto you; Ye shall find the babe wrapped in swaddling clothes, lying in a manger.

"And suddenly there was with the angel a multitude of the heavenly host praising God, and saying,

"Glory to God in the highest, and on earth peace, good will toward men.

"And it came to pass, as the angels were gone away from them into heaven, the shepherds said one to another, Let us now go even unto Bethlehem, and see this thing which is come to pass, which the Lord hath made known unto us.

"And they came with haste, and found Mary, and Joseph, and the babe lying in a manger.

"And when they had seen it, they made known abroad the saying which was told them concerning this child.

323

"And all they that heard it wondered at those things which were told them by the shepherds.
"But Mary kept all these things, and pondered them in her heart."

"I knew the story would be beautiful," Thecla whispered when he finished. "Jesus really is the son of God."

"Yes, dear," Luke told her. "The world will know it now."

She drew a sigh of relief and happiness. "Read it to me from the scroll, Luke," she begged. "You know the part we both love."

Luke took the stained and torn roll of parchment from the table beside the couch and unrolled it to the passage he meant. They had read it many times together since Mary had given Luke the scroll, but as he read it again his mind went back to a night long ago on the road from Jerusalem to Joppa when he had first seen the now familiar words.

"Blessed be ye poor: for yours is the kingdom of God.
"Blessed are ye that hunger now: for ye shall be filled. Blessed are ye that weep now: for ye shall laugh."

And even when he knew that the pulse in the wrist under his fingers had ceased to beat, Luke continued to read until he came to the sentence which summarized the thing Jesus came to tell the world and which both he and Thecla had loved and made their creed:

"As ye would that men should do to you, do ye also to them likewise."

Even though his beloved's heart no longer beat, Luke could not bring himself to believe that she had really gone away. Somewhere, he knew, perhaps out there upon the terrace she had loved, or down along the shores of the lake where Jesus had walked, or even in far-off Bithynia, the real Thecla still existed and would go on existing until the end of time.

And as he knelt there he heard a calm voice say: *"Fear not, for I am with thee. Be not dismayed. I will strengthen thee, I will help thee; yea I will uphold thee with the right hand of my righteousness."*

For a moment Luke thought Peter had come into the room and had spoken the words. But when he raised his head no one was there. He knew then who it was who had spoken to comfort him in his hour of greatest sorrow.

xii

The leaves were turning from green to the gold and red of autumn and the air was crisp with the promise of winter when Luke returned to Caesarea. All through the summer he had labored at his writing on the sunny terrace of Mary's house at Magdala, close by the tiny glen where they had laid Thecla's body to rest upon the mountainside, overlooking the blue lake which both she and Jesus had loved so much. And as he wrote, not only did the beautiful story of Jesus take form and substance in words, but the man himself grew in stature within Luke's mind. Simply, yet beautifully, the words upon the parchment revealed Jesus to the world as the son of God who had chosen to become a lowly carpenter and to give up his life on the cross that a new hope might come to the world and men might learn the way to God through humility, love, and denial of self.

Now as Luke walked through the streets of Caesarea toward the palace of Herod, where Paul was still a prisoner, he saw little change in the months that he had been away. The waves still washed endlessly against the stones of the mole which Herod the Great had built. The streets echoed to the rumble of carts and the cries of vendors shouting the virtues of their wares. And in the grim forbidding headquarters of Roman might, soldiers tramped the battlements on sentry duty, as they did throughout the far reaches of the Empire.

The Voice which had taught the gentle precepts of brotherly love along the shores of Galilee and in Jerusalem was stilled, but the message continued to be spread through the tongues of those who had seen and loved his Way and followed it. And the Way would soon be known even more widely through the words set down upon the bulky scroll beneath Luke's arm. Another voice had carried the good news by Roman highways and sea routes to province and continent. Now it was momentarily stilled within the palace of Herod, but the message continued to be spread through the letters which Paul was writing from his prison, letters which one day might bring even more people to know the Way of Jesus than Paul's own inspired words had ever been able to do.

At the palace Luke was admitted to the room where Paul was kept, still guarded only by a single Roman soldier who stood outside the door. The room was more like a study than a prison, for Felix had imposed no harsh measures upon Paul. When Luke came in Paul was pacing the floor, dictating to Timothy, who was writing with a metal stylus upon a wax-covered tablet, just as when Luke had seen them last. Paul stopped his dictating and ran to embrace Luke. Timothy, too, greeted him warmly. Prison had been kind to the apostle, Luke saw. He looked better than Luke remembered seeing him in many years; some of the restless energy had been curbed, and the fire in his eyes which only death would quench burned more quietly, if just as intensely.

The three friends gathered about the table while Luke gave an account of the happenings since he had left Caesarea. When he came to the scroll, Luke took it from his robe and put it into Paul's hands.

"So you found it, Luke," Paul said, turning the small parchment roll reverently in his hands and touching the dents where the stones had struck it at his own order so long ago. Then the apostle added thoughtfully, "I wonder if its story is ended yet."

"Peter let me keep it," Luke told him. "But I promised to guard it always."

"We must keep it safe," Paul agreed. "It is our only relic of Jesus. But what is that other scroll you carry, Luke, the larger one?"

Luke told them then of his writing the life of Jesus and the strange and thrilling story he had heard in Bethlehem. With Paul and Timothy listening, he began to read; nor did he put down the parchment until he came to the final paragraphs:

"And he led them out as far to Bethany, and he lifted up his hands, and blessed them.

"And it came to pass, while he blessed them, he was parted from them, and carried up into heaven.

"And they worshipped him, and returned to Jerusalem with great joy:

"And were continually in the temple, praising and blessing God. Amen."

Timothy had long since lighted the lamps when Luke lay down his scroll containing his story of Jesus. Paul was silent while he rolled up the parchment again, then he said, "The pattern is clear now, Luke. God intended you for this from the first."

"Do you approve of the writing?"

"It is the most beautiful story ever written," Paul said sincerely, and Timothy gave eager assent. "No one but you could have set it down in just that way. What do you do next?"

"I plan to have copies made," Luke said. "Theophilus is in Rome, and I am thinking of sending him one, asking that he have it published abroad there."

"Why not take it to Rome yourself?" Paul asked, smiling. "Unless you are unwilling to travel again with an old companion of the road."

"Is Felix letting you go free?" Luke cried.

Paul shook his head. "Felix still hopes for a bribe. Besides, he is afraid to release me for fear of angering the high priest and the council, so I am determined to appeal to Rome. Then he will be forced to send me before the Emperor's courts, and they will release me, for there are no real crimes charged against me."

"Then we can go together," Luke said happily, "and take the story of Jesus with us."

Timothy and Luke walked back together through the darkened city to the house of Philip, stopping at the foot of the great stone mole that formed the harbor of Caesarea to watch the play of phosphorescence in the water as it battered the stone barrier which formed a safe haven for ships. The sky was clear and brilliant with stars. To the north, one shone far more brightly than all the others.

"I have never seen the North Star so bright as it is tonight, Luke," Timothy said. "No wonder the mariners use it as a guide. Look how its light makes a path of silver across the water."

Luke looked up at the brilliant star which did seem to glow tonight, not with the cold brilliance of the other heavenly bodies, but with a warmth of its own. Watching it, he felt the sense of loss which he had experienced ever since he had laid Thecla to rest there on the mountain above the Sea of Galilee begin to fade. Instead, some of the star's warmth crept into his heart, filling it with a quiet joy, for he knew now that the star was not shining of itself alone. Like the lamp in the window which guides the weary traveler homeward through the dangers of the night, his beloved was there, directing his footsteps toward the place of beauty and of peace which waited below the star to the north, now that his great task was done. His road might lead to Rome or to the ends of the earth, but he knew that she was keeping her promise to wait for him there. In token of it she had set the warm brightness of the star to guide him always along the Road to Bithynia.

Author's Notes

WHILE the name of Thecla does not appear in the New Testament, she is in no sense a fictional creation, for she appears prominently in apocryphal literature. The vivid and dramatic Acts of Paul and Thecla tells of the adventures of a beautiful young girl of Iconium who was converted by Paul and later, because of her faith, bound to a wild beast in the arena from which she was miraculously saved. The biblical historian, Harnack, says, "There must have really been a girl converted by Paul at Iconium whose name was Thecla, and who took an active part in the Christian Mission." Another biblical authority, Sir W. M. Ramsey, said, "Thecla was a real person and . . . she was brought into relations with the greatest figures of the Galatic province about A.D. 50—viz., Paul, Queen Tryphaena, and the Roman Governor." For a very interesting account of the complete adventures of Thecla, the reader is referred to *More Essays on Greek Romances,* by Elizabeth Hazelton Haight, page 48, Longmans Green & Co., New York, or to any one of several volumes of apocryphal literature.

Of all the many odd customs of the early Christian faith, none is stranger or more startling than the true history of men living with virgins as husband and wife in everything except a physical sense. Paul says in I Corinthians, 7:36-38, "But if any man think that he behaveth himself uncomely toward his virgin, if she pass the flower of her age, and need so require, let him do what he will, he sinneth not: let them marry. Nevertheless he that standeth steadfast in his heart, having no necessity, but hath power over his own will, and hath so

329

decreed in his heart that he will keep his virgin, doeth well. So then he that giveth her in marriage doeth well; but he that giveth her not in marriage doeth better."

Of this same custom, Arthur Darby Nock (*St. Paul,* Harper & Brothers) says: "A second matter, presumably raised by the Corinthians in the letter brought to Paul, now follows—the problem of 'virgins'; it apparently relates to a curious custom whereby men were spiritually betrothed to virgins and even lived with them without having any physical relations; difficulties were liable to arise. Once more Paul prefers continence, but regards the concession of ordinary matrimony as right if it is the way to avoid sin. In the same manner he permits the remarriage of a widow 'only in the Lord,' that is, presumably to a Christian for the prevention of moral evil." Many other references substantiate the authenticity of this odd custom in the early church.

Historically, Luke did reach Bithynia, for the Monarchian Prologue to Luke's Gospel, thought to be written about A.D. 200 and considered by most biblical authorities to be authentic, states: "Luke, by nation a Syrian of Antioch, a disciple of the Apostles, was afterward a follower of Paul till his martyrdom, serving the Lord blamelessly. For having neither wife nor children, he died in Bithynia at the age of seventy-four, filled with the Holy Spirit" (Graham Chambers Hunter: *Luke, First Century Christian*).